THE MUSIC OF BEES

Also by Eileen Garvin

HOW TO BE A SISTER

THE

MUSIC

of

BEES

· *A Novel* ·

EILEEN GARVIN

DUTTON

DUTTON

An imprint of Penguin Random House LLC
penguinrandomhouse.com

LIBRARY OF CONGRESS CATALOGING-IN-PUBLICATION DATA
Names: Garvin, Eileen, author.
Title: The music of bees: a novel / Eileen Garvin.
Description: New York: Dutton, [2021]
Identifiers: LCCN 2020043236 (print) | LCCN 2020043237 (ebook) |
ISBN 9780593183922 (hardcover) | ISBN 9780593183946 (ebook)
Subjects: LCSH: Bee culture—Fiction. | Friendship—Fiction. |
Farm life—Fiction. | Grief—Fiction. |
Self-actualization (Psychology)—Fiction.
Classification: LCC PS3607.A782894 M87 2021 (print) |
LCC PS3607.A782894 (ebook) | DDC 813/.6—dc23
LC record available at https://lccn.loc.gov/2020043236
LC ebook record available at https://lccn.loc.gov/2020043237

Printed in the United States of America
1st Printing

Interior art: Bees and flowers © AVA Bitter/Shutterstock

BOOK DESIGN BY KRISTIN DEL ROSARIO

For all the wild creatures

and

everyone who loves them

THE MUSIC OF BEES

ORIENTATION FLIGHT

Those who suppose that the new colony consists wholly of young bees, forced to emigrate by the older ones, if they closely examine a new swarm, will find that while some have the ragged wings of age, others are so young as to be barely able to fly.

—*A PRACTICAL TREATISE ON THE HIVE AND HONEY-BEE*, L. L. LANGSTROTH, 1878

Jacob Stevenson had the tallest mohawk in the history of Hood River Valley High School. Even before it was listed as an official yearbook record, he was pretty sure about it. In his senior photo, it was a blue-black masterpiece that flared up to a height of sixteen and a half inches. Well, almost. It was more like sixteen and three-eighths, but close enough to silence any quibblers. Jacob had put six months into growing the spiky mass, which he sculpted into four sections, and it had reached its optimal height right before spring finals last year.

On this morning, he surveyed the masterpiece of his hair in the mirror and felt no little satisfaction that he'd managed to maintain it for more than a year now, despite unforeseen challenges. The undeniable truth of a mohawk was that you were always fighting gravity, and at a certain point, you lost. You had to be realistic. The idea was to aim for maximum volume that would hold over an entire day. A fallen mohawk would be a terrible embarrassment, especially for a boy of eighteen. Jacob had experimented with various products to maintain the loft. He'd tried egg whites, mustache wax, hair spray, and even some adhesive from wood shop—an unfortunate episode. All that experimenting revealed that a mixture of extra-firm sculpting wax and professional-grade hair spray was the best choice to sustain that sixteen-and-nearly-one-half-inch height of achievement.

Noah Katz had taken the official measurement the night of the spring jazz band concert. Both of them had been dressed in the traditional black tuxedos that members of the Hood River Valley High School jazz band had been wearing for the past twenty years. Jacob thought then that his hair contrasted nicely with the powder-blue cummerbund and bow tie. He posed with his trumpet as Noah snapped a photo, cackling, the phone dwarfed in his big paw. His cheeks shook as he laughed.

"Sick, Stevenson!"

Katz was a good-natured lumberjack of a guy. The two had become friends at May Street Elementary in fifth-grade band—Jacob on trumpet and Noah on trombone. Noah did not have a mohawk. Noah's hair was crazy curly, and he referred to it as "The Situation." Unlike Jacob, he did not need any product to make his hair resist gravity. He grew his curls up and out, chiefly to irritate his mother.

"Look out, ladies!" he crowed, tugging on his curls with one hand so that he resembled a human dandelion in fluff stage. He snapped a selfie. Then they hustled into Noah's truck and sped across town to the high school. They had been late, as usual, and Mr. Schaffer was mad, but their band teacher seemed always to be looking for a reason to yell at the two boys, so it was no big deal.

Remembering that night made Jacob smile. He turned his head from right to left. On either side of the mast of hair he could see bits of stubble on his otherwise cleanly shaven skull. He turned on the faucet and dampened a washcloth under the tepid stream to wet his head. He squirted a soft puff of shaving cream into his hand and patted it on the stubble. The lemony white foam smelled institutional, like the hospital, and made him feel slightly nauseated. He breathed through his mouth and picked up his razor.

A mohawk took discipline. He had to wash or at least wet his hair, then comb it out, apply wax to the wet mop, part it into sections, and dry it with the high-power blow-dryer before spraying it into place and then shaving the stubble. The process made him sweat on warm days like this one. It was a big investment of time, really. But that was cool. These days he had nothing but time. Two hours to do his hair was no problem at all.

The reality of that hit him like a punch in the throat, as it often did when he sat in front of the bathroom mirror in the morning. The dark little hairs on his scalp poked through the white lather, standing up unwaveringly while Jacob Stevenson—or Jake, as everyone but his parents called him—could not. Jake swallowed hard. It seemed so stupid—the mohawk itself and the mohawk record, considering that in addition to having the tallest mohawk in the history of Hood River Valley High School, he was probably also the only kid there who'd *ever* had one in this farm town, which was short on punk and big on rodeo. It was also stupid because he no longer went to school there, having sort of graduated last spring. But mostly it seemed stupid because it was pretty much all he had to do on a given day, fix his fucking hair, now that the doctor's appointments had tapered off and his physical therapy was down to once a month and he had all the time in the world to face the rest of his life in a wheelchair.

Jake pushed back from the mirror and looked at his body—lean and muscled in his torso and arms. His legs didn't look terribly different than they had before. But sometimes he almost felt like they belonged to someone else.

The wheelchair was why he had "sort of" graduated. The school administration had mailed his diploma to his parents' house while Jake lay in the hospital sixty miles away in Portland. His teachers had all passed him even though that was a stretch for a couple of classes, like PE, since he was in the habit of skipping to go to Noah's house after second period to get high before lunch. He hadn't darkened the gym door since before Christmas break. But even Mr. McKenna wasn't enough of a dick to fail a PE student who was going to spend the rest of his life as a paraplegic. Irony, yo.

Jake's mother had told him he'd be graduating when he was still doped up during those first days at the hospital. She sat next to his bed, her eyes puffy behind her pink-framed glasses. She tried not to cry in front of him, though she barely left the chair next to his bed. She sat for hours, holding his hand and murmuring that God was watching over him. She'd run through the list of people who had called and emailed to send their thoughts and prayers—his teachers, the neighbors, the mailman, people from church. People he'd never heard of, but he didn't say that because it would have hurt her feelings. She brightened when she got to the part about the graduation cere-mony, which, at that point, was still weeks away.

"We're so proud of you, honey," she said. "Your name will be in the program. They asked Noah to receive the diploma on your behalf, since you won't be able to . . ."

Her voice faltered, and she stopped.

Jake winced, his smile a grimace. "Since I won't be able to *walk*, you mean?"

His laughter came out in short barks, and then he couldn't stop. He blamed the drugs, but there was more to it. He laughed and laughed at the word "walk," which had taken on such a different meaning now that he had lost the use of his legs, his young, strong boy legs, legs that had skateboarded and run and climbed, legs he had completely taken for granted every single day of his stupid life until the day he couldn't use them anymore. He couldn't stop laughing even when his mom put her face into her hands and wept. He was such an asshole, he thought now, sitting in front of the mirror. He rolled forward and peered at himself, noticing how much thinner he was than he had been last spring.

He had laughed because the word "walk" had made him think of his father, Ed Stevenson, and his fleshy, angry face.

"The least goddamn thing you can do is walk your lazy ass down the aisle at graduation," Ed had said. "You turn eighteen, we're gonna give you a knife and fork and send you on your goddamn, merry way."

That had been winter break of his senior year, when Jake realized his grades didn't matter, now that he'd lost his music school scholarship, and it seemed like he might actually flunk out.

"Don't worry about me, Ed," Jake replied.

He'd begun calling his father by his first name when he started high school, knowing it bugged him.

"I'll be out of here so fast you won't even see me go."

Jake had decided to move to Portland after the dream of music school faded to impossibility last year. He figured he'd work in a music store or a coffee shop someplace near the eastside clubs. He hadn't worked out the details, but how hard could it be to get a job in a city that big?

However, since Jake had injured his spinal cord, his lazy ass was firmly stuck at his parents' house. He wasn't going anywhere anytime soon, and there was nothing Ed or anyone else could do about it.

He touched up the right side of his head, toweled it off, and started on the left, dragging the razor along the curve of his skull. The scraping sound was half-thrilling, half-sickening.

His father was part of a six-man building crew for Klare Construction. That meant he worked long hours on weekdays like this one, and those hours, even when they yawned wide and empty, were a relief to Jake. Weekends were harder, when Ed parked himself in front of the TV with a half rack of PBR and a bag of peanuts. Then Jake stayed in his room, listening to music or surfing the web. His earbuds muffled the sound of his father's rattling cough, the ping of peanut shells into the bowl, the white noise of screaming fans, which always sounded the same whatever the sport or season.

Jake looked around the bathroom at the lowered sink and mirror, the shower chair, grab rails, the widened doorway. An experienced carpenter, his father could have easily made these renovations in a couple of days to prepare for his only son's return from the rehab center, where Jake had gone after the hospital. But Ed hadn't lifted a finger. His mother's church group had done it, all eager to help Tansy Stevenson, their pastor's administrative assistant, during this difficult time with her son. They took up a collection to pay for it and assembled a volunteer work crew before Jake returned home.

His mom told him this when she came to visit him. She sat next to the therapy table in a flowered dress and sensible shoes, an outfit usually reserved for church or holidays. He could tell she hadn't wanted to make too much of the renovation to save his pride. But Jake knew his mom read it as a sign of God's love that all those people had come out to their crummy double-wide to help Tansy Stevenson by helping her son. Jake lay on the table and his PT showed his mother the exercises she'd need to help him do to prevent contractures— permanent shortenings of the muscles that would make him even more of a freak. He watched his foot move toward and away from his face in the PT's hands. He didn't ask if Ed had sat in front of the TV sipping tall boys while the earnest members of the congregation remodeled the bathroom. He didn't have to ask because he knew Ed wouldn't even have had the decency to leave the house while they were doing the work he should have done. That must have been hard on his mother too. Anyway, he was grateful he could use the damn bathroom by himself.

Jake cracked the window and heard a car rattle past, its radio blaring Mumford & Sons' "I Will Wait." That song. His stomach dropped. He swiveled the chair and reached for the hair spray. He surveyed his bare chest and shoulders in the mirror, flexed his biceps, and smiled grimly. His upper body was stronger than it had ever been, as he'd started lifting weights to fill the long days.

When he'd returned from the rehab center last fall, his mother tried to get him to keep going to his support group in Portland. She nagged him to call the local mentor he'd been assigned—a Paralympic skier who lived nearby in Mosier. She stood in the doorway of his room, her purse over her arm, as she got ready to leave for church.

"You should get out of the house, Jacob," she said. "You need to see people and start getting on with things."

Getting on with things. His body flushed with anger, but he didn't say anything. He just stuck his earbuds in and turned back to his computer. He was playing *Tomb Raider* and winning—a hollow victory since he was playing against himself. At least he didn't say something horrible to her. She was sweet, his Jesus-loving mom. It wasn't her fault that her only son, who was kind of a screw-up to begin with, had fucked himself up so badly.

They hadn't been drunk, not even a little buzzed, on that weirdly warm April day last year. Someone had set up a Slip 'N Slide in the yard at Tom Pomeroy's house, and they had taken turns belly-flopping down the slick yellow plastic. There were about twenty people, all juniors and seniors. The guys whooped and the girls screeched as they careened down the lawn. When Jake threw himself into the wet tongue of the slide, he felt a streak of joy. He let himself forget about the pressure of life after graduation and the stress of finals that he was pretty sure he would fail. He pulled his thoughts away from the lost scholarship to music school, which had hurt so much at first and finally settled into a dull ache that he could ignore from time to time. As he walked among his friends in the warm sunshine, he felt like a kid again. He went up onto the porch as someone cranked the stereo. Mumford. That song. It was just a few moments, an ordinary collection of seconds that had an extraordinary impact on his life.

Jake grabbed a beer out of the cooler and bummed an American Spirit. He didn't smoke, but it was a party, so why not? He climbed the stairs to the second floor behind Megan Shine, who was telling some story about her spring break trip to Mazatlán, where her rich parents had taken her and her sisters. Megan was super nice even though she didn't need to be because she was also gorgeous. Cheerleader hot. Blond and all that. Not his type, but still. She laughed at something he said and took his beer away from him, tipping her head back to drink, and he snuck a look at her beautiful breasts. Surely she wouldn't mind even if she noticed his eyes diving down into her bikini top, her lovely flat stomach, her short pink shorts. Someone grabbed him from behind. Pomeroy squeezed Jake with one arm and gave him a playful smack on the side of his shaved head.

Pomeroy was a good guy, if kind of an ape. He was one of those dudes who always had to be doing something physical—a push-up contest or jumping off the train trestle into the river or skateboarding through the Mosier tunnels in the dark—and rallying everyone else to do the same. Nothing fazed him. The guy was always doing shit that should have gotten him hurt, but he was like a cat, always landing on his feet.

He was bigger and stronger than Jake. Pomeroy played football, so Jake would usually have dodged this kind of wrestling match. But for some reason, he dropped his cigarette and spun around to grab Pomeroy's meaty torso. Maybe because Megan was watching and laughing. Jake threw himself at the bigger boy, wrapping his arms around Pomeroy's waist. His friend staggered under his weight.

"Christ, Stevenson!" he yelled as he slipped.

It would have been no big deal, except they were standing on the second-story roof over the patio. Jake fell, his body twisting in the air, and landed with a sickening thud on the low wall separating Mrs. Pomeroy's rose garden from the driveway. He looked up and saw Megan and Pomeroy peering over the edge of the roof. He wanted to laugh up at them that he was okay, but he was not. And things would never be the same again.

Unlucky, the doctors told him later. That was what they called his incomplete spinal cord injury to T11 and T12 in his lower back.

Jake felt sick remembering. He took a deep breath and wheeled himself down the hall to his room. The loop had started in his head.

He would never walk again, the surgeon said, but at least he had good control of his upper body since the injury was only partial. *"You can be grateful for that."*

Jake had stared at the guy. Grateful? Gratitude was far, far from his mind then.

He pulled on his favorite gray Dickies shirt, buttoned it up, grabbed his backpack, and slung it over his chair.

He was lucky to have the use of his hands and arms, the redheaded nurse had told him, despite the asymmetry of strength on one side.

He slid his sunglasses into his shirt pocket.

He was young and otherwise healthy, his PT said over and over again. He could have a really great life.

Jake lifted one leg onto the foot rail with both hands and then the other. He pulled on his Doc Martens, laced them up, and wheeled through the house, out the door, and down the ramp.

"A successful career," his therapist said.

He put on his sunglasses and stuck in his earbuds. He turned up the volume on his iPhone, and the familiar rasp of ska-punk filled his head.

"Computer programming, maybe," his mom suggested, nodding at the social worker and then at Jake. *"You like those games so much, don't you?"*

He maneuvered his chair down the gravel driveway and out into the bike lane that snaked along Belmont. His wheels kicked up dust and bits of gravel. He smiled at his speed. The chair was pretty fly. His classmates had taken up a collection for it. Otherwise he'd have the

crap-assed one his dad's insurance would have covered. They had announced it at graduation, Noah told him. He was glad he hadn't been
there to have to thank them, which would have been so humiliating,
though he was grateful for it. He would spend the afternoon, as he
had been lately, now that the spring rains were tapering off, out near
the orchards where he knew he wouldn't run into any of his friends.
Those who weren't at college—like Noah, who was working to save
money to travel—would be at work or hanging out at the skate park.

The air smelled green and fresh. It pricked something in his heart.
This season—when unexpected rain showers swept across the valley
floor and the wind turned the orchards into waves of blossoms—had
always filled him with hope. The chorus frogs sang in the irrigation
ditches, and the days lengthened imperceptibly. Hawks perched along
the fence line of county roads, and tiny finches darted through the air.
Flickers keened in the shadows of the forest. He never told anyone he
noticed these things. But spring always brought him a secret joy, the
promise of something new. Now he felt his heart try to rise toward it
and fall back defeated.

He turned up the music. It was Spring Heeled Jack's *Connecti-
cut Ska*, which launched the band into the U.S. punk scene in the
early nineties, just before Jake had been born. Jake would focus on Pat
Gingras's trumpet and parse how the band's sound was changing before Gingras was replaced by Tyler Jones. He would make up argu-
ments in his head, today taking the position that Jones's style
maintained the band's classic ska-punk sound, but who believed that,
really? If you had any ear at all, you could hear Spring Heeled Jack
working toward the mainstream sound of the Mighty Mighty Boss-
tones, which would eventually swallow some of its members. Other
days he would conjecture that Gingras's sound was authentic and true
to the real mission of the music, which was what he really believed.
So did every other genuine ska fan. It didn't matter. It was like his
Tomb Raider games. Just killing time in the jail that was his life. This

life had replaced the life he was supposed to have—one of music and promise, the other life that now felt like something he had imagined.

Jake's musical ability, which had been obvious from an early age, was a mystery to his parents, who were not musical people. Luckily his teachers noticed and had suggested he join the school band. He'd been playing trumpet since middle school. He couldn't remember life without music. He didn't have words to explain it, this vivid thing that lived in him.

In the fall of his senior year, Jake had been offered a three-quarter scholarship to Cornish College of the Arts in Seattle, mostly based on his musical ability and letters of recommendation. If his grades had been better, it might have been a full ride, but 75 percent was enough. He was going to study music theory, history, and performance with trumpet as his primary instrument. He kept the acceptance letter in his trumpet case for months and pulled it out to reread when he was alone even though he pretty much had it memorized.

"Dear Mr. Stevenson, It is with great pleasure that we welcome you into the Cornish College of the Arts community . . ." The words made him giddy. But then, when it came time to send the school a down payment on the balance, his father had refused to lend him the money. Ed wouldn't listen to his wife's pleading and barely took his eyes off the TV to respond.

"Music school? Please," he scoffed. "I was working full time at his age."

Case closed. Jake didn't want to think about it, that crushing loss. But under the wail of Gingras's trumpet, his mind was invaded by questions with no answers that played in an unending loop: What if his father had lent him the money? What if he'd earned more than a 2.3 GPA and gotten the full ride? What if he'd worked a weekend job and saved some money of his own? How pathetic to have this thing he'd so wanted slip away because he hadn't tried harder a little earlier.

The questions unraveled from there like always, becoming more and more impossible. What if he hadn't been at Pomeroy's that day, but had cleaned up the yard for his mom, like she'd asked? Instead he stepped around the rake and leaf bags, promising himself he'd go to the party for an hour and finish the yard before she got home. What if he hadn't been showing off for Megan Shine? What if he could do it all over again?

Jake turned up the music to drown his thoughts. He hit the bottom of the hill by the Indian Creek Golf Course and threw himself into the climb. The clouds had lifted, and the sky was turning from orange to yellow over the ridgeline. The apple and pear trees had unfurled into an embarrassment of beauty, their blossoms rippling along the valley floor to the foot of snowcapped Mount Hood. The temperature dropped, and Jake inhaled the wet green scent of the irrigated orchards. He could taste the faint, acrid tang of whatever they sprayed on the trees in the back of his throat. He told himself the pesticides were making his eyes sting.

He sailed down the next hill, ignoring the old dude who had stopped his golf cart to gawk at the boy with the mohawk in the wheelchair flying toward the four-way intersection. Don't worry about me, old man, he thought. The worst has already happened.

Was that true? Maybe the worst thing was that nothing else was going to happen in his miserable life. A month from now, Hood River Valley High School would host another graduation. Class of 2014. Hip, hip hooray! Two hundred young people would move forward in their lives to college or work or at least someplace other than this hick town. He'd been thinking about it all week. It was right there in his face, the anniversary of the day his life stopped. Nice job, Jake. You fucked up. Just like your old man has been saying your whole life. Nice job, fuckup.

The afternoon deepened into dusk, and Jake sped past the old Oak Grove Schoolhouse, which cast long shadows into the apple orchards. Out in the trees he watched lights coming on in the fruit workers' shacks. He could see figures up on ladders, their shadows lengthening between the rows of trees. He rolled south toward the shape of Mount Hood, which was kissed with alpenglow against the green-yellow horizon.

"Give you a knife and fork and send you on your goddamn, merry way."

The words echoed in his head, and he turned the music up as loud as it would go. He could smell his sweat, which was different now than it had been before. He smelled like an old man, like someone sick, like a stranger to himself. He tried to focus on the white line of the road, which wasn't a bike lane this far outside of town in the orchards, just a skinny shoulder.

He fought a flood of images: Megan Shine's smile and the sun bright on her bikini top. His fingers flying along the valves as he blasted a trumpet solo with his heart in his throat at the state jazz band competition. Watching Noah rip the half-pipe at the skate park. Passing around a can of chew in the back of the band bus. Running after his brindled dog on the sandbar. All of it gone. Those things were part of the life he used to have, the one that was lost to him. His heart ached, and he hated himself for it. He hated the tears that were coursing down his cheeks, which he could no longer pretend were sweat. He hated what he had done to his stupid life and that he had no one else to blame. In that moment he felt broken in a way that could not be undone.

Jake was turned so far inward that he didn't hear the sound of the pickup truck coming up behind him. He was facing away and wouldn't have seen one wheel riding inside the white line of the shoulder. A truck whose driver didn't see the boy in the dusk until the headlights hit the back of his chair. Then Jake heard the squeal of brakes over the sound of the music and everything stopped.

2

Twelve Queens

The queen bee is the only perfect female in the hive, and all the eggs are laid by her.

—L. L. LANGSTROTH

Alice Holtzman would have rated her mood below average even before she hit the wall of traffic creeping down Interstate 84 back to Hood River. She blamed the young imbeciles at Sunnyvale Bee Company in Portland who had mixed up her order, which had delayed her departure and landed her in this late-afternoon sea of cars and trucks. To be more precise, they had lost her order, which was frustrating because Alice was a regular customer at Sunnyvale and also because, as a point of personal pride, she tried hard to be conscientious.

Things were always crazy on Bee Day, an annual event in April, and she acknowledged that. After all, the Sunnyvale Bee Company saw hundreds of millions of bees move through their yard on that single day. When Alice arrived, she saw hundreds of bee packages awaiting pickup. Each small, screened crate held ten thousand bees, all buzzing with confusion at their recent sorting in the bee yards of southern Oregon from whence they came. The precious cargo, trucked in before dawn, had to be picked up, transported, and hived within twenty-four hours.

Hundreds of beekeepers would descend on Sunnyvale to claim their bees on an average Bee Day, so things could get hectic.

The car in front of her crept forward and slammed on its brakes. Alice exhaled through her nose with impatience. She looked at her watch and sighed. Yes, Alice knew Bee Day would be crazy. That was why she had taken the day off. It was a Thursday. You could never count on the bees arriving on a weekend. They came, like babies, unpredictably and often inconveniently. Alice and other expectant beekeepers had to wait until those southern hives grew strong with populations of young bees and the early-spring showers tapered off. Pickups were rescheduled all the time. A betting man wouldn't put money on Bee Day, as intransigent as it was. Alice knew that. That was why she had called two days before, like she always did, to reconfirm her order with Tim, the cheerful shop manager who'd been there, she knew, for more than twenty years. It was impossible to tell how old Tim was. He was one of those men who'd looked old at twenty, probably, losing his hair right after high school, and now seemed ageless. Unflappable Tim. Alice didn't even know his last name, but for the past several years, Tim had been a regular part of her life. Not a friend, exactly. More like a friendly milepost, a happy marker that said it was spring, Oregon's winter was finally over, and it was time for fresh life in the apiary. For all its inconvenience, Alice usually loved Bee Day.

But this year Tim hadn't answered the phone when she called. Instead a young woman picked up and identified herself as Joyful.

"How can I help make your day amazing?" she'd asked.

Alice gave her name and order number while wondering if Joyful could possibly be her real name. Joyful had assured her that all orders would be filled as usual and that they would be thrilled to see her in two days. She hadn't actually refused to look up Alice's order, but she hadn't looked it up either.

"Be well!" she'd said, and hung up before Alice could say anything else.

So as Alice stood watching Joyful with her blond dreadlocks hanging in her face as she pawed through the stack of orders and failed to find Alice's, she had wanted to say, I told you so. She had wanted to say other things—things that would have disappointed her mother. Alice folded her arms over her chest, took a deep breath, and leaned on the counter.

"Miss, I called you two days ago. My name is Holtzman. Alice Holtzman. Hood River. I ordered twelve Russian nucs. Twelve nucleus hives."

She tried to sound calm and shifted back slightly when she noticed she was tapping a blunt finger on the counter.

"No extra queens and no packages. Tim usually sets my stuff aside in the overflow yard." Alice pointed to a gated area on the left. For years now, Tim had separated the orders of experienced beekeepers, like her, from those of the beginners who were more inclined to linger with questions, thereby creating their own buzzing confusion on Bee Day.

"Why don't you just let me have a look over there? I'm sure I can find them myself."

But Joyful, with her brows in a crease and her dreads in her face and who was not having an amazing day, would not be moved. She looked up from the mess of papers and fixed Alice with a stern gaze.

"Ma'am, I hear you saying that you are a longtime customer, and I do respect that. But we have a system in place here, and you are just going to have to wait your turn like everyone else."

Alice flushed with embarrassment and drew back, pressing her lips together and feeling like a chastised child. She felt her breath catch and thought about Dr. Zimmerman, who asked her to note such moments. Alice hitched up her overalls and joined the clutch of other beekeepers milling around and chatting as they waited for their orders. Alice did not chat.

The spring sun grew warm on her head. She took off her sunhat and pulled her hair off her neck, which was damp with sweat. She glanced at her hands, her nails chewed to the quick, and shoved them in her back pockets. She shifted her weight from one foot to another, her feet swelling in her work boots. She glanced up and saw herself on the security monitor and looked away, tugging on the straps of her overalls. Being motionless made her nuts. Half an hour later, her order was discovered on the floor under Joyful's Birkenstocked feet.

"Alice Holtzman, Hood River. 12 Russian nucs. No extra queens. Side yard. ***VIP!!!" was scrawled in red across the page.

Joyful looked miffed but didn't apologize. She handed Alice the crumpled paper and pointed toward the overflow area.

This situation was nothing new to Alice. She was a Holtzman, after all. German-American, rational, she always planned ahead and thought things through like her parents had taught her. She tried to anticipate what might go awry and work in advance to avoid hiccups. She knew most other people were not as conscientious. She often found herself waiting for others to catch up with her thinking, having fallen short before they even started. So how did she account for this feeling now, this impatience, the childish urge to reach across the counter and yank Joyful's dreadlocks? She took the paper and walked to the side yard.

A couple of regular staff, Nick and Steve, helped Alice duct-tape the tops of the cardboard boxes and carefully load each one into the back of her pickup. She tightened a tie-down strap around the bases of the boxes to keep them from sliding around.

"Sorry, Alice," Nick said, rolling his eyes toward Joyful. He was a nice guy about her age with a handlebar mustache.

"New management while Tim's in Arizona. Family stuff, I guess."

Alice shrugged, tried to smile, and failed. She shut the gate of the truck harder than she needed to. It wasn't Nick's fault that she'd wasted more than an hour on what was meant to be a fifteen-minute stop, but she wasn't going to stand around making small talk.

"Thanks, Nick," she said. "Tell Tim to give me a holler about that honey extractor when he gets back."

Now on the clogged highway, Alice huffed with annoyance. She reached across the seat and grabbed the bag of mini Chips Ahoy! cookies she knew she shouldn't have bought at Costco earlier that day. She pulled out a handful of cookies and tossed them into her mouth.

She hated to admit it, but she'd been running late long before she got to Sunnyvale. She stopped at Tillicum Lumberyard and then at Costco, that great behemoth of retail they didn't have in little Hood River. People shoved past her, and one harassed-looking mother of two banged her cart into Alice's heels and didn't even apologize. Alice waited forever in the checkout line, which made her stressed. Then she'd lost an hour waiting for her bees and was now smack in the middle of the afternoon traffic she'd tried so hard to avoid. It was why she'd called ahead two days ago. It was why she'd taken the day off and gotten up early. She tried so hard to have everything organized. It was other people who fouled things up. She felt a bloom of anxiety then. The line of traffic inched along, and her chest felt tight. She cracked the window, but the hot smell of asphalt stung her nostrils, so she shut it again. She looked at the cars on either side of her. Nobody else seemed to mind sitting here. They were all looking at their phones. She gripped the steering wheel, feeling the tightness creep up into her throat. Then she heard Dr. Zimmerman's calm voice in her head: *"Do you know where that feeling comes from, Alice? Can you follow the thread?"*

Alice inhaled deeply and flexed her hands. Being still was so hard for her these days. If she stayed focused, kept working, her thoughts couldn't blindside her. No, Dr. Zimmerman, she thought, she couldn't follow the thread. Not with 120,000 Russian honeybees in the back of the pickup.

She ate another handful of dusty cookies and glanced in the rear-view mirror at the nucleus hives wedged together in the back of the truck. The spring sunshine was mild enough, so she wasn't worried about the bees getting overheated on the ride home, slow as it was. Once there, she intended to get them hived before sunset. She could do it quickly, all twelve on her own, she was sure. She was efficient and had laid out her tools in the shop the night before, all cleaned and polished. Remembering that made her anxiety rise again. She stayed up late to set things up so she could get back early and install her hives before dark. She took a deep breath, trying to slow her thudding heart. She tossed the cookie bag into the back seat, where she couldn't reach it.

At the exit for Multnomah Falls, which marked the halfway point to Hood River, Alice saw two cars pulled over on the shoulder—a fender bender, from the looks of it. The lane was cleared by the time she reached it, but everyone was still rubbernecking. Two men stood next to their dinged-up cars talking on their cell phones. Probably some tourist trying to take a photo without the inconvenience of stopping. It happened all the time—people leaning out the window to snap a photo of the 611-foot waterfall.

After the wreck, the highway opened up, and soon she was doing eighty, heading east as the sun dropped behind her. The freedom of movement made her feel calmer. Alice took off her hat and sunglasses. She unhooked one strap of her overalls, an admission that they didn't really fit anymore, but she didn't care. She turned up the music—Springsteen's "Born to Run."

Alice disliked Portland, with its confusing network of bridges, snarls of traffic, and aggressive panhandlers. But the open road leading away from it, she loved. Basalt cliffs overlapped each other in a view that unfolded mile after mile along the Columbia River. She knew the distinct monoliths by heart—Rooster Rock, Wind Mountain, Beacon Rock. In the early sunset, the green hills and rocky crags were cast in a pink veil. It looked like a painting, like a dream. Alice never grew tired of looking at it, this impossible beauty that she had lived within for forty-four years. She passed a semi and glanced at the wide river on her left. The dark green water was frothy from the wind, whitecaps whipped-up and pushing against the current. She saw a mass of white pelicans resting on a gleaming sandbar and towering Douglas fir trees leaning out over the water. An osprey circled the river, keening. On the right, she saw the headlight of an oncoming train. It passed her, and she heard the whistle blow and recede. The setting sun threw a gauzy light over the water, and Alice felt her body relax.

She took exit 62, slowed, and stopped at the top of the ramp. She rolled down the window, and the cool wind off the Columbia River blew through the truck and teased strands of hair around her face. She could smell the water, the pines along the road, and the faint scent of woodsmoke. She could smell the distinct green breath of spring. She passed the Red Carpet Tavern, its roof sagging sadly, and noted that the parking lot, as usual, was full of pickup trucks of guys stopping for a beer on their way home from work. She smiled to recall her father so often in their midst—slender and reticent, but drawing others to him with the force of his kindness under his cutting sense of humor. The road past the bar would take her south to her little house outside of town down in a dell at the end of Reed Road. There was orchard on one side and forest on the other. It was the perfect spot for honeybees— sheltered from the wind and with Susan Creek running down off the hillside providing water for her girls, as she liked to call them. Beside the irrigation ditches were tangled miles of clover, blackberry, and dandelion. Bee heaven.

The dell was perfect for Alice too, because she hardly ever saw anyone out there. Other than Doug Ransom, whose large orchard sprawled pleasantly to the west of her, she had no real neighbors un- less you counted Strawberry Hollow, a messy collection of trailers at the foot of Anson Road. She didn't know anyone who lived there and kept her distance. Meth heads and pit bulls, she imagined. Rapists and creeps of all sorts, she thought. She started making up headlines.

"Ten Arrested in Trailer Park Drug Bust."

"Shallow Grave Discovered at Strawberry Hollow."

Then she stopped herself. Like the anxiety, this was also new—making up ugly stories about people she didn't know.

"They are just thoughts, Alice, and the pattern promotes a negative outlook," Dr. Zimmerman had said to her. "But you can shift those patterns and rewire your thinking. It just takes practice."

Dr. Zimmerman was obviously very smart. She had diplomas from Harvard and Stanford on her wall. She had worked in Palo Alto, ostensibly fixing the tech crazies, before moving to Hood River for semi-retirement. Despite the diplomas and her chic looks, which were unusual in this rural outpost, she wasn't arrogant. Just confident. And kind. Still, the fact that she, Alice Holtzman, was seeing a therapist was absurd. You had to laugh, she thought. Only it wasn't funny, was it?

Alice steered the truck south toward Mount Hood, toward the home she had bought with the help of her mom and dad. They were third-generation orchardists, both of them. It was hard work, but they had loved it.

"Never be afraid of hard work, Alice," her mother would say.

"Or I'll come back from the grave and kick you in the rear, my dear," her dad would say with a wicked grin.

A life lived outside, they always said, was a good life.

"A good life," she said aloud, glancing into the rearview mirror at the twelve nucleus hives, each holding a queen and her workers and so much promise.

"Almost home, girls. You'll have a good life. I promise."

Though it was no longer the quiet backwater it had been when Alice was born, Hood River was still a great place to live. The 1980s brought the windsurfers with their vans and long hair. There were some fights between them and local loggers and farmers, like the ones who hung out at the Red Carpet. But the hippies who caused trouble ultimately left. The ones who stayed started families, fixed up the town's old houses, and opened businesses—cafés, pizza places, and windsurfing stores. The town grew. The last decade had seen an explosion of wineries, fancy boutiques, breweries, and restaurants. It wasn't the same town anymore, but for locals like the Holtzmans, who lived outside all that, it didn't matter. Their lives kept chugging along the same tracks. The sunburned tourists who plodded through downtown clutching iced coffees had no idea that the heart of this place was far from Oak Street, up the valley, and out in the orchards. Those long rows of trees were far more than a postcard backdrop for their scenic drives. They were history, part of a tradition that was more than one hundred years old.

Alice's family was part of that history. The Holtzman orchards were small, but they were all heirloom stock from the 1900s—Gravensteins, Pippins, and Winesaps—nothing like the mushy Red Delicious apples from your average school lunch. This was fine, flavorful fruit. Al and Marina Holtzman had taken over the orchard from Al's parents, who had taken it over from his grandparents—German immigrants who'd arrived in the valley before World War I. Al and Marina had made a living for themselves and Alice, their only child. They'd been happy there.

Alice rolled to a stop at Country Club Road, signaled right, and glanced left, alert for the plodding tractor one was apt to see on a spring evening like this. The quiet lane was empty. She hung a right and continued toward home.

Alice had been planning to take over the orchard from her parents since she was ten years old. When the time came, she knew she'd have to work hard and keep her job at the county to make ends meet. But to her shock, Al and Marina had decided to sell eight years ago. Her dad had become disheartened by changes in the industry. The big producers had forced spray laws on the county that the smaller farmers couldn't stomach. Not that the Holtzman operation had ever been fully organic. Al Holtzman was too much of a libertarian to let those words cross his lips. But he was German, after all. Sensible. He sprayed minimally and by hand. The county regulations were too much, he said, and went too far.

"It's poison, Alice," he said, shaking his head. "The fools are cutting off their noses to spite their own faces."

She hated to see her parents pushed aside by the demands of the larger orchardists, who were too stubborn, busy, or just plain wrongheaded to consider different options. As for the county, well, Alice worked in the county planning department. She knew how backward things could be. It could take years to change a simple mailbox ordinance. Alice had later wished she'd argued with him about it, wished she'd told him how much she wanted it. But she didn't want to make him feel worse. Her eyes prickled with tears remembering. She wiped them away with the back of her wrist.

Al and Marina gave Alice some money from the sale of the orchard, which she used to buy her place in the quiet dell—a single-story rancher on a couple of acres. She thought they might eventually move in with her. But they had wanted to be independent, and they'd moved into a town house. They died within six months of each other—Al first. Alice missed them.

She talked to Dr. Zimmerman about them too. She mentioned she seemed to hear their voices in her head and sometimes she talked back to them, though that might sound nuts. Dr. Zimmerman looked at Alice over the tops of her glasses. Alice blushed. She supposed it wasn't polite to say "nuts."

But Dr. Zimmerman simply nodded. "It must be a comfort to you," she said.

But they both knew the reason Alice went to see the nice lady doctor was not because she missed her folks.

Alice slowed for a large fruit packing truck barreling through the intersection near the road to Kingsley Reservoir. She glanced south to find Mount Hood on the horizon, kissed with sunset. She turned up the stereo, which was now playing one of her favorite Springsteen songs, "Thunder Road."

Alice had started seeing Dr. Zimmerman after she'd had what felt like a heart attack in the middle of the produce section in Little Bit Grocery and Ranch Supply three months earlier. She'd been standing next to Carlos, the friendly, handsome clerk, the one who always called her "Madame" or "Miss Alice" and always had a story to share about his kids or the news. For the first time she had felt that invisible band ratcheting down across her chest, and she couldn't catch her breath. She slid to the floor, pulling down a pile of kale with her. Carlos eased her into a sitting position against a rack of absurd, uncut Brussels stalks. She could see his lips moving but couldn't hear any sound. She was close enough to see that he had a tiny bit of shaving cream on the smooth brown skin behind his ear. She felt she needed to tell him and wanted to laugh at that urge. The paramedics came, and then it seemed like half of Hood River County was standing around looking down at Alice Holtzman sitting on the floor, her chest heaving and red in the face. Her face flamed now, remembering.

She knew almost everyone at the small ER too. Jim Verk, who she'd known since second grade, was on duty that night and told her she'd had a panic attack. She went to see Dr. Zimmerman at his recommendation. Nobody in the history of the Holtzman family had ever been to a therapist, but the experience at Little Bit had embarrassed Alice so much that she was willing to try anything to avoid a repeat episode.

Alice stared at the road and realized she was gripping the steering wheel as she remembered. She willed herself to relax. The sunset was winning their race when she reached the Oak Grove Schoolhouse. She sped up the hill, which was shadowed by tall Douglas firs that marked the boundary of county forest land. Through the window, she felt the cool air at the top of the rise and glanced at the bees again in the rearview mirror. The new nucs were the root of her anxiety, she realized. Every step of her carefully planned day was bent toward successful hive installment. These bees depended on her. But at this hour, the temperature would be even colder down in her shady ravine, and she didn't want to stress the girls with exposure to the cold, dark air and the artificial light of the shop. They would have to wait until tomorrow, she told herself. They had honey in their combs to eat and would be fine for one night in their nuc boxes. Better for her to make the transfers when she was fresh to avoid any silly mistakes.

"Be sensible now and pull yourself together," her mother's voice said.

Alice sighed and surrendered the idea of that chore.

"Tomorrow morning before work, then," she said aloud.

Alice relaxed back into the seat and palmed the wheel as she followed the familiar curves of Reed Road. She let her mind drift, trusting her thoughts to behave, expecting her customary self-discipline to keep any worrisome memories rounded up like obedient sheep by a collie. But then she recalled her last session with Dr. Zimmerman. The therapist had been leading Alice toward the forbidden topic for some time, but they hadn't ever quite arrived. Alice kept certain thoughts behind a firmly closed door in her mind and had resisted Dr. Zimmerman's gentle prodding. Now, without warning, the door opened a crack. Later she would blame fatigue for her careless bargaining with herself. I'll just think of his face, she thought. Just that. Then the door burst open and the memories flooded her.

Bud laughing as he stood behind the counter at the John Deere store. A photo of Bud in his parks department uniform on the front page of the *Hood River News*. Bud looking so serious that she thought he was breaking up with her, but he asked her to marry him instead. That day at the courthouse, the day he moved in, the day they brought the baby chicks home from Little Bit and sat on the floor watching them peep and hop around under the heat lamp. Buddy waltzing his laughing mother around the living room after Sunday dinner to Sinatra's "Fly Me to the Moon." Buddy loading the little nephews in the truck to go fishing and running back to the house to kiss Alice goodbye.

Alice didn't realize she was speeding when she hit the curve at the top of the hill. She was thinking about her husband, Robert Ryan, who everyone knew as Buddy. Buddy, who had arrived so suddenly in her quiet life, bringing such unexpected happiness. Buddy, who was now gone.

The pressure ballooned in her chest, and her throat caught. Her breath grew ragged and shallow and then exploded into hot sobs. Her vision blurred as her eyes filled. Triggered, her grief loosened like a load of big timbers from one of the logging trucks she had passed on the highway.

Alice wiped an arm across her streaming eyes as she swerved toward the edge of the road. In the twin arms of her headlights, she saw a shape in the shoulder. She slammed on the brakes, swerved, and banged to a stop against a fence post.

Alice felt 120,000 Russian honeybees crash together in the back of her truck. Her head bounced as the seat belt arrested her. Time slowed. Her head rang. She saw spots of white and blue zipping around her field of vision. She looked in the rearview mirror and saw a wheelchair on its side, one wheel spinning like a runaway Ferris wheel.

Alice scrambled out of the truck and ran across the road. She could not move fast enough and felt like she was swimming through the cool air. She began to pray, her eyes searching the tall grass in the waning light. She saw a person on the ground next to the chair. Was he hurt? Alice crouched, her hands on her knees, and peered down. The figure rolled onto its back. Alice expected to see some confused old person, a little guy in his bathrobe and slippers doing a runner from Riverdale Retirement Center up the road. But she saw a boy—a teenage boy with crazy hair and a tangle of earbuds and sunglasses on his face. Holy shit! She'd hit a damn kid!

The boy pushed his sunglasses off his face and looked up at her. He smiled. Relief surged through her, and she wanted to cry. Instead she yelled.

"Christ on a crutch, kid! What in the hell are you trying to do? Get yourself killed?"

3

FORAGING

The drones begin to make their appearance in April or May; earlier or later, according to the forwardness of the season, and the strength of the stock. In colonies too weak to swarm, none as a general rule are reared; for in such hives, as no young queens are raised, drones would be only useless consumers.

—L. L. LANGSTROTH

If Harry Stokes had to choose one word to describe how he was feeling on this particular morning, he would have said, unequivocally, "hungry." But it was just a medium kind of hungry, nothing serious. This was not "famished" or "ravenous." And yet it was well beyond "peckish." It was the kind of hunger that made him pay attention, a hunger that left him keenly aware that his present situation was untenable.

He sat on the steps of his uncle's trailer and dragged his finger along the bottom of the Jif jar. He sucked his fingertip, confirming that the plastic container held nothing but a faint memory of its previous contents. He peered wistfully into the bottom and then lobbed it toward the trash pile. It fell with a thunk and rolled back toward him. A light breeze rose and circled his thin neck like a cool scarf. Harry shivered and pulled up his hood. It was midmorning, but the sunshine had not yet penetrated the wall of towering Douglas fir trees that rose around the clearing in which the trailer sat. His stomach growled, uncoiling like a cartoon spring.

To distract himself from the empty yawn of his appetite, Harry pulled out his notebook and opened it up to a half-full page upon which he'd been tallying the pros and cons of his current situation. He picked up his pen and glanced around. What Harry liked best about where he found himself, he decided, was the setting. The Klickitat River roared behind the trailer, a white-water highway that drowned out all other noise. You couldn't even hear the county road from here where the trailer was tucked away in the woods. Harry also liked the view of Mount Adams. The sleeping volcano crouched under heavy spring snow to the north like a white monster.

"Pastoral Beauty," Harry wrote in the left-hand column of his notebook. He couldn't remember what "pastoral" meant, exactly—something outdoorsy—but it had a nice ring to it. Anyway, it was a good list word—short and punchy.

This list-making strategy was something Harry had employed for at least two decades of his young life. It was a habit conceived of the day he perched in a booster seat in the back of his mother's Lincoln Town Car, clutching an orange crayon in his four-year-old fist. That was the day his mother had driven out of Mississippi and toward New York City, leaving his father and the sweltering South behind. Harry could barely remember his father. But he remembered the wet heat of the summer day and the joy on his mother's face when they reached the city limits of Hattiesburg. She lit a cigarette and rolled down the window.

"What's in New York, Mama?" he asked.

She blew smoke out the window and looked at him in the rearview mirror.

"The Statue of Liberty, son. And the Empire State Building. Broadway, where all the famous actors go. Central Park has a pond and a zoo. In New York, they have policemen on horses. You're gonna love it, Harry."

She smiled, waving the smoke out of her face, and Harry wanted to believe her because he liked it when his mother smiled.

"What about Daddy?" he asked.

There was a pause, and then she said, "Nope. Not your daddy. Your daddy will not be in New York."

At least that was the way Harry remembered it—the smell of cigarette smoke, Patsy Cline on the radio, and his mother singing along. In his mind's eye, Harry could see the orange crayon and the paper. He'd drawn a horse, a policeman, and a caged tiger on one side of the page and a stick figure of his father on the other—thereby marking his first tally of life's pros and cons. Harry continued to use this strategy as a young man. The list-making helped, or at least Harry liked to believe it did, as he so often found himself stuck between the now and the next.

"Analysis paralysis," Sal teased him. *"Kid couldn't decide his way out of a paper bag."*

His mother would shush his stepfather, saying Harry was doing just fine, that he was actively considering his options when he made the lists. However, not even she would say that Harry was doing anything remotely active now—living in his uncle's trailer off of Highway 141 in the woods near BZ Corner. Harry had been content with his situation until recently. He liked the peace and quiet. Those were two more items for the left-hand column. And privacy. Harry hadn't seen a single person since his uncle left. Only chattering birds and flashes of small creatures in the underbrush.

"Wildlife," he wrote under "Privacy," although wildlife wasn't always a positive element to rural life. The golden grosbeaks that flashed down onto the sunny driveway were beautiful. But the aggressive raccoon guarding the trash pile was not. Harry was almost certain he'd seen a coyote, its lanky brown body slung low to the ground, skulking around the edges of the property.

"My propity!" Uncle H was always saying, his Mississippi accent still strong even after decades out west. "Private propity! They got no reason to trespass up here into my bidness, do they?"

Harry was unclear about who "they" might be, seeing as nobody had visited his uncle in the two months Harry had been staying there. Feisty Uncle H—short for Harold, last name of Goodwin—didn't welcome visitors. Harry conjectured there'd been a fire sale on "No Trespassing" signs at the hardware store since dozens of them hung along the overgrown driveway all the way to the mailbox. Uncle H had affixed them with nails, tacks, and duct tape. Tattered and windblown, they added to the general atmosphere of neglect that surrounded the dilapidated trailer.

Harry wondered whether his uncle really owned any "propity" here in the dark woods near BZ Corner. It seemed possible that he was just squatting and whoever owned the land couldn't be bothered to move him or didn't know he was there. BZ was really nothing more than a wide spot in the road just north of Hood River. In his short time there, Harry had determined that people who lived in BZ seemed to be of three types: 1) God-fearing retired loggers who liked to hunt, fish, and keep to themselves. 2) The cagey and unemployed, who were shifty-looking enough that you wanted to steer clear. 3) Second homeowners from Portland who'd built rustic vacation homes they rarely occupied.

Harry wouldn't say it to his face, but Uncle H seemed to be firmly in the second category. It was unclear how the old man had landed here or why he'd stayed. He had a daughter and grandchildren in Mississippi still, Harry's mom said. Harry had no idea where he got his money, of which there seemed to be little. When he sent Harry to the store, he'd pull crumpled ones and fives out of his pockets to pay for groceries. Harry's status as a guest was tenuous enough that he didn't ask questions. The only thing that kept his uncle from lumping him in with those other trespassers to his "propity," Harry thought, was that Uncle H always liked Harry's mother, Uncle H's sister's daughter.

"Your mama, she's a good woman. Bona fide heart of gold," he'd say whenever she came up in conversation. "Genuine article."

Still, the issue of "propity" was part of the reason Harry was staying with his uncle in the crummy little trailer in the woods. Namely that Harry didn't have any.

The trailer. That would definitely go in the right-hand column.

"Sorry, Uncle H," he said aloud, "but it is a genuine, bona fide piece of crap."

The trailer had seen better days. Among its failings: Loose siding that banged in the wind and ragged insulation spilling out of cheap paneling. It had no running water, spotty electricity, and great holes in the floor. At night Harry could hear mice skittering behind the walls. At some point the stairs had given way, so when Harry had arrived in February, the old man, who was nearing ninety, was using a homemade ladder to climb in and out of the trailer. He seemed as unfazed to see his great-nephew walking up the muddy drive unannounced as he was to climb in and out of the trailer for twice-daily trips to the outhouse. Uncle H hadn't questioned the young man's story about wanting to see the West. If he had talked to Lydia about Harry's "trouble," as his mother liked to put it, Uncle H didn't let on.

Harry liked his uncle, who seemed content to hold up the conversation for both of them for hours on end. He talked about his years as a railroad engineer for BNSF, traveling from coast to coast. How he hitchhiked through every province in Canada as far as the remote territory of Newfoundland, facing the wild Labrador Sea. He regaled Harry with tales of the fine-looking women he'd met on his travels. Harry was a good listener. Perhaps that was why, after he had been there for a week, his uncle didn't ask when he was leaving. Instead,

Uncle H sent him into BZ for groceries and ice for the cooler, which he used since the refrigerator was broken. Harry procured the small supply of what Uncle H deemed staples: Jif, macaroni and cheese, Spam, potatoes, light beer, toilet paper, and Cheez-Its. After that, Harry did the shopping every three or four days.

The two fell into an amicable routine. Uncle H enjoyed a captive audience for his stories and endless games of cribbage. Harry, stuck as he was between the recent debacle of his past and the uncertainty of his future, was happy to pause there, suspended between what he had done and what he might make of himself. As the spring rains swept through the great woods, the two of them sat at the dinette in the mildewed trailer playing cards or reading from Uncle H's library, which consisted of wildlife guides, Pacific Northwest history books, and a few ragged mysteries. Uncle H yanked gleefully on his shock of white hair whenever he beat his great-nephew at cards, which was often. In the afternoon, Uncle H curled up and napped. When the rain lightened, Harry poked around in the woods above the river. Once he had tried to tidy up around the trailer, sorting through the trash to see what might be salvageable or recyclable, but his uncle yelled at him to mind his own goddamn business and get his hands off his things. He stomped up the ladder with a ferocity that alarmed Harry, given his age and the integrity of the ladder, and slammed the flimsy door. Harry had spent the rest of that day down by the river. By the time he came back, Uncle H was frying up Spam and potatoes for dinner. He waxed Harry at cribbage for the hundredth time and didn't mention the incident.

After that, Harry stuck to sanctioned chores, like repairing the exterior of the trailer and reinforcing the ladder. Harry was handy with that sort of thing, and his uncle seemed to appreciate it. He'd also walk or hitchhike to the small grocery store. He stood with his thumb out, willing himself to look safe and friendly in his greasy pants and knit cap. People probably stopped faster for the old man tottering down the shoulder of Highway 141, he thought. The sight of Uncle H in his long johns worn under shorts and tube socks might have been the reason social services had shown up two days ago. Or, rather, the not-sight of him, after Harry took over the shopping.

BZ was a small community. Someone must have noticed that Uncle H hadn't made the trip for a while. Nobody would have recognized that his great-nephew was shopping for him. Harry never spoke to anyone at the grocery store. Uncle H had no phone, so nobody could call to check on him. Harry had heard him grumble that his doctor nagged him to get a phone. So, although Uncle H might not have been surprised to see the county folks, Harry had been.

When the white sedan and ambulance rolled slowly up the driveway two days ago, the old man was sleeping, as he had been doing more and more, and not just on rainy days. Harry was outside taking a leak, standing on the edge of the clearing where the woods began. A car emblazoned with a "Hood River County Official Use" seal led the way. Two women climbed out—a passenger in pink hospital scrubs and the driver in khaki pants and a navy cardigan. Harry saw a guy about his age climb out of the ambulance. The sedan driver said something to him and he nodded, leaned against the door of the ambulance, and began thumbing through his phone. The two women walked toward the trailer.

"Hello! Mr. Goodwin?"

The driver pulled off her glasses as she approached the door.

"Mr. Goodwin? Are you home?"

Harry felt an urge toward hospitality mixed with a sense of protectiveness. He moved to step into the sunlight and introduce himself as the great-nephew to and namesake of Harold Goodwin. He would ask these people who they were and what they needed. He would climb inside and help his uncle down the ladder, even though Uncle H got mad when Harry offered help.

But Harry didn't do any of that. Instead, he turned around and ran. He couldn't say how long he sprinted the narrow game trail above the river, but when he finally stopped, sweating and panting, he found himself deeper in the woods than he'd gone before. He collapsed on the loamy dirt and tried to slow his hammering heart. He thought of his mother. "Exasperating!" she would say. Like when, in first grade and unable to work the stiff button on his new jeans, Harry had wet himself at school. When she picked him up, she asked, "Harry, why didn't you ask a teacher for help?" Harry just shrugged and wiped his nose on his sleeve. "Exasperating," she had muttered for the first of a thousand times.

Sitting with his back against a log, Harry would not have argued. He had no reasonable explanation for running. He could not put this childlike panic into words befitting adult behavior. Surely, he could do better than this. At least no one had seen him. He stood up and started back to the trailer. He breathed deeply and rehearsed the words in his head.

"Hello. My name is Harry Stokes. I'm Mr. Goodwin's great-nephew, visiting from Long Island. How can I help?"

That was what he would say. When he got back to the trailer, however, the driveway was empty. Harry sighed with relief. He wouldn't have to say anything after all, but he would be ready next time. He climbed into the trailer, buoyed by the luck of the near miss.

"Hey, Uncle H," he called. "You awake in here?" His uncle didn't answer because his uncle wasn't there. Harry climbed outside and checked the outhouse to confirm the sinking truth. Those people had taken him away.

That was two days ago. Harry figured they had taken Uncle H to the hospital in that ambulance, and part of him was relieved. Uncle H had been sleeping a lot and acting strange. Last week he had looked up during a hand of cribbage and scowled at Harry.

"Who let you in here?" he growled.

"You did, Uncle H," Harry said nervously.

The old man's frown relaxed, and he laughed.

If Uncle H had mentioned his great-nephew, the county people might not have believed the kooky old man. Harry planned to hitchhike down to the hospital and check on him. But he hadn't gone that first day or yesterday. Today was day three. He could have at least called from the pay phone in BZ Corner. He didn't want to think about why he hadn't. He was ashamed of himself, which made his hunger disappear briefly. He put the thought away and cast his gaze down the overgrown driveway.

"Security," Harry wrote in his now-full left column. However, those assets were growing decidedly less attractive in the face of other facts: he was dirty, hungry, a little worried about food poisoning with the cooler situation, and slightly miserable waking up alone in the dark woods. He didn't feel close to his uncle, exactly, but Uncle H had been someone to talk to or at least listen to. However, the weeks Harry had spent at his uncle's hadn't put him any closer to solving his own problems, which were considerable. He flipped back to that list, which was growing.

Under the header "Spring 2014 Status Report," he had written the following: "Problems: Homeless (not counting trailer), Jobless, Checking account: $318.57, Owe Mom and Sal $1,468.25."

He sighed. Harry needed money. He knew his mother would send him some if he asked. She always did, saying it was just to help him get on his feet. But this wasn't a crisis. He'd simply run out of money like he always did when he hit a dead end because he had no plan. No, he couldn't call his mother. Besides, she'd ask about Uncle H. He felt a lead weight in his stomach thinking of the old man alone at the hospital.

Harry turned the page and wrote a new list.

"April 2014 Tasks: Update résumé, Apply for jobs, Go see H, Call Mom." He drew an arrow and moved "Go see H" to the top of the list, which made him feel better.

The idea of looking for work made his stomach clench. Work was not the problem. Harry was a hard worker. The problem was interviewing, talking to people, closing the deal.

"You don't follow through, kid!" Sal would yell. *"That last place offered you a job and you never called back! What the heck is wrong with you?"*

Exasperating.

Harry had no reasonable explanation. How could he describe the paralyzing set of questions a new situation would present? What was the best route to drive to work in the morning? What was he supposed to wear? Did people bring a lunch, or did they go out? What if he had to use the bathroom, like, really use the bathroom? He couldn't ask anyone those questions, so it was easier to come up with white lies: the pay was bad, the hours were lousy, the manager seemed like a jerk.

Harry tapped his pen against his upper lip. Getting a job would be harder than usual this time, not just because he was living in the woods without a car. There was also the nagging detail that Harry was a criminal. Or had been. Past tense. But he had served his time for that. It was behind him, he told himself. First things first. He had to find his uncle.

He grabbed a towel, soap, and a change of clothes and walked into the woods toward the river. For all the vagueness of the term "pastoral beauty," Harry had truly become enamored of the great dark woods around Uncle H's place. The days he rambled through the trees above the river he found himself shocked by the beauty of the simplest things: the electric-green moss growing on a tree trunk; an unexpected sunbreak lighting up the ghost of a tree snag. Once, as he tramped along, a handful of small birds, squabbling among themselves, had flown out of the trees and directly across his path. They'd been so engrossed in their spat that they hadn't even noticed him. "A quarrel of sparrows." That was what the bird book called them. Another night, just before bed, Harry stood outside in the darkness and looked up at the stars, which were so bright there far from any city, brighter than any he'd ever seen. Then he heard the deep, pulsating call of an owl throbbing through the woods around him. Harry could not have said which tree the great bird sat in, as the call seemed to be everywhere at once. The hoot came again, and Harry felt it settle into his chest and fill his heart. A child of the suburbs, he had never been so close to such wildness and had not known it would stir such feeling in him. He would have called it happiness if someone had asked him. But there was nobody to do so.

Harry walked the trail to a small sandbar on the river where the wild current circled back on itself and created a calm eddy. He stripped to pale gooseflesh, took a deep breath, and jumped into the icy water, which shocked the breath out of him. He toed the sandy bottom before scrambling out to soap his hair and body in the fragile sunlight. Then he jumped in again, scrubbing himself clean.

Back on the bank, he dried off and pulled on the cleanest of his two pair of pants and one of his uncle's shirts, a tartan wool with the tags still attached. His body tingled as he walked back to the trailer. He shaved in the small mirror his uncle had hung on a tree. Bald at twenty-four, or balding, anyway, he sighed. He had considered shaving it all off but remembered how a high school dare had revealed his bumpy Neanderthal skull.

Yet he wanted to do something to mark a change and a fresh start. When he'd first come west, he planned to get a tattoo but couldn't decide on the right image. He'd spent an hour in the tattoo shop in Seattle, flipping through the books before leaving with a sheepish wave. The big guy looked up from the customer he was working on and jerked his chin at Harry.

"Sometimes it takes a while to decide, bro," he called.

Was he sneering? What if he was? Harry felt like such a nerd. Why did he care what that guy thought, anyway, some stranger?

Harry shaved his skinny jawline and chin but left the stubble on his upper lip. He'd grow a mustache. Out on the river, he'd seen some kayakers with mustaches lately. Guys his age. It could be cool.

He pulled his beanie over his damp hair and grabbed his backpack, which contained his notebook, a pen, a bottle of water, and a slightly dented orange. Harry walked down the gravel drive past the collection of tattered "No Trespassing" signs to the highway and turned south, warming up as he went and looking up at the great dark trees.

"Where you off to, little Harry Stokes?"

He could almost hear his mother's voice. She always asked that when she saw him readying to leave the house when he was a boy.

Harry, short for Harold. Harold Stokes. Middle name of Courtland. The whole thing was ridiculous, really. Harold Courtland Stokes III. It sounded like some country club member you'd read about in the *Times*. His parents' families were poor, but ostentatious names were common in the South. Of Harold Courtland Stokes II, Harry had a fuzzy memory of a tall man laughing as he dabbed whiskey on Harry's tongue with his pinky, cigarette smoke curling around his big hand.

One afternoon when he was in high school, he'd screwed up the courage to ask his mother about his father as he helped her unload a truck full of compost. How did they meet? Why did she leave? Did his father ever ask about him?

"Your father is a jackass," she said, mashing out her cigarette with the heel of her boot and pulling on her gloves. He didn't ask again.

When she took Harry north to New York, Lydia had wanted to become an actress. Instead she ended up waitressing at a Long Island golf club, where she had met and married a nice guy named Sal Romano. Sal ran a landscaping business and had been the only father Harry had ever known. Good old Sal.

Harry heard an approaching car and turned, sticking out his thumb. It was a Subaru wagon with a young family inside. The father never took his eyes off the road. The mother flicked her gaze at him and away. Guilt. Fear. Two car seats in back. Harry couldn't blame them. He kept walking.

Sal and Lydia had announced in January that they were selling the Long Island house and moving to Florida for good. Sarasota, where they'd been wintering, had won them over. Sal was sick of the landscaping business, especially after Hurricane Sandy. Lydia was tired of the snow. In Sarasota, she'd taken up pickleball, and Sal wanted to sit by the pool and read the tomes of military history he favored. Harry struggled to hide his disappointment.

"That's great!" he'd managed. "Here's to you guys!" He raised his beer to clink with their wineglasses. His enthusiasm was feeble, and he knew it showed. It wasn't lost on him that their announcement coincided with his parole officer signing off on him two weeks earlier, leaving him free and clear to leave the state if he liked. Living in their basement was always meant to be temporary, but it weighed on him, the thought of moving on by himself. His mother set down her wineglass and reached a hand across the table, her eyes misty.

"You're gonna be just fine, Harry. Fresh start, honey. And if you ever need a place to stay, you can always—"

"Bup-bup-bup!" Sal held up his big hand like a stop sign. "Don't get carried away, Lydia hon."

He raised his glass again.

"To Harry's future," he said. "May it be as bright as his mother's eyes."

Lydia sniffled and raised her glass. Harry had forced a smile and swigged his beer.

The wind picked up, and a chill spiked down his neck. He buttoned up his uncle's wool shirt. The sun went behind a cloud, and the pavement in front of him freckled with raindrops. Harry pulled his cap lower and hunched his shoulders.

He heard the whine of an approaching engine and stuck out his thumb. A Ford Econoline van lumbered past and pulled over. Harry jogged up to the window and saw a young woman behind the wheel. Bright blue eyes under a red trucker cap over brown braids and a plaid flannel shirt. She smiled and rolled down the window.

"Hi! Um, I'm, like, totally lost! Do you know the pullout for the upper Klickitat run? I'm delivering lunch for a Wet Planet rafting trip."

Harry knew the pullout was just down the road. He often saw the bright yellow rafts clear the rapids behind Uncle H's place and eddy out at the sandy beach. He pointed south and explained where to turn off.

The young woman giggled and rolled her eyes. "I'm terrible with directions. Can you just show me?"

That was how Harry found himself in the warm, dry van, munching on an enormous pastrami sandwich from River Daze Cafe in Hood River with the beautiful Moira. After she dropped off the lunches, she climbed back behind the wheel and asked Harry where he was headed.

"I'm going down to Hood River if you want a ride," she said.

He hesitated. He didn't want to explain about his uncle, so he just told her he was looking for work.

"I don't know what you're looking for, but there's more jobs in Hood River than BZ," she said.

Harry nodded, deciding he would go see Uncle H on the way home from Hood River.

Moira turned up the music. Harry smiled, bit into his sandwich, and stole a glance at her long, tanned legs in cutoff jean shorts. She drove the van with her knees and lit a joint, threw her head back, and sang along with the Dead.

"What a loooooong strange trip it's been!"

She inhaled, coughed, smiled at Harry, and passed him the joint. For the first time in a long time, Harry felt like things were looking up.

· 4 ·

CALLOW BEE

Let all your motions about your hives be gentle and slow.
Accustom your bees to your presence: never crush or
injure them, or breathe upon them in any operation.

—L. L. LANGSTROTH

The year had finally turned a shoulder on Oregon's bleak winter and
was hinting at the promise of summer. Nights like this, after sunset,
the sky darkened and then turned that improbable green-yellow
against the black hillside. Jake had always loved the bruised light that
clung like an anti-shadow to the ridgeline. He gazed at it now, remembering the first time he'd been old enough to be outside this late in the
evening. On the school playground, a parent-teacher night. He spun
in circles on the tire swing, watching the sky darken as he waited for
his mother, feeling like such a big kid.

He could hear the spring runoff coursing through the irrigation
ditch that ran alongside Reed Road at his shoulder. By late March, the
snowmelt off Mount Hood flooded the drainages of the valley and
filled the night air with a clean green scent, that distinct smell of
young spring. It was one reason he had always loved being out in the
orchards at twilight even before the accident.

He shifted onto his back and tuned into the raucous song of

chorus frogs in the ditch. He recalled his eternal debate with Noah about where the thumb-size creatures went in winter. Did they hibernate or die off? How did they know when it was time to reemerge and start singing so hopefully into the cold air? Why was he lying next to the ditch? Time had slowed, and the tiny frogs bleated like a metronome for this in-between place. Metronome. Keeping time, like Cheney's enormous, drumming tail.

Noah's sister Angela had found Cheney running around after school one day the fall of the boys' junior year. His skinny brindled rump and lack of a collar marked him as a stray. A pair of hilarious helicoptering ears couldn't decide whether to stay up or down. His tail banged out the beat of his happiness as he romped around on huge paws, with white stockings on three legs. His nose was a thick, short snout, and his wide mouth was split in an eternal grin. One eye was blue and the other brown. Noah was the one who said the dog looked like former vice president Dick Cheney if the man had ever smiled. The name stuck.

That day Angela brought him home, Cheney jumped on Jake and then Noah, his big paws raking down their arms and legs.

"Ow! Oh my God! Down, dog. Down! Off! Beast!" Jake yelled.

The dog tore off, running in tight, happy circles around the living room.

Noah and Angela's hope of keeping the big mutt evaporated the second their mother walked in the door.

"Absolutely not," Mrs. Katz said. "Take it to the county shelter. Immediately."

Nobody argued with Mrs. Katz. Jake wished his mother got angry once in a while or at least talked back to his father. Maybe it was out of spite for Ed that he decided to take the dog home.

"I think he's cool. You little punk rocker!" he said, tugging on the dog's big ears. "I'll get him a spiked collar. Want to come home with me, boy?"

The dog boxed Jake's shoulders.

Mrs. Katz stopped chopping onions and pointed her knife at Jake. "Jacob Stevenson. Do not tell your poor mother I encouraged you to take this dog home."

"He was never here, Mrs. K," Jake said, holding up two fingers. "Scout's honor. I found him at school."

Mrs. Katz laughed and shook her head. "Good luck, Jacob."

Once Cheney was in his life, Jake couldn't imagine life without him. Cheney lying on his back to have his belly scratched in the morning. Cheney's thrilled face peering through the bedroom window when Jake skated home after school. His joyous bounding at the end of the leash. That time he found a turtle, surely someone's escaped pet, and nosed it with such a hilarious combination of worry and surprise. Cheney wading farther and farther into the river until he discovered he could swim. Once he flushed a dozen wild turkeys up in the east hills as Jake and Noah scouted a deer hunt with Noah's dad. He bounded after the awkward birds, which seemed more annoyed than afraid, occasionally tearing back to Jake and barking as if to say, "OH MY GOD! Isn't this AWESOME? TURKEYS!"

Jake had never minded being an only child, but after Cheney came, he felt like there had been an empty space in his life, a small closet of sadness that was now filled by this eternally joyful creature. The dog was a cheerful presence in the Stevenson family home, which had grown quieter and sadder with each passing year. When Jake's father wasn't around, Jake thought that he, his mother, and the dog almost felt like a family again. It made him happy to see his mom laugh at Cheney's antics, the way he would try to climb in her lap, all eighty pounds of him. For Jake, Cheney was simply and completely his first true love.

Ed had been on a job in Salem when Jake brought Cheney home. His mom was already smitten too, but Jake was pretty certain his argument for having a guard dog was what won Ed over. He didn't like his neighbors and was constantly complaining about their use of the driveway or where they put their garbage cans or the noise from backyard parties. Something always pissed Ed off. He warmed to the idea that Cheney might scare people.

"I don't want to see it or hear it or smell it," Ed said, jabbing his cigarette and glaring down at the dog. "Take care of the animal or it goes."

"The animal"—of course that was how his father would put it. He wouldn't see what a friend the dog was or how hard Cheney tried. When he failed, Cheney was so sorry—like when he stole a block of cheese off the counter. Or when he broke the screen door during his wild greetings. He wanted to be good, you could tell. After he'd clobbered Jake's mom a couple of times, he understood he needed to be calm around her. He would sit at her feet, trembling, as she scratched his ears and the white star on his chest.

His father was sure he wouldn't be able to take care of the dog and was waiting for Jake to make a mistake. But Jake did it all: walked him, fed him, brushed him. He filled his water bowl and kept him tied up when they were outside in the yard together. Jake got him neutered, and poor Cheney banged around the house in that great plastic cone. His mom helped pay for the surgery and dog license, but they didn't tell Ed that. Anyway, he promised to pay her back.

What had Noah's mom said that day?

"Good luck, Jacob."

Dean had said the same thing. *"Good luck, kid."*

Dean was his big, buff physical therapist at Providence Rehab.

"You're gonna do great."

Wait. That was later. That was after. Cheney came before the accident.

His memories were all jumbled together. Where was he? The ditch.

He opened his eyes again and saw the darkening sky above him.

He could make out the Oak Grove Schoolhouse rising against the east hills. He'd been out on Reed Road listening to Spring Heeled Jack. So how had he fallen out of his chair next to the irrigation ditch?

And Cheney, where was Cheney, his fireplug of a dog, his constant companion?

The day of Pomeroy's party, Jake had shut Cheney in his room. He'd only be gone for an hour. Then the dog could hang out in the yard with him while he raked. Cheney looked mournful as he watched the boy lace up his Doc Martens. Jake tossed him a peanut butter–filled KONG from the freezer. The last he saw of his dog was Cheney bounding around like a giant brindled bunny with the red KONG in his jaws.

Jake put a hand to his face. He tried to sit up and everything whirled. He lay back on the cold ground and remembered the day he came home from rehab. His big dog's absence was the first thing he noticed. He pushed his way into the house and saw the hook by the door empty of the leash. He listened in vain for the staccato click of nails on linoleum. There was no happy bark from his room. That one tiny spark that held the crushing depression at bay went out.

He would never know exactly what happened to Cheney. His father glanced up from the TV. Ed, who had come to visit Jake in the hospital only once and had stared down at his son, his face clenched like a fist, now wore the same look. He turned back to the TV and sipped his beer.

"Like I said. Take care of the animal or it goes."

"I'm so sorry, honey," his mom whispered behind him. "I didn't know."

Jake wheeled himself to his bedroom. The doorway had been widened to accommodate the chair. His old twin bed with the Star Wars sheets was gone, and there was an accessible bed in its place. There was an overbed lifting pole attached to the wall. His posters and games were still there, and his desk and computer. All clean and tidy, too tidy. He closed the door behind him on the sound of his mother's low voice and Ed's rising to drown hers out.

He was exhausted but couldn't sleep. He lay awake watching the moon move across the sky until all was dark again. He wanted to be anywhere else but there. Yet where could he go? Finally, he slept. He dreamed of a golden river. It flooded its banks, swept him out of his wheelchair, and away he swam, light and happy. He awoke in the morning to the crushing weight of his future.

After that Jake slipped into a dark place. Winter 2013 set a record for rain—124 inches in three months. He thought he might go crazy. He woke up in the dark listening to his parents leave for work and watched the darkness fall by 3:00 p.m.

Each day he faced the empty hours. Another day of waiting. Another day of PT exercises that seemed to have plateaued. Instagram posts from friends who had moved on to other things. Email messages he couldn't bring himself to open. He slept as late as he could to kill the time. He was eighteen years old and killing time. His life was like jail. He would have cried, but he had already done that for months and it hadn't helped.

He thought briefly about killing himself then. He sat in front of Ed's rifle case one afternoon, considering how he would manage it. One thing that stopped him was the thought of his mother and what would happen to her if he botched it and ended up even worse off than he was then. And anyway, he was still himself, wasn't he?

He listened to music—the Clash, the Ramones, the Dead Kennedys, and all the U.S. ska bands, the louder the better. But he couldn't touch his trumpet. That music was too close to his heart. Just the thought of playing made him feel absolutely shredded. The trumpet case sat in the corner of his too-tidy room until one day he couldn't stand it anymore and shoved it in the back of his closet.

He faced his physical limitations head-on then. Yes, he was supremely grateful that he could shower, use the bathroom on his own, and transfer in and out of his chair by himself. Learning to use a catheter to empty his bladder several times a day. Tracking his bowel movements to avoid the kind of situation that had given the term "shit storm" new meaning. That had been a steep learning curve, but he'd done it all, thank God. The humiliation of the nurses and his mother helping him remained fresh in his mind.

However, the list of things he could no longer do was overwhelming. He couldn't drive—not without some kind of modified vehicle, which felt like an insurmountable goal—or even hop into Katz's truck without a thought. No more skateboarding, which also meant no more skate park. What was he going to do—have his mom drop him off by the half-pipe? Just moving freely in public was a thing of the past. Like the one time he went to the pharmacy with his mom after a doctor's appointment. The memory made him feel sick. The bright overhead lights in his eyes, the stupid Halloween displays blocking the aisles. He just wanted some damn Chex Mix and had gotten his fucking wheel caught under a cardboard cutout of a grinning jack-o'-lantern jutting out into the aisle. Some little old lady tried to help him, which made it so much worse. "Humiliating" didn't even begin to describe it. He didn't have the words. He was only eighteen and shouldn't have to have the words.

He stayed home after that. He played *Tomb Raider*, ignored his email, and didn't return texts. They were only from Noah by then anyway. Katz still texted every couple of days and even called him occasionally, leaving funny messages, pretending to be someone else, most recently a Scottish whisky salesman named Headachy McDrinkerstein. They hadn't spoken in person since before Christmas Eve. Noah had stopped by with Celia Martinez, and Jake couldn't come out of his room. He could hear their voices rise and fall talking to his mom, the sound of the door closing, Noah's truck driving away. It was easier to be alone. Being with his old friend was too painful, especially with his new girlfriend. He liked Celia, but she was a reminder that their lives were changing and his wasn't. Now what? That was the eternal question. The last thing he thought of at night and the first thing in the morning was, What the fuck am I supposed to do now?

He'd pulled out his sketchbook once or twice, but it depressed him to look at the scenes he'd drawn from his old life. He tried to comfort himself with the idea that he could still draw sitting down. But that thought made him so angry that he threw the book across the room.

He'd started lifting weights just to pass the time, and felt surprisingly better. When the weather improved, he ventured out on his own, waiting until his parents were at work. He went farther each time, getting stronger, until he was doing this orchard loop at least twice a week. Moving his body was such a relief.

At his last checkup in Portland, his neurologist was thrilled.

"You're fit as a fiddle, kid," Dr. Gunheim said, tugging at the waistband of his chinos as he sat at the computer.

Except I can't use my fucking legs, Jake wanted to say.

"Any questions?"

Jake was glad he'd asked his mom to stop coming into the exam room with him. He wasn't even embarrassed to ask, and Dr. Gunheim didn't seem surprised. What eighteen-year-old boy wouldn't wonder about his dick? Unfortunately, Dr. Gunheim didn't have any definite answer.

"It's very likely you'll have adequate sexual function, but we'll just have to wait and see. I'll make you a urology appointment in a couple of months. You're still healing, Jake. Try to be patient."

Patient? He liked Dr. Gunheim, but at moments like that, he felt like punching the guy in the side of the head.

Now his own head throbbed. He looked across the orchard toward the tree line where the forest began. The green light of dusk had swallowed the sun. Venus brightened among the first faint stars. The evening breeze blew down off the hillside carrying the smell of pines. Jake's gaze drifted. His eyes landed on his chair, which was on its side.

Next to that, he saw a person, a short woman in overalls who looked older than his mom. She leaned forward and peered down at Jake. Her expression was worried and relieved at the same time. She reminded Jake of Cheney when he had brought Jake that turtle in his teeth—his brow furrowed with curiosity and worry at this unknown thing. It made Jake want to laugh, remembering that. Then the woman's face folded into a frown.

"Christ on a crutch, kid! What in the hell are you trying to do? Get yourself killed?" she yelled.

5

SCENT FANNING

Members of different colonies appear to recognize their hive-companions by the sense of smell, and if there should be a thousand stocks in the Apiary, any one will readily detect a strange bee; just as each mother in a large flock of sheep is able, by the same sense, in the darkest night, to distinguish her own lamb from all the others.

—L. L. LANGSTROTH

When a honeybee colony experiences a disturbance, even something as slight as a beekeeper opening a hive to evaluate honey caches or pollen sources, the bees' first instinct is to communicate with each other. A few guard bees will fly out to evaluate the threat at hand, but most bees will immediately drop into the crouch that exposes their Nasonov gland and fan their wings, thereby spreading queen phero-mone throughout the hive. This action, called scent fanning, is like a soothing roll call that tells the inhabitants all is well.

Alice, by contrast, was alone in this moment of urgency and had no one to lean on for guidance or comfort. She hadn't been in so much as a fender bender since high school, but she quickly recognized that yelling was inappropriate, especially given the circumstances— namely, that she might have injured a minor in a wheelchair. She peered down at the boy and lowered her voice.

"Are you okay, kid? Can you . . . can you sit up?"

The boy didn't say anything, but he was still smiling. That didn't seem right. Was he mentally delayed? Or what was it—cerebral palsy? Holy hell! Alice fumbled for her phone.

"I'm calling 911," she mumbled to herself.

The boy's smile disappeared then, and he put a hand up. "No. Don't do that. I—I'm okay. I just need a minute. Catch my breath."

His voice was quiet but otherwise sounded normal, and it made Alice realize that she was crouching too close to him. She stepped back. What was he doing out here in the near damn dark? She looked around into the falling dusk and saw no one.

"Are you by yourself?" she asked.

The boy nodded.

Alice felt guilt and shame pump through her body like a drug. She could smell her own sweat. She looked up and down the road, which was dark and quiet. Then she ran back to her truck, turned off the engine, and clicked on her hazard lights. When she returned, the boy hadn't moved.

She plunked herself down, crossed her legs, and watched the kid's face. He blinked up at her, and she saw his chest rise and fall.

"That's good. Take some deep breaths. We'll just sit here a minute," she said.

The dusk deepened, and the air darkened. The cockeyed headlights of the truck threw two arms of light into the orchards. In their beams she could see bees zipping around. The hazard signals ticked like a frantic kitchen timer, and Alice's heart raced to match it. The kid was staring up at the sky.

"I'll be right back," she said. She returned to the truck, grabbed her water bottle, and looked at the wreckage of nucs in the truck bed and the ditch. Hundreds of bees had alighted on the truck bed and were scent fanning madly. With their abdomens raised and their Nasonov glands exposed, they were spreading pheromone trying to locate their queens. What a mess. It would have to wait.

She returned to the boy and held up the bottle. "Thirsty?"

He shook his head, and Alice sat down next to him again.

"Are you hurt?" she asked, and then cringed. He was in a wheelchair, for God's sake. "Are you in pain?"

He shook his head again. That hair! His beak-like nose stood out sharply on his pale face. In his skinny jeans and combat boots, he was as alien to Hood River County as if he had dropped from the sky.

"Did you hit your head?"

He nodded. "Not hard. It just kind of . . . bounced when I fell."

Alice realized she was holding her breath and exhaled.

"What's your name?"

"Jake."

"Jake. I'm Alice. Alice Holtzman."

He looked directly at her then and nodded. Alice felt herself relax a notch. She could smell the cold water of the irrigation ditch below them and was thankful the kid hadn't fallen in. She squirmed as the gravel poked through her overalls. In the faltering light, the boy's pale face was luminous under the crazy hairdo. Alice glanced at her watch.

"Listen, Jake, I should call your folks and let them know where you are. Can you give me their number?"

He shook his head and winced. "No. It's okay. I'll be up in a second. They aren't home anyway."

That last part sounded like a lie and, given that they likely had cell phones, irrelevant.

"Right," she said slowly, not sure what else to say. Alice hadn't been around teenage boys since she was a teenager herself.

"I think I can sit up," he said.

He pushed himself up on his elbows and pulled the tangle of earbuds and sunglasses off his neck. He blinked and glanced around.

"What's that noise?" he asked.

The air around them pulsed and vibrated. Alice could see the bees in a throbbing cloud above the truck in the waning light. Agitated questions thrummed through the air. Where was the queen? Was the brood safe? Were the guard bees on duty? Where was everybody? Where was home? Despite the more urgent situation of the boy in the chair, she felt hot tears spring to her eyes at what she had done to her bees. She cleared her throat.

"It's bees. Honeybees," Alice said. "I had some beehives in the back of my truck, and they are a bit confused right now. I'm so sorry about this. I just didn't see you. I was probably going too fast, but this is my road and I hardly ever see anyone out here. I certainly didn't expect—"

She stopped, flustered. The boy was watching her, and she thought she saw the corners of his mouth twitch.

"You didn't expect to see a wheelchair ripping down Reed Road?" he asked.

She didn't know what to say to that.

The boy shifted his weight and looked over her shoulder toward the truck.

"So, honeybees? Why do you have bees in your truck?"

"I'm a beekeeper," she said, grateful for something to talk about. "Just a hobby, really." She gestured down the road toward her house. "I have a few hives."

"Beehives. Whoa."

He watched the bees zipping in and out of the headlights.

"They sound mad," he said.

Alice shook her head. "No, they aren't mad. More like confused."

What had he said his name was? God, her memory! She tried to keep her voice calm.

"They're just kind of talking to each other right now, making sure everyone is all right. They're supposed to be in their boxes. Some fell out of the truck when I hit the fence."

She looked at the side of his thin face. What were you supposed to do when someone hit their head? Ask them questions? Jake! His name was Jake.

"How's your head, Jake? Any better?"

He touched a hand to his bald pate and nodded.

"Do you know where you are? What were you doing out here?"

He smiled at that. "Don't worry. I don't have a concussion. I'm on Reed Road. It's April 10, 2014. I live in Hood River, Oregon, and Barack Obama is the president of the United States."

His grin faded, and he frowned.

"But I can't remember your name," he said.

"Alice Holtzman," she said.

"I'm fine, Mrs. Holtzman."

Well, the kid did seem okay. She glanced at the truck. She'd have to deal with the mess to get the boy home.

"Listen, Jake, if you don't mind, I'm going to check on the bees."

"Oh, yeah. No problem."

"You sure?"

"Totally."

"You sit tight," she said, rising.

"Okay. I won't go running off," he said.

She hesitated. Was that a joke?

He waved a long arm. "Really, I'm fine. Go check your bees, Mrs. Holtzman."

"Call me Alice," she said. "My mom is Mrs. Holtzman."

"Okay, Alice," Jake said.

Alice pulled on her gloves and veiled hat and flicked on a red flashlight, steeling herself for the damage. Seven nucs remained in the truck bed. She righted them and tamped down the lids. The other five were strewn alongside the road. She knew there would be lots of dead bees, but she had to focus on what she could salvage now.

"Sounds like a horror movie over there," the boy called.

"No, it's fine," Alice called back. "I just need a few minutes to sort this out. You all right?"

"Yup," he said.

In about twenty minutes she'd collected all the frames and put the nucs in some order. She was stung twice on her forearms. That couldn't be helped. She had to concentrate on the ones she could save. Alice returned to Jake, who was sitting up with his back against a rock. With that hair and his long legs, he looked like some sort of exotic bird.

Alice reached down and grasped one side of the wheelchair, and the kid glared at her. She recoiled, embarassed, and wondered how she had offended him.

"I thought I'd have a look at your chair?" she said.

His face relaxed, and the boy nodded. Alice righted the wheelchair and ran her flashlight along the right side. She noticed scuffs, presumably from his fall. But when she spun the wheel, it seemed true, which was good. She could still hear the bees, though the buzz was receding. There must have still been hundreds flying in the air.

The kid shifted against the rock and gazed past her. "So, they, like, live in those boxes?"

"Just temporarily," Alice said. "They all have nice hives waiting for them at my house. Those boxes are for the commuter stage, like a cattle truck," she said, now surveying the left side of chair, which seemed unmarred.

"How do you get them back in?" Jake asked. "Tiny cattle dogs? Little lassoes?"

She glanced at him and saw that he was smiling again. Funny kid, she thought.

"Well, they'll go back as soon as it gets dark and cold enough out here," she said. "I need to give them a few minutes. Then I'll give you a ride home."

"No rush," he said.

"Look, I'd feel better if I called your folks, though, Jake. Really."

He sighed and pulled his phone out of his pocket.

"It's fine," he said. "I got it."

He thumbed a message into his phone.

"Done," he said, and smiled.

"Thanks," she said. "I don't want your parents to worry. I feel bad enough about all this . . ."

Alice tilted the chair to the right and spun the left wheel, which also moved freely and seemed true. She wasn't the best mechanic, but the wheelchair seemed okay. She would insist on paying for any repairs. Did you tune up a wheelchair like a bicycle? she wondered.

"Well, technically you didn't do anything. I fell over trying to get out of your way. So I'll just tell them you ran me off the road."

Alice frowned, still looking at the chair, and didn't reply. Was he trying to be funny?

"I'm fine, really. I was just . . ."

His voice trailed off, and he looked past her at the truck. Then he shifted slightly to face her.

"About the bees, Alice. Do you just wait until they get in those boxes?"

She nodded. "Yep. They'll find their way back. They want to get home."

"What happens if they stay out after curfew? Does the mom bee lock the door?"

Alice set the chair aside but didn't look at him. "If they don't get home before the temperature drops, they just don't make it."

"What do you mean?"

"Well," she said, "if they don't make it back to the hive at night, then they die outside. It's too cold."

She saw a look of concern cross his face, surprising her. She clicked off her flashlight.

"Most of them will be just fine. They're hardy," she said, wanting to reassure him. She was touched that a teenage boy might care about the fate of the small creatures.

"My dad always called them tough little broads," she said.

He grinned at that and looked past her.

"So, they can just go into any one of those boxes?" he asked.

"You really want to know?"

He nodded.

Alice looked up into the twilight at the small bee cloud buzzing over the truck. She loved the story of the bees, which was like a fairy tale. Even if you were a scientist or a religious person, there was no denying that the bees had real magic.

A hive of sixty thousand honeybees, she explained, had one queen—leader and mother to them all. And 97 percent of the other tiny golden bodies buzzing away in there were her daughters. The remaining handful was made up of males, called drones. Daughters and sons recognized the queen by her scent, which was called her pheromone. The queen pheromone said, "All is well." It said, "We are together." It said, "You belong here."

From the time they emerged from their capped cells, those golden creatures knew exactly what to do. The daughters were called worker bees, Alice explained to Jake as the light faded between them. The very first thing they did after hatching, when they were known as callow bees, was clean up the cell they were born in. Then they started taking care of the other baby bees, feeding them and capping the larvae cells and helping other newly emerging callow bees learn how to contribute to the hive. She told Jake how workers got promoted up the ladder as they got older, moving toward the front door to receive nectar and pollen from the bees that flew around collecting out in the field; those were called foragers. Some workers eventually graduated to foraging or became guard bees, she explained. Guard bees kept watch at the entrance and only let in the other bees that belonged there.

"How do they know?" Jake asked. "Who's who, I mean?"

They knew by the scent, Alice told him. As long as the queen was healthy and laying eggs, her pheromone kept them all united. If they had any worry, they would immediately stop what they were doing and expose the Nasonov gland in their abdomens, passing a distinctive lemony scent from bee to bee. The bees that foraged carried that smell with them and brought it back to the hive. The scent allowed the guard bees to identify them as residents and not robbers.

"What do you mean? They rob each other?"

She nodded. "Bees from hungry hives will steal honey, so everyone gets checked at the front door. Yellow jackets try to get in too. They'll actually eat the larvae and eggs—carnivorous little bastards."

Whoops! she thought. Language! She glanced at her watch. How long had they been sitting there? She felt anxious to get the boy home.

The buzzing had died down, and few bees remained in the air.

"Almost done. As done as they are going to get, anyway."

Alice stood up, brushed off the seat of her overalls, and turned toward the truck. She didn't want the boy to see her face. It upset her to think about losing even one bee.

She shivered, feeling the sudden drop in temperature that was common on April nights like this one. She turned to face Jake and the problem of getting him up, choosing, as she usually did, to be direct.

"Well, all right, then," she said. "Tell me how to help you get up and I'll drive you home."

Jake explained how to position the wheelchair with the brake on and then he pulled himself up into it. Alice moved to help him but stopped when she saw that he was clearly able to manage it. He lifted his rear into the seat and then used both hands to lift each leg and place his feet on the foot rail. He looked down at the dark, uneven ground and hesitated. Alice sensed his embarrassment.

"Look," she said, "I'm going to push you over to the truck. Humor a nervous lady, okay?"

He gave a shrug of acquiescence but didn't meet her gaze.

Alice maneuvered him next to the truck and opened the door. Her cab, as usual, was a mess. Flustered, she threw a pile of papers and books into the back seat to make room. Then she stood aside and watched the boy evaluate the space. When she asked if she could help, he shook his head. Jake maneuvered knees first into the truck door. He lifted his feet, one at a time, onto the floor of the cab. Then, with the precision of a rock climber, he reached in and gained opposing handholds on the seat and the door handle and pulled himself up and in.

Jake sat back, and Alice could see he was sweating from the effort. She handed him his backpack, and he explained how to fold the chair. It was lighter than she expected, and she secured it in the back of the truck with a strap. She slid behind the wheel and glanced over at Jake, who was scanning the dark sky.

"Looks like you were right. I don't see any more out there."

Alice nodded but didn't say anything. She thought about the still, golden bodies she'd seen strewn alongside the road.

"Okay, then. Where to?"

"Greenwood Court. Over behind NAPA Auto," he said.

"Are you kidding me? Good Lord! Just out on a ten-mile spin?" She shook her head with admiration and saw him hide a smile.

She turned the key, and Bruce Springsteen's voice roared through the cab: "Oh, oh, oh, oh! Thunder Road!"

"Jesus!" she yelled, and snapped off the stereo. She felt a cold sweat spring up on her face and hands.

The boy threw back his head and hooted with laughter. "No wonder you didn't see me, Alice," he said. "Rocking out to the Boss! And you have a tape deck! That is so awesome!"

He clapped his hands together, and Alice let herself smile, catching her breath. He spotted her collection of tapes in the center console.

"May I?" he asked.

"Knock yourself out," she said, and drove toward town as he dug through the cassettes. She turned the stereo back on with the volume down low.

"Let's see . . . Bob Dylan. Classic. The Fixx. Passable. Of course, their only good album was *Reach the Beach*. And here we have— Holy hell, Alice. Phil Collins? This is criminal. Too tragic! You'd better just let me out here."

They were at a stoplight, and he pretended to open the door.

"Genesis is perfectly respectable!" she protested. "I don't know how his solo stuff got in here!"

"Really. I'm embarrassed for you, Alice."

What a little smartass! She leaned against the steering wheel and laughed. When was the last time she had laughed?

He was accusing her of harboring a secret cache of Madonna as she turned onto Greenwood Court, but then his smile disappeared. She slowed down on the bumpy driveway and passed a ceramic donkey with crumbling legs and a basket of tattered plastic flowers. The ruined donkey depressed Alice for some reason.

"You can just let me out here," Jake said in a low voice.

In front of a blue manufactured home, Alice's headlights lit upon a woman's legs and then her crossed arms and anxious face. She turned off the engine. "That must be Mom?"

"Yeah."

"I'll go explain," she said, and jumped out of the truck.

"No, Alice. Wait!"

The boy's mother marched across the gravel drive, closing the gap between them and pulling her gray cardigan tight around her. Before Alice could fully explain what had happened, she'd moved swiftly toward the truck.

"Jacob, honey! Are you all right?"

"I'm fine, Mom," the boy said. "And it wasn't Alice's fault. I wasn't paying attention."

"Wait. What?" His mother whirled on Alice. "You said you *found* him. You hit my son?"

She pointed a finger in Alice's face. "Have you been drinking? What kind of irresponsible—"

"No, that's not—"

Jake's mother started yelling then, and Alice raised her voice trying to be heard.

"Ma'am! If you could just calm down, I can—"

The door banged open on the house, and a man strode toward them, his sunburned face clenched with anger.

"What in the hell is going on out here?!" he yelled.

Jake's mother was now struggling to open the truck tailgate and weeping audibly.

Jake leaned out the window and called back at her. "Mom! Just calm down!"

Alice turned toward the father to reassure him that his son was all right but quickly realized he was simply upset about having his evening interrupted. He leaned down, jabbing a finger in Alice's face, and said a series of unrepeatable things. Suddenly the kid was right next to her.

"Ed! Shut up!" he yelled. The man sneered down at the boy, spat on the driveway at Alice's feet, and walked back inside.

"Alice—" Jake said.

She looked at him and didn't speak. She spun on her heel and strode to the truck.

"Wait!" the kid called.

She climbed behind the wheel and watched Jake pull away from his mother and move toward her. She was overwhelmed by the feeling that she was abandoning him. Ridiculous. She didn't even know him. She shook off the thought as she drove away. She flew toward home like an errant worker bee trying to find her way to the safety of the hive as darkness took hold of the valley.

6

HIVE SITING

A hive of the simplest possible construction, is a close imitation of the abode of bees in a state of nature; being a mere hollow receptacle, where, protected from the weather, they can lay up their stores.

—L. L. LANGSTROTH

The wind banged around the house all night like it was looking for something it had lost. It stole under the windowsills and crept into corners, rattling doorknobs and whistling along the hallway. Alice lay in bed listening. Living there in the valley between the old volcano and the river gorge was to live with the wind. She'd grown up with the near constant westerlies that whipped the river into a froth all summer and pummeled the forests with snow in winter. When she was a girl, she thought of the wind as a live thing like some enormous winged creature galloping across the valley. Some days it danced above the orchards with its voluminous skirts flying about. Other times it was arrow-thin and dove between the storefronts and tight alleyways of the town core. Tonight, the wind was small and fretful, buzzing around like a stray honeybee caught in the corner of the room. It was like a memory, a wish, or a forgotten dream.

She heard the throbbing call of an owl, a sign that dawn was distant and night was still holding sway. She dozed until she awakened to the cooing of the mourning doves that descended in a gray flurry to the chickens' water trough around 5:00 a.m. Then Red Head Ned, her ever-faithful bantam, began his predawn shouting. It was the wind, the birds, and the chickens that kept her up, she told herself as she came fully awake. Not the boy. She surrendered to wakefulness when that thought arrived and sat squarely on her chest, like a stubborn cat, unwilling to leave. The boy. She swung her feet out of bed and sat up sighing. Of course it was the boy. She'd thought about him all day yesterday at work too.

Alice made coffee and sat, her elbows on the Formica table, looking out across the yard. The kid was clearly fine. The chair was probably okay too, but she hadn't had time to talk about it before all the yelling had started two nights ago. She understood his mother was just worried about him. She wasn't even bothered by what the kid's moronic father had said to her. But she wondered about his well-being. What did Jake do all day? Did he have a job? Go to school? She thought he said he'd graduated from high school. But what did he have to fill up his life? What was life like with a father like that?

"Alice, dearie. What could you do for the boy, anyway?"

She could almost hear her own father's voice—the quick cadence and the remnants of a German lilt.

"He's not your responsibility. He has people."

That was what Al would say. He was one to talk, though. For all his insistence that people should mind their business, Al Holtzman had been a serial philanthropist. He hadn't gotten involved in people's problems. He had gotten involved in their *solutions*. That was what he said. Alice grew to understand that he'd always asked that question— what could you do, anyway?—because if he could see some specific way to help, he would. He assisted in his quiet way, not wanting to draw attention. He paid for Mrs. Travis's groceries when he was far enough ahead of her white, curly head in line at Little Bit that she wouldn't hear him, because he knew she was living on a widow's pension. He dropped off a cord of wood at Tom Connolly's drafty house one cold fall day, complaining it wouldn't burn worth a damn. He paid off a lien on Juan Garcia's auto repair shop. Marina hit the roof about that one. But Al just said Garcia was a nice man and he had four little kids. He'd been in the hospital with a herniated disk. How Al learned these things was a mystery. Her unassuming father knew the intricacies of so many lives.

"What can you do for the boy, anyway, Alice my dear?"

Unless there was a clear answer, there was no reason to consider the question any further. That was Al's clear counsel, even from the grave.

Alice sighed. "Nothing I can think of, Dad."

She shook some Raisin Bran into a bowl and ate standing over the sink. She spooned sugar into another cup of coffee. She knew her eating habits were terrible, but she didn't care. She'd finished off the Chips Ahoy! the night before, one by one, like it was work. She knew the emptiness she felt all the time was not hunger, but sugar was a short-term solution.

Alice took her notebook out to the bee yard to plan her day, grateful that it was Saturday and she didn't have to go into the office. The wind had ceased scuttling, and the morning was glorious. Sunlight streamed through the branches of the cottonwoods by the creek. It warmed the white sides of her hives so that the girls were out in full force, their golden bodies flitting over the clover and into Doug Ransom's orchard, then beyond that to who knew where. They could forage more than three miles. Alice wished there was a way to follow them and learn their bee secrets. Little web cams, she thought, which made her think about Jake's joke about the tiny cattle dogs and lassoes.

She sat on a stump and looked at her notes from yesterday, when she had installed the nucs early before going into work.

Friday, April 11, 2014 Sunrise: 6:27 a.m., Temp: 63F/43F, Wind speeds 10–18 MPH, Precipitation: 0 inches, Sunset: 7:47 p.m. Hive totals to date: 24. Notes: Installed 12 Russian nucs in northeast side of the bee yard. Each hive with five frames of brood, pollen, and honey. Hives dated and marked No. 13–24. Transition without incident.

She smiled wryly at that last part. The nuc transfer had gone fine, but she felt there should be some way to note the unusual episode of running a teenager in a wheelchair off the road the night before she installed the bees. She put an asterisk after the word "incident" and wrote "(Jake Stevenson*)" as a footnote at the bottom of the page and then turned to the work for this day.

"Saturday, April 12, 2014," she wrote. She jotted down the time of sunrise, the forecast high and low temperatures, and wind speeds. Then she wrote, "Tasks: complete regular inspection of hives No. 1–12." That would keep her busy for hours.

Alice donned her veiled hat and gloves and began the careful work of inspecting her original twelve hives, which were each two brood boxes tall. She cracked the first top open with her hive tool, set it aside, and removed the inner cover. She loosened a frame and eased it out. Holding it up she looked for eggs, larvae, and capped brood. She checked for pollen and honey stores. She set that frame aside and pulled out the next one. As the sun climbed in the sky, she completed this action for all ten frames in the top and bottom brood boxes of the twelve hives. Only two weren't thriving. Probably their queens hadn't made it through the winter. In those she saw lots of drone brood, which was the sign of a laying worker, but no queen cells had been created. Alice decided to add frames from healthier hives to give them a boost.

She looked through her notes and identified two of the strongest hives. In the first she found frames ringed with capped honey, bands of golden and orange pollen under that, and row after row of healthy brood cells. Alice breathed in the sweet scent of wax and honey. This would do quite nicely. If the queens in the ailing hives had died, robust workers like these could produce another one within three weeks. She made a note to check for queen cells in five days and then set to work, humming to herself, transferring healthy frames into the two fragile hives.

Alice had always enjoyed the problem-solving part of beekeeping. Each hive was a living organism with different needs. The bees fascinated her, these single-minded creatures that each worked tirelessly for the whole. And they created such beauty—the honey stores, yes, but also the wax foundation and the brilliant caches of pollen, which ranged in color from lemon to pumpkin to ruby. She marveled that her simple hobby had grown from one hive to twenty-four. She stood in the sunlight with bees buzzing around her veiled head as the number sank in. Twenty-four was almost halfway to fifty. It felt like a tipping point. She pulled off her hat, sat in the noon shade, and looked out at the bee yard, chewing on her pencil. There was plenty of room to grow here. She could get to fifty hives by the end of the summer if she was methodical about splits and capturing swarms.

The idea excited her in a way she couldn't remember being excited in a very long time. Practical by nature, and prone to consider obstacles first, now she just thought, Why not? She paged back through her notebook to last summer, where she had noted the details from the honey harvest that had yielded seven to ten gallons from each of the twelve hives. She'd sold it for $20 per quart at the fair and netted $6,000 after expenses. A tidy little sum. Her excitement grew. What might she do with more hives, more honey? The thought came immediately: she could afford to put in an orchard. She scanned her field where the land was flat and sunny. Something small, nothing like the historic Holtzman family orchard. But hers. Yes. Why not?

She would need help. That was certain. The August harvest alone would be massive, and then she'd need help with tree planting in the fall. But she could afford to hire someone, especially with the anticipation of honey sales and maybe even raising queens. She paced the apiary to determine how many hives would fit, and her enthusiasm grew.

Back at the house, she pulled up the farmer's market page on her computer and scanned the classified ads. People weren't offering that much. Ten to fifteen dollars an hour or less for WWOOFers. Alice scoffed.

"You can keep your WWOOFers," she said aloud.

Volunteers from Worldwide Opportunities on Organic Farms. She saw them, youngsters from Australia lately, running the booths at the farmer's market. Dirty hair and hippy clothes, like Joyful. They worked in exchange for room and board. No thank you, she thought. She didn't want to be a tour guide, and she wasn't keen on having someone live at her place. Alice liked being alone down here in the dell. The phrase "communal living" made her skin crawl. Ever since she was a little kid, she had enjoyed her solitude. Alice Island, her mother teased her. Alice All Alone. Her father understood. His parents had been solitary people too. It suited her just fine. Most days, anyway.

She opened the ad-posting form and typed: "Help Wanted: Part-time summer worker for bee farm. No experience necessary. Must be able to lift up to 100 pounds. Light construction skills a plus. $13–$15 per hour, negotiable. Call 541-555-2337 for info or email al.holtzman @gorge.net."

She figured she'd get a high school kid for that much, and the bulk of the work would be completed by the time school rolled around.

That afternoon Alice ran errands—Ace Hardware for sandpaper and paintbrushes, and, as much as she dreaded it, the damn grocery store for something other than cereal. She dreaded going to Little Bit, and not just because of the panic attack. Hood River's single grocery store was like the town square, and Alice hated small talk. Old people shopped in the mornings and young families in the afternoons. Both of those times she was liable to run into some friend of her mom's or someone she knew from high school. She did her shopping at night and never on the weekends. Weeknights it was just young men and Latino families. They didn't want to stop and chat either, at least not to her. But the fridge was empty, so she'd just have to cope.

Outside Ace, she jumped in the truck and slung the paper bag of supplies onto the floor. She tossed her windbreaker aside to make room. Then she saw the small backpack. Already knowing it must be Jake's, she opened it and pulled out a wallet. There was the kid's big grin and that crazy hair disappearing out of the top of the frame. Jacob Todd Stevenson, born February 2, 1996. Hazel eyes, black hair. Height: five feet ten; weight: 145 pounds. Sure, kid. Maybe if you were wearing a weight belt. Boys and women lied about their weight in opposite directions, apparently. I'll have to drop it off, she thought, and for some reason her heart brightened.

Alice suffered through the grocery store, where she ran into Mary Condon. Mary had been close to Alice's mom and told Alice about her recent hip surgery. Alice didn't really mind listening. It was easier than talking to her own old friends, who would get that sad look on their faces and touch her arm.

"How are you *doing*, Alice?" they'd ask. What a question.

As she steered toward the cereal aisle, she saw the back of Debi Jeffreys, the office manager from the county planning department, her cart piled high and three little boys hanging off the sides yelling like pirates. Alice decided she didn't need cereal after all and headed to the checkout line.

She drove down Twelfth Street and turned onto Greenwood Court. The yellow Ford Focus parked in front of number eleven had a bumper sticker that read: "God is my co-pilot." Her pulse quickened as she thought of the scene there two nights before, and she took a deep breath. She turned off the engine and sat, letting the seconds tick by. This was small-town politeness—waiting in the driveway when one wasn't expected. After a couple of minutes, the door opened and the kid's mom came out, shading her eyes with her hand. She waved and walked down the steps toward Alice, smiling. Alice climbed out of the truck and held up the backpack like a flag of surrender.

"Hi!" she called. "Don't mean to intrude. I just wanted to drop this off."

Jake's mother was still smiling. As she got close to Alice, she held out her hand.

"I'm Tansy. Tansy Stevenson," she said. "It's Alice, right?"

Alice nodded and smiled. Tansy grabbed her hand and shook it. She held on to it a second too long, which embarrassed Alice, it felt so intimate. She pulled away, but Tansy didn't seem to notice.

"I'm so sorry for the other night. I felt terrible once Jacob explained what happened. Edward and I are so grateful that you brought him home safe. We thank the dear Lord that you were there to help him."

Alice doubted that Tansy's husband thanked the dear Lord for anything, but she could see tears welling up behind the woman's pink-framed glasses under curled bangs and felt sorry for her. Tansy was younger than she was and dressed in an A-line polyester skirt and nylons with low heels. Alice was suddenly self-conscious of her dirty overalls and her sun hat jammed down over her hair.

"It was nothing," Alice said. "It was the least I could do. I feel terrible about the whole thing. I just didn't see him in the dark out there."

Tansy sighed, put her fingers to her temples, and shook her head. "I tried to get him to promise me he wouldn't go running around alone, but he's stubborn."

She tried to laugh, but Alice could see the tears still bright in her eyes.

"There are so few things Jacob enjoys these days . . ." She trailed off.

Alice didn't know what to say. The sorrow in the woman's voice spoke volumes about her son's young, arrested life.

"Well," Alice said, "I'd like to pay for any repairs needed on the chair."

Tansy smiled, pulled a Kleenex out of her cuff, and dabbed her eyes. "The chair seems fine, but thank you for offering."

Just in case, they should exchange numbers, Alice said. She walked back to the truck to get a pen. She scribbled her email address and phone number on her receipt from Ace and realized she was stalling, hoping to see the kid. The screen door creaked open, and there he was, mohawk and all. She noted the dark circles under his eyes and his pale face. His smile bloomed tentatively.

"Hey, Alice!" he called. He rolled down the wheelchair ramp and braked at her feet. Alice noted his fluid, even graceful, maneuvering of the chair. In the clear light of day, he looked even younger. She regretted having left so abruptly two nights earlier, never mind what his stupid father had said.

He spotted the backpack at his mother's feet.

"Thanks. I was missing that," he said.

"No problem," she said, and smiled back.

"How are the ladies doing?" he asked. "Everyone okay after their big adventure?"

Alice chuckled. "Yes, they're settling in okay."

"Right. Like you said, tough little broads. Everyone hard at work raising the babies?"

Alice was pleased that he had remembered her words.

"You bet," she said.

Tansy looked from Alice to Jake and back again.

"Bees, Mom! I told you. She's a beekeeper," Jake said.

He waved his hands in the air, his eyes wide. "She has thousands of bees at her house. Thousands!"

"Well, tens of thousands, actually," Alice said. "Each of those boxes in my truck had about ten thousand bees in it."

"Holy crap! That's amazing!"

"Jacob. Language, please."

"Sorry, Mom," he said. "But seriously."

He cocked his head and lowered his voice. "You should have seen them flying around after Alice hit the fence. The boxes fell all over the place. She just walked right in there like it was nothing. Picked them up and put them back in the truck."

Tansy shuddered. "Do they sting you?"

Alice shrugged. That was everyone's first question. "Sometimes. But like I told Jake, they only sting when they feel threatened."

Though Alice hated small talk, she loved bee talk. She thought she might tell Tansy about the guard bees, if she was really interested. But Jake was already telling her. He glanced at Alice.

"Yeah, I looked it up yesterday. Pretty cool. It's like Gandalf in Lord of the Rings. 'You shall not pass!' I was reading about yellow jacket robbing too. What do you do? Bait traps or let them fight it out?"

Alice started to respond but then heard the low growl of a diesel engine in the driveway behind her. She turned and saw Jake's father glaring out the window of a silver Ford F-250. The engine whined as he reversed and parked on the street. He walked toward them, his face creased in anger, every step weighted with the tragedy of this inconvenience.

". . . Park in his own damn driveway!" he was muttering as he approached. The smile had left Jake's face, and Tansy looked nervous. Jake's father scowled at them. Something told Alice this happened all the time.

"What are *you* doing here? Besides blocking my damn driveway?"

He was wearing Wranglers ironed to a crease and a plaid shirt with a name tag that read, "Hello! I'm Edward!" in cheerful female handwriting, clearly from some work event. The contrast with his cranky face made Alice smile involuntarily.

"You think that's funny, huh?"

"Edward, dear," Tansy said. "Alice brought Jacob's backpack—"

"I think I told you to get off my driveway," he said, ignoring his wife. "And I meant stay off. Is that so hard to understand, lady?"

His voice rose to a whine, and he looked like a petulant child.

Alice didn't say anything. She'd grown up with such a kind father, his colorful language aside. But she'd met this kind of man before. Every woman in America had by the time she was twenty-five. She'd worked with men to whom bullying was a standard management style. Testosterone poisoning, she and her friend Nancy joked. And yet it was women who were called hysterical. They were like little children, these angry men, she thought. Always throwing their tantrums.

Something clicked in Alice's mind then. Little boys. Edward Stevenson. Eddie.

"Eddie Stevenson," she said aloud. "Eddie Stevenson from Hatch Street."

Edward's face went slack in surprise.

"I'm Alice Holtzman," she said, looking closely at him. Yes, he was in his late thirties, which would make him about seven years younger than she was.

"I was your babysitter's neighbor. Jeannine Sharp. Remember?"

She snapped her fingers and laughed. "I helped her give you a bath when you were three years old."

The memory flickered through her mind. Funny Jeannine, always so patient with little kids. Alice sat on the bathroom floor watching the boy splash in the tub while Jeannine changed his little sister's diaper.

Ed shifted uncomfortably and grew pale. Jake looked skeptical, as if he couldn't believe his father had ever been a small, naked child. Alice saw something in Ed's face like shame. And fear.

What was it? The ugly story came back to her like a sour smell. She was a junior when she heard about it at a football game. The little boys had caught a feral cat on the playground after school. Tortured it to death. Alice looked at him and saw the little boy in this man's face. Imagined the dirty streaks on his nose, sunburned neck, crew cut, and torn shorts. He would have been nine or so then. They'd sent him to live with relatives in Spokane.

"Yeah," she said slowly. "You got expelled from May Street Elementary. You and Craig Stone."

Such cruelty from children was rare in their little town, something you didn't forget. The poor helpless creature, not deserving of such an end. And Jake, with a father like that.

Alice felt her throat catch, and her breath grew shallow. Time slowed. She held herself very still and waited for her breath to leave her, waited for that tightening in her chest. But it didn't happen. This was different. Her vision, instead of blurring, sharpened, and so did her hearing. She heard the scornful yawp of a crow and felt the brisk breath of the spring chinook on the back of her neck. Instead of feeling like she might splinter into a thousand pieces, she felt a hot, white coherence. It hovered over her head like a blessing.

Ed still said nothing, his face pale and sharp. He seemed to shrink into himself. Alice glanced at Tansy, who was gripping the railing of the wheelchair ramp with one hand, her eyes closed, her mascara making tracks down her cheeks. She knew who she'd married.

"What can you do for the boy, anyway, Alice?" her father's voice murmured in her ear. Alice stepped back and exhaled.

"I should go," she said, looking away from Ed and down at the boy. "But I have a proposition for you."

She handed him the Ace receipt with her phone number and email address.

"Thing is, I'm hiring. I need help around the bee yard. No experience necessary, and it's part-time. I just posted the ad today. Check the job board on gorge.net. If you want to give it a whirl, call me."

She heard herself telling him that room-and-board was negotiable as part of the wage. Never mind that she had scoffed at the idea of WWOOFers that very morning. The words just kept tumbling out of her mouth.

The boy looked at the paper, expressionless and clearly as surprised by the idea as Alice was herself.

Ed roared back to life then. "Lady, you need to mind your goddamn business! I'll kick your ass from here to Odell if you don't get off my driveway!"

"Edward, please!" Tansy grabbed her husband's arm.

Alice felt the white heat descend again and entertained the joyful fantasy of harming this man. She could hear the neighbors opening their windows and doors to listen. The rational part of her knew she could never hurt anyone. Of course not. She was a Holtzman. Still, she felt that strange feeling course through her—a wildness that somehow made her feel deadly calm. She looked directly into Ed's eyes.

"You go ahead and do that," she said evenly. "And I'll call the sheriff. He's my brother-in-law."

"Lady, if you know what's good for you—" Ed hissed.

"Sounds great to me, Alice!" Jake exclaimed at her elbow. "I'll come with you now, actually. Have a look around."

The boy's mother had retreated, her arms folded, against the porch. "Jacob," she sobbed.

Ed sneered down at his son. "Working man, huh? How do you think that's gonna go for you?" he spat.

Jake's eyes blazed as he stared up at his father. "I guess we'll just have to see, won't we? Eddie."

When he called his father Eddie, Alice saw the man shrink back. He opened his mouth and nothing came out.

The boy drew himself up taller in his chair, as if Alice's fury lit something in him too. It burned bright in his eyes and bore him forward. And then Alice found herself driving out of the dusty yard, past the vanquished donkey, and into the bright April sunshine with eighteen-year-old Jake Stevenson on the seat next to her, his eyes blazing and Bruce Springsteen blaring through the speakers.

What in the hell have I done now? Alice thought.

7

BUMBLING

I discovered that bees often recognize strangers by their *actions*, even when they have the same scent; for a *frightened bee curls himself up with a cowed look*, which unmistakably proclaims that he is conscious of being an intruder.

—L. L. LANGSTROTH

If Harry had learned anything in nearly a quarter of a century of life on earth, it was that upon first impression, most people thought he was a dumbass. He couldn't really blame them. He was a follower and sometimes went where others led despite the "Wrong Way" signs posted at every turn.

"Don't be such a people pleaser," his mother said. She'd been saying that since fourth grade, when he let some older boys "borrow" his lunch money and came home hungry. She was trying to help him, he knew, but it was really just a nicer way of saying he was a dumbass.

"Those boys don't want to be your friends, son," his mother said. "You know how you can tell?"

Harry shook his head and bit into the peanut butter sandwich she'd made him.

"Because they want to take something from you. Friends should just be friends because they like each other."

Harry nodded, not really understanding. He would think of her words the next time he lost his lunch money. And the day he let the neighborhood kids ride his bike off the jump in the vacant lot and came home with a bent wheel. Then there was the time he got arrested for helping his friends move a truck full of stolen flat-screen TVs.

"What were you thinking!" his mother yelled in the car after she bailed him out. It wasn't a question he could answer. Harry slumped against the seat with shame and fatigue. He'd spent the night in jail next to a drunk old guy who smelled like pee and mustered up the courage to call his mother when he couldn't take the smell any longer.

"Harry! Explain yourself, son!"

His mother rarely yelled, saying it was undignified, so her doing so then underscored the seriousness of the situation. But Harry had no explanation for her. He could only acknowledge that he'd been stupid enough to let his friends talk him into driving a truck of stolen TVs to a buyer who had turned out to be an undercover cop.

What had he been thinking? Certainly not that Marty's rationale made any sense.

"Dude. Nothing has changed since Occupy," Marty said one afternoon, as they stood outside the Three-O-One Saloon. "The one-percenters still have all the power. System's rigged. They owe this to us."

Marty dragged on his cigarette and flicked it out into the street, where it lay smoldering. Sam nodded, and Harry had nodded too, though he wasn't really agreeing. He just didn't want them to think he was a big puss. He was thinking that Marty was kind of a one-percenter himself. At least his father was—a man who owned a string of assisted-living facilities along the Atlantic Coast. Marty often bragged about how his father skimmed off of Medicare and about the family's vacation home in the Florida Keys. His father employed him too. And although Marty purported to hate working for him, he would inherit the family business. Thus, the Robin Hood rationale didn't make much sense. Harry knew this—Marty's proposal that they remove a shipment of electronics from the store where his cousin worked—wasn't a revolution. It was just a side hustle.

Harry ended up as driver and later wondered if Marty and Sam had agreed upon that in advance. They ran when the cop pulled out his badge. Harry was sitting in the cab looking at his Facebook feed and hadn't noticed. The cop had to tap on the window to get his attention. Harry was the only one who got arrested.

The judge sentenced him to twenty-four months in a low-security prison for attempted grand larceny. He looked disappointed, which made Harry feel even worse.

"Mr. Stokes," he said, "this would be a good time to turn yourself around. Make a change before you go too far down this road."

His mother blew her nose and suppressed a sob. Sal sat next to her with his big arms crossed and his nostrils flaring.

Harry had hoped to leave his poor decision-making behind with the move west, which had felt like a change. His parents wanted to believe that it signaled some sort of new direction. Accepting the idea that Harry was finally leading his own life would allow his mother and Sal to move to Florida guilt-free. Harry didn't want them to worry about him anymore. But Seattle had been too big and confusing. The high school friend who told him to come visit anytime hadn't seemed pleased when he showed up. I should have called first, Harry thought then.

Still, it was cool of Jeff to let him stay for a week. Jeff's girlfriend, Sylvia, made it very clear that she didn't want him there. She had stayed in the bedroom when she was home from work and stalked through the living room to the kitchen without speaking to Harry or Jeff as they sat reminiscing about high school. Sylvia's angry silence made him uncomfortable, and he started looking for his own place. He even talked to the manager of Jeff's building and began filling out an application. But then he got to the part about the background check. He stuffed the paper in his bag and mumbled something about forgetting his ID. Who would rent to a felon?

He walked the dreary Seattle waterfront where huge container ships docked against bulky piers. The air smelled of creosote and seawater. Seagulls hopped about on the sidewalk, screaming and fighting over garbage. The blustery February wind blew in over the stormy Puget Sound and dark clouds obscured the Olympic Mountains. Rain spattered in fat drops and then began in earnest, falling in a blinding torrent. Harry ducked under the dry roof of Pike Place Market and found himself standing next to a tower of polished apples. "Heirloom selection: Pippins, Braeburns, and Gravensteins from the Hood River Valley!" the sign read. Harry picked up a sample, and as the sweet pulp slid down his throat, he remembered that his mother's uncle lived somewhere near Hood River. He said goodbye to Jeff, hopped on a Greyhound to Hood River, and hitched his way to BZ Corner. After Sylvia, Uncle H's welcome seemed pretty warm. Harry didn't know if it was hospitality or senility, and he didn't want to know. However, any momentum he'd gained had stopped there in the woods.

At River Daze Cafe, Moira let Harry use her laptop and showed him the local job classifieds. He looked at the landscaping listings first since he'd worked for his mother and Sal for years, but the pay was terrible. Migrant workers from Mexico were hired for those jobs, Moira said, and it drove down the wage.

"Look at the restaurant section," she said as she loaded a tray of loaves into a huge oven. Harry watched the smooth muscles of her beautiful sun-browned back ripple beneath her tank top. He sighed and turned back to the computer.

He pulled out his notebook and started a list of job prospects. Waiting tables paid better, but he didn't have the experience or clean clothes for that. He'd washed dishes at a Long Island pizza parlor in high school. But a hot, wet kitchen seemed like a hellish place to spend the summer. He looked at the farmers section. There was one interesting post from a beekeeper. It didn't pay great, but it mentioned light construction. He preferred working outside, he decided, more than he'd ever realized living in New York.

At Uncle H's even when you were inside, you were almost outside, what with the state of the trailer. Harry had grown to love the voices of the wild river and the ever-present wind in the huge trees. The woods were thick with birds and small animals that roamed freely in the absence of humans. He only saw the occasional kayaker hitching back to the launch as he made his way to the grocery store. And Uncle H often didn't speak for hours apart from muttering to himself. Harry had grown accustomed to listening to the murmuring outside world.

He emailed three of the listings—the pizza place, a farmer's market stall, and the beekeeper. He could put Jeff down as a reference. Jeff didn't know he'd gone to jail, and Harry hadn't mentioned it. Who else? His parole officer? Stupid idea. His parents? No. He swiveled on his stool to look at Moira, who stood rolling out a pile of dough.

"Hey, Moira. Can I put you down as a personal reference?"

She laughed and pushed her hair out of her face. "So forward, Harry! I mean, I just met you."

His face flushed. "Oh, right. Sorry. I just—"

"Kidding, dude! Sure, you can put me down. You're not an ax murderer or anything, right?"

No, just a small-time criminal, he thought. Not even a good one.

She gave him her last name and her email address. She also invited him to a party at her house. She told him to come back to the café at 5:00 p.m. and he could ride with her.

"My friends are cool. You'll like them."

Harry's heart thrummed. She was so pretty, and she smelled like cinnamon and melted butter. Things were looking up. He waved and left the café, pretending he had somewhere to go. Killing time until

5:00 p.m., he walked through Hood River's small downtown to the waterfront.

The wind picked up as he neared the river and whistled in his ears. He could see whitecaps out in the green water and a flash of activity in the middle of the channel. He'd seen windsurfers at the Jersey shore, and there were a couple of those out there, zipping around like furious plastic sharks. But there were these other things—large paraglider-like things flying high over the water. Harry walked closer and saw a sign that read, "Kiteboarding launch. Spectators use caution."

People in wet suits were pumping air into the big kites. Harry watched as one guy holding a bar signaled to a woman clutching a kite at the other end of the lawn. She released it, and the man steered it overhead. Harry watched the guy walk down to the river with the kite flying above him. Then he hopped on a wakeboard and sped off across the water. It was mesmerizing. People zoomed across the river and back. They launched high in the air, suspended for long, impossible seconds. They did flips and complicated tricks. Out on the large sandbar that spilled into the river, he saw dozens of wet-suited figures launching and landing the great colorful kites.

Harry bit into one of the cinnamon rolls Moira had given him, still warm from the oven. Drizzled with honey, it made his teeth ache. A big guy crossed his field of vision with a bright pink kite under one arm and a board under the other. He put his gear down next to Harry.

"Damn! Well, that was a day for paying dues," he said with a laugh, and flipped his long, wet hair out of his face. "I prolly shoulda stayed home and organized my sock drawer."

The guy seemed to be talking to Harry. So he asked, "Bad day?"

The big man cracked his neck. "Nah. Not too bad. The wind's dying. Been fluky," he said, swimming his hand through the air. "Up and down. But hey—any day out here is better than a day at the office, right?"

The guy flipped his kite over and pulled a valve open. Air rushed out, and the kite deflated into a limp pink sheet.

Harry watched as he began to fold it up. "Is that hard to learn?" he asked.

The other man laughed and jerked his thumb at a collection of trailers near the water.

"The kite schools will tell you it's easy. But I'm a reasonable man, so I tell people the truth. It's a challenge. You have to get out there and stay out there and figure it out on your own. Schools have Jet Ski support and walkie-talkies and all that, but the bottom line is you gotta learn what the wind wants to do, and then hold on when shit goes sideways!"

He eyed the cinnamon rolls. "River Daze? Oh, man, I love their honey buns."

"Have one," Harry said, pushing the box toward him. "I can't eat both."

Harry insisted when the big guy protested, and he picked up the pastry, dwarfing it in his big paw.

"I bet it's expensive," Harry ventured.

The kiter unpeeled the cinnamon roll and shoved a piece in his mouth and nodded as he chewed. "Well, brand-new gear, a full set of kites, lines, harness, and board—you can spend four or five grand."

Harry looked closely at him. The kiter didn't look like he had four or five grand lying around.

"But you can get used gear for a fraction of that. Around here at the end of the summer, sometimes people just give shit away."

Harry looked skeptical, and the guy grinned.

"Serious, man. Some of these people don't know what to do with all their money. That's why we need a revolution!"

He pumped a fist in the air. Harry thought of Marty and blanched, but the big guy laughed.

"Just kidding! I'm way too lazy for that shit. Besides, all's I need is wind."

He shook his wet hair out of his face. "And beer," he said. "Now I really need a beer."

He wiped his hands on the grass, stood, and reached down for the folded kite with one hand. He held out the other for a fist bump.

"Thanks, brother. Name's Yogi," the guy said.

"Harry," Harry said.

"See ya around, Harry."

Harry looked out at the water again, at the sandbar, where two dozen kites had landed and people were wrapping their lines around the control bars. Maybe Moira would think it was cool if he became a kiter, Harry thought, and he stroked his upper lip.

What Moira thought was cool became clear later in the evening at her party. Harry was one of a dozen guests—all guys except for one sour-faced girl, who stared at her phone and didn't talk to anyone. When Moira said he would like her friends, she must have thought he'd be into kayakers—hulking guys with loud voices and big beards that made Harry feel scrawny and lamer than ever.

She'd been so nice to him, but now he understood she was nice to lots of guys. She buzzed around the party, flirting with everyone without focusing too long on one person. She had delegated the grill to the biggest guy, named Hootie, who ran a food cart somewhere in Portland. He looked like he could have picked Moira up in one hand and flipped burgers with the other. Clearly the alpha. The others surrounded him, all bragging about their afternoon river sessions.

It felt like high school all over again, only it was the kayakers instead of the football team. Harry had never managed the macho camaraderie necessary to fit in. Instead he went to the shop after school when he didn't want to go home to an empty house. Mr. O'Brien, the crusty old shop teacher, had shown him how to use every tool—the table saw, the chop saw, the jointer, the planer, and the router. But nobody under thirty knew what a router was. Making dovetail joints was definitely not as cool as shredding Class V white water.

In his uncle's wool shirt and his dirty pants, Harry felt like Bilbo Baggins when the trolls were about to make a meal of him. He sat by the bonfire and sipped his beer, morose, and thought of the long journey back up Highway 141 to BZ. What an idiot to think someone like Moira could actually like him. She had offered to lend him a bike, at least—an old Schwinn her last roommate had left behind.

Moira was giggling at something Hootie said. Harry would not be crashing on her couch, as she had suggested earlier. He could see there would be lots of competition for that. Harry stood and stepped out of the light of the bonfire into the shadows. He walked around to the side of the house, grabbed the old Schwinn, and rode away.

The wind rose in the dark and blew over him like a blessing as he climbed the highway toward Uncle H's trailer. He felt better and realized that being alone wasn't always bad. Sometimes being by yourself was better than keeping the wrong company. He felt happy, choosing that. He still had no clear plan, no job, and no friends here. But it was okay. Somehow, he knew it was going to be okay. And he would go see his uncle at the hospital tomorrow.

The wind gusted and buffeted the bike. Harry, who rarely had confidence in his ability to make good choices, felt briefly, wildly happy and didn't know why. He looked up at the sky above the highway. A band of stars shimmered in the long corridor of trees. He could hear branches creak and groan as the wind blew through the forest, building in force as a front moved through the deep river gorge. He thought of the kites and the white froth of waves out on the wide green river. He rode twelve miles uphill and didn't even feel tired.

He dismounted at Uncle H's mailbox and walked down the rutted road to the trailer eating a River Daze kitchen sink cookie, his last bittersweet taste of the day with Moira. He made a list in his head of the good and bad things that had happened and thought about how he would write them down in his notebook. He leaned the bike against a tree, climbed the ladder, and stood at the door, looking up at the stars before crawling into bed. He didn't feel the eyes on him in the dark just beyond the first row of trees. Watching. Hungry.

8

BEE SPACE

Requisites of a complete hive . . .

5. Not one unnecessary motion should be required of a single bee.

—L. L. LANGSTROTH

Alice awoke with a crick in her neck and a sense of foreboding. She hadn't slept well, listening for sounds from the guest room indicating that the boy might need help. Though she hadn't heard anything, her worry kept her vigilant. It was like when her mother was in hospice and Alice had spent those last weeks sleeping on the couch in her parents' town house. Even though there was a night nurse on duty, Alice only dozed for a few hours at a time with an ear turned to her mother's room. One night Alice fell into a heavy sleep, and the nurse shook her awake to tell her that Marina had passed.

Last night she had listened, heard nothing, and asked herself again just what in the hell she'd been thinking bringing the kid home with her. It was so unlike her, so impulsive. And getting up in Ed Stevenson's grill! It just wasn't her way. She didn't involve herself in other people's dramas. Well, apparently, she did, because she hadn't paused to think. It was like stepping off a dry bank and entering a rushing river before gauging its depths.

Not a mile from the Stevensons' driveway, the white heat had evaporated and the victorious rush of confronting a bully had drained out of her like air from a birthday balloon. For one thing, her threat of calling her brother-in-law was a bluff. Though Ron Ryan was, in fact, the Hood River County Sheriff, he hadn't spoken to Alice in months and would not have picked up the phone if she'd called. And though it was true that she was looking to hire someone, she didn't have a job for Jake. She needed someone able-bodied to help her on the farm. Someone who could lift heavy things and dig holes.

And the idea of offering room-and-board—where in the hell had that come from?

She heard her parents' voices in her head.

"Aggressively compassionate!" Al hooted. *"That's my girl."*

"Pot, kettle, black," said Marina.

She had glanced at Jake, who sat with his head back and his eyes closed, smiling, and bit the inside of her cheek in frustration at herself.

Once they had arrived at the farm, it seemed like the right thing to invite the kid to stay the night. She made dinner and they managed an awkward conversation that expressly avoided the particulars of the job description on her side and any mention of his father's behavior on his.

Now Alice lay in bed looking up at the ceiling, her eyes grainy from lack of sleep. She had no idea what his physical needs were. She'd been the one to invite him, but did she have to take care of him now?

"The boy isn't a puppy, Alice," her mother's voice snapped in her mind. *"Make him breakfast and save the hard questions for later."*

Sensible even in the afterlife—that was Marina Holtzman. Alice got out of bed and pulled on her clothes. She heard a door open and the sound of running water from the guest room. That was something. Her anxiety eased a notch, and she went into the kitchen.

As she made coffee, Alice reflected wryly that the accessibility of the house had proven itself, anyway. She'd renovated the one-level rancher thinking that her parents would move in someday: the ramp, widened doorways, and a fully accessible guest room and attached bathroom. But no one had maneuvered through its hallways until last night. Jake wheeled himself in the front door and down the hall. He'd spun the chair and smiled.

"Nice digs, Alice," he said.

Despite the smile, he looked tired. Alice was exhausted too and happy to turn in early when they finished dinner and he said he didn't need anything.

Alice looked out over the field, where the sun lit upon the white beehives. She could see it was windy already as she watched the cottonwoods and Doug firs tossing their branches. Not ideal weather for checking the new nucs as she had planned.

"Coffee first, dearie. Always coffee first," her father's voice said.

She sat at the table and pulled up the weather forecast on her laptop. It would be windy early, tapering off in late morning. She could do her hive check later. For now she could show Jake around the farm and introduce him to the bees. She'd find a way to broach the subject of the actual work involved and ease him into an understanding that he couldn't possibly do what she needed him to—lift bulky brood boxes and hundred-pound honey supers and dig holes for fencing and the like. There was no way he could do any of that from a sitting position as far as she could see. But she could let him stay for a couple of days, until his father cooled down. That made sense, and surely, he would understand.

She heard the sound of wheels on the linoleum behind her and turned, smiling with the false cheer of someone who was accustomed to being alone in the morning and liked it that way but who was brought up to make an effort to be polite.

"Good morning," she said, and then stopped cold at the sight of his long, wet hair draped behind one shoulder like a punk mermaid.

He looked embarrassed and pulled the long shank with one hand.

"Pretty rad, huh?" he said, trying to smile and shrugged. "I really needed a shower."

He looked so young and vulnerable with his wild hairdo undone, and Alice felt herself soften.

"Not too formal around here," she said, waving a hand at her rumpled shirt and Carhartt overalls. "This is standard coffee-hour attire."

His face brightened, and he looked over her shoulder to the kitchen. "There's coffee?"

Alice moved to stand, but Jake rolled up to the counter and poured himself a cup. He maneuvered over to the table and sat next to her and looked out the window.

"Wow! I've never been this far out in the orchards. Your place is amazing. Is that all yours out there?"

Alice loved the beauty of the sunlit meadow and adjacent forest land, but it surprised her that a teenage boy would notice. She nodded and gestured south. "Out to the fence line is all my place. And on this side, past the barn. Then north to the road. I'll show you after breakfast. You hungry?"

He nodded and moved to follow as Alice rose and went to the kitchen.

"Let me help," he said. "I make a mean piece of toast."

Alice turned and smiled the polite smile of the reluctant host. "I'll do breakfast this morning and then we'll see—" She stopped.

Hearing her hesitate, Jake's smile dimmed. Surely, he understood that this would never work.

He cast his eyes down and then back up at her as if steeling himself. "Listen, Alice. You did me a solid last night. I won't be a burden around here. I'll carry my own weight. I'll—"

She waved a hand at him, feigning lightness. She thought of what her mother would say in a situation like this, though Marina Holtzman would never do something so rash as insert herself in another family's conflict. And then there was the wheelchair. She had no idea what kind of needs the boy had.

"Don't worry about it, Jake. We'll figure something out."

She said the words with an ease and confidence that she didn't feel, and it did the trick. The kid smiled and rolled back to the table. He rifled through a copy of yesterday's *Hood River News* while Alice made breakfast.

Over scrambled eggs and toast, she explained the apiary, which was currently at twenty-four hives and which she hoped to grow to fifty or more over the course of the summer. She explained the bee year, which started in spring and ran into fall. Her hives were all Langstroth hives, which were designed by Lorenzo Langstroth in the mid-1800s and had revolutionized beekeeping in America. Because they had removable frames, they were the easiest for beginning beekeepers, Alice said.

Jake said she didn't seem like such a beginner with twenty-four hives, but she just shrugged. It still felt that way to her. When they went out to the barn after breakfast, Alice walked more slowly than usual and tried to act like she wasn't. Unlike the house, the yard had not been modified for a wheelchair, and it seemed suddenly bumpy and rough to her as she watched him navigate it. The chickens clucked an alarm at their approach and scattered. Red Head Ned stalked out in front of Alice, and glared at them, reminding her that he was on duty. Alice pointed at him and smiled.

"Watch out for that guy. He's a real hothead."

The barn was divided into the shop area and the bunkroom. In the shop Alice showed Jake an empty hive and took out the frames to show him what the foundation looked like before the bees built out the honeycomb. Bits of old beeswax clung to them, and Jake took one of them from her and put it to his nose, breathing in the ghost of honey.

Alice explained the difference between a brood box and a honey super, which was really just a question of location. Honey supers went on top of the brood boxes, which were baby bee nurseries or brood nests. She talked about how the bees built their comb out and the way a hive developed with its brood nest in the middle and honey and pollen around the edges as food stores. The excess honey in the supers was what she could harvest because it meant the bees had ample stores for the winter when they clustered up and couldn't fly.

Jake put his finger on some sticky brown residue. "Is this honey?"

Alice shook her head. "No. That's called propolis. They gather it from trees around here and use it to plug up any cracks or holes. Kind of like natural caulk."

"They go get it and bring it back to the hive?"

She nodded. Propolis, which bees used to secure every gap in a hive, was just one of many dazzling bee miracles.

The kid actually seemed interested, so she checked the wind reading on her phone and decided it didn't seem too strong after all. She grabbed her hat and gloves and looked squarely at Jake.

"If you're game, I can open up a hive so you can see the girls at work. I have a full bee suit if you want to put that on. I also have a jacket and another hat and veil. That might be easier, but your legs won't be protected. They aren't aggressive, but they might sting you if they are feeling protective. It just depends on how comfortable you think you'll be."

"Jacket's fine, Alice," he said, smiling.

"You sure?"

He nodded. "I can't feel my legs anyway, so if they start stinging the shit out of me, I won't notice," he said.

Alice looked at him closely, seeing a glint in his eye. Mischievous or bitter? She couldn't tell, and she didn't know what to say.

He waved a hand at her. "I'm not allergic. I promise," he said.

Alice handed him the hat and jacket.

"At least my hair fits under this thing today," he said with a chuckle, pulling the hat on his head and deftly zipping the jacket.

She grabbed her tool bag and led the way into the yard. The ground was flatter there, and Jake seemed to have an easier time rolling over it.

The apiary was surrounded by a fence to deter raccoons, which were everywhere, and bears, which were less frequent but occasional visitors. Alice opened the gate to the enclosure in which the white wooden hives were set in orderly rows. Twelve of them—the oldest hives—were two boxes high. The twelve new hives, inhabited by the newcomers Alice had brought home from Sunnyvale, were single boxes. The air was full of zinging bees, but they were too busy to take much notice of the two humans.

Alice stopped next to one of the two-level hives. "Italians, 2013, No. 11" was scrawled on the side in black grease pen. A warm buzz emanated from its core, a steady pulse like a heartbeat or a small engine. Golden bees crawled in and out of a slot entrance a few at a time. Alice pointed out how they each paused for a moment, and then headed off in more or less the same direction. The kid watched them catch the wind and disappear.

Alice took a small metal can out of her bag and tucked pieces of paper and burlap into it.

"This is called a smoker," she said, lighting the paper and pumping the can's small leather bellows. "I use just a little bit to calm them down."

She used a metal hive tool to loosen the top of the hive and then eased it off to one side along with the inner cover. The buzzing went up a notch. A couple of bees drifted out from the front of the hive and hovered around Alice's veiled face.

"Good morning, girls," she said almost under her breath. "Just coming in to have a look. No need to worry."

She pumped cool smoke into the hive in three short bursts. The bees climbed down inside and out of view. Alice set the smoker aside and used the tool to loosen one end of a wooden frame and then the other. She maneuvered it out of the box and held it in her gloved fingertips for Jake to see. In a quiet voice she explained what he was looking at—capped honey, uncapped honey, pollen, worker larvae cells, and a sprinkling of drone cells. If he looked closely, she said, he would see tiny bee eggs at the bottom in some open cells like grains of rice. Climbing around on all that material was a murmuring mass of black-and-gold bodies. Each diligent to her task, the bees moved around the frame with purpose.

Alice took his silence for nervousness and moved to slide the frame back into the box.

He reached out with his gloved hands. "Can I hold it?" he asked. "I'll be really careful."

Surprised, she nodded and transferred the frame from her gloved hands to his. Jake held it in front of his face and looked at the workers, some scent fanning, some oblivious.

Not a scaredy-cat, anyway, Alice thought.

After they had examined every single frame from that brood box, after Alice had shown him the difference between a drone and a worker bee, and after they had identified the long, slender body of the queen bee in the middle of the box, Jake had a hundred questions.

Why was the queen in the middle, and why did she live longer than the others? Why did she have a green dot on her? How did the workers know what their jobs were? What happened to them in winter? What about the drones? Where do the bees get the pollen and nectar, and what was the difference between nectar and honey? How did they know where to fly? Where did the wax come from? Why did only the queen lay eggs?

Most people restricted their questions to stings and honey. A few asked about winter. Jake's interest pleased Alice. She talked, and the boy listened. Really listened. The sun climbed over the field as they sat at a picnic table under the big cottonwood and watched the dance of the bees. Alice told him about royal jelly, gestation periods, bee space, and drone congregating areas. They talked for a long time.

Alice went back to the house and brought iced tea. They sat in a companionable silence, watching the honeybees stream from their hives into the forest and fields. Alice was surprised to feel easy sitting there with the boy. As a woman without children, Alice was not accustomed to teenagers, who, as a rule, made her uncomfortable. The only ones she saw regularly were the sullen progeny of her co-workers, who barely looked up from their phones to address her when prodded by their parents.

"You started with just the one hive, then?" Jake asked.

Alice nodded and smiled. She pulled her hair off her neck and wrapped it in a rubber band. She pointed out Hive No. 1 near the west fence line. "That one was my very first. I never thought I'd have twenty-four."

"And you want to have fifty by the end of the summer?"

"Yep. If I don't take as much honey and split the strong hives, I think it could work. Most of them are doing really well because we've had a good spring. I can probably capture some wild swarms to make new hives too."

As long as no unseasonably hot spring days shriveled the delicate blossoms, she was thinking. As long as no big storms blew through the orchard, decimating the blossoms. She thought the kid would ask her next about how to catch a swarm. Instead he asked the one question she hadn't seen coming, the most obvious question someone would ask.

"How did you get your first hive?"

There was a long pause, and Alice set down her glass with a bang. She couldn't speak. Stalling, she looked back across the field and then up to the house. He was waiting for her to answer. The weight of her not answering sagged between them like a line of wet laundry. Alice felt her breath grow shallow and her chest tighten. Not here. Not now. She could not freak out in front of this kid, and she could not answer his question without freaking out. She punted.

"Damn!" she said, jumping up. "I forgot I was supposed to— Listen, I'll be back in an hour. I've got to run into town. Sorry!"

Without a backward glance, she hustled over to the truck, picked the keys off the seat, and disappeared up the long driveway.

As soon as the house was out of sight, she pulled over and turned off the engine. She leaned her head back and tried to slow her breathing. Her heart hammered like mad, and a high-pitched tone rang in her ears.

Follow the thread, Dr. Zimmerman had said. Her laugh was a sob. No problem this time. An innocent question was a booby trap of memory. That was why it was easier to avoid talking to people. Invariably someone would blindside her with a simple question like Jake's.

Alice had seen her first hive at the Hood River County Fair on a date with Bud Ryan more than ten years ago. It was not the first time Bud had asked her out, after months of flirting with her at the John Deere store. He had worked in the maintenance department then and befriended her dad, who had taken the tractor in to get the belt replaced. Tall, handsome Bud Ryan. What he saw in her, she never understood. Al couldn't understand why she wouldn't go out with him.

"It's just lunch, Alice!" her father railed at her. "Just have lunch with the man, for the love of Pete!"

She said no. She said she worked during lunch. She said she had plans with her parents. She said she had a work thing. She was helping Al with the pruning. Finally, Bud invited her to the county fair.

"The 4-H awards are tomorrow, Ms. Holtzman. It's a big day for all of our future farmers. Do it for the children, won't you?"

She had laughed at that, happily defeated, and said yes. What was the big deal anyway? Her unease returned while she waited for him to pick her up that morning. She should be spending the day helping her dad in the orchard, she thought. They had so much to do. She reached for the phone to cancel, and then stopped. When he stepped out of his truck, smiling, she felt glad. Bud was kind and easy to be around. He was at home in his own skin and made her feel that way too.

Alice had always loved the county fair and was pleased when Bud steered her toward the animal competitions. At the lamb judging, they applauded for a tiny girl named Luz Quinto, who won a blue ribbon for her perfectly behaved little lamb. She led it around the circle on a loose rope, and anyone could tell the animal adored her. When the bidding started, Alice's heart sank. It was part of it, but she hated the idea of seeing that little girl separated from her pet, though Alice knew she would use the money to buy another. With dismay, she saw Bud put up a hand. She didn't want to participate in the little girl's sorrow. Bud offered an outrageous sum for the animal, far more than it was worth for breeding stock or meat. When the bidding was over, Luz Quinto handed him the stock ticket with big tears in her dark eyes. Bud leaned down and whispered something in her ear and handed the ticket back. Her face lit with joy. She ran to her parents, the lamb kicking its little hooves behind her.

"You are a big softy," Alice said.

"It's just I'm thinking about going vegan," Bud said, slapping his big belly, and they both laughed.

They spent the afternoon walking through the corrals of cows, goats, and pigs. They sampled pies, jams, chutney, and fresh apples and pears. They avoided the noise and lights of the midway without even talking about it. Bud seemed to understand that Alice wouldn't like that—the rides, the day-drunk adults, and the crowds of roving children. They strolled through the barns, looking at the heritage chickens, the sows and boars, the enormous bulls that would later be used in the rodeo. On the far side of the stock area, they found the beehives.

Later, Alice would know the names for the different hives she saw that day—Langstroth, top bar, leaf hive. There was even a woven reed and mud in the style of an old-fashioned skep. These demos were set there by the local beekeeping association. They were all empty except for one Langstroth hive that had a Plexiglas viewing window on one side.

Alice sat on the bench in front of the hive, enthralled by what she saw. Thousands of bees crawled over the comb, unhurried, each proceeding single-mindedly in her task. Pollen-laden bees stuffed bright orange powder into cells and packed it down with their legs. She watched one bee feed a clumsy, white larva. She saw a bee emerging from a cell, complete and perfect. What a tiny, amazing, orderly world.

Bud read the sign in front of the hive. "'This hive, built in the style of American beekeeper Lorenzo Langstroth, contains approximately fifty thousand bees when fully functioning. A healthy hive will produce between five and ten gallons of honey per year. Local honeybee hives are a boon to orchards and farms. Langstroth hives are available at a discount through the Hood River County Beekeeping Association.'"

He sat next to Alice, and they watched in silence for some time. Alice had never been so comfortable with a man. She hadn't thought it possible. Bud just slipped into her quiet world like that.

"You should get one," he said after a while. "They would love the orchard at your folks' house."

Alice shook her head. "I wouldn't know the first thing," she said.

Bud had thought otherwise and showed up at her parents' barn the following Saturday with an unassembled Langstroth hive in the back of his truck.

"I thought maybe you could help me put it together," he said, grinning and holding up his big hands. "I'm all thumbs with these little nails and stuff."

Alice went along with his ruse. Because why not? Together they assembled forty wooden frames, two brood boxes, and two honey supers. They primed the boxes and painted them and built a hive stand. The process took several Saturdays, and Marina invited Bud to join them for dinner every week. By the time the hive was assembled, it was too late to say no to anything Bud Ryan asked of her. This big, laughing man didn't mind her silence. He didn't read it, as many did, as unfriendliness. Bud understood her in a way most people didn't. Alice felt like herself around him. She didn't even think about things like love or marriage. There was no decision. They just were.

"As it should be," Marina said three months later, though still irked that her only daughter had gone to the courthouse on a Friday afternoon and gotten married without telling anyone.

But those days were long past. Now Alice gripped the steering wheel and felt her whole body shake. There was a hole inside her gaping open. Dr. Zimmerman said it would take time and hard work for it to grow smaller. She said it would never heal completely. Her grief was part of her life now. She had to name it and learn to regulate it so she wouldn't feel that panic and loss of control.

Alice clenched her fists and fought for her breath. She thought of the kid back at the farm, and that just made everything worse. She couldn't handle having another person at the house. Not when she could fall apart like this. Jake would have to go home and soon—that much was clear. The thought calmed her. At least she still had control over her house, her farm. She could be there on Alice Island with her drawbridge up. Her breathing slowed. She wiped her eyes and felt a calm weight settle in her core.

She turned the ignition and drove toward Little Bit to pick up some bales of hay. She needed to make a new windbreak anyway, and the bales would offer a plausible excuse for her hasty departure. She tried to think of the words she would say to let the kid down easy. Even her parents would agree with that plan, surely.

"It'll be fine, right?" she asked aloud. "He'll understand that's just how it's got to be?"

But her parents' voices were silent as the grave.

9

WORKER BEE

The Workers, or common bees, compose the bulk of the
population of a hive . . . It has already been stated, that
the workers are all females whose ovaries are too imper-
fectly developed to admit of their laying eggs.

—L. L. LANGSTROTH

When Alice Holtzman was ten years old, she stood in front of her
fourth-grade class and told the story of how Holtzmans had farmed
her family's orchard for three generations. She recounted how her
great-grandparents had come to the Hood River Valley from Germany
and planted the first trees. She explained how they passed the orchard
to her grandparents, who passed it to Al and Marina. Colorful drawings went along with her presentation as she explained the seasons of
pruning, irrigation, and harvest. She detailed annual crop tonnages
and the Holtzmans' prize varieties of heirloom fruit, including Pippins, Gravensteins, and Braeburns. For the last picture, Alice had
drawn herself in overalls driving the green tractor between the rows
of apple trees. This was how she imagined herself as a grown-up, taking over for her parents as the fourth generation of Holtzman family
farmers.

When she finished, her teacher, Miss Tooksbury, patted her pretty
hands together and urged Alice's classmates to do the same. Alice was

rolling up her pictures when David Hanson yelled from the back of the room.

"You can't be a farmer! Farmer's wife, you mean!"

He collapsed across his desk with hilarity, and the room erupted with laughter. Alice stood frozen at the front of the class. Miss Tooksbury scolded David, saying that Alice could be anything she wanted.

"Yes, even an astronaut, David," she said, frowning.

But as Miss Tooksbury glanced at her and away again with narrowed eyes, Alice realized that her teacher didn't really believe that she could be an astronaut or a farmer. It was the first time she understood that adults sometimes lied. After school, she told her father about it as she helped him cut and sand tree stakes for the new grafts. Al listened, nodding, but didn't say anything. She pressed him, even though she knew that her father spoke only when he had something to say.

"But she's my teacher," she said, her voice rising to a whine. "And she thinks David was right!"

Her father stopped sanding and looked down at her, sawdust motes floating in the air between them. "Is Miss Tooksbury here cutting tree stakes?"

Alice shook her head.

"Will she be here tomorrow when we start grafting new seedlings?"

Again, Alice shook her head.

"Well, I guess we know that Miss Tooksbury is not learning to be a farmer. But who knows? People change."

And that was all he said about it. Alice hugged him harder than usual when she went to bed that night. Al Holtzman was a man of few words, but she knew he thought she would be a great farmer.

And yet, thirty-four years later, Alice was not staking trees or grafting stock. Al was dead, the orchard was gone, and Alice was still working at the county planning department. She wasn't a farmer or even a farmer's wife.

On Monday, as she drove to work, she considered what had happened between fourth grade and the age of forty-four. Her situation was not unusual. People let go of their childhood dreams and repackaged their lives into practical, predictable boxes, right? The idea depressed her and made her feel even worse about Jake.

It had been late afternoon when she returned from Little Bit and unloaded the hay bales from the truck. Jake was out in the apiary when she got back, so she waved and called out what she was doing. He watched her use the tractor to position the bales in a windbreak, and the activity eased the strangeness of her departure since they couldn't talk. When Alice finished and walked over to the apiary, he beamed and gestured around with wordless happiness. Her heart sank. She couldn't tell him then. Anyway, it was nearly dinnertime. One more night wouldn't hurt, she thought.

After the kid disappeared into the guest room, she drafted a concise explanation of why he needed to go home. She would just be matter-of-fact about the physical part of the job. She rehearsed it, so that he could only agree and call his mother. The whole thing would be over after breakfast and he'd be gone when she got home from work. She was cheered at the thought of how quiet her house would be. She slept well, and when she awoke that morning, she knew it was the right thing to do. She just needed to be alone.

Alice found Jake waiting in the kitchen with a pot of very strong coffee. She choked on her first sip, but Jake didn't notice because he was talking about the bees. He'd been up until 2:00 a.m. reading her *Backyard Beekeeping* book and had all kinds of questions about drones, their gathering areas, whether the drone population could be used to measure the health of the hive. Varroa mites and the controversy over treating or not treating. Against her will, Alice was drawn into the conversation because they were very interesting questions. Then she was running late and realized she would have to talk to him about leaving after work. She swore under her breath as she sped toward town.

She parked in the county lot and stood on the sidewalk, looking down the hill toward the water. It was windy already. Kiteboarders and windsurfers formed bright clusters on the white-capped river, most likely locals stealing a bit of water time before work. The waterfront would be packed with tourists by June. She could see the long strip of green grass where people congregated—wind chasers and spectators.

She had been looking at that view for her entire life and never tired of it—the emerald swath of grass, the sandbar spilling into the river, and the craggy cliffs of the gorge rising up out of the water. Memories of summers past burbled to the surface of her mind. Not now, she said, and put them firmly away.

"Morning, Alice!"

The voice at her shoulder made her jump. It was Rich Carlson, the county's human resources and finance manager. As usual, Rich was in a suit when everyone else adhered to the dress code Alice described as "farm-casual." In twelve years Alice had never seen Rich without a tie. Not even at the summer picnic. He stood on the sidewalk batting a rolled-up newspaper against his thigh. Rich was a black hole of time on two legs. He could suck up the better part of an hour just stopping by your desk to shoot the breeze. Alice had felt uneasy around Rich even before the office Christmas party six years ago when he'd cornered her under the mistletoe. She jerked away, and his dry lips grazed her neck. Whenever she found herself alone with Rich, she remembered that—the feel of scratchy polyester, his aftershave that smelled like car freshener.

"Morning, Rich," she said, faking a smile.

"Big day today," he said, flashing a toothy grin. "You folks in planning ready for our meeting with CP?"

Alice kept the smile on her face and groaned inwardly. Like so many western towns, Hood River had grown with the arrival of the railroad in the nineteenth century. Cascadia Pacific, for its part, had developed from a rail line company into a huge conglomerate that now included fiber-optic lines and right-of-way contracts with tech companies as well as other seemingly unrelated twenty-first-century diversifications. Alice had completely forgotten that the Cascadia Pacific reps were coming that day for the annual interagency meeting. Representatives from Forest Service, farmers alliance, and the watershed group would be there too. Alice knew it was an empty gesture to show CP shareholders that they had good relationships with their small-town nodes, but it was mandatory.

"Ready as we'll ever be, Rich," she said.

Rich loved meetings. He took copious notes on his laptop and filed them away for who knew what use. Alice felt sorry for the employees in his department. Sifting through Rich's constant email thread must be a part-time job alone. Alice stole a glance at her watch. She had a little over an hour to pull herself together.

". . . Spent the weekend reformatting my reports," Rich was saying, "so everyone can have access. I keep a master copy on the server. I'm grabbing a coffee at Ground. Care to join me?" He gestured down the street.

Alice couldn't think of anything she'd rather do less. She held up her mug. "I'm all set. Thanks anyway."

Rich made no sign of moving out of her way.

"Well, I'd better get to it," she said, and stepped around him.

"Go get 'em, tiger!" Rich swatted her shoulder with the newspaper as she passed. Alice flinched and felt a lick of anger pass over her.

As usual she was the first one in the planning office. Nancy's chair was empty, and Bill's door was closed. She flipped on her computer and found the department profile, which she would need to submit for the CP meeting. She copied last year's report and began updating it. It wouldn't take her long. The financials were the main thing. She shot an email to Debi Jeffreys, the office manager, sweating as she typed and marking the subject line "urgent." Debi was often crabby when asked for such things. Alice would have preferred to get the financials from the accounting department directly, but because Debi was also hugely passive-aggressive, she insisted that all requests go through her. In her email Alice apologized for waiting until the last minute. Debi wrote back immediately with the attached files.

"You're not the only one who forgot," she wrote. "But the only one to apologize for waiting until this morning! ;)"

Alice sighed with relief to have caught Debi in a good mood. She opened the spreadsheet, scanned it for the pertinent information, and cut and pasted it into her report, working quickly through the first three pages. The numbers were solid across the board—building permits, transportation filings, taxes. She could do this work in her sleep.

The Hood River County Planning Department was supposed to be a stepping-stone for Alice. But when she looked back, it was easy to track how she'd become lodged there. After high school, she went to OSU and double majored in ag and business. At home, Al was the tree specialist and Marina handled the books. Alice wanted to be prepared to do both. She had graduated with honors and worked for a couple of years at a wheat farm with a small cattle operation in the Willamette Valley as operations manager. By the time she went to Eugene to do her master's, the little farm had been gobbled up by the booming wine industry. She didn't think much about it because she planned to return to the orchard.

She moved home in 1996 and worked alongside her father on evenings and weekends. The planning department would be temporary until Al and Marina were ready to hand off the farm. Only that hadn't happened. Alice had watched things get increasingly difficult for her parents—regulations, fees, and prices too low for the small producers. Then came the spraying regulations. When they decided to sell, she understood, though it pained her.

So she dug in. Her boss, Bill Chenowith, had made it clear that she was first in line when he retired. It was the one carrot Bill always held up—his position as county planning director.

At her annual review in March, he'd thrown it out as a parting salvo.

"You know I'm thinking of retiring soon, Alice," he said. "I've always said you would be the best candidate for the transition."

She was ready for that challenge. And this past year, work had given her something to focus on, disappear into. Her job might be boring and predictable, but it provided neat, safe borders to operate within. She took a sip of coffee and focused on the spreadsheets. Mindless, mechanical work—it was a relief.

In the conference room, Alice noticed that the Cascadia Pacific rep, a trim blond man from Seattle, was the only person wearing a suit besides Rich. He seemed like a nice guy, despite the meaningless corporate language: "community building," "shared prosperity," and "blue-sky thinking." This was just a demonstration of a small town's fealty to a big corporation that funded their local grants and made big donations to the schools and parks. In exchange, CP got the right of way to run their fiber-optic cable along the county easement and down the heart of the Columbia River Gorge to support the tech companies that were moving in. Better to call it what it was—a financial exchange, an arranged marriage, if you will. But nobody would do that.

Many of her colleagues had their laptops open. Rich was banging away, taking meticulous notes. Others, she could tell, were reading their email. Nancy was looking at pictures of her kids on Facebook. Her big silly grin gave her away. Alice's mind wandered to the bees. She jotted down some notes in her notebook—building materials, paint for new hives. She would stop by the salvage lumberyard and see what she could find for hive stands. She thought about Jake again and his wild enthusiasm. He had followed her through full checks on three hives, asking questions and holding her tools as she worked her way down the row, which was helpful.

She felt a flash of anger at herself. What are you going to do? Have the kid follow you around and hold your tools?

". . . Celebrating twenty years of interagency partnership!"

The CP rep was wrapping up, and everyone was clapping.

"And as part of our mission to diversify, we have become the regional distributor for SupraGro, which produces value-added products for the farming and ranching sector. We hope to be the bridge between SupraGro and local farms, ranches, and orchards. Here's this year's catalog, and my contact information is on the bottom. Please get in touch with any questions, and thanks again!"

The shiny catalogs were shuffled around the conference room table. Bill thanked the CP rep for the presentation. There was more clapping, and people started to leave. Alice pushed her chair back but found the one next to her still occupied by Stan Hinatsu, from the Hood River Watershed Alliance. Stan was about Alice's age, Japanese-American, with salt-and-pepper hair. A nice-looking guy, she had always thought, but now, brandishing a handful of the colorful cardstock, he looked angry.

"SupraGro!" he sputtered. "Are they kidding? They destroyed the salmon watershed in the north Sierras. In Truckee. There was a huge lawsuit."

Alice vaguely recognized the name of the little California town.

"They're going to just slip this in like we won't notice?" He stood and called down to the other end of the room. "Excuse me! Bill? Bill! Can we have a conversation about this last item?"

Bill was talking to the CP rep. He hitched up his khakis and threw an empty smile in Stan's direction.

Stan gathered his things, muttering, ". . . Completely unacceptable. I can't believe—"

He strode toward the door and called out, "Bill! I'm going to call you and set up a meeting!"

Bill smiled blandly and waved. Stan shouldered his way out of the room.

"What was that all about?"

Nancy stood next to Alice's chair with a Styrofoam cup in her hand, shifting her pleasant bulk from side to side, her pink floral skirt swinging. "What's ol' Stan-o upset about now?"

Nancy had a new perm and was wearing earrings to match her purple-framed glasses. Like Alice, Nancy was a longtime county employee. They'd gone to high school together—Nancy graduating two years before Alice. Nancy laughed often and still carried herself with the same enthusiasm she had as a cheerleader at Hood River Valley High School. They were both Bill's assistants by title but tacitly accepted that Alice really did most of the work. Bill came in late, left early, and couldn't be bothered with paperwork, which was pretty much what the department was all about.

"Something about SupraGro and a California lawsuit," Alice said.

"Drama queen," Nancy said, rolling her eyes. "Always upset about something, those tree huggers."

Alice felt defensive. She liked Stan. "I don't know, Nancy. Remember when those Cascadia trains derailed in Mosier? Stan's group was the one that made them clean it up."

Nancy made a face and laughed. "Jeez! Don't be so serious, Alice. It's Monday morning. By the way, did you get in touch with the Heights folks last week? I was waiting for those housing numbers from you so I could create the forecast."

They walked back to their office together.

Alice felt restless for the remainder of the day. At lunch she walked down to the river, past the kiteboard beach, and east toward the waterfront hotels, the museum, and the little marina, sheltered from the wind. Sailboats bobbed in the light breeze, their rigging clanging lightly. She saw Bill's boat among them—the *Kathy Sue*, named for his wife of forty years. She looked up at the old brick build-ings climbing the hillside above Oak Street. Hood River was still a nice little town. Everyone turned out for the Fourth of July parade and the high school homecoming game. People refrained from honking and braked for turkeys, which ranged through town in the fall.

Alice walked to the middle of the bridge and looked down at the river. Two fly-fishermen stood hip deep in the water, and the sunlight glinted off their lines as they swirled them back and forth in the air. Mount Hood rose up to the south, placid under spring snow.

She loved this place, but she had never expected to end up parked at the county planning department for her entire career. A life lived outside was a good life, her parents had always said. Her heart surged as she thought of her plan of growing the apiary and earning enough money to put in a little orchard at her place. She needed to hire someone to help get things going. That was even more reason she needed to send Jake home, Alice thought. The kid would understand. And if he didn't, well, that wasn't her problem. He had parents, didn't he? He wasn't her responsibility.

She spent the rest of the day immersed in the mammoth task of scheduling assessments for the town's commercial buildings. One by one her colleagues left until it was just her, Nancy, and the red-haired college intern, Casey. Nancy had talked him into happy hour at the taqueria and tried to convince Alice to come too so it wouldn't look like she was hitting on the poor kid.

"Margarita Monday, Alice!" Nancy sang, and did a salsa step next to Alice's desk, snapping her fingers.

She begged off, saying she had chores at home.

"Suit yourself, amiga," Nancy said. "Guess it's just you and me, Casey."

Her laughter rang through the lobby as they left.

Alice knew she was stalling. She drove south toward her house and thought about picking up tacos at Nobi's on the way home. She felt a flash of impatience. She was not cooking dinner for the kid again. She wanted to be irritated, she realized. She needed to justify sending him home. But she liked the kid, which was not insignificant. As a rule, Alice didn't like most people she met. But there was something special about this boy. And she was the one who had invited him. What had that grand gesture been about, anyway? She argued with herself all the way home.

Alice descended the long curve of the driveway and saw a truck parked in front of her house. Her stomach dropped as she heard rising voices, then yelling. Another Stevenson family fight? Of course Ed Stevenson would come looking for his son. Why hadn't she thought of that? Her heart raced. She dreaded confrontation, but she'd be damned if Ed Stevenson thought he could scream at anyone at her place. She rushed up the walkway and threw open the door, ready for a fight.

10

Hive Maintenance

Requisites of a complete hive . . .

1. A good hive should give the Apiarian such perfect control of all the combs, that they may easily be taken out without cutting them, or enraging the bees.

—L. L. LANGSTROTH

Jake didn't have the words to explain what he felt when Alice handed him the frame from the beehive that first morning. He was simply overwhelmed by the beauty of it. The wooden rectangle hung heavy in his fingers as he drew it toward his face. He saw a tapestry of multi-colored pollen, capped honey, and glistening nectar. He breathed in the sweet aroma of fresh beeswax and fermented honey and felt the thrum of a thousand tiny bodies vibrating in unison. It hit him in the heart like a drug. The reverberation ran through his hands and up into his arms. His chest ached, and he thought his heart might explode. It was a calming weight, an invisible touchstone, a "You Are Here" marker.

The pollen-dusted frame was covered with delicate white wax. Across this surface, fuzzy golden bees moved with purpose. They paid no attention to Jake. Some were busy packing away pollen; others wriggled deep into cells filled with honey. Bees were feeding larvae or carrying away the bodies of the dead. Forager bees, nurse bees, undertaker bees. Alice named them as Jake watched the living tapestry of gold, ochre, and scarlet. He breathed in the scent of it all, a fragrance sweeter than cotton candy, and felt the urge to press his face into it. But what he would remember most was that the buzzing mass seemed to inhabit his body. He could feel the resonance in his chest, like when he had played the trumpet. The feeling traveled from his solar plexus through his rib cage all the way into his beat-up, eighteen-year-old heart—a vibration of happiness and contentment. It made him want to sing. He didn't say anything to Alice. He thought he would sound crazy. But the experience made him sure he wanted this job. He pored over Alice's books late into the night, and the more he read, the more it felt like fate, like some sort of door opening.

After Alice left for work, Jake sat on the porch and felt the west wind blowing over the ridgeline as the morning heated up. He watched the wind move through the trees on the edge of the woods, heard a flicker call from deep within the forest. The chickens fussed, and a dog barked. By force of habit, he stuck his earbuds in and turned on his iPhone, but then shut it off. He listened again to the wind, the birds, the faint song of chorus frogs in the distance. It was its own kind of music, and he wanted to hear it.

He wheeled down the ramp to assess the limitations of the yard. Slowly, he moved along the perimeter to gauge where he couldn't go with the chair. He was glad there was no one to watch him struggle across the uneven ground around the yard. He rolled past the apiary and moved toward the barn, maneuvering for the best line.

He recalled the recent events at his parents' place. His kind mom, who worked at the church and helped people all day long, losing her shit on Alice. Tansy Stevenson was a sweet, God-fearing woman who believed in helping her neighbors and loving her enemies. She decorated the kitchen with ducks and geese dressed in bonnets, and she loved watching funny cat videos on the Internet. But if anything appeared to threaten her only son, well, it brought out the pit bull in her. It was a small pit bull, more like an angry Chihuahua, but formidable.

And that fucking story about Ed! Alice filled him in, briefly, in the truck. Jake had no trouble believing it, though it made him sick. Ed had used the belt on him when he was little. The whippings had stopped when a neighbor saw Ed smack Jake, then twelve, and threatened to report him. Ed never hit him again, but Jake knew he wanted to. No surprise Ed had been violent as a child.

An unexpected wave of sadness washed over Jake then. His dad hadn't always been so mean. He recalled the feeling of his father's large hand over his as he walked to the edge of the pool for his first swimming lesson. Only five, he was afraid of the deep water and shivered in his SpongeBob SquarePants trunks. He started to cry when Ed handed him off to the teacher and turned to go. His father usually got angry when he cried. But this time, Ed squatted down and put his big hands on Jake's shoulders.

"I'll be right over there," Ed said. "You're gonna be just fine."

Jake felt his worry leave him as his father squeezed his shoulder and went to sit in the bleachers. He stopped crying and climbed down the ladder to join the class in the shallow end. He kicked, paddled, and blew bubbles. His confidence grew until he did the inconceivable thing and put his head under the water. He shook his head to get the water out of his eyes and searched the crowd of parents for his dad. He saw him then, his face charged with something Jake hadn't understood at the time. Jake thought Ed was mad that the lesson was taking so long. But now he knew it was fear. Ed was afraid Jake wouldn't come out of the water breathing.

Jake paused in his circumnavigation of the yard. He considered this memory almost against his will, but he knew it was true. There were others. The smell of cigarette smoke as his dad ran behind Jake's bike, holding on to the seat to balance him and clapping like crazy when Jake rode away. When he turned eight, his dad gave him a remote-control dune buggy and they spent the afternoon racing it up and down the bumpy driveway. His dad had laughed and looked like a kid himself. There were Sundays they all went to church together and his dad had walked with Jake to get a donut and a cup of hot chocolate from the parish hall afterward. That was all before Ed had stopped going to church, before he'd gotten fired from Middle Mountain Surveyors, where he'd been a supervisor, and gone to work for Klare Construction. Jake had been too little to understand why his father had gotten fired. He just knew things were different after that.

Jake stared out at the ridgeline and chewed his bottom lip. He shook his head. To that handful of good memories, there were just too many years of bad ones. He remembered Ed throwing down the Christmas turkey because his mother suggested he go to mass with her in the morning. Ed yelling at the Chavezes, their nice neighbors, for playing ranchero music during a Sunday afternoon barbecue. And later, kicking their little dog when it wandered over into the Stevensons' flower bed and lifted its chubby leg to pee. When Jake grew the mohawk, his father sneered at him once or twice about his freak hairdo and then stopped speaking to him. Jake preferred the heavy silence to the ugly things Ed said, like those he had screamed at Alice.

The thought of going home made Jake feel cold to his core. He wasn't physically afraid of Ed, but the idea of being back in that man's house made him feel trapped. He pushed himself along the perimeter of the yard, feeling the emotion rise in his chest. He couldn't possibly go back to that cramped house, the air so thick with tension you could almost smell it. The hours of waiting to be alone, which was only slightly less terrible than being in the house with them. So, what then? Could he live and work here? What if Alice changed her mind? He barely knew her, and she didn't owe him anything.

Jake hit a divot, and his front right wheel stuck. He rocked back and forth to free himself. As he struggled, his certainty grew. He could not go back to his parents' house. Impossible. He'd move into adult foster care first, or that shitty group home in The Dalles that his caseworker took him to. Everyone else there was twice his age, and some of them were mentally retarded. "People with intellectual disabilities" was the correct terminology, his caseworker reminded him when they were back in the car. The language didn't matter; he could never live there. He wasn't like them, he told her. But now even the group home seemed preferable to living with Ed. He felt sick at the thought of rolling back up the ramp under his father's gloating gaze. No way. No fucking way!

He pushed harder, and the chair went over. Jake's shoulder hit the dirt with a thump. He could feel gravel on the side of his face, and the familiar weight of despair began to descend on his heart. This was his life now, his fucking body. He heard a low growl then, and when he looked up, he saw the plucky rooster standing on one leg, glaring at him. The sight of the overly confident little bird made him laugh out loud, and Ned stalked away. Jake lay gazing across the barnyard, willing himself to slow his breath. No one was likely to come along, which made him feel grateful. He picked a pebble off his cheek and gathered himself.

First things first. To stay here he had to pull his own weight somehow. To begin with, he had to get off the fucking ground. Slowly, he dragged himself over to the fence, pulling his chair with one arm, grateful for the hours he had spent lifting weights out of boredom. It took some time, but he managed to sit up and right his chair. He set the brake and pulled himself up and in it. He sat in the sunlight, sweating, victorious, and exhausted. Then he rolled back up to the house.

From the kitchen he surveyed Alice's small, tidy rooms, which were conveniently wheelchair-accessible in the most basic ways. The living room was a problem, though. A big bookcase stuck out into the hall, and a labyrinth of small tables crowded the room. The path to the barn and around the apiary was problematic too. He knew he needed help.

Jake hesitated, then pulled out his phone and dialed. Noah Katz picked up on the second ring and acted like they had just spoken the day before, calling him the usual host of disparaging names. Like a true friend, he didn't mention the months that Jake had avoided his visits and failed to return texts, emails, and phone calls. Good old Katz.

After trading insults for a couple of minutes, Jake got down to business.

"Listen, bro. I need a favor," he said. "Can you come by today for, like, an hour? And bring someone with you who can lift things? Right. Cool. Yeah, now-ish would be great! Oh, and I'll need to give you directions. I moved."

Jake hung up. It was so like Katz to say he could come right over, that he was already headed that way on some errand. Katz always had his back, even when he didn't deserve it—like when Mr. Schaffer kicked him off the band bus in The Dalles for fucking around on the way to a football game. What had he been doing that time? Oh, right—lighting matches and flicking them at Matt Swenson in the back seat. The band director's thin face was red with anger as he ordered Jake off the bus in the Walmart parking lot and told him to call his parents for a ride. He would not be performing with the jazz band at the HRVHS game against The Dalles, which would be the last game of his senior year. Schaffer hoped he understood that.

"Poor me!" Jake said as he rose to leave. "No more football. Wah! Wah! Wah!"

The girls around him tittered, and Schaffer flushed redder. Jake grabbed his trumpet case and slouched off the bus.

"Later, skaters!" he yelled over his shoulder. Once off the bus he found Noah on his heels, leaving in solidarity. Schaffer yelled at Noah to get back on the bus. Noah just shook his head and waved, smiling. The band director slammed the door of the bus and drove off. Jake called his mom for a ride. While they waited, the two of them busked in front of the Walmart.

Jake remembered how happy he felt to have Katz stand by him, even when he was being a jerk. Then his mom showed up, tight-lipped with disappointment, and Jake felt the deep, hollow regret of missing the last game of his senior year. At his mom's suggestion, he'd apologized, and Schaffer had agreed to let him play in the spring concert, which was scheduled for the week after he had ended up in the hospital. Busking at the Walmart with Noah was the last time he had played his trumpet for any kind of audience.

The two boys had always shared music, ever since they were in band as little kids. In high school, Noah had gotten more into old school jazz while Jake leaned further into the hard-core punk stuff— the Misfits, Black Flag, and the Dead Kennedys. He turned it up loud when he skated or when he was at home to drown out his father's voice and the drone of the TV.

Noah was the one who had turned him on to Slapstick, a Chicago band from the nineties that mixed punk and ska. He liked the way the trumpet worked in there as the band laughed at itself for what it was or wasn't, like in the song "Almost Punk Enough." That described Jake. So much of it was posturing, for him. He knew that— the music, his hair, his clothes. But he did truly love his trumpet. As they sat in front of Walmart that day, Katz played the melody line of "Almost Punk Enough," and Jake played mockingly over the top on his trumpet.

"You need to start taking yourself seriously, Mr. Stevenson!" Schaffer had yelled at Jake's back.

Jake scoffed, but he knew Schaffer was right. Schaffer was the one who had suggested Cornish College of the Arts in the first place. It was Schaffer's letter of recommendation that helped him get in, he knew. The band director came to see him once in the hospital, and Jake pretended to be asleep. What could he possibly say to him?

Jake watched Noah's truck descend Alice's long driveway and smiled at the familiar sight of his beefy friend unfolding himself from the cab. Goofy Noah with his big hair and toothy smile. Jake groaned inwardly to see Celia in the passenger seat. He hadn't banked on Katz bringing her. Jake thought he might have rounded up one of the guys to help.

"Dude!"

Noah high-fived Jake and leaned down for the acceptable man-hug shoulder bump. He stood back and appraised him. "The hair is looking super sad. What's up with the ponytail? And look at this place! What the hell? You've gone country on me!"

"You know it's been my lifelong goal to be a farmer," Jake said, leaning back and bracing his hands on his knees. "I'm just exploring my 4-H dreams."

"You are rocking it, dude!" Noah said, gesturing at Jake's skinny jeans and Doc Martens. "I barely recognized you."

The passenger door creaked opened, and Celia, who everyone called Cece, climbed out. He had to smile at her, though he wished she hadn't come. She leaned in to hug him, and Jake breathed in her girl smell of minty gum and perfume.

"Hi, Jake! It's so good to see you!"

She looked down at him and pulled on her long black braid with one hand. Her brown eyes shone, and she looked like she might cry. Jake felt a flash of anger. Why did people think it made him feel better that his life made them sad? He threw up his hands in mock outrage.

"Jesus, Katz! I told you to bring someone with muscle. Not this skinny little girl. *La flaca, wey? Cece es la flaca.* Maybe you shoulda brung your grammy instead."

Noah laughed, and Celia squealed in protest.

"No soy la flaca, wey! Órale!"

She flexed her muscles and gritted her teeth. Jake laughed. That was better. And Celia was strong enough to help Noah with what Jake needed anyway. He didn't pause to let himself feel the awkwardness of asking for help. He led them into the house and showed them the furniture he needed them to move. Noah kept up a steady stream of jokes about Jake's new farm boy identity, which helped.

"How did you meet this lady?" Celia asked as she and Noah repositioned the coffee table. "Is she a friend of your mom's?"

Noah rolled his eyes at Jake. Girls always asked questions.

"It's kind of a long story," Jake said. And left it at that.

The kitchen had less furniture but was a bigger deal, and here Celia was the hero. As the oldest girl in a big family, she knew all about cooking. She sorted the pots and pans and pantry items, putting what he would use every day close at hand. She also explained the difference between cooking and baking stuff. They considered the microwave, mounted too high above the stove to reach, and she scoffed.

"You don't need that thing. They stink and make a big mess anyway."

Jake took them outside to see the barn, the chicken coop, and the apiary. He avoided their eyes and briskly pointed out the rough sections in the path. He didn't mention his fall. Noah found shovels and rakes in the barn, and Celia helped him work the dirt to level the path. Jake did a lap to test it and confirmed it was easier to manage. Noah said he would come back and give it another going over, but he didn't make a big deal out of it.

Jake offered to show them the hives, and though they were intrigued, they wouldn't venture inside the fence of the apiary. As Jake told them some of what he had learned, the honeybees seemed to sing to him. The air was full of golden bodies, some zipping off to forage and others returning. In front of a close hive—one of the new nucs from Sunnyvale—several dozen bees zinged wildly back and forth in short bursts. This was an orientation flight, Alice had told him.

"The big kids are teaching the newbies how to find their way home. Isn't that cool?" Jake said.

Noah stood behind Celia, who stood behind Jake. Very cool, they agreed.

"When you get the honey, I'll give you my abuela's recipe for torta de miel. It's awesome. You'll love it," Celia said.

Jake turned and smiled up at her. "Cece, you're a genius. I need your help with one other thing."

Home ec class had been pass/fail and based on attendance, so Jake and Noah had goofed off in the back of Miss Trainor's class and learned nothing. Celia, on the other hand, already knew how to cook for a houseful of people. She sent Noah to the store with a list, to which Jake had added hair product. While they waited for Noah, she talked Jake through some basics—scrambled eggs, pancakes, grilled cheese sandwiches, and burritos. When Noah returned, she helped Jake make his first dinner—chicken enchiladas with chile verde sauce.

"And a salad. You need to eat your vegetables. No, seriously, you guys!" she protested as they mocked her, calling her the Veggie Nazi.

It was after 5:30 p.m., and Alice still hadn't come home. Jake was nervous, wiping down the counters and checking his phone.

"Why don't you guys stick around?" he said.

Noah set the table for four. Jake took the enchiladas out of the oven and covered them to keep them warm. He started the rice like Celia told him to. Noah pulled out his phone to show Jake a video of their friend Mikey landing an Impossible at the skate park. Celia had already seen it several times and rolled her eyes as the boys leaned over the screen. She paged through the newspaper instead. Jake felt tired and happy. He'd missed Noah. Celia was a good one too. Not whiny or clingy. He thought about the last time they'd all gone to Lost Lake. Noah and Celia hadn't been officially dating then. Celia had ridden in the back seat with Cheney draped across her lap. Cheney. The thought of his dog made his heart fold in half. Still, it was good to be with his friends.

Celia noticed the smoke first.

"The rice! The rice!" She dashed across the kitchen and grabbed the smoking pot by the handle with a dish towel. The smoke alarm screamed in short bleats.

"Open the windows!" Jake yelled.

Noah threw open the windows of the kitchen, and Celia jumped on a chair and flapped the dish towel in front of the smoke detector.

"This is not a drill!" she yelled, laughing. "Proceed to the nearest exit and your teachers will direct you!"

"Holy shit! Do your cooking classes always end in a crisis, girl?" Jake shouted.

"I fell into a burning ring of fire!" Noah sang.

The kitchen was filled with smoke and laughter and yelling.

"Noah, take the damn thing outside!" Jake hollered. Noah grabbed the pan and threw open the door, nearly colliding with Alice.

"What in the hell is going on in here?" she yelled.

11

SCOUTING

That bees send out *scouts* to seek a suitable abode, admits of no serious question. Swarms have been traced directly to their new home, in an air-line flight, either from their hive, or from the place where they clustered after alighting.

—L. L. LANGSTROTH

The dancing catfish clock over the dinette wriggled and slapped its freckled head and tail to announce that it was 7:00 a.m. Harry had awakened hours earlier to the predawn snarling of raccoons in the garbage pile. They looked like small bears scuttling around in the weak moonlight and sounded like crazed human babies. When he threw open the window and yelled at them, they seemed more irritated than frightened but finally slunk off into the woods.

His own hunger had been sated by the discovery of a cache of food under the bench where his uncle usually slept. His eyes had lit on the handle as he scoured the trailer for any remaining supplies. Bingo! A jar of peanut butter, three Hershey bars, two loaves of unfortunately moldy bread, a box of saltines, and a quart of whiskey.

He shivered in the cold damp of the trailer, went outside, and sat on the steps in the morning sunlight with a plate of peanut butter crackers. He held up the whiskey, unscrewed the cap, and took a swig of the golden liquid. It burned all the way down his throat. He coughed and put the lid back on, realizing the impracticality of getting drunk while waiting for the library to open so he could check his email. He brushed his teeth and examined his face in the chipped mirror.

In many ways, Harry's twenty-four-year-old face was the same face he'd had as a child. His kindergarten photo showed a small boy with red-brown hair, a sprinkling of freckles across alabaster skin, and a worried brow. His pale blue eyes stared out of the frame, uncertain. Surely, he was being admonished to smile, but his lips were pinched in a straight line. The neutral expression made him look old-fashioned, like a miniature man in daguerreotype. His mother laughed when she saw it.

"You look just like my paw paw!" she exclaimed.

If everyone had a core, Harry's was five years old—skinny, not brave, but not a tattletale. He didn't ask for help, not wanting to be a bother. He suffered through things. He attached himself to people in a quiet way, hoping they wouldn't notice, just wanting to belong. All the way through school, he was the boy just outside the circle, making enough noise to fit in but not stand out.

However, as the episode with the stolen TVs had shown, Harry was not what you'd call a great judge of character when it came to friends. Sam had come to see him once. He thanked Harry profusely for not ratting him out and promised to visit often. Harry hadn't heard from him after that. Marty never bothered to come at all. It took six more months of silence from his supposed pals for it to sink in that Marty and Sam had never been allies. He had known them since high school but couldn't remember a single kindness either of them had ever done him. He lay on his bunk at night, his face burning with the shame of it. They didn't even like him. What a dope.

He met with his lawyer then and handed over their names, an act that reduced Harry's sentence considerably. He walked out of the

Stonybrook Correctional Facility after nine months, still skinny, still not brave, and now a tattletale.

His lawyer tried to help him see it another way. "What would Sam and Marty do in your shoes, Harry?"

Harry knew they would have thrown him under the bus. The realization shocked him—not that his friends weren't trustworthy, but what he'd been doing his whole life. He'd always been the fall guy. No, the problem with Harry's life was Harry. He knew that. He needed to change. He just didn't know how.

"Follow your bliss!"

His teachers had been saying that since the sixth grade.

What did that mean? Did everyone else really sense some Oprah-like compass directing their lives?

"Work, Harry. Hard work, son. That's my passion," his mother said, when he'd been assigned to write about the power of personal passion for school. She pushed her hair out of her eyes with a gloved wrist and opened the tailgate of the truck.

"And pink zinfandel. Now help me unload these trees."

Sal was no help either.

"My passion is blondes, kiddo. Like your mama," he said, and winked.

Harry wrote his paper about having a passion for long-line trolling, which really didn't interest him at all. He got a C+.

Forget about passion. Harry's problem was far simpler and more daunting. How do you move forward? All he knew after a stint in jail, a cross-country bus trip, and two months in the woods was that he still had no idea how to direct his own life. Harry sighed and ran his fingertips across his upper lip. He needed to get his shit together.

He thought of Uncle H and felt a wave of guilt. He hadn't gone to see him at the hospital yesterday as planned. He'd gotten as far as calling, but the nurse said she couldn't release patient information outside the family. He hung up without saying he was family, the only family in the area. He should have gone straight to the hospital then, but he didn't. Why he didn't was another question he simply couldn't answer, and really the same question that had dogged him his entire life—like the lunch money, the bike, the heist, his general failure to thrive. Why was Harry a passenger in the vehicle that was his life?

He washed up in the frigid eddy behind the house and hopped on the old Schwinn, which was rickety but faster than hitchhiking. The cool wind on his face cheered him. He rode the two-lane highway, swerving back and forth between the lanes as he went. He heard the chug of a big engine behind him and moved right to make way. As a logging truck blew past, he swerved to miss a pile of red and brown that he realized was something dead, a dog or a coyote. Harry could see its head and face intact like it was smiling above the torn body. He gagged as he passed and wished he could unsee it.

There was nobody in the little library in BZ besides the librarian, who nodded at Harry and said good morning. She gave him the computer log-in code, which hadn't changed in the two months he'd been coming, but neither of them acknowledged that. He opened his email, and his stomach dropped at the five messages from his mother. They all had the same subject line: "Call me!"

He sighed and didn't open those messages.

He scrolled down, deleting as he went. Spam. Political newsletters he never read. A message from a guy he met in jail who Harry had, regrettably, given his email. Then a message from the gorge.net job board. It was a reply to one of his applications, the bee thing. In his notebook he had listed the pros and cons of each job he'd applied for, and under the bee farm he had written: "Positive: working outside, learning opportunity, farming, carpentry." The last and most important: "No background check request." In the negative column he had simply written "bees." He shuddered. He hated insects, all kinds. But the idea of carpentry work cheered him. He shot a quick message back to the farmer. Yes, he could be there the following afternoon at 1:00 p.m. for an interview. He printed the email, paid the librarian, and left.

Harry wheeled his bike to the gas station and leaned it against the worn fence at the pay phone. Harry hadn't seen a pay phone since he'd been a kid, but the poverty and poor cell service in BZ meant this one got plenty of use. He called his mother collect, and his heart sank when he heard her agree to receive charges. It reminded him of calling her from jail. Twenty-four years old and he still couldn't afford to call his mother.

"Son! I've been worried sick. Listen, honey, I want to hear all about your new job, but first, how's he doing? Is he still unconscious? Are they keeping him on oxygen again today?"

Harry felt the weight of shame descend. Of course the hospital would have called her.

"I, um. They wouldn't release any information to me when I called. So, I'm not sure what the story is right now," he said.

"What do you mean? Aren't you at the hospital?"

Harry looked up at the big fir trees leaning over the highway like he might find the answer there.

"I-I've just been really busy with work," he said. "It's been hard to get the time off during visiting hours."

Did hospitals even have visiting hours anymore? He hated lying to his mother, but he didn't want to try to explain why he hadn't set foot in Skyline Hospital in the four days since his uncle's capture by social services.

Why his mother always chose to believe him was a mystery, but he was grateful now.

"Listen, son. You tell your boss that this is an important family matter. We are Uncle H's only people. Well, the only good ones, anyway. I called Jenny. 'He died years ago as far as I'm concerned,' she told me. Can you believe that? She's just mad because he lost all his money in that Ponzi scheme at Powder River. Well, she should have been looking out for him, so she has no one to blame but herself."

She paused, and Harry heard her light a cigarette and exhale.

"Listen, Harry. I wish I could be there, but I can't get away right now. Sal isn't doing great. It's nothing serious, but he needs eye surgery, and I have to drive him to appointments the next couple of weeks. I'll get out there as quick as I can. Meantime, I'm counting on you to keep me updated. Call me collect until you get a phone. Now, how are you doing? Are you eating enough? Making friends? How's your job?"

Harry told his mother some more lies about how great things were and promised to call her the next day. He felt like such a loser.

Down the hill at the small hospital, he forced himself through the doors. He presented himself as Uncle H's nephew, and the woman at the front desk directed him down the hall. Harry walked slowly, glancing into the rooms. TVs blared, and old people lay flat on their backs, mostly sleeping.

Uncle H was at the end of the hall. Curled up under a blanket, he looked smaller and frailer than Harry remembered. His white hair stood up in its usual bird's nest. His eyes were closed, and his breath was shallow and ragged. He was attached to a bunch of machines that beeped and flashed. Plastic tubes ran into his nostrils. His lips were sucked in around his gums, as someone had removed his dentures. His face was gray and papery.

"Uncle H?" Harry whispered, hoping the old man would open his eyes and say something feisty. But he didn't. His breath dragged in and out. The machines beeped; their lights flickered. The room smelled antiseptic and was brightened only by a vase of flowers on the table. Harry knew they were from his mother before he read the card.

"Get well soon, Uncle H! Much love, Lydia and Sal," it read.

Harry swallowed hard. He sat and looked out the window. He

could see the river from up here, but he doubted his uncle had appreciated the view. Harry stared at a calendar on the wall. April. How was it already April? He'd been living with his uncle for two months.

A doctor came through the door, peering down at a tablet in his hands. He was tall and thin and looked irritated until he saw Harry. Then he smiled and held out his hand.

"Hi. I'm Dr. Chimosky."

Harry stood and shook his hand. "I'm Harry Stokes, sir. His nephew."

The doctor nodded and looked back down at his tablet. "We've been in touch with your mother, I think?"

Harry nodded and hoped the doctor wouldn't ask where he had been for the past four days.

"Well, your uncle had a rough night. He was recovering well from the initial stroke, but he's pretty fragile, and his heart went into an arrhythmia for a bit and then bumped itself back out. He's been on oxygen since he got here. He's stable now, but there's not much we can do for him. Legally we have to follow his advanced directive."

Harry struggled to make sense of the flood of information. "A stroke? What's an advanced directive?"

The doctor looked impatient. "From what we can tell, your uncle had at least one stroke before social services brought him in. An advanced directive outlines what kind of care he wants to receive if hospitalized. He signed it last fall. It says he doesn't want to be admitted to the ICU or put on a ventilator or have a feeding tube put in. We can only offer him limited intervention, like IV fluids and comfort care."

Harry shook his head. "I didn't know."

The doctor shrugged, seeming unsurprised. "You're living with him now?"

Harry nodded.

The doctor frowned down at his tablet.

"Sounds like his trailer is in pretty rough shape. If he recovers, he'll likely move to a rehab setting for a while, but then he'd need a more stable living situation. Will you be staying with him? He'd need help with bathing, eating, getting to follow-up appointments, and such."

Harry, who was down to $297.75, half a jar of peanut butter, two sleeves of Saltines, a Hershey bar, and a quart of whiskey, said, "Yes, sir. Of course, sir."

The doctor smiled. "That's great to hear," he said. "It's much easier when folks have family step up."

He tucked the tablet under his arm and reached out to shake Harry's hand again. "I'll check in later. Let the nurses know if you have any questions."

The doctor strode out of the room.

Harry sat down and looked at his uncle, who struggled to breathe, and was unsure how to feel. He was fond of Uncle H, but he didn't really know him, not like his mom did. He mostly felt guilty for not feeling something more deeply—sad or worried. But he could be there on his mother's behalf. That was something.

Around 5 p.m., one of the nurses brought in a dinner tray.

"Oh, I don't think he can eat that," Harry said.

"Anybody else hungry in here?" she asked with a wink.

Creamed chicken and rice, corn, salad, a cookie. Harry ate every bite, ashamed and grateful. He fell asleep in the chair and awoke when another nurse came in in the morning. Through it all, Uncle H hadn't opened his eyes or uttered a sound other than the rasping breath that escaped his mouth. Without his glasses and his dentures, he looked like a baby. His thin arm was bruised around the IV. Harry took his hand, which felt cold and papery.

"I'll be back this afternoon, Uncle H," he said. "I'll bring some cards with me, and we can play rummy."

Harry rode down the hill to Hood River and across the bridge. He passed River Daze and caught a flash of Moira's face in the bakery window. His heart clenched, and his stomach growled. He thought wistfully of the hospital breakfast trays he had seen passing the door. The morning nurse hadn't offered him one or seemed very friendly, so Harry hadn't asked.

He stopped at a food truck just outside of downtown and bought a breakfast burrito. He knew a little Spanish from working with the guys in his parents' landscaping crew. So he said good morning and ordered in Spanish. The guy beamed at him and said a bunch of stuff Harry didn't catch. He gave Harry an orange juice for free and gestured to a plastic chair next to the food cart. Harry sat and wolfed down the burrito, licked his fingers, and drained the juice box. He looked out over the methodical rows of trees that made up the orchards. Their white blossoms stirred in the breeze. The valley opened up there, and he could see Mount Hood to the south and more orchards marching across the landscape. He heard the cough of a diesel engine and saw a man driving a red tractor between rows of trees. The engine startled a flock of birds, which burst across the road, crying in alarm and flapping their nearly useless wings. A covey of quail, Harry remembered from the bird book as he heard their alarmed peeping. He wiped his hands on his pants and grabbed the Schwinn.

"*Gracias, señor! Buen día!*" the man said.

"*Gracias!*" Harry said, waving as he pedaled off.

He parked his bike in the shade by a creek to wait until it was close to 1:00 p.m. He tried to think of what to say to the farmer. Should he have brought a copy of his résumé with him? The thought ratcheted up his anxiety. He hadn't thought about job interviews since his coaching meeting at the correctional center.

His counselor was a skinny Italian guy named Anthony Barone. Anthony wore a crisp blue shirt and tie and had a small gold earring in one ear. His office smelled strongly of cedar aftershave, which was not unpleasant. Harry sat in the chair he gestured to. One of the wheels was coming loose, and the whole chair tipped backward if Harry shifted his weight. He sat forward and watched Anthony flip through his file, feeling like he was in the principal's office.

"Mr. Stokes. Okay. So, you graduated from high school. Good. Oh, college boy! Don't see that every day. How the heck did you end up in here with a college education?" He looked up from Harry's file and raised a thick eyebrow.

Harry hung his head. "It was just community college," he mumbled.

Anthony folded his hands and glowered at Harry. "Mr. Stokes, most of the guys in here didn't get past the eighth grade. Do you know what it's like looking for work with no diploma? And then a record on top of that? And brown skin?"

Harry shook his head, reddening.

"No, you don't. That's right. Remember that. Don't take your advantages for granted. Be grateful you've got that education, okay, Harry?"

Harry nodded.

"Now what skills do you have, then? Let's see. You've done some landscaping. Looks like that was for your folks' company. What else? You worked at a restaurant for a little while. What did you do there?"

Harry shrugged, and the chair tipped. He saw Anthony frown, and he sat up straight.

"Um, I did a little bit of everything? Busboy, dishwasher, prep cook, stock boy, delivery driver. All those things," Harry said. "It was a small place."

That about captured Harry's problem. He wasn't good at anything in particular.

Anthony looked disappointed when he saw that Harry hadn't filled out his goal sheet. The older man slid it across the desk with one hand.

"Take it back with you, Harry. Spend some time on it. You'd be surprised how it might help. We'll talk it through next time."

He smiled briefly, and Harry left feeling encouraged. Unfortunately, there was no next time. The counselor at Harry's second, and last, appointment was an impatient woman who was older than his mother and didn't introduce herself. She looked irritated when he asked about Anthony and said it wasn't her job to keep track of personnel. She didn't ask about his goal sheet either. She slid a pile of forms across the desk for him to sign and worked on a crossword puzzle while he filled them out. She took them without a word when he was done and pointed at the door, signaling that he was ready to face the world of employment outside of jail.

Harry consulted the email for directions to the farm and pedaled down the road. Tall fir trees grew close together here and curved overhead, forming a green tunnel. Harry sped down the hill, hoping he was going the right way so he wouldn't have to backtrack. He saw the name "Holtzman" on a mailbox at the end of a driveway, hopped off his bike, and walked toward the neat blue house, tucking in his shirt as he went.

He heard voices out by a large barn, and when he rounded the corner, he saw a short person up on a ladder under a tall pine. The woman wore a floppy white hat and had a cardboard box balanced between her hip and the ladder. She held a pair of loppers with one hand.

A boy sat at the foot of the ladder in a wheelchair. He leaned back and called up to the woman, who murmured back. Harry couldn't hear what they said.

Sal had taught him never to surprise anyone on a ladder, so he stood back and watched as the woman dropped the loppers, held the box up, and broke off a branch. A great black clump fell into the box. Harry watched as she shut the box, lost her balance, fumbled, and dropped it. The box seemed to hang in the air for a long second as she grabbed for it and missed. Then it bounced off the ladder and landed in the lap of the kid in the wheelchair.

Harry could hear everything the woman said after that. The string of swear words that carried loud and clear would have bested his cellmate at the Stonybrook Correctional Facility. Harry watched her clamber down the ladder to the boy in the wheelchair, who sat in a buzzing cloud of what Harry realized were bees, laughing his head off.

12

DISRUPTION

As the extremity of the sting is barbed like an arrow, the bee can seldom withdraw it, if the subject into which she darts it is at all tenacious. In losing her sting she parts with a portion of her intestines, and of necessity soon perishes.

—L. L. LANGSTROTH

While swarming honeybees can be heartbreaking for their beekeeper, a swarm is actually the sign of a healthy, productive hive. The older daughters decide the colony is overcrowded and, leaving half their sisters with healthy virgin queen cells, abscond with their mother to greener pastures. If those greener pastures happen to belong to another beekeeper, that loss is transformed into an opportune gift. That was how Alice had viewed the swarm in the fir tree, at least before she had bungled it so badly.

She grasped the last barb with a tweezer and eased the stinger from her hot forearm, which had swelled like a ham hock. She saw the young man's faint mustache twitch as she plucked it out.

"Well, that's done," she said, and rubbed her hands over her arms.

"Does it hurt?" Harry asked.

"No. Just a little itchy."

She wanted to downplay the entire embarrassing episode with the swarm, which wouldn't have happened if she hadn't been rushing.

Every mistake she'd ever made with the bees she'd made in a hurry. Today she'd come home at lunch to interview Harry and spotted the fat swarm while she was waiting for him. She was sure these bees were not hers and couldn't pass up the chance to grab a feral swarm. In hindsight it was a terrible idea—going after the bunched-up bees without a second pair of hands. Not to mention dropping the box on Jake.

What a marvel the kid hadn't been stung. He was still laughing when Alice reached him and pulled the box off his lap.

"Jesus H. Christ," she swore under her breath. "Well, that was a damn stupid idea."

The docility of a swarm had its limits, and this one rose to guard their queen as Alice pushed Jake's chair away. She'd been stung three times, but Jake was untouched.

Jake clutched his stomach and gasped for breath. "Oh, Alice! Your face! You were so surprised, like now how did *that* happen?"

Though Alice felt for the three workers who died in their stinging, Jake's ribbing had finally made her laugh, especially once she understood he was not hurt. Jake vowed to refer to the event ever after as his bee baptism. Not many people, he said, could claim they'd had an entire swarm of bees dropped in their lap. As he wiped the tears out of his eyes, he noticed Harry frozen at the edge of the field.

"I think your interview is here, boss," Jake said.

The young man glanced over his shoulder as if considering a run in the other direction, then raised a tentative hand in greeting and walked toward them.

Alice introduced herself and then Jake. The young guy, who said his name was Harry, looked past her like he was expecting someone else.

"Um, and Mr. Holtzman, ma'am? Al Holtzman?" Harry asked.

Alice chuckled. "Oh, my email address? I'm Al Holtzman. Al for Alice. There's no Mr. Holtzman. That okay with you?"

Harry blushed and stammered, "No, ma'am, I mean, yes, ma'am," and managed, "Thank you for the interview."

Alice watched him struggle, amused. He hesitated and then asked if the thing with the ladder was a regular part of the job.

"No, no. That was what you might call a bad decision," she said dryly. "It was more irregular than regular."

This statement renewed Jake's mirth, and he laughed until tears ran down his cheeks. Harry looked at him worriedly as Jake rolled himself up toward the house.

Harry and Alice sat at the picnic table, and after she'd dealt with the stingers, Alice opened her laptop to glance through Harry's résumé again. She asked him where he was living, and he said BZ, that little nothing town high up in the woods. She ventured that must be boring compared to New York. Harry shrugged and mumbled it was fine.

Not a talker, then, Alice thought. She pushed her hair out of her eyes and gestured out at the bee yard. "I have twenty-four hives now, and by the end of the summer I would like to be up to fifty. My goal is to have one hundred by next summer."

The job was pretty simple, she explained. She wanted someone who could follow directions, lift up to one hundred pounds, and take initiative in seeing what else needed to be done. She needed new hives built as part of the expansion process. Besides the beekeeping, there was the field to mow, fences to mend, and a few apple and pear trees to tend to. There was no end of small projects, she realized, looking around. Things had gotten away from her in the past year.

"So, a little carpentry, some heavy lifting, and help keeping the place shipshape," she said in summary.

Harry nodded.

Alice waited for him to say something, realized he wasn't going to, and glanced back down at the computer screen, searching for something else to ask.

The back door banged open, and Jake rolled toward them with a tray of iced tea and glasses balanced on his lap, whistling.

Harry glanced at him and back to Alice. "Is your son, I mean. Is he . . . sick?" Harry asked in a low voice.

Alice felt a flare of anger on Jake's behalf.

"He's not sick. He's paraplegic," she said flatly. "And he's not my son. He's—"

She stopped, flummoxed, not knowing how to explain Jake. "He's a friend of the family," she finished.

Harry reddened and mumbled an apology.

Jake lifted the tray onto the table. "Okay if I sit in, boss?" he asked.

Alice nodded and turned back to the computer. "So—light construction skills. What can you tell me about that?"

She saw Harry take a deep breath and sit up straight.

"I'm good with a table saw, planer, jointer, sander—the basics. I learned to use all that stuff working for my mom and stepdad. That's Romano Landscaping," he said, gesturing toward his résumé on her screen. "We worked small commercial and residential jobs on Long Island. A little bit of everything."

Landscaping, irrigation systems, and pruning, Alice read. That could all come in handy with the future orchard, she thought.

Alice nodded with approval. "You worked for your mom. Trustworthy, I guess?" she said.

Harry said nothing. There was a long pause. Alice shut her laptop and suggested they all have a look at the bees.

From outside the apiary, Alice explained the basics of the hive setup and the orientation of the yard. The air was full of darting golden bodies. The untrained eye would see only random motion, but if you watched the flight patterns as she did, you could see that each group was working its way to a specific destination and back again. The yard hummed; a breeze stirred the grass and then the branches of the big fir trees. A flicker called, "Cheer!" from the shadowy woods. Alice swung the gate open and eyed the closest hive. She grabbed a pair of clippers from the toolbox and trimmed the grass down in a few quick snips. The mower couldn't get this close, and the ladies didn't like the noisy weed eater. This was the kind of random task she needed help with, she explained. Proper ventilation was key to hive survival. That meant keeping entrances clear of grass in summer and snow in winter. She leaned down to trim another entrance as she talked.

The three of them moved along the perimeter of the bee yard, and Alice pointed out the difference between the brood boxes and the honey supers. She explained how they became heavy with honey and brood later in the summer. That was why she needed a strong back. A full honey super could weigh up to one hundred pounds.

She talked briefly about how she could increase the number of hives with splits and swarms but didn't want to go into too much detail. She gestured at the fallen ladder and the cluster of bees that had regathered in a buzzing clump in the same tree.

"That was a swarm capture gone wrong," she said. "It's usually fairly easy."

Harry nodded, looking unconvinced, and Jake snorted. Alice eyed the swarm and considered asking the young man to help her capture it as a kind of test. A glance at her watch on her still-throbbing arm told her she needed to get back to the office. So she walked Harry to the barn, where she showed him an empty hive, pulling out the frames so he could understand where the bees built the wax, laid the eggs, and stored the honey. Jake sat listening, his face intent.

"I can teach you everything you need to know. I'd probably start you on yard maintenance and grass cutting. Like I was saying, ventilation is pretty important as it gets hotter, so grass is a daily chore."

Was she offering him the job? The idea of interviewing more people tired her, and he seemed fine. Still, she wished he would say something. Harry was silent, pulling apart the empty hive and peering in at the frames. He lifted the cover on and off, turned it around in his hands. The seconds ticked by. Alice was impatient to get back to work and annoyed that he didn't seem to be listening. She cleared her throat.

"So? Any questions about the job, Harry? I imagine it seems fairly—"

"Why don't you make the entrance at the top?" he interrupted. "It's like their front door, right? If the grass and the snow blocking the entrance is a big problem, then it seems like you should just move the front door to the top. That one over there has a top door. Why don't the rest of them?"

Alice followed his gaze to one of the new splits she'd created and returned to the apiary. The front entrance, she realized in exasperation, was choked with crabgrass. The bees were flying in and out of a gap in the top where the brood box was cracked and the cover hadn't seated properly.

"What the hell—" she grumbled.

Alice grabbed her hat and veil, pulled on her gloves, and opened the hive, drawing out a middle frame. It looked just like it should—layered with brood nest and honey and pollen. She put it back, careful to leave the cover tipped to keep that entrance open. Her thoughts whirred. She'd never heard of anyone doing a top entrance on a Langstroth hive, but she couldn't think of a reason it wouldn't work. And if it did work, the kid had just eliminated countless hours of maintenance.

She walked back over to the boys, as she was already calling them in her mind, and smiled.

"When can you start?" she asked.

That evening after work she sat at the kitchen table going over the hive calendar and looking at her banking statement as she willed herself not to scratch her itchy forearms. Her budget would be tight, but she'd only be paying Harry for twenty hours a week. She shook her head. He was an odd duck—either silent or blurting paragraphs. She had to laugh at herself. Alice Holtzman with an awkward part-time employee and teenage roommate. Who'd have thought?

Alice opened a bag of Nutter Butters and looked out the window at Jake, who was slowly rolling the perimeter of the yard. With his black hair back in its crazy spikes, he resembled a Roman sentry. She sighed and munched a cookie. She had a teenager living with her. Alice the introvert. Alice Island. He and his friends had managed to convince her to let him stay for a while. She smiled, recalling how she'd barreled through the door ready to battle Ed Stevenson and instead found three teenagers and a pot of burned rice.

After the smoke had cleared and Alice had stopped yelling, she'd met Jake's two young friends—Noah and Celia—who'd rearranged her furniture, which was disorienting. But they'd also made her dinner. It would have been impolite to refuse, she knew. She sat down to eat with them, begrudgingly, and told Jake they had things to discuss after dinner. Alice's dark mood settled over the table. The silence was broken only by the sounds of forks on plates and chewing.

"These young people are guests in your home, Alice!" she could hear her father's voice hissing in her ear. She sighed and put down her fork.

"This is really delicious," she said, forcing a smile. "Thank you, Celia."

Celia jumped in like she'd been waiting for an opening.

"Actually, Mrs. Holtzman, Jake made dinner. I just helped him with the recipe. He did all the work."

She looked at Jake, who looked down at the table.

"I asked them to help me organize your kitchen so I could reach the cooking stuff," Jake said. "We'll put it all back. Don't worry."

Alice glanced at her rearranged living room, understanding. She took another bite of the chicken enchiladas, which were quite good. So were the beans. The kid had made a salad, for God's sake. Alice couldn't remember the last time she had a home-cooked meal or a dinner she hadn't eaten over the sink. When she was finished, she wiped her mouth on her napkin and stood.

"Show me," she said.

Jake explained Celia's thoughtful reorganization of the cooking and baking utensils. Tentative at first, his confidence grew as he saw Alice was intrigued. His friends stood behind the counter, interjecting like his cheerleading squad.

"Show her the pantry stuff," Noah said. "And how we hung the skillets so you could reach them."

"And the ice cream maker is way up high there with the canning stuff, Mrs. Holtzman," Celia said.

Alice nodded, impressed. After all, Holtzmans admired initiative and organization. She was also won over by their teenage enthusiasm, which was unfamiliar to her. There it was, a force to be reckoned with.

"Well," she said. "Nice work. I'm impressed. Thank you for dinner. Now I have a little work to do. Can you three handle the dishes before Noah and Celia head home?" she asked Jake.

She excused herself and went to her room so she could pretend not to see them high-fiving each other and celebrating. That had been two weeks ago, and she was surprised by how she had grown accustomed to having him there.

Hiring Harry had solved her labor problem. As for Jake, he would be her guest for the time being. From the kitchen table, Alice watched him pause at one of the new hives. After his friends had left that night, she talked to him frankly about the physical demands of the job she was hiring for, and he agreed it was more than he could do. His face had fallen, and Alice felt her stomach plummet.

"I'm sorry, Jake," she said. "I should've been clearer about it."

He shook his head and tried to smile, saying he knew she was just trying to help. Sitting there looking into his young face, she could not bring herself to send him home. She suggested he stay for a while until he could figure out his next move. That idea seemed to cheer him, and he thanked her. Her heart sank a little as she realized she had backed herself into a corner, but it wouldn't be forever. Besides, she was surprised by how much she liked this funny, smart kid. She had always liked being alone. She'd preferred it, really. Being around other people made her feel tired, almost lonelier. But then Bud changed things, she thought.

The thought of Buddy blindsided her, and loneliness reached up and grabbed her by the throat. She reached for the sleeve of cookies and ate them one after the other, trying to stuff back the growing ache. It didn't work. She grabbed her keys, banged out the door, and waved at the kid.

"Errands!" she called.

He waved back.

Alice jumped in the truck and sped up the road into the blinding light of the setting sun. Being in motion helped calm her. Somehow being in the truck with the windows rolled down and the wind in her ears made it easier to hold her grief within the confines of her body. Otherwise she might have split in two. Once she had driven halfway to Seattle with no memory of the long drive. Just mile after mile of telling herself to pull it together now, Alice. You can do this. Shove it back down in there. As long as she made it to the county planning department by 8:30 a.m. five days a week, no one had to know that Alice Holtzman was made of a million tiny broken pieces held together by cookies, solitary driving, and the sheer determination not to go crazy in public.

She felt the warm evening air blow across her face and she focused on her breathing. She named the familiar landmarks as she passed them, only letting her mind settle on the surface of things. McCurdy Farms, Twin Peaks Drive-in, Western Antique Aeroplane and Automobile Museum, Eagle One Thrift, Novedades Ortiz, Bette's Place, Hood River County Library. Just this building and the next. Concrete and bricks and no need to think of her feelings. She worked her way into town with this strategy and found herself at the waterfront. She decided a walk would clear her head.

The sunset turned the river into a ribbon of gold, easing her clenched heart with its beauty. A handful of kiteboarders were riding the evening wind, early-season keeners who were milking every minute. Up near the park, she could see a small crowd gathered under the picnic shelter. Alice drew closer and moved toward the curb to maintain her solitude. She spotted Stan Hinatsu up on a small rise on the lawn with a sign that read, "Keep SupraGro Out of the Gorge!" Alice recalled how angry he had been at the end of the CP meeting. She drew closer and stood at the back.

". . . Coal they ship through our communities and along the river. I don't need to remind you that the Cascadia Pacific train that derailed in Mosier spilled a load of Bakken crude oil less than one hundred yards from the Mosier Community School. Now it's not just the trains. Cascadia recently bought SupraGro, a pesticide company that's being sued by community groups in Nebraska and Northern California for devastating local watersheds. And as part of that partnership, Cascadia is offering their products at a deep discount to local farmers and orchardists for use here in the Columbia River Gorge. That will affect every single water source in the valley. I'm talking about communities from Parkdale and Pine Grove to Mosier and the Dalles. And water sources from Dog River and Hood River to the White Salmon and the Klickitat. The runoff will go directly into those watersheds we get our drinking water from, that our kids swim in, and that the salmon spawn in."

It was absolutely urgent, he said, to take action. Stan asked people to call their county commissioners, attend the city council meeting next week, and volunteer to canvass locally.

Alice listened, nagged by a thought. She pulled out her phone and googled SupraGro. There it was. SupraGro had decimated local honeybee populations in those California and Nebraska towns—commercial outfits and hobby farms like hers. Even a research farm that was associated with the University of Nebraska. Thousands of hives had died. Millions of bees.

Alice had read about it on a bee blog, which linked to an article in the *Washington Post*. The bee part was buried at the bottom of the story about the lawsuits, which centered on drinking-water safety. The story said that the bees had been devastated either through the water contamination or the spray. Years later they hadn't recovered, and losses continued year after year in those towns where the pesticide company still had a stronghold.

Alice heard the click of a camera next to her and saw Pete Malone snapping a photo of Stan and the crowd. She liked Pete, who had been in her AP English class senior year. He had been writing for the *Hood River News* for decades. Pete was always there asking questions and taking photos—the county fair, city council, the annual Wild Weiner Days and Dachshund Dash. Pete caught her eye and nodded.

Stan was wrapping up. He thanked everyone for coming and asked them to like the Facebook page for Hood River Watershed Alliance. As he finished, people turned to each other and started talking, for in Hood River, even environmental activism offered a chance to chat. She saw Stan shouldering his way through the crowd and was startled when he stopped in front of her.

"Hey, Alice," he said. "Thanks for coming out. It's nice to know that someone from the county is paying attention."

"What? I— No, sorry. I was walking by and stopped to hear what you were talking about. I'm not here for the county or—"

Stan smiled at her and rocked back on his heels, his arms crossed over his clipboard. "Sure. I know. You aren't on the clock. You aren't a county employee right this moment. You are Alice Holtzman, concerned citizen. Right?"

She heard the click of the camera and saw Pete out of the corner of her eye.

"No. I mean, yes. I am a concerned citizen. I care about this community and who we do business with. Of course I do."

Click, click, click, went the camera.

"Right, that's all I'm saying," Stan said.

Click, click, click.

"But I don't— I'm not— Dammit, Pete. Would you stop?"

Alice's voice rose. She glared at Pete, who seemed only half-embarrassed.

"Public meeting, Alice," Pete said, and shrugged as he swung his camera toward the rest of the crowd.

Alice turned back to Stan, who was still smiling.

"Look. Yes, I am a concerned citizen, but don't quote me and try to make me out as some sort of envoy for the county. I don't even understand the situation yet."

But she understood enough. She just didn't know what in the hell she was supposed to do about it. Stan must have seen that on her face. He held out the clipboard.

"Just give me your email, Alice. We want to keep you informed."

She exhaled, took his pen, and scribbled her email address.

Click, click, click.

When she looked up, Pete had blended into the crowd. She was irritated to notice Stan was even more handsome when he smiled.

"Thanks, Alice. I'll be in touch, okay?"

"Sure, Stan. See you later."

She walked along the river where the sun had fallen behind the ridgeline and the sky had turned light green above the trees. The west wind caressed her face.

What had Dr. Zimmerman said? Disrupt old patterns. Find a path out of the old way of doing things to forge a new one. It might feel uncomfortable, but the only way out was through. Things needed to feel different to become different, she said. Well, "different" was one word for it, Alice thought. She walked until the path ended at the water, and then, because she had no other choice, she turned around and went back the way she'd come.

13

OVERTONES

One who carefully watches the habits of bees will often feel inclined to speak of his little favorites as having an intelligence almost if not quite akin to reason.

—L. L. LANGSTROTH

Jake sat in the afternoon sunlight in front of the hives and closed his eyes, feeling a warm hum in his chest. He marveled at the sound he heard, the everyday noise of the bees at work. He wondered why none of the beekeeping books talked about this musical droning, this golden anthem, this song. It seemed so significant to him. He'd asked Alice what they were saying, but she hadn't known either. She said the how of it involved the vibration of their delicate wings, which was easily heard when a bee was in flight. But she didn't know what they were communicating inside the hive. The queen and most of the workers lived their entire lives within the pulsing, lightless interior, so sound must have been some kind of tool. Maybe they heard the tone as Jake did. To him it said, "We are here and all is well." It said, "We are home."

Jake hadn't felt at home since he was a very small child, but he felt something close to it now. This new feeling had lodged in his chest. He put a hand on his sternum and felt his breath rise and fall. What was this feeling? It took him some time to name what he felt. Calm.

The time he spent with the bees, those minutes and hours, were building a sense of calm in him, slowly but surely, just as honeybees built out their honey stores.

Even though he had been living with Alice for more than two weeks, Jake still felt a burst of relief each morning when he awoke and realized that he was not at his parents' double-wide. This morning he'd lain in bed and listened to the alarmed call of quail and the whirring of the birds Alice said were mourning doves. He pulled himself out of bed when the rooster had been shouting for a while. Alice rose first, and he could hear her making coffee in the kitchen. That made him miss his mom a little, but not enough to want to be back in that house.

His mom hadn't said much when she stopped by the other day. Though he had assured her over the phone that he was fine and Noah could grab his stuff, she'd insisted on seeing him. She brought a duffel bag of his clothes, boxes of single-use catheters, his laptop, and his trumpet, which she must have dug out of the back of his closet. Lastly, she pulled his longboard out of the back seat of her car, which made Jake smile. Good old Mom. She would think of that.

They sat at the picnic table under the shade of the great cottonwood tree, and Jake told her about the bees—the queen, her workers, and the drones. He described the pair of owls he heard calling to each other in the woods at night and the coyote he saw at the edge of the pond at dusk. He didn't tell her that every time he saw that coyote, his heart clenched thinking of Cheney.

His mom sat with her hands balled in her lap, and Jake knew she wasn't really interested in the bees. Tears welled up in her eyes and rolled down her cheeks. She took off her glasses, pulled a tissue out of the cuff of her sweater, and dabbed at her eyes.

"Mom, it's okay, really. I'm fine here. You don't have to worry."

She shook her head and reached across the table to squeeze his hand. "I'm your mother, Jacob. It's my job to worry about you."

The unspoken questions hovered there, pressing down on them. What would happen to Jake? What kind of life could he have? Could he take care of himself? Could he get a job? Go to college someday? These questions had arisen when his life exploded a year ago, and no clear answers had yet emerged. Jake avoided talking about the specifics of his circumstance with his mother, but he knew she was just as aware of them as he was.

"Look, Mom. You're awesome, but I'm still . . . I'm stuck in this town. I need to figure things out. And living with Dad really wasn't helping. At all."

She wiped her eyes and nodded. She didn't even try to defend Ed, which was a relief. Jake hated it when she said his father didn't mean the things he said and that he really loved Jake. Blah, blah, blah. Anger flared in his belly, thinking of that red, jeering face. He clenched his fists on the table.

"He's such an asshole, Mom!"

Tansy shook her head, reached into her purse, and took out a cough drop. Jake watched her unwrap it, put it in her mouth, and fold the paper into a small square that she tucked into her purse. In this way she composed herself and donned the serene face she wore whether she was praying or watching her meathead husband shout at the TV or something worse. Jake had first seen that look when Ed threw his dinner plate at the wall and stormed out of the house. His mom swept up the mess and made macaroni and cheese for ten-year-old Jake, humming "Make Me a Channel of Your Peace."

Now she tried to smile.

"You're a smart boy, Jacob. You're going to make a good life for yourself. If you want to stay with Mrs. Holtzman for now, that's fine. She seems like a good Christian woman, and we are grateful for her kindness."

Jake smothered a smile as he recalled Alice swearing a blue streak when she had flooded the tractor engine the day before.

His mom squeezed his hand again. "I will always help you, honey. And I will pray for you every day."

She hugged him and made him promise to call her at least once a week. He watched her drive away and felt a little sad. Sweet Mom.

When he dug through the duffel bag later, he found his sketchbook among the neatly folded jeans, shirts, socks, and underwear. He was startled to realize he hadn't drawn anything since before the accident. He flipped the book open, and images jumped out like scenes from someone else's life. Noah riding an ollie at the skatepark and Noah with his trombone. There was one of the cheerleaders in a lineup behind the jazz band at a football game, their faces blurred. There was a group of kids in the bleachers, and one girl with blue hair and braces was making the others laugh.

He turned the page, and his heart somersaulted. Cheney's sleek body leaping off the dock at Lost Lake. Cheney with his face out the car window, smiling into the wind. Cheney asleep at the end of Jake's bed, his great monster head resting on his paws, looking somehow dainty. It hurt to remember, and Jake shut the sketchbook.

He picked up an envelope with "Jacob" written on the front. Inside were ten $20 bills and a couple of prayer cards—one of the Virgin Mary Queen Mother and one of St. Giles. His mother had jotted a note on the back of that one: "Son of an Athenian, and a hermit, Giles is the patron saint of the disabled." Jake laughed. Only Mom. Under the cards was another piece of paper. It was an official form from the state of Oregon. His mom had filled it out, removing herself and Ed as his guardians. As a fully emancipated adult, Jake would now receive all disability checks directly, the form read. She'd filled out the change-of-address section as Alice's and stuck a stamp on the envelope for him. His monthly disability check was paper-clipped to it, signed over in her perfect script.

Jake shook his head. "Wow! Way to go, Mom."

He underestimated her. The flowery dresses, carefully curled hair, and polite Christian demeanor concealed a woman of action. Most of the time, she kept the peace and sailed around her brooding husband. She had her limits, though. Jake remembered the time she grew tired of asking Ed to pick up his empty beer cans from the living room in the evening. One day when he was at work, she gathered them in a trash bag and put them on the floor next to the couch with a pillow and a blanket and went to bed early. Ed came home to a dark house, no dinner, and a locked bedroom door. They never spoke of it, but after that his cans went into the recycling.

Jake's stomach dropped when he thought of what would happen when his father noticed the check was missing from the joint bank account. Jake had heard them arguing about it a couple of weeks after he'd returned home from the rehab center in Portland.

"Jacob needs to be saving for his future, Edward." His mom's voice came through the thin wall of his room. Ed said something he couldn't hear.

"That is not true, Edward," his mom said.

Jake cracked the door.

"Boy ain't going nowhere. Always been lazy. Sure as hell not giving him any more of a free ride than he's already getting."

Jake clenched his jaw, remembering. Right, Ed. Just joyriding over here in my wheelchair. Still, he hoped his mother wouldn't suffer the brunt of that.

Now he listened again to the golden reverberation of the hive in front of him. He itched to get closer and see the intricate interior life. He thought about Harry, and his belly roiled with jealousy. The guy didn't even seem interested in the bees. Jake already knew so much from what he'd read. But the damn hives were too tall, and Jake knew he couldn't do the work Alice needed.

He looked at Hive No. 6, which included two brood boxes and one honey super stacked above the hive board. The cover was well above his head. There was no way he could even open the top as he had seen

Alice do, let alone see the frames. It was so frustrating. In all the time since he'd been home from rehab, he hadn't let himself care about anything. Nothing had penetrated the dark bubble he lived in as he relinquished any expectations for the future. Now this shining, living thing called to him—this magical hive life. He flexed his hands, wanting to work. It was right in front of him, but it was impossible.

Jake rolled past the newest hives that Alice had brought from Portland and stopped dead. Painted white and marked No. 13 through No. 24 in black grease pen, these new ones were just one brood box tall. Jake paused next to No. 13. He could easily reach the frames of this hive, he realized with growing excitement. He should wait and ask Alice, he thought. She would be home in a couple of hours. But then he thought, What the hell? What harm could it do?

He closed his eyes and saw the steps he'd watched her take so many times—lighting the smoker, cracking the top, a puff of smoke, easing the top off. He could do that. He listened to the hum, felt it buzz in his chest cavity like there was a golden hive inside his own body. Then he heard something else. The new sound was a completely distinct tone. He listened closely and heard it again. It was an ethereal note somewhat higher than the others, like an overtone. What was that? He had to know.

He grabbed a hive tool and a pair of gloves. When he tried to pull a hat and veil over his head, it wouldn't fit over his hair. He dropped the hat and eyed the smoker. He'd read that not all beekeepers used smoke anyway. The beekeeper in the OSU videos he'd been watching didn't even wear a veil or gloves. He dropped the gloves too. He was just going to go in like that—light and fast. He maneuvered his chair in close so No. 13 was on his right, which was his strong side. He closed his eyes and listened. The hum settled in his chest. His breathing slowed, and he heard it again, that golden note above everything else. He hummed along, matching it. He inhaled, exhaled, and cracked the top. It popped off easily because the hive was new and not yet well sealed with propolis. Then he jimmied the inner cover off and set it aside. A trio of bees buzzed up and out, flying around Jake's face. He sat very still with his hands in his lap and his eyes closed.

"Hello, ladies," he murmured, mimicking Alice. "Just coming in to have a look. No need to worry."

The guard bees frisked his face and neck for a minute or so. Jake was motionless as they zipped in front of his closed eyes, his ears, his mouth. Then they went back into the hive, having decided he was no threat. Jake marveled at his own calm, which then became a self-fulfilling enterprise. He used the hive tool to loosen a frame in the brood box, lifted it slowly with two fingers, and held it in front of his face. This one didn't have much going on. A few bees, and just the start of a wax layer. Jake leaned it against the side of the hive, loosened another, and pulled it out. He worked through the next two frames, noting that each showed more activity. The fourth frame was harder to extract. He pried up one side, sticky with propolis, and it slipped back down. The bees buzzed in complaint. Jake froze as the guard bees flew up, hovered, and dispersed again. He eased the frame up and out. It hung heavy on his fingertips. Just like the photos in the books, it had a ring of honey on the outside with a pollen band in the center and capped brood cells at the bottom. The frame began to slip in his fingers, and he willed himself to concentrate. He exhaled and slid the frame back into place and kept going.

The fifth frame was also packed, but he felt something different when he lifted it out. He heard a shift of sound. There it was—that bell-like note. He would swear it was a G-sharp. He lifted the frame to eye level. There in the middle of the wax-covered surface the worker bees moved slowly around one central point. And there she was. In the middle of the golden crawling bodies, Jake saw the queen. Her long, tapered figure was marked with a bright green dot, just like Alice had said. She was discernably larger than the worker bees—her wings reaching far down her torso. Her movements were slower and more graceful than the others. He leaned forward. Yes, now he was sure of it. This other sound, this note, was coming from the queen.

He closed his eyes and breathed in the smell of honey and wax. His heart thumped; his whole body felt the vibration. Jake knew that he was holding the absolute life of the hive in his hands. If anything happened to the queen, the others would not survive. He felt strangely calm and confident, he realized. He would never let anything bad happen to her. He opened his eyes and looked at her again, and then lowered the frame back into the brood box, replaced the other frames, and put the cover back on.

As the sun moved across the meadow, Jake went through six of the twelve new hives—hatless, gloveless, and without a smoker—with slow and methodical care. He was not stung once. After shutting the second hive, he remembered Alice's record-keeping book and retrieved it from the barn to take notes. He mimicked her entries as best he could with the date, time, temperature, hive number, and a description of what he saw inside. He made a few sketches. He also highlighted that extra tone with an asterisk at the end of the note. In all six he heard that sound and located the queen—six green-dotted beauties. He was elated. He thought about Harry, who would be there tomorrow evening to get his first instructions for work. Jake didn't want to share the bees with him, and he didn't want to share Alice's place either. He thought of inviting Katz over again when Alice was at work. But now this guy would be hanging around half the day.

The wind picked up, and Jake rolled into the shop. He cleaned off the hive tool with mineral spirits and put it back in the toolbox. He was physically tired like he hadn't been in months. A good tired. He moved back over to the shade, drained his water bottle, and fell asleep.

He didn't remember the details of his dream, only that in it he was on his skateboard again, flying along the trail by the river at the waterfront. And Cheney was with him. He was so happy. When he awoke, he felt a piercing sense of loss. It came to him like this sometimes. In sleep he forgot. Then he awoke to the understanding that he was no longer just Jake the average fuckup with his whole life ahead of him. He was Jake the particular fuckup—eighteen years old, jobless, not at music school, and using a wheelchair. A knot rose in his throat, and a weight settled on his heart as he considered the state of his life. But then he looked out at the apiary. He flexed his tired hands. He remembered the sound he had heard and the beauty he had seen. He thought about everything he would tell Alice. The weight shifted, and a spark of joy bloomed in his heart. This new thing, this wonder.

14

DRONE LIFE

Bees issue from their hives in the most peaceable mood
imaginable; and unless abused allow themselves to be
treated with great familiarity.

—L. L. LANGSTROTH

The sun beat down on Harry's shoulder blades as he rode away from
Alice Holtzman's farm. His stomach yawned. He hadn't eaten since
the breakfast burrito. Landing the job had cheered him up but had not
changed the fact that he was almost out of money. He and Alice had
agreed upon the hourly rate, and she asked him to return the following
evening to make a plan for his work schedule. Then Alice asked if
there was anything else he wanted to discuss. He almost asked for
lunch but stopped himself, sensing that would be an odd request.

His hunger grew as he rode up the long hill toward town. He
stopped at the grocery store to use the bathroom and cruise the deli
samples. He nibbled cheese and piled bits of salami on a napkin until
the deli lady glared at him. He left, shoving the tiny pieces of meat
into his mouth and feeling hungrier, as if the tidbits had only sharpened his appetite. He hopped back on the Schwinn and headed north
toward the bridge, the hospital, and his uncle with growing dread.

At the waterfront, the bike chain jammed and Harry jumped off to unkink it. He washed his greasy hands in the public restroom at the waterfront, and as he came out, he heard a man's voice over a sound system. "Check one. Check two. Check three. Check, check, check. Hello, Hood River! Yeah, I think that's good, Doug," the voice said.

Harry saw a band setting up on the grass—three guys with a bass, drums, and a guitar. He smelled the scent of grilling meat and saw a woman opening a tall sleeve of red plastic cups next to a sweating beer keg. Harry wandered closer and spotted a long table covered in aluminum serving trays—piles of potato salad, baked beans, green salad, and pie. People were queuing in front of the grill for burgers and hot dogs. He felt dizzy with hunger.

"Hey, brah. You in line?"

Harry turned and saw the big guy from the kite beach. His long hair hung in his face, and his tank top revealed muscled, suntanned arms.

"Oh, hey! Honey Buns Man! S'up?" The guy high-fived him like they were old friends. "Harry, right?"

Harry nodded, surprised. Harry was not used to being remembered.

"Yogi," the big guy said, tapping his own chest with a thick thumb. "Good to see you, dude. Grab me a plate, will you?"

Harry handed him a paper plate, and Yogi began to pile it high with food.

"Get in here, man," Yogi said. "I didn't mean to take cuts."

"Oh, no. I didn't pay, I don't—" Harry started, but Yogi shook his head, his long hair flapping around his face.

"Nah. It's free! The port does this every spring at the beginning of the season. It's an appreciation barbecue for the kiteboarding crowd. Keeps the natives docile."

Yogi laughed and shook his hair out of his face. Harry, unable to believe his luck, filled a plate and followed Yogi to the grill. With two burgers and a cold beer each, they sat on the lawn in the shade of a tree. Between mouthfuls, Yogi launched into an interesting if confusing monologue about his morning kite session and a new trick he was trying to master called "Dark Star."

Harry nodded as he listened, not understanding any of it, and tried to make himself chew between bites and swallows.

Yogi sipped his beer and wiped his mouth on his wrist. "You been out there yet, man? Body dragging or on a trainer kite?"

Harry shook his head. He hesitated, not one to talk about himself, and told Yogi he'd been busy looking for work and had landed a job.

"Most excellent!" Yogi said, and threw up a hand again, and Harry slapped his big paw for a high five. Harry usually hated it when guys did that, but Yogi seemed sincere. He thought he might tell Yogi about the bee farm, but Yogi was talking about kiting again.

"Listen. Your next day off, come down here and I'll give you a little intro lesson. I've got extra gear, and I can hook you up, show you the ropes. Seriously, it's not that hard to learn. You don't need to pay hundreds of clams to one of them," he said, jerking his thumb at the cluster of kite school trailers.

"I mean, they're okay for people with money. But we regular joes need to stick together."

Harry nodded, uneasy. The last time someone had told him they needed to stick together, he wound up in jail.

Yogi set his beer on the grass. He pulled his hair into a ragged ponytail with a rubber band.

"I'll tell you the secret, the thing the kite schools won't tell you, if you want. You seem like the kind of dude that could get it."

Harry nodded.

Yogi held his hands out in front of him, his palms up. His voice dropped to a whisper. "Okay. The secret is: You have to feel. The wind."

He closed his eyes, leaned back, and rolled his big shoulders.

Harry started to laugh but realized he was serious. Yogi, his eyes still closed, sat with his palms up. His voice dropped to a murmur.

"You have to ask yourself, What is the wind doing and how can I capture it? How can I move within that? What is my place within this beautiful atmospheric moment? Just this one. Right here. Right now. You have to listen to the universe and hear what it is telling you."

The big man inhaled through his nose and exhaled out his mouth.

Harry didn't know what to say. Yogi opened his eyes and laughed, his voice returning to normal.

"It's magical, man. Seriously. Super Zen. I try to live like that. Moment by moment."

He punched Harry in the shoulder. "And you are going to fucking nail it! I can tell!"

He wiped a thick finger across his plate and licked it off. "Right. Gotta motor. I'm meeting some brothers for a downwinder from the Viento launch. But seriously, dude, your next day off—come find me. I'm here every day. Catch ya later, Harry."

He held out his fist, which Harry bumped awkwardly. He watched Yogi stride away, waving and calling to people as he went.

I have a job, Harry thought. And maybe a friend. He smiled and lay back in the shade of the tree, his belly full. He would just close his eyes for a minute, he thought, and then he fell asleep.

When he woke up, the party was gone and the sun was flirting with the horizon. He remembered his uncle and his promise to call his mother. He jumped on his bike and rode across the bridge. By the time he got up the hill to the hospital, twilight had settled along the ridgeline and the river below was a ribbon of darkness. The hospital doors hissed open, and the sting of antiseptic hit his nostrils. Harry hurried down to Uncle H's room and stopped in the doorway. The clicking and beeping machines were gone. So were the flowers his mother had sent, and so was his uncle. Harry's scalp prickled like someone had poured cold water over his head. He walked quickly back to the front desk.

"Um, I'm looking for Harold Goodwin. He was in room nine?"

It was the nice nurse, the one who had snuck him dinner. She stood and came around the desk, her face grave and her arms folded.

"I'm so sorry. Your uncle passed away this afternoon. He went into a respiratory arrest, which is not uncommon after a stroke."

She waited a beat, letting Harry take that in. She explained that swelling in Uncle H's brain had caused him to stop breathing. She reminded him about the advanced directive and said his uncle had not been in any pain.

Harry's head spun, and his hands felt clammy. His ears rang, and sweat sprang up on his forehead. The nurse was saying they had called his next of kin. So his mother would already know. The body had been transferred to the morgue. She took Harry by the elbow and guided him into a chair. The scratchy pink upholstery reminded Harry of the visiting room at jail. She sat down and pulled a pen and pad out of her shirt pocket.

"I'll give you the number, and you can call them tomorrow to make arrangements," she said, scribbling on the paper. "And I'll put Dr. Chimosky's cell number on here too. He said to call if you had any questions."

She handed him the paper. Harry folded and unfolded it and didn't know what to say. How was he supposed to feel? The nurse cocked her head and looked at him.

"Your uncle was pretty sick, you know? Boy, he was a tough little guy," she said.

She told him Uncle H had been admitted three times since Christmas. The last time he had been so fragile that the staff had decided to move him into residential care. But Uncle H had heard them talking about it and rallied. He took off while no one was looking, and they found him trying to hitchhike up 141 in nothing but his hospital gown and a pair of socks.

Harry tried to smile. That sounded like Uncle H.

The nurse asked if she could call anyone for him. He shook his head.

"Look—sit here for as long as you need to. I'll be right over there if I can help with anything."

He mumbled a thank-you and stared at the floor. He felt weirdly self-conscious about not crying. Was this a loss? Harry had grown fond of his crazy little uncle over the past two months, though they weren't what anyone would call close. And yet poor Uncle H had died alone. Worse, his mother would know Harry hadn't been there. Whether or not they were close, Uncle H had helped him. The old guy accepted him as someone to play cards with and share a Spam sandwich with. Harry hadn't needed much more than that. He'd never had many friends, despite the fact that his mother was always telling him that he needed to meet people.

"You don't have to like them that much, Harry. You just need to hang out with people. It's normal, son."

But he never knew what to say to people. Marty and Sam had been his friends since high school just because they were in the same class, and look how that had turned out. Years ago, there was Shane, who lived with his mother in the same apartment complex as Harry.

Go play with Shane, his mother would say. Harry didn't like Shane. Then Shane smashed up his Hot Wheels collection—bringing a heavy rock down on the roofs of the little model cars—and wouldn't stop, so Harry socked him in the nose. Shane ran to his mother, and Harry got a spanking. His track record with friendships hadn't improved much since then. But he knew his mother was right. He needed to make friends. He just didn't know how.

Harry rode slowly toward the phone booth in BZ, dreading the conversation with his mother. How to explain why he hadn't been with Uncle H when he died? What had he told her about his job, the imaginary one he had before the real one? His white lies almost always tripped him up.

"Jesus! Just tell the truth, Harry!" Sal would bellow. *"It's easier to remember, kid!"*

But Harry didn't have to explain anything. He could hear his mother crying as she accepted the charges for the call. She told him she was so glad that he was there. She would have felt terrible if Uncle H had died alone. Family was family, and Harry had done a great thing reminding him that he had people.

It cheered Harry to listen to his mother's version of things. It was all technically true. After all, he had gone to see his uncle. Even though Uncle H was unconscious by the time he arrived, maybe he knew Harry was there with him. Maybe it helped. Harry told his mother about the morgue. He told her that he would pick up Uncle H's remains. She blew her nose.

"He was such a kind man. Harry, I wish you'd met him when he was younger. Look, son, I'll come out there soon, and we can scatter Uncle H's ashes together. That will be nice, won't it?"

Harry hung up the phone and stood straighter. He tipped his head back and looked up at the black dome of the sky—star-studded and brilliant. He had been there for his uncle, sort of. He would start his new job, and things would be okay. He would work hard. He would be reliable. Thing were going to be different. He could feel it.

Riding up the highway, he entered the corridor of tall trees, and the dark swallowed him up. Harry forced himself to trust that the road was in front of him as he rode the rickety old bicycle along in the night. He thought of the dead animal he'd seen on the shoulder and shuddered. It made the hair on the back of his neck stand up. To distract himself, he thought about what he would buy with his first paycheck—pizza, mac and cheese, some of the Spam Uncle H had got him liking. A six-pack of beer, maybe. When he reached the bumpy driveway, he got off his bike and walked to the trailer, trying to ignore the sensation that he was being followed. He stood in the darkness and tried to shake it off, but he imagined someone watching him as he climbed the ladder. From the doorway, he looked into the woods and willed himself to see whatever might be out there. Nothing. Then a twig snapped, and a bird startled into flight in the dark. Harry felt a streak of fear knife down his spine. He closed the thin door and locked it and put a pillow over his head. It took him a long time to fall asleep and he slept badly, waking every hour or so thinking he heard something rustling around outside the trailer. He got up at dawn for a glass of water and finally fell into a deep sleep.

When he awoke, the woods were quiet. The previous day's events came at him out of order, like cabinet doors popping open—the deli-samples lady frowning, the bees falling out of the air, Yogi with his eyes closed, the kid with the mohawk, the burrito man, his uncle struggling to breathe, the empty hospital bed. He sat up and swung his legs over the bunk. The catfish clock said it was after 1:00 p.m.

He looked at himself in the mirror, his shirtless skinny torso above sagging long johns. He stood up straighter and took a deep breath. This was the first day of a new life, he pledged to himself. He would fix this place up—get the water going again and rewire the electricity. He could start over here. He would save up and get a car. He would meet people. He thought of Yogi and the kite beach. Why not? Maybe it wasn't so hard to make friends. He opened the door and climbed down the ladder to take a whiz.

Something shifted in the trash pile, and a shape moved toward him with an animal swiftness. Cougar? Coyote? Rabid raccoon? It was large and white and brown. It was that thing lurking in the woods last night. He was sure of it.

Harry yelped, scrambled for the ladder, and lost his footing. He heard a strange whining sound. He turned to see the creature standing stock still. It had a broad brindled body, large paws, and a long, thick tail. Where a head should have been there was a large plastic bucket labeled "Premium Chicken Feed." The dog's bark was muffled by the plastic. Harry stood and approached slowly, grasped the container, and pulled. As it came free, Harry saw an enormous pair of ears, wide eyes, and a giant mouth, which the dog opened to reveal a huge set of teeth. Harry stepped back, and the dog exploded at him.

The big snout hit him first and then the paws pummeled his chest before stopping abruptly. When he opened his eyes, he saw the dog cantering away in a wide circle around the clearing. It turned on a dime and galloped back to Harry, threw its paws on his chest, and licked his face before running off again. Harry watched the big animal running in wide, happy circles. It tore into the woods toward the river and then loped back, soaking wet, and dropped at Harry's feet with a soggy thump.

Harry had never been around dogs much, but this one seemed to be smiling. He reached down, tentative, to pet its head. The animal shoved its snout into Harry's hand and snorted, then flipped over on its back, exposing matted fur and a pink belly. Harry patted it, and the dog wriggled on its spine. A squirrel scolded, and the dog jumped up and bolted away. Harry laughed, relieved, and realized he still needed to pee. As he reached into the fly of his now muddy long johns, he heard the sound of an engine and turned. A Jeep rumbled up the driveway and stopped. The seal on the door read "Hood River County Sheriff's Department."

The short man who stepped out was dark-haired and wore a neatly pressed brown uniform. He glanced at Harry, who still had his hand down his fly. He took it out and then didn't know where to put it, so he clasped his hands behind his shirtless back. The officer reached into the car and pulled out a hat, which he placed on his head and straightened with both hands. It seemed too big and somehow made him look like a Boy Scout. He shut the Jeep door and marched up the driveway, his shiny shoes kicking up dust. The guy was Latino and about Harry's age. He was handsome and had a super-clean shave. Harry fingered his upper lip regretfully.

"Good morning, sir," the man said. "I'm a deputy with the Hood River County Sheriff's Department."

With two fingers, he extended a business card, which Harry took, glanced at, and then, having no pocket, closed in his hand. The deputy asked if this was Harold Goodwin's residence.

"Yes," Harry said, finding his voice, "he's my uncle. Was my uncle."

The man nodded, his face impassive. "I'm sorry for your loss, sir. We understand Mr. Goodwin passed."

Harry nodded. "Thank you," he said. "He'd been sick for a while, so . . ."

His voice trailed off as he followed the deputy's gaze around the mess of the yard, the outhouse, the garbage pile, the crazy ladder.

"We've been trying to get in touch with your uncle for some time," the man said. "I went to see him at Skyline the last time he was admitted. The county condemned this trailer in January, but your uncle refused to talk to me."

He held up a piece of paper with a formal-looking stamp on it. "I'm going to have to ask you to vacate the premises. There's a crew coming to pull it out."

They'd be hauling the trailer to the landfill, he said. Harry should clear out anything he wanted to keep immediately.

His heart sank. So much for his plans to fix up the trailer. So much for a fresh start.

"But I—I don't have anywhere else to live," he said. He needed two weeks, he explained. He had just started a new job, and he'd have some money to get a place when he got paid.

The cop was unmoved and said there was nothing he could do about it. He shrugged and tucked the paper inside his jacket.

That shrug. Flickers of memory. Sam sitting in front of him during his one visit to the jail.

"You volunteered to drive, man," he'd said, and shrugged.

The school principal picking up the phone to call his mother as Harry sat, snot running down his upper lip, insisting he hadn't been the one stealing money from the little canteen at the junior high.

"Don't be such a follower, Harry," the principal had said.

Moira catching his eye at the barbecue and waving but not coming to talk to him.

Harry felt a small flame ignite in his chest. The flame formed a word, and the word was no. He was tired of being the nice guy and not getting a break. He just needed a break. Two weeks was all he needed.

He heard a thumping noise, and the dog thundered out of the woods behind the deputy, his body sleek and wet from the river. He tore between the two men, then back again, grazing their knees. The cop yelped, and Harry started to laugh, but then he saw the gun. A squirrel scolded, the dog disappeared, and the gun flashed in the sunlight. Harry's eye followed the barrel as it whipped up to the sky and past his face. He closed his eyes.

The sound of the gunshot was deafening, and Harry put his hands over his ears as time slowed. When he opened them, the small guy was on his knees with his hat off and his face the color of paper.

"Oh, fuck! Oh, fuck!" he said. "I didn't hit you, did I? Did I?!"

Harry looked down at his bare arms and chest, which were streaked with mud from the dog, and shook his head.

The deputy stood and paced, swearing and clutching his hat. He said something about getting written up again and how they were going to dock his pay or fucking fire him this time. He was such an idiot, he said, clearly to himself and not to Harry.

"Thought it was a fucking wolf or a coyote or something!" he said, his voice rising. "I mean, they send me up here into the damn woods by myself and this *hijo de puta* comes flying—!"

Then he lapsed into rapid Spanish that Harry couldn't understand.

Harry felt bad for the guy and started to reassure him, to tell him it was fine, that nothing had happened. That was what he would normally have done. But then that flame came back, the small coal in his chest. No, it wasn't fine. He could have been shot! He just needed two lousy weeks. And he still needed to pee. He watched the cop stop pacing to check the safety again on his gun. He felt some kind of resolve settle in him then. Harry squared his shoulders and looked the guy in the eye, stating his case again. Please, he said.

The deputy shook his head. "I'm really sorry, man. I wish I could help you, but the crew is already scheduled. And I'm new. Nobody listens to me. They think I'm a moron. And if anyone finds out about the gun—"

He looked like he might cry and looked away. He really did seem sorry. Harry asked him to wait a minute, saying that he had to take a leak. While he was peeing, he looked around the yard, at the trailer, and at the Schwinn, and he formed a plan. He walked back to the deputy, who was leaning against the Jeep and turning his hat over and over in his hands.

"Can you give me a ride to town?" Harry asked.

The guy sighed and looked out toward Highway 141.

"I can't take you now. I have a meeting at the Mt. Adams Ranger Station. But I can swing back by here in a couple of hours, on my way down the hill."

Harry nodded.

"Thanks."

The deputy left and Harry gathered his stuff, which didn't take long.

While he waited for the guy to return, he sat on the steps with his notebook and made a list about his goals for the new job. The dog returned from its sprint through the woods and curled up at his feet. They both dozed in the afternoon sunshine.

When the deputy reappeared, Harry climbed into the front seat of the Jeep and slung his backpack at his feet. From Uncle H's trailer, he took only two of his uncle's wool shirts, the bird book, and the cribbage board. He cast a final look back at the trailer as they pulled away. It would soon be in the landfill. The garbage pile would be raked clean. The angry raccoons would return in the dark and find nothing.

The dog paced happily in the back seat, thrilled to be on the move. The deputy, who said his name was Ronnie, had agreed to take him to the animal shelter after he dropped Harry off.

Harry looked out the window as the Jeep sped down the highway. He would go to work. Then he would figure out where to stay. He thought of Yogi. He leaned back in the seat and felt the breeze on his face. He asked himself what his place was within this beautiful atmospheric moment—just this one. Right here. Right now. He waited, listening to the universe, listening hard. But there was no answer.

· 15 ·

QUEEN RIGHT

There is one trait in the character of bees which is worthy of profound respect. Such is their indomitable energy and perseverance, that under circumstances apparently hopeless, they labor to the utmost to retrieve their losses and sustain the sinking State.

—L. L. LANGSTROTH

Honeybees have been clocked flying as fast as twenty miles per hour—a speedy clip for an insect that weighs about a tenth of a gram. But that is nothing compared to the velocity at which news travels in a small town. Alice found the *Hood River News* propped on her desk in the morning. Pete's front-page photo had captured Alice and Stan holding the clipboard between them like a couple cutting a wedding cake. Stan was smiling, and Alice was not. The headline read, "Watershed Alliance Rallies against Cascadia Contract." Alice was identified as Alice Holtzman, county resident. Someone, probably Nancy, had drawn a smiley face over their heads in ballpoint pen.

Alice scanned the story, which said nothing she didn't already know. Pete detailed the watershed group's objections to the county contract with SupraGro and briefly mentioned the lawsuits other communities had filed against the company in the past. There was no quote from her, although the caption said she was among other "concerned citizens" at the rally. Thanks for nothing, Pete. The county had offered no official comment, the story read.

She dropped the paper into the recycling, sat down, and turned on her computer. The door to Bill's office opened, and Nancy came out, giggling as she closed it. She grinned at Alice. Nancy was forty-six years old but would wear that naughty little girl face to her grave, Alice thought.

"Good morning, Miss Front Page!" she said, wiggling her fingertips at Alice. "It's all paparazzi and tall dark strangers these days, eh?"

"You're here early, Nance," Alice said. Nancy never got to work before Alice.

Nancy pointed over her shoulder at Bill's door. "He's in this morning."

She opened her email and saw the message: all-staff meeting, Wednesday 9:30 a.m. It was dated 7:36 p.m. yesterday. Since when were they supposed to be checking email after hours?

Her stomach dropped as she read the message. All county employees were expected at a mandatory review of compliance agreements with privately held stakeholders. It was about the watershed protest, Alice thought. Alice had been through this before when the Cascadia oil train had derailed in Mosier and threatened the county drinking water, orchard irrigation, and the entire watershed along that stretch of river. The normally polite citizens were angry and had staged a protest downtown. The county lawyers had convened a similar meeting then to remind them that as county employees, they were bound to silence respecting local contracts. Translation: don't talk about the oil spill.

At the time, Alice hadn't thought much about the county's defensive posturing. She'd been busy helping her parents move, and though the oil spill distressed her, she really believed the county would do the right thing, which was to force Cascadia to clean up the sidelined railcars and greasy oil before they began running trains along the river again. They should also make Cascadia set speed limits to decrease the likelihood of a future derailment. Only the county hadn't made Cascadia do any of that. It had taken a lawsuit from the watershed group, hadn't it?

Alice fumed as she scrolled through the rest of her email. Why not let people talk to each other? They were members of this community, not county robots. And wasn't the county supposed to be looking out for its residents?

Apparently, Alice wasn't the only one who missed the after-hours email. There was a scramble for seats in the conference room. Bill sat at the head of the table, breathing through his nose and drumming his fingers on the table. He tugged his sweater down over his belly as he waited for people to settle.

Nancy was teasing the new intern, Casey, about a picture of his girlfriend on his phone. The kid was blushing up the back of his neck into his red hair. Alice could smell the hot plastic stir stick in Nancy's eternal cup of coffee. Chairs squeaked and groaned as people made room for each other.

Bill cleared his throat. "Good morning. Thank you, everyone, for being here. I think you all know why we've gathered, so I'll get right to it."

And back to my golf game, Alice thought.

Bill put on his glasses and read from a piece of paper. "'All employees of Hood River County are bound by the individual nondisclosure agreements they signed upon entering employment, and which are understood to renew automatically each year. Said agreements include any and all county business as well as affairs among and between individual contractors and private corporations.'"

Bill dropped the paper on the table and pulled a handkerchief out of his pocket, coughed, and mopped at his mouth. "I'll turn it over to Legal now for the specifics."

The county's lead attorney, Jim Murphy, gave a general wave from where he sat at the front of the room. Skinny and amicable, Jim wore a faded button-down shirt and rumpled khakis. He opened his laptop and began to explain the fine print of the nondisclosure agreement. Alice wasn't really listening. She was thinking about the Cascadia oil spill in Mosier. She was thinking about the neonicotinoids in Supra-Gro pesticides that had killed the bees in Nebraska and other states. Out of the corner of her eye she saw Bill lean back in his chair and thought he was looking at her, but he was looking past her at Nancy, who was still whispering to Casey.

Jim, reading through the legalese, suddenly stopped. "Yes, Rich. Question?"

All eyes turned to Rich Carlson, who had his hand up. Rich lowered his polyester-sheathed arm and folded his hands in front of him like an altar boy.

"How would that last article affect an employee of the county? That section about communication with the media, I mean?"

Jim looked down at the screen and back at Rich. "Well, I think the terms are pretty clear, Rich. It just means that no county employee is authorized to speak to the media regarding any county policy unless so directed by the leadership of the organization. In other words, no interviews."

"Thank you, Jim," Rich said. He glanced at Alice, leaned forward, and typed on his laptop, his thin lips curled into a smirk.

Alice thought of Pete's photo, and her face grew hot.

"Anything else there, Rich? Okay, then. I'll keep going," Jim said.

After the meeting, Alice waited for her colleagues to file out of the room. She could see Rich talking to someone in the hallway and blocking everyone's way out. He tapped his bald spot with his fingertips as he talked. The memory arose of the mistletoe, Rich's dry lips. She shuddered. Jim, one of the last to leave, caught her eye and winked.

Alice returned to her office, hoping to find Bill. She wanted to go over the drafts of the waterfront project regulations for her afternoon meeting at the building site. But Bill's office was dark. Alice sighed. He'd probably headed home already. Nancy's chair was empty too. Alice sat down, knowing she should work on the weekly compliance reports. Instead, she opened Google and typed "SupraGro honeybee death."

There it was, story after story, and not just on beekeeping forums. There were articles in the *San Francisco Chronicle*, the *Oklahoma Observer*, and *Huffington Post*. The most recent lawsuit was in Sacramento, where commercial beekeepers had reported losses of 75 percent over the year before. Scientists had traced the deaths to SupraGro used on almond orchards in and around California's Central Valley. That lawsuit was significant because the almond industry was so heavily dependent upon commercial beekeepers. California had so few honeybees remaining that it had to truck in hives from all over the West to pollinate its crops. That meant that the bees that had died had come from Oregon, Washington, Montana, and Canada. An estimated seven million honeybees died during a five-day period.

Alice kept reading, poring over the stories about SupraGro's refusal to even consider the science behind the complaints in county after county around the West. When Nancy returned, Alice reopened her reports and ignored her colleague, who wanted to gossip about Jim Murphy and his much younger wife. She pouted when Alice wouldn't join her for a smoothie at Ground and left. The morning dragged. Alice tried to focus on work, but her mind was drawn back to the news stories about the bees and the multistate lawsuit against SupraGro. Stan had to know about that, didn't he? Was the Watershed Alliance in that fight? Alice itched to make some phone calls, calls she couldn't make at work—to Stan, Chuck Sauer from the local beekeeping club, and that guy at the state ag office . . . What was his name? Michaels?

The door clicked open, and she looked up, expecting to see Nancy saunter in with a whipped cream–topped smoothie in her hand. Instead, Rich Carlson stood in the doorway, batting a magazine against his leg and smiling aggressively. His close-together eyes and narrow teeth made Alice think of a ferret. His right front tooth was slightly yellowed, she noticed.

"Alice. Glad I caught you! I've got a small item to discuss."

Rich grabbed a chair and propped his elbows on Alice's desk. She leaned back abruptly.

"I don't think Bill will be back today," Alice said, knowing he wasn't there to see Bill.

He gave her a tight smile and said it was Alice he wanted to talk to. She braced herself.

"Look, Rich," she said, "I was just walking by the waterfront and Stan said hello. You know how Pete is."

Even as the words came out of her mouth, she felt stupid. She sounded like a girl in trouble with the teacher.

Rich feigned confusion.

Alice pulled the newspaper out of the recycling bin and held it up.

Rich leaned forward and squinted at it. "Ah! I hadn't seen that. I just wanted to talk to you about your vesting plan."

"My vesting plan?"

Rich nodded and rocked back in the chair with his hands behind his head, stretching his elbows and knees away from each other in a way Alice had always found slightly obscene. Why did men do that?

". . . Been at the county for almost twenty years," Rich was saying. "Your pension disbursement would kick in two years from July 1, should you choose to retire."

Twenty years. She knew that, of course, but the stark reality of it struck her then. Almost twenty years ago she was an energetic young graduate student and the county job was a temporary thing until the orchard passed to her.

Rich was saying something about annual review baselines and how the penalty clause affected the vesting date. A poor review could bump back the vesting period two to four years depending on what the committee decided. Multiple bad reviews could nullify the pension agreement altogether, he said.

"Of course, that has never happened before," he said. "Not during my tenure. It's just the official county policy, you understand. And the committee has to get a formal complaint through Legal about employee noncompliance. Jim Murphy says there's nothing too much to worry about right now."

He sat forward again, still smiling that non-smile, and pulled a pack of gum out of his jacket pocket. He popped a bright green stick into his mouth and chewed vigorously, snapping the gum in his teeth.

"Let's keep it that way, shall we, Alice?" He stood up and slapped the magazine against his palm. "Well! Please tell Bill I thought the meeting went great today. You have a good day, Alice."

He left the door open, and Alice could hear him whistling as he walked down the hall. She felt sick, and her ears rang as his words sunk in. He was threatening to mess with her pension over this photo of her with Stan, over nothing. She pushed her chair back and stood, looked at the air where Rich Carlson's narrow face had hung. The air was sticky with electricity. Alice grabbed her bag and headed for the front of the building. Nancy stood next to the copier, teasing Casey and sipping on her smoothie. Her floral knit dress stretched tight across her rump, and she leaned toward the intern, laughing her big toothy laugh as he shrank away. She grinned at Alice.

"Where's the fire?" she asked.

"I've got a meeting at the waterfront building site. Back after lunch," Alice said, not slowing.

"Yes, sir, Alice, sir. Important business to attend to." Nancy laughed and looked at the intern, trying to draw him in.

Alice stopped and turned. "I'm just trying to do my job, Nancy. What are you doing?"

She pushed through the front door, leaving Nancy's astonished face behind her, and walked quickly down the sidewalk. She didn't know where she was going and found herself striding down Oak Street. Her clothes felt tight, and she tried to catch her breath. That empty feeling yawned inside her, and the hole in her center gaped wide open. Dammit. Damn Rich Carlson.

She passed Bette's Place, and it was all she could do not to push through the glass door and rush to the counter. She pictured herself demolishing an entire pie by herself, banana cream or strawberry rhubarb, in front of Bette and Grace, who had worked there for thirty years and had known Alice since she was born. Alice saw Bette through the window, her white hair above that silly pink apron, waiting on a full table. She waved. Alice waved back. She couldn't do that. That was far too much drama for a weekday morning in downtown Hood River—a public display, taking her grief by the hand like a small, monstrous child and parading it for everyone to see.

She turned toward the waterfront and struggled to control the anxiety, her heart racing and her breath accelerating.

"Where did it begin, the feeling?" Dr. Zimmerman had asked her months ago, during what had been her third appointment.

The therapist worked out of a mother-in-law apartment behind an elegant, two-story Craftsman that overlooked the river from a high bluff. Alice felt at ease there. It didn't feel clinical, like the hospital would have. She also valued the privacy, which was hard to come by in a town this small. The fact that Dr. Zimmerman was somewhat new to Hood River helped too. Dr. Zimmerman hadn't known her since she was a child. She'd never met Al or Marina. She wasn't from an orchard background and didn't understand the complex network of old alliances, grudges, and gossip that formed invisible fences around the people who lived there. It also made things harder to explain because Alice couldn't fall back on the customary small-town short-hand.

An October rain had lashed the windows and the skylights as Alice leaned back into the rose-colored love seat. She felt like she was playing hooky from school. She had left work for that appointment, telling Nancy only that she had a doctor's visit. Nosy Nancy. Even there in the private office, Alice felt as if the residents of the little town were leaning in, craning an ear to listen to her talk about her very private thoughts.

"Can you think about how it started? What were you thinking about when that anxiety was triggered the first time?"

Alice described standing in the grocery store parking lot and noticing it was crowded. It was a Sunday morning, and Spanish-language mass had just ended at church. She thought about coming back later, but told herself she was being silly avoiding people and forced herself to walk through the door.

Dr. Zimmerman nodded and made a note. Alice was distracted by the woman's casual elegance—a slate-blue cashmere sweater and dark wool slacks. She wouldn't know that the clothes she wore on a rainy Tuesday were more expensive than what some would spend on special-occasion clothing in this town. Not that it mattered. Dr. Zimmerman looked like she belonged wherever she chose to be—comfortable in her own skin.

Alice crossed and uncrossed her legs. She dug her thumb into her waistband. She described how she had grabbed a blue plastic shopping basket, only meaning to get a few things, like milk, cereal, and Tylenol. She moved through the crowd—mostly Latino families all dressed-up from mass. In the checkout line, she saw a little girl in a flouncy pink dress, patent leather shoes, and white ankle socks. She had one hand in her mother's and was looking up at the older woman, asking a question in Spanish. Her glance fell on Alice as she passed, and Alice recalled Luz Quinto from the Hood River County Fair when she and Buddy were on their first date. Luz and her lamb. Luz and her little face blooming with joy when Buddy gave it back to her.

Alice felt her breath catch recounting the story to Dr. Zimmerman. Of course that hadn't been Luz Quinto in the store. She would have been in high school by then. But the heart-shaped face, the soft brown eyes, and the bright smile brought it all back. Alice wheeled around and headed to the produce department to get away from the little girl and the memories that flooded her mind: Buddy at the fair. Buddy in the kitchen. Buddy leaving for work that last time.

Dr. Zimmerman nodded. "So it was the little girl, and the memory of that day?"

Alice shook her head and rubbed her hands across her face, trying to find the words. No, it wasn't just the memories, she said. It was the realization that time had moved on. Alice was no longer a young woman with options. When she first met Bud, her life opened up in ways she'd never imagined. She'd expected to be alone in life, and she had been content with that. But then she gained this extraordinary life partner. She even thought they might have kids—something she'd never considered possible before. Her, Alice—somebody's mom! Al and Marina could have been grandparents. Bud would help her run her parents' orchard, and she could leave the county job to lean into the family farm. She could teach their children all that Al and Marina had taught her about the fruit business and how to behave in the world. She would leave something behind. But not now. All those possibilities were gone. Alice was a childless, middle-aged widow and the last of her family. The treasures she never even knew she'd wanted before had evaporated overnight. She felt—she searched the edges of the emotion for the right word—robbed. Her biggest dreams had disappeared just as she'd become aware of their existence.

She felt safe talking about these things to Dr. Zimmerman in her cozy office. And the doctor had given her a strategy to help whenever she felt overwhelmed, when she lost her breath. Follow the thread. What was it that made her feel out of control? What stole her breath?

Alice walked on toward the river. She thought of Rich Carlson's pointy face and mean smile. She remembered the long-ago Christmas party, his face too close to hers. Usually that memory brought shame and discomfort, but now she felt a flash of indignation. How dare he touch her. And now, this threat to mess with her pension, that money she had worked so hard for. She, who never called in sick. Alice, who came in early and stayed late. Loyal Alice. Why would he do that? More to the point, why did it make her feel this rising panic? Everyone knew Alice was doing Bill's job. If they fired her, nothing would get done. The waterfront project, the biggest development the county had undertaken in years, would be stalled for months as they cajoled the old man off the golf course. Even if they got him back to work, they would discover that Alice had been doing his job for so long that he truly didn't know how things worked anymore. Or they could hire someone new to replace her. Either way, they couldn't afford to lose the time.

This wasn't about her fear of getting fired, then. And she wasn't embarrassed at being linked with Stan either. Like she'd told Nancy, she respected what Stan's organization had done for the farmers and orchardists like her parents. It was something else. What was it?

"You're too nice, Alice."

Out of nowhere, out of the clear blue, she heard Buddy's voice.

"You know it, sweet pea."

The sudden realization was like a curtain pulled aside to reveal a hidden room, the interworkings of Alice's heart, her motivations, misguided and hidden even from herself.

How often had she stayed late on a Friday to finish something Nancy had dumped on her? Not that she had plans anyway.

"You're so good to me, Alice!" Nancy called as she left. "Thank you!"

Too nice.

Why had she been doing Bill's job for him instead of demanding a promotion? Staying after the Labor Day picnic to clean up. Volunteering for the high school football team fund-raiser every year when she was the only employee without kids. Sitting there at the booth all day in the rain, and she hated football.

Too nice. Too nice to say no.

Her face flushed with shame. No, too *afraid* to say no. Afraid to stand up for herself and speak her mind. Afraid of being herself.

She had never understood it so clearly before. But now it was all she could see. She had felt the shape of it that night she confronted Ed Stevenson. It was buried way down deep, that white heat, the anger that had seemed to come from nowhere. Alice was deeply angry at having pretended to be someone she wasn't for so long. Why would she do that? Just to avoid making other people uncomfortable, like Rich Carlson? She saw his ferret face, his comb-over. Fury rose up in her like a wall of fire. How dare she fail her parents that way. How dare she fail herself.

She kept walking past the waterfront beach. She climbed down the rocky bank and out onto the wide sandbar that spilled into the confluence of the Hood and Columbia Rivers. She hiked around the big logs and boulders that had tumbled down from Mount Hood in flood after flood. That powerful rushing water had pushed those obstacles down the mountain one mile at a time. The wind stung her face as a squall blew in from the west. When she reached the end of the sandbar, she stood in the spattering rain and let it all spill over— her anger, sorrow, loss, and despair. That was where the thread took her, Dr. Zimmerman.

She named it all: Buddy, her parents, the orchard, the children she might have had, and the irrevocable passage of time. She let it all course through her, everything she had lost and could never retrieve. Her body throbbed with the understanding that she was alone in the world. She had been alone before Bud and now would be until she died. Alice Island, drawbridge up. Alice All Alone.

But she hadn't minded before, had she? That was essentially who she was in her core. Just Alice. So it would be okay. Yes, she thought, her breath slowing. She could be content with that, content with exactly who she was. She could be herself. She would belong wholly to herself. And like water from a turned-off faucet, the anxiety just stopped. She could feel the clean edges of her grief, but it was a contained, manageable thing. Alice stood at the river's edge, not caring how she might look—a pudgy, middle-aged woman bawling her head off in the middle of a spring rain shower.

The knot loosened in her chest and released its grip in her throat. She saw them all lined up in her mind's eye—Buddy, Marina, and Al. They had all loved her. That still mattered. And they expected her to be herself. Then the last bit of fear flew away like a balloon cut from a string. She smiled, wiped her eyes, and laughed. She felt 100 percent Alice Holtzman—daughter of Al and Marina, wife of Buddy Ryan, and keeper of bees. She was very much herself, and she was deeply pissed off.

She reached into her pocket, pulled out her phone, and dialed.

"Hello, Stan," she said. "It's Alice Holtzman. Do you have time for coffee?"

16

COLONY COLLAPSE

If the Apiarian keeps his stocks strong, they will usually be their own best protectors, and, unless they are guarded by thousands ready to die in their defence, they are ever liable to fall a prey to some of their many enemies.

—L. L. LANGSTROTH

The guiding principle of the hive was order, Jake understood. And the first element to be ordered was food. A queen could lay upward of two thousand eggs a day, but if the harvesters didn't locate enough nectar and pollen, those eggs simply wouldn't survive. The second element of order was cooperation. The most experienced bees, the foragers, often visited several thousand flowers in a single day in the course of collecting resources for the colony. The house bees were responsible for delivering that food to the nurse bees, who fed the eggs, larvae, and callow bees. The queen's retinue kept her fed and clean so she could keep doing the work she needed to do. It was a perfect system of interdependence, a high-functioning, interconnected household.

Not unlike humans, Jake thought as he chopped kale for white bean chicken chili. In his family home, he had never felt a sense of cooperation. It almost felt like the three of them lived together separately. But at Alice's, once he started cooking, he felt like he was making a contribution. They had eaten together every night at the dining room table since Jake had moved in. He liked sitting down with her at the end of the day and talking about the bees. He was also surprised to find that he had a knack for cooking. No matter that Noah was now calling him "*la dueña de la casa.*"

"All you need is a flowered apron, man!" Noah teased when Jake offered him a dish of flan—one of Celia's family recipes.

Celia elbowed Noah, accepted her plate graciously, and handed Jake a small package wrapped in tissue paper. He opened it to find a retablo of St. Pasqual painted on hammered tin—the patron saint of kitchens, Celia explained.

"From my mom," she said, rolling her eyes. "'*Cada cocina lo necesita, mi'ja,*'" she said, her voice rising to imitate her bossy little mother. "You're supposed to hang it near the stove."

Under that there was a second retablo, this one from Celia—St. Deborah.

"Patron saint of bees," she said, smiling shyly.

Noah, meanwhile, was wolfing down the flan.

"Man, this is actually really good. No, I'm serious!" he said when Jake scoffed.

Celia and Jake pored over the new cooking app he was using. It linked to a grocery list, which he texted to Noah and Celia so they could food shop for him. It pained him to ask for their help, but he knew he couldn't handle that right now. The idea of rolling through Little Bit Grocery and Ranch Supply for the first time in over a year—well, he might as well do it naked, he thought. All those people staring at him and wanting to stop and talk to him. No way. Not yet. He'd made a troubled peace with the fact that depending on his friends allowed him to contribute to Alice's household and gave him some value as a guest.

After they put away the groceries, Celia wanted to see the bees again. This time she donned Alice's full bee suit and walked right up to the hive with Jake, who approached them, as always, bareheaded.

Noah stayed back by the gate. "You're gonna get the shit stung out of you, Cece! Don't come crying to me, sissy."

"*No soy nena!*" Celia called back at him. "You're the sissy!"

"I can see one on your shoulder right now. It's going to bore into your ear and eat your brain!"

Noah soon tired of heckling and began bouncing a tennis ball against the side of the barn.

They eased up next to one of the more mature hives, and Jake told Celia to crouch down near the entrance so she could watch the bees flying in and out. She moved slowly like he told her to, and the bees carried on unperturbed. One guard bee buzzed around Jake's bare face. He closed his eyes and breathed, holding himself still until she decided he was not a threat and went about her business. He heard Celia gasp.

"Oh my gosh! Look at their legs! So orange! And yellow!"

Jake smiled. The bees were landing on the hive entrance like tiny planes, one after the other. Their pollen baskets were loaded with exaggerated hues of orange, yellow, and red. Some were dusted from head to toe and sat on the hive board, combing the pollen over their heads and down onto their legs. Jake pointed to one with a bright yellow pair of back legs.

"That's called the corbicula. It's a little compartment she can stash the pollen in. She'll go in and hand it off to another bee that will pack it away to feed to the babies later. They fill up whole sides of the frame. It almost looks like a painting."

"I want to see!" Celia said.

Jake hesitated before leading Celia over to one of the new hives. He felt a pang of regret that he hadn't told Alice he'd opened them while she was at work yesterday. He couldn't keep away from them that morning either. He'd completed inspections of the other half of the new hives that Alice had brought home from Sunnyvale Bee Company—Nos. 19 through 24, which were all still single-level brood boxes and positioned on the east edge of the apiary. He was fascinated by their industry, their beauty, and the mystery of the queen's music. Now Jake put his hand on the top of No. 17 and closed his eyes. The box hummed, calm and even. He listened longer, envisioning the center of the frames, his breath slowing until he could hear it, the faint sound of that G-sharp—the note that told him the queen was in there and that the hive was "queen right."

Jake jimmied the hive tool under the top. He set the top off to the side with the inner cover and pulled out a frame, which was still empty of wax and bees. He slid the other frames over, eased out the center frame, and held it up for Celia to see.

Jake heard her quick, sharp breath.

"Amazing!" she whispered, and clasped her hands.

Jake propped the frame on the arm of his chair. The bees went about their business, unhurried and steady. He pointed out the band of brilliant pollen packed into cells. He showed her where the honey was stored, where the larvae were capped, and which were the un-capped egg cells. In the middle of the moving mass of bodies he saw the elegant body of the queen, still marked with a bright green dot from the breeder.

"There she is, Cece," he said. "The lady who makes it all happen."

Jake had read about how early beekeepers and scientists assumed that this larger bee was a male and called her the king. It wasn't until the mid-seventeenth century that a Dutch naturalist dissected the ovaries and discovered this error. Celia thought that was funny too.

"Typical man thinking. This makes total sense to me, though," she said, gesturing at the mass of quivering bodies encircling the queen. "This is like Christmas at my house. That's Abuelita in the middle and all my aunties and mom running around doing whatever she tells them to. She would love this! And the part about the drones hanging around doing nothing—*órale!*" She snapped her fingers.

Personally, Jake found the fate of the drones a bit distressing.

They lived only to mate once and then died after the act. Those that never mated were kicked out of the hive in the fall because, since they weren't wired to raise brood or forage, they were excess baggage.

The sound of the tennis ball ceased.

"Sorry to ruin the party out there, Neil Armstrong," Noah called, "but I gotta jet to work!"

Celia walked toward him in slow motion, breathing through the screened face shield.

"Luke. I am your father," she rasped.

"Wrong color, Cece! Vader's black, not white," Noah said.

Jake helped Celia take off the bee suit and followed his friends to the truck, not wanting them to leave. He dreaded the arrival of Alice's new hire, Harry, that evening.

Noah leaned against the door and scrolled through his phone. "We're jamming at Pomeroy's this weekend. You should come hang out, man. Everyone wants to see you."

Pomeroy's garage was the perfect man cave, with two old couches, a Ping-Pong table, a beer fridge, and a beefy sound system. His mother let him take it over after she divorced his father. Jake's heart rose as he remembered being there. Shooting the shit, drinking beer, and taking leads on his trumpet.

"I'm sure I could still kick your ass at Ping-Pong, Stevenson."

Jake shrugged.

"I'll give you a handicap," Noah teased, bumping Jake's chair with his knee. "Just to be fair."

Jake tried to smile, knowing his friend didn't mean to be unkind. But then he said, "Dude, you know that isn't really funny, right?"

Noah flushed red to the tips of his ears and looked stricken. "Fuck, Stevenson. I'm sorry. I just—"

Jake punched him in his side to cut him off. "I know," he said. "I just don't want to have to kick your ass."

Relief flooded his friend's face.

"I'll think about Pomeroy's," Jake said.

Celia leaned across the seat and poked Noah in the side. "I thought you were in a big hurry, *wey!*" she said.

"Text me if you want a ride, bro," Noah said. He bumped Jake's fist and folded his big body behind the wheel and left.

Jake sat at the kitchen window watching the golden bodies flit toward the neighbor's orchard. He thought about hanging out in Pomeroy's garage. All the guys staring and pretending not to. It was too much. Never mind that he hadn't picked up his trumpet in forever.

He put in his earbuds and scrolled through the music on his phone. There was nothing he wanted to listen to there, so he took them out again. He realized how often he'd been blocking out the sound of his parents moving around the house. It was so quiet at Alice's, and there was so much more to listen to. Just sitting there he could hear the wind in the trees, the cluck of the chickens. A bee buzzed past the screen door and flew away.

He opened the recipe app on his phone and pulled the kale out of the fridge and set it on the cutting board.

"*Sissy*," Celia had called over her shoulder at Noah.

"*Sissy*," Ed hissed in his mind.

His father would not be impressed that Jake was learning to cook. Ed hated everything that didn't seem outwardly masculine in the most redneck sense. Men drove trucks, drank beer, ruled the roost, and hunted in the fall. Manual labor was a thing to be admired, but only if it took place outside the walls of the house. As for his wife's daily cooking, cleaning, and managing of the household, that was simply expected, even though she worked full time too. Jake had never once heard his father thank her for making dinner or offer to clean up.

"*Sissy*," his father said when he had come home to find twelve-year-old Jake practicing an ollie in the driveway on his new skateboard.

He had lit a cigarette. "*You should be playing football, not messing around on that stupid thing.*"

Jake didn't tell his father that there was no football team in seventh grade. Nor did he mention that some of the best Olympic snowboarders, like Shaun White, had started out on skateboards. His father probably thought snowboarding was stupid too.

By the time he was in high school, he was riding a longboard, the one his mom had brought over, and it had been his freedom. It got him to school, the skate park, and Katz's house. That board was still precious to him, even though he couldn't ride it now. It sat in the corner of his room at Alice's. Would that make Ed happy?

He put the chili on low to simmer. With the afternoon ahead of him, he decided to go through the new hives again. And when Alice got home that evening, he would confess.

The inspection took him the better part of the afternoon. As he worked, he reflected that his time with them was growing short. The bees had already built out these first brood boxes almost to capacity. Soon Alice would add another brood box to each so the bees could make more wax comb for the brood. Then the hives would be too tall for him to open while sitting in his chair. He was becoming adept at spotting eggs, uncapped larvae, capped larvae, and drone and worker brood. The art of locating the queen was like a game. Listen, find the G-sharp sound, open the hive, and find the queen. His chest swelled with pride each time he managed to locate her.

The sound was the same with every hive. Last night he had found a reference on the Internet to explain it. A researcher at Washington State University had verified that queens had a tone all their own— G-sharp/A-flat. Why that same tone? he wondered. Was she singing to her children or to herself, and what was she saying?

He worked his way through the hives without issue, and then something weird happened when he got to Hive No. 23. He had to strain to find the sound. And when he opened the hive and looked inside, his stomach dropped. The queen was on the fifth frame, but she seemed lethargic. Her attendants were circling her, cleaning her body and her wings. Her buzz was intermittent and weak. Jake shut the hive with a cold feeling in his gut. No. 24 was worse. There was no queen sound, and he could not find her long, tapered figure among the vibrating mass of workers.

A layer of sweat sprang up on his scalp and upper lip. What had he done? He should have just left them alone. Fuck. Alice was going to be so pissed. Without the queens, these two new hives were doomed.

She had patted No. 23 the first day she had shown him the hives.

"You girls are the future," Jake had heard her say. "You just do your thing and I'll keep you safe."

Jake spent the next couple of hours online looking at bee forums, but everything he read made him feel worse. When he heard Alice's truck descend the driveway, his stomach flipped over. He'd briefly considered not saying anything to her about the stricken queens. He didn't know how long it would take her to notice—probably a few days. But he had quickly dismissed that thought. The longer he waited, the more likely the hives wouldn't survive.

Alice banged through the door and threw her bag on the couch. "Hey, kid," she said. "It smells great in here. I guess I'm off the hook for dinner again, huh?"

She smiled, and Jake hated himself for what he was about to tell her. "Hey, Alice. Good day?"

She gave him a crooked smile. "Yeah, you could say that. In a weird way," she said.

When she came back into the living room in her overalls, Jake pulled out her beekeeping diary and put it on the table.

"Alice, I need to tell you something," he said. "You'd better sit down."

Quickly and succinctly, he told her about going into the new hives.

"Jesus! You what? How did you—" Her voice rose, and she gestured at his chair.

"Using a wheelchair doesn't make me helpless, Alice," he said quietly. "Now, if you would just hear me out."

Her face grew red, and she apologized and nodded. Jake told her about hearing the queens in her new hives. He handed her the hive diary with his notes. He'd been as detailed as he could be, using her entries as a model: date, temperature, time of day, queen sightings, egg sightings. He had also drawn pictures to document what he'd seen—drone comb, pollen patterns, emerging larvae.

She nodded as she looked at the pages and turned them slowly. She put the notebook down.

"This is good work, Jake. The drawings are impressive too," she said, and smiled ruefully. "I'm sorry I lost my temper. I didn't mean to insult you. I just didn't expect this. It's really helpful, actually. Your records are amazing."

Jake felt his shoulders relax. "You're not mad?"

She shook her head. "No, I'm not mad," she said. "I think I'm replaced."

She pushed the notebook across the table at him. "From now on, you're in charge of the hive diaries."

Jake glowed with joy and momentarily couldn't speak. He didn't know how to explain what he felt—that the bees were drawing him toward something new and wonderful. That feeling, that golden thrum in his core when he watched them, was something he'd never expected.

"There's something else," he said.

He told her about the G-sharp sound that he had distinguished over the tone of the rest of the hive. Alice looked confused and then astonished. He told her about the WSU researcher and showed her his notes on the topic in the diary. He felt like he was sharing his most precious secret with the one person who might understand.

"Ain't that something?" she murmured, glancing at the pages and then looking up at him. "I wonder why they do that. You heard it every time, huh?"

Jake's smile faded then. He looked out the window, then back to Alice, and told her about the ailing queens.

Alice's face fell. She sighed and rose from her chair. "Let's go check it out."

In the apiary, Alice donned her hat, veil, and gloves. She looked surprised when Jake said he didn't use them or the smoker.

"Okay. Whatever you say, kid."

She gestured for him to open No. 23. His hands trembled at first, but he closed his eyes, took a few steady breaths, and went in as carefully as always. It didn't take long to confirm what he had said. The queen in No. 23 wasn't even moving anymore, and they couldn't find the queen in No. 24.

"Dammit," Alice said.

She thrust the notebook at him. "Queen failure. Write it down, just like that," she said tersely. "For Hives Twenty-three and Twenty-four and the date."

Jake felt sick as he wrote the notes.

"Those two will have to be re-queened right away, and the hives might fail anyway. They're too young to make their own queen, so I'll need to order a couple," Alice said.

She took off her gloves, sat on the windbreak, and looked at him closely. "Hey, kid, don't take it so hard. Sometimes that happens. My wrecking the truck couldn't have helped. These two hives are young and will probably be just fine with new queens."

Jake looked at her, his stomach in a knot. "So, I didn't— You don't think I did it? Hurt them, I mean."

"Oh, no. Uh-uh," she said, shaking her head. "No—you didn't hurt anything. I can see how careful you are. You have real talent with beekeeping. Going in bareheaded like that? And that sound thing? Damn, I've been doing this for years. I'm jealous, to be honest."

Jake felt his body relax as his worry left him. He felt that golden buzz in his chest cavity, like he was a hollowed-out tree filled with a honeybee colony. This feeling had been growing in him, and he finally remembered what it was. He'd felt it the first day he woke up with Cheney in his room. He felt it when his mother bought him his first skateboard and when Noah had showed up to help him at Alice's with no questions. And now with the bees. That feeling was just love. It was just everything. He held that knowledge in his heart, and he didn't speak.

Alice glanced at her watch. "Harry should be here soon," she said.

They moved along the west side of the bee yard past the older, well-established hives that were two or three brood boxes high. Though Jake had not been able to go into these hives, he had been monitoring the sounds of the queens. Now he was disturbed by what he didn't hear. He stopped and put his hand on the closest hive.

"Alice," he said. "I think we'd better check these."

What they found inside those hives was a shocking and complete devastation. In five of Alice's oldest hives, all the bees were dead or dying. The bodies of workers were piled up on top of each other, a still mass of once-golden creatures desiccating and turning brown. In one hive, bees were in the final throes of dying. They spun in circles and buzzed on and off like they were short-circuiting as they crawled over the bodies of their dead sisters.

"No!" Alice said. "No, no, no, no!"

She grew more frantic the deeper she moved into the hives, swearing under her breath. No. 6 was still healthy, still queen right. She put the top back on and sat, staring at the dead hives. Jake didn't say anything. He gripped the notebook and waited for her to explain how an entire hive could die at once—or five, for that matter.

". . . Doesn't make sense . . . never even read about that in the normal spring cycle . . . ," she was saying to herself. Her eyes ran along the western border of the bee yard, across her field, and into the neighbor's orchard. The west wind had picked up as it did on these warming spring days, and the apple trees in the neighbor's orchard tossed their blossomed branches. Alice took a deep breath, smelling the air.

"Drift," she said. "Shit."

She paced the field to the far western edge, and Jake followed. She inhaled, and Jake did too, recognizing the acrid tang of pesticide. He remembered seeing workers out there just days before but assumed they were pruning the trees.

Alice dug out her phone and called her neighbor, Doug Ransom. She put her phone on speaker. Jake listened to her patiently wading through neighborly pleasantries until she could ask her question. Why yes, Doug had recently finished his spring spraying and he hoped the smell wasn't bothering her. He had changed products this year. He got a free sample from his farm rep, and everyone seemed to think it was a superior product. Alice should come by and see him. He sure missed seeing her and Buddy. Come by any time, Doug said.

Alice hung up, shoved her phone in her pocket, and put her hands over her face. She walked away from Jake and toward the row of devastated hives, which were closest to Doug's orchard. She turned back toward him, and he saw the naked grief on her face. A knot of empathy rose in his throat. He heard an engine, and they both looked up to see a sheriff's department Jeep rumbling down the driveway.

"Jesus Christ. What now?" Alice muttered, and they moved together to meet it.

17

GLORY BEE

Although bees will fly, in search of food, over three miles, still, if it is not within a circle of about two miles in every direction from the Apiary, they will be able to store but little surplus honey.

—L. L. LANGSTROTH

For all the solace provided by his notebook—lists of pros and cons, goals and aspirations, to-do lists and checklists and thoughtful word choices—Harry knew it was of no real use to him in moments like this, moments that really counted. Life was rushing at him, and no end of careful journaling could help him figure out what to do. The only words he could conjure to describe this present moment were "uncomfortable," "unavoidable," and "inevitable." Only now did he recognize the main drawback of asking Ronnie for a ride. Namely, that he had to explain to his new boss why a sheriff's deputy was dropping him off for his first day of work.

"Tell the truth, kid! It's easier to remember," Sal's voice echoed in his head.

Nothing about that truth seemed worth sharing with Alice Holtzman. The truth was he was a homeless convicted felon. Even so, as he climbed out of the Jeep, Harry prepared to give it his best shot. This was a fresh start, after all.

As Alice crossed the yard to meet him, Harry noticed the boy coming along with her. The sight of the chair and the hair, still surprising, distracted him. He dropped his bulging backpack at his feet and wiped his sweating palms on his pants and tried to rally. Surely, there was a shred of confidence in him somewhere. He lifted his chin and tried to feel brave.

"Hello, Mrs. Holtzman," he said. "Sorry I'm late."

Alice nodded at him, frowning.

"So, this funny thing happened," Harry began. "It's kind of a long story. I was in Seattle in February, and it started to rain, and I went to Pike Place Market—"

He stopped, kicking himself. Get to the point, Harry, he thought. Don't tell her your life's story. He started again.

"And, so, my uncle lives in BZ Corner. You know, up north on 141?"

No, he couldn't start there, with the trailer and Uncle H's death. Flummoxed, he lost his momentum and didn't know what to say. Alice Holtzman had shifted her withering gaze to the cop.

"Hello, Ronnie. I heard you joined the team," she said.

The deputy took off his hat, ducked his head like he was in trouble, and said, "Hello, Auntie Alice."

Alice frowned at him and looked back at Harry, who wanted to get back in the Jeep and go far, far away. Any scrap of bravery drained out of him under Alice's gaze. He was a disappointment, plain and simple. There was nothing he could say to explain himself. He wanted to grab his bag and disappear up the road.

Alice glanced down at his backpack like she'd read his mind.

"Going somewhere, Mr. Stokes?" she asked.

He heard his mother's voice in his head.

"Where you off to, Harry Stokes?"

He shook his head and looked down at the gravel in the driveway, feeling vertiginous. The ground tilted, and each blue-gray pebble seemed to magnify and shrink away again. He dragged his eyes back up to Alice's frowning face and opened his mouth.

"It's just . . . the place I was staying . . . the county condemned it. And then Ronnie came . . . and they are tearing it down, so I need to . . ."

Harry ran out of words and breath at the same time. He didn't know what else to say. Alice's face wore the look he'd seen on other people's faces his whole life: "dumbass." He could already imagine the conversation with his mother, which would end with her offering bus fare to Florida. He'd ride back across the country on a smelly Greyhound like the one he'd taken west in February. Sal would be pissed off but would let him move in. Then what would he do?

But now Ronnie was talking.

"We had a big party for Abuela and Abuelo's fiftieth last month at Aunt Connie's," he was saying. "We missed you. Man it was something! We did a whole roasted goat, you know. Birria and all that. Everyone was there but you and . . ."

He faltered and then finished, "Everyone but you."

Alice just looked at him but didn't say anything. Ronnie, who barely looked old enough to shave, had just turned twenty-one when his uncle died and Alice had only seen him once or twice since—at the funeral, of course, and once near the post office last winter, when she'd crossed the street to avoid being seen by her dead husband's family. She didn't return their calls and had pulled the shades when they drove to the house, which they'd stopped doing months ago. She watched Ronnie, her face blank, as he shifted his weight from one foot to the other. He turned his deputy's hat over and over in his hands.

She heard the crunch of Jake's wheelchair on the gravel behind her. Ronnie looked over Alice's shoulder at the young man with the mohawk in the wheelchair. Confusion passed across his face and then embarrassment as the silence bore down on them all. His eyes lit upon the beehives, and he smiled, as if grateful for something to talk about.

"Oh! The bees! How are your bees doing, Auntie?"

Ronnie's mother, Evangelina, was from Michoacán, like so many Mexican immigrants to the valley. Consequently Ronnie was short and dark, but his dad was Buddy's older brother, Ron. And when he smiled, her nephew looked so much like her dead husband that she could barely stand to look at him. He beamed at her now and pointed at the hives. She thought of her first hive, now dead along the western fence line, and how Buddy had brought it to her parents' house that Saturday after the fair. Buddy laughing at himself in his bulky bee suit. Buddy tap-dancing across the yard in it to make her laugh. Alice's heart, which had folded in two at the sight of her nephew, now broke wide open.

She put her hands on her knees and struggled to breathe. The feeling came crashing down on her, and she couldn't get away. She felt the hole inside her open up right there in the driveway. Her darling Buddy. The stupid, pointless circumstances of his death. Alice felt herself split in two, and her anguish poured out. It was a primal, animal grief.

Ronnie froze, and Harry looked ready to run. The sounds that spilled from Alice's mouth didn't seem like English or even quite human. The two young men were at a complete loss—both silent and terrified.

But Jake was unafraid. Sitting behind her in the driveway, he heard only her terrible sorrow. He recognized very clearly that Alice was in pain, which was something like the others probably couldn't. He pushed his chair forward until he was right beside her. Then he reached out and took her by the wrist with his slender hand.

"Hey, Alice. Take a breath."

He didn't raise his voice, and he didn't have to.

She fell silent. She looked down at Jake and then back at her nephew.

"Buddy," she said.

Her legs failed, and the ground caught her. She put her hands over her face and wept like a child, like she hadn't since that day the state police came to her front door and told her that her funny, kind husband had been in an accident and pronounced dead at the scene. It washed over her again, the terrible loss that opened up and opened up until it was impossible to contain. It had finally flooded her life.

Jake put his hand on her shoulder and patted her lightly. Alice sat in the driveway and wept with the sun shining down and the thoughtless beauty of spring swelling around them.

"It's okay, Alice," he murmured. "It's gonna be okay."

It was all he could think of to say, but in that moment, it was enough. His mother had said the same thing to him, over and over again last year as she sat next to his hospital bed. He hadn't believed her then, but it had helped somehow, to hear it.

Jake knew what it felt like when you finally understood that the life you had was gone and you would never, ever get it back. For him, it had come in a brutal moment, early in rehab, when he lay on a therapy mat, drenched in sweat and trying to relearn how to sit up on his own. That day he had felt like a broken version of himself.

He had lived with that loss for more than a year now. Every morning the sight of the chair would bring it all back. His old life was gone, and he would never be okay again. But that wasn't the truth at all. Now Jake understood that his life had been shifting imperceptibly for months. He didn't feel broken, and he hadn't for some time. He was becoming something else. Sitting there with Alice, he realized he had come out the other side. His reference point for the accident had been "before." Now there was "after." His after was the farm. His after was the bees. His after was helping his new friend Alice bear her terrible sorrow simply because he could.

Alice sat with her face in her hands, her shoulders heaving. The three young men looked at each other and didn't speak. They just waited, not knowing what else to do.

Then they all heard it—a terrible sobbing bark, an anguished ca-
nine shout from the back seat of the Jeep and a scrabbling of nails at
the window as the dog tried like mad to get to the boy he hadn't seen
in over a year.

Years later, Jake was certain he would never forget the vivid details
of the day Cheney came back. The sweet smell of lilacs hung thick in
Alice's yard. A thrush called out of the forest just past the meadow. He
was wearing his favorite Ramone's T-shirt. And he felt an impossible
burst of joy when he heard the beloved, familiar bark that he'd thought
was lost forever.

Harry struggled with the Jeep door. It was bad enough that Alice
Holtzman sounded ready to castrate them all. Now this stray he'd
found was raising holy hell.

Cheney leapt out of the Jeep and threw his lanky body at Jake,
threatening to tip the wheelchair backward. He lapped furiously at the
boy's face. Then he ran to Alice and shoved his snout into her hair,
before returning to Jake. Then he bounded off across the field like a
giant brindled jackrabbit, singing a happy cry as if his joy was too large
to be contained in his body and must be shared with the great wide
world.

Alice came back to herself then. She took out her bandana, wiped
her face, and blew her nose. She pushed herself up off the ground
with a small grunt and looked at Jake. The boy watched the dog sprinting in a wild figure eight with tears streaming down his face. He
laughed and laughed and couldn't speak.

Harry was now certain he'd lost this job before he'd even started.
"I'm so sorry. I just— I found him in the woods, and I couldn't leave
him up there. Ronnie said he'd take him to the shelter for me," he said.

Alice watched the dog tear back to the boy and collapse in his lap.
Jake put his arms around Cheney's neck and buried his face in the
dog's big crazy ears.

Alice cleared her throat. "That's all right, Harry. I think this dog belongs to Jake. Well, okay." She took a deep breath. "Why don't we all go sit down for a minute and get ourselves sorted? Come on, Ronnie. You can help me get some drinks."

And that was how Alice Holtzman, aged forty-four, assistant to the county planning director, beekeeper, orphan, widow, and mother to no one, found herself sitting under the cottonwood tree with three young men, drinking lemonade and listening to their stories. It was an odd little group gathered there, crying and laughing by turns. But it happened like that sometimes. Sorrow released a person from common constraints, and in their grief they could be their true, bald selves. If others chose to witness that, to truly see others, well, it changed everything.

Jake sat with one hand on Cheney's neck as if he couldn't bear to stop touching him. He told them that Cheney had disappeared while he was in the hospital. Harry explained how he'd mistaken Cheney for a wild animal. Ronnie surprised them all by breaking down in tears as he told Alice how much he missed his uncle. Of course he did, Alice thought. Ronnie had grown up with Buddy. He'd been like a second father to the boy. Of course they missed him, all of the Ryans, as much or maybe even more than she did. Buddy had belonged to all of them.

Ronnie wiped his sleeve across his eyes and sniffled. "I miss you too, Auntie. We all do," he said.

Alice reached across the table and squeezed his hand. "I've missed you too, Ronnie. I'm sorry I haven't been to see you all. I really am."

Ronnie smiled and shook his head. "It's okay, Auntie. We understand. Mom said you just needed time."

She smiled back. "I guess so," she said.

"Look out now, though. Once they hear, you won't chase 'em off. The Ryans are going to be crawling all over this place. Salazars too. You know how we do! Always somebody's birthday or anniversary or quinceañera. Oh, right. Angie's is next weekend. Connie's youngest.

See, I told you! Now you are officially invited. All of you!" He gestured to include Harry and Jake.

Alice laughed and said that sounded just great. She knew Ronnie's dad would feel differently, but she didn't want to hurt her nephew's feelings, so she didn't say anything. Ronnie probably didn't know what had passed between her and Ron Senior on the day that Buddy died, all that had been said and could never be unsaid.

Alice asked Jake to give Harry a tour of the farm. In the barn, he pointed out the tool bench, the chicken supplies, and the beekeeping equipment. Cheney padded alongside them, sniffing and marking fence posts as he went. Jake watched his skinny butt shift from side to side and saw his ribs poking through his dirty fur. The two young men stopped at the entrance to the apiary. Cheney nosed the air and snapped his big teeth at the darting golden bodies.

"I guess Alice will show you the hives later," Jake said, running his hand along the dog's body from shoulder to flank, thrilling to touch him again. He hesitated, then said, "She had some bad news about them earlier today, so don't ask too many questions, you know?"

Harry nodded. He was shocked that he was still employed and wasn't going to ask anyone anything. His stomach uncoiled loudly.

Jake grinned. "Come on. You can help me with dinner."

The two young men went in the house, and Cheney ran around to the back porch to the slider door. Jake put the chicken chili on simmer and dug in the fridge for some scraps for the dog—leftover pancakes, which he mixed with four eggs in a pie pan. Balancing it on his lap, he opened the slider, lowered the pan to the porch, and watched the dog gulp it down. Jake retrieved the pan and filled it with water. The big dog emptied it three times and then collapsed with his nose on his paws and gazed up at the boy with loving eyes.

Jake felt his heart swell and closed the screen door. "Tell me how you found him again?"

Harry repeated the story about the chicken feed bucket, and Jake laughed until tears ran down his cheeks. They both pretended it was because the image was hilarious and not because Jake's heart was mending back together.

Jake filled a pitcher with water and handed it to Harry. He pulled plates and glasses out of the cupboards, and together they set the table.

"So, is Mrs. Holtzman a friend of your folks or something?" Harry asked, laying out the silverware.

Jake laughed. "No, she's not. And don't call her Mrs. Holtzman, or she'll kick your ass. It's Alice. Just Alice." He paused and rubbed his scalp. "She, kind of, rescued me? I guess that's the easiest way to put it. My parents . . ."

He trailed off and shook his head. "I'm just staying here for a while."

Harry nodded. He wasn't about to quiz anyone about their origins.

"So, are you excited about the bees?" Jake asked, trying to keep the jealousy out of his voice.

Harry shrugged. "I don't know. The ad said light construction and chores. I don't know anything about bees."

Jake grinned at him. "They're pretty cool, man. That's all I can say. They'll kinda blow your mind."

Alice and Ronnie came inside, and the four of them sat around the kitchen table and ate Jake's chili. Alice wanted to laugh but knew she shouldn't. These poor boys had seen enough lady crazy for one day. Still, it was funny. Three dinner guests on Alice Island.

Harry shook hands with Ronnie before he left. "Thanks, man," he said.

"No, thank *you*, man," Ronnie said, his voice low. "Fucking gun. Jesus!"

"No worries," Harry said.

Alice walked Ronnie out to the Jeep. She hugged her nephew and promised she would call the family about Angie's party. Ronnie kissed her on the cheek and left.

Alice turned back to the house and saw Cheney, his head cocked, considering Red Head Ned, who had locked the dog in his glare and was stalking toward him. Alice pointed at the chicken yard and said, "No chickens. Understand? Watch yourself there, big dog. Or you'll be homeless again."

Cheney looked at her, blinked, and trotted back toward the house. She sighed. First a teenager, and now a dog and a twentysomething. She shook her head. She'd told Harry he could sleep in the bunkroom until he found a place.

Alice shoved her hands in her pockets and cast a glance at her hives. Her eyes landed on the dead ones. Even from a distance, they looked so still. She would start there with Harry, she decided. She would have him take them apart and scrape out all the wax and bodies. First things first. There was still enough light to show Harry the bees.

Harry's introduction to the bees was quick, but not in the way Alice had expected. It took less than ten seconds for Harry to communicate to Alice, Jake, Cheney, and any neighbors within a mile that the bees scared the absolute shit out of him.

Taking his cue from Jake, he declined a hat and veil. So, when Alice opened the first hive and the guard bees flew gently up around his face, Harry yelped and slapped at them. The guard bees responded with a stress pheromone, and then Harry was under attack. He took off up the hill, with Cheney bounding after him.

Alice eased the top of the hive back on and watched Harry disappear into the woods.

"Well," she said with a sigh, "my fault. You've clearly skewed my sense of newbies."

Jake grinned at her.

"We'll have to take things slowly with young Harry. If he ever comes back, that is," she said.

She sat on the windbreak and pulled out the hive diary to look at Jake's notes again.

"Count estimate," she said, looking up at him. "Now, how did you figure that out?"

Jake shrugged. "Just something I read on the Internet. You count the bees on either side of the middle frame and multiply it by ten for a week-old nuc hive."

She raised an eyebrow.

"I had some time on my hands," he said, trying to sound casual.

Alice flipped through the entries and came to the series of sketches again—bee bodies, wings, antennae, legs, and pollen baskets. The face of a bee emerging from its cell, the bee waggle.

"Wow, kid! These are really good."

He shrugged, embarrassed.

"No, really, Jake. This is great detail. I mean it. Now, tell me about the sound again."

This was a story he'd never tire of. Jake closed his eyes and described the thrum of a healthy hive and that magical queen song, that ringing G-sharp.

"Show me," Alice said.

The two of them traveled a row of hives, and Jake paused by each one and sat with his eyes closed and his head cocked.

"Queen," he would say when he heard it.

She believed him. Clearly this kid had some special talent with bees.

"Come over here." She strode toward the west edge of the field, toward the dead hives, and stopped at the row right before them, hives No. 7 through No. 12. She gestured down the row.

"What about these?" she asked.

Jake rolled down the row, listening.

Seven, he nodded. Eight, he nodded again. Nine was fainter but he could hear it. At Ten he shook his head. Alice sighed and looked out toward Doug Ransom's orchard and then back at the hives. She turned to Jake and smiled grimly.

"Got any plans tomorrow night?" she asked.

Congregating

Honey-Bees can flourish only when associated in large numbers, as in a colony. In a solitary state, a single bee is almost as helpless as a new-born child, being paralyzed by the chill of a cool Summer night.

—L. L. LANGSTROTH

Life in a honeybee colony is ruled by the seasons. In summer, diligent field bees head out to forage as soon as the first rays of dawn warm the hive, and they work tirelessly into the cool hours of twilight. Fall foragers venture into wet woods and meadows between rain showers and blustery winds. Winter hives sit snow-covered and still until spring, when the bees break their tight cluster to take up their work again— cleaning the hive, building new comb, and gathering nectar and pollen to build the family up again.

The lives of humans are similarly ordered, especially in a farming town like Hood River. Each spring, the citizens were drawn back outside into each other's company. As the lilacs bloomed, snow melt swelled the river, and the days lengthened almost imperceptibly. People drew together with the sense of anticipation that only spring can summon. Even Alice, who enjoyed her solitude, felt the pull as she drove through town with Jake.

They passed the library and saw that the parking lot was packed.

The sandwich board on the sidewalk announced two simultaneous evening events: the Hood River Valley Beekeepers meeting and a live demo from "Karl the Snake Man." Alice swore under her breath and circled the block again, glancing at Jake. Parking was something she hadn't thought of.

After Alice circled the building for a third time, Jake sighed and dug a skinny arm into his backpack. He pulled out a disabled placard and stuck it on the rearview mirror. He looked at Alice, his face impassive.

"Let me help you out, Mrs. Holtzman," he said. "I hate to see you walk too far, being so old and all."

"Oh, dear Harry," Alice said, laughing as she pulled into a disabled parking spot by the front door. "He's really one of a kind, isn't he?"

She knew Jake was referring to the previous evening. After Harry had returned from his sprint through the woods with Cheney trotting at his heels, he'd offered to meet the bees again, determined, it seemed, to redeem himself.

Alice had shaken her head. "Tomorrow," she said. "It's getting dark. Let's get you settled."

The young man looked so relieved she almost laughed.

Alice led him to the small bunkroom in the barn that Buddy had built so many years ago for the nephews. It was simple but neat and had a small bathroom. With a pang she recalled the summer nights Ronnie, his brothers, and his cousins had spent there. There was a photo of Buddy on the wall, his arms draped around the nephews, each holding a fishing rod. Alice had taken the photo when the boys still had their baby faces. Even then, the resemblance between her nephews and her husband was uncanny. She turned away from the photo and the memories it threatened to trigger.

The next day, she arrived home after work to find Harry in the barn. She noticed he had swept the shop floor and restacked the wood into a neat pile.

"I see you are settling in," she said. She wanted to thank him for tidying up, but the words stuck in her throat. It was just so jarring to see another person in Buddy's space.

"Hang on. I've got a project for you," she said.

She took a cart out to the apiary and retrieved the five now-silent hives. Jake, who was making notes in the hive diary, waved hello and followed her back to the barn.

Alice set one of the brood boxes on the worktable. She glanced at the pegboard where Buddy's tools hung. Among the dusty screwdrivers, pliers, and hammers was another photo—a faded snapshot of the two of them sitting on the front steps of the house their first summer together. Buddy had his big arm around Alice. Oh, how it had felt to lean into his shoulder. Safe. Loved. She forced her eyes away and opened the brood box for Harry.

"This sticky stuff here is called propolis," she said. "The bees gather it from trees to seal up all the cracks."

Harry nodded.

"Some people call it Nature's cement."

He didn't say anything. The kid sure was quiet, she thought.

Alice loosened a frame and pulled it free from the brood box. Her heart sank as she surveyed the devastation—eggs dried up in their cells, desiccated larvae, and full-grown workers hanging dead from the wax.

No use being sentimental, she thought. "I want you to clean it all out," she said.

She demonstrated how to brush the adult bodies into a large plastic tub with a bee brush and then use the hive tool to scrape the wax into another.

"I want loose bees in this first container and everything else in the second. All the wax and the eggs and larvae. Scrape it down to the foundation, okay?"

She looked him in the eye, and he nodded.

"Okay, Mrs. Holtzman," Harry said.

"Call me Alice, Harry," she said. Her mother was Mrs. Holtzman. Or had been.

Harry blushed and nodded. Nervous little rabbit, she thought. She passed the frame to him, and he took it gingerly with the tips of two fingers.

"Don't worry, kid. You won't get stung. These bees are all dead," she said.

She was trying to lighten the mood, but she didn't think it was funny, and she knew she sounded impatient. Harry reddened, and she felt bad. She glanced at Jake, who was watching the exchange. Harry was young, she thought, not much older than Jake, really. She should be more patient. She mustered a smile. "Got any questions, Harry?"

He shook his head, and after an awkward silence, Alice turned to leave.

"Okay," she said. "Holler if you need anything."

"Do they always look like this after you take the honey out?" Harry blurted at her back.

Alice turned around and looked at him. "I beg your pardon?"

"The bees," he said. "Do they always die when you take the honey? What did you call it—harvest?"

She paused and took a deep breath. "No, Harry," she said, her voice low. "I didn't harvest the honey. This hive died."

Harry swallowed. "I'm sorry, Mrs. Holtzman—I didn't . . . ," he stammered.

"Don't worry about it," Alice said. She gestured at the workbench. "Use anything you need in here, okay?"

Harry nodded, looking around, and his eyes fell on the snapshot of her and Buddy.

"Oh!" he said. "So this is your son's shop?"

The seconds ticked by as Alice stared at the photo. She was afraid to open her mouth and then decided she could trust herself to speak, if just. She shifted her gaze back to Harry.

"No, that's not my son," she said slowly. "That is my late husband."

Harry's face turned from white to pink and back to white. She looked at Jake, and he held her gaze. It was, after all, true. Bud Ryan was her late husband.

"I'll come check on you in a bit," Alice said.

She left the two young men in the barn and took a long walk along the fence line. She could feel the knot in her chest tighten, and she willed herself to inhale and exhale, inhale and exhale. She looked out at Doug Ransom's orchard, where the trees tossed their frothy branches. The pain eased a notch, and she could breathe again. She let herself think of the photo of Buddy and the little boys. Such wonderful days past. She thought of her conversation with her nephew. Sweet Ronnie, it was clear, didn't know what his father thought of Alice.

The day Bud died last spring, Alice had watched Ron's Jeep speed down the driveway toward her house. She wanted to go see his parents but hadn't been able to move from the kitchen floor, where she collapsed after the two state troopers left.

They told her the accident had taken place near Boardman. A car traveling east crossed the center lane and nearly collided with Bud, who was heading west toward home in his truck. Buddy swerved to avoid the car, smashed through the guardrail, and rolled into the slough. He was pronounced dead at the scene. The other driver was drunk, had previous DUIs, and would be prosecuted, the officers said. Their words sounded far away. Could they call anyone for her? She shook her head.

She pulled herself off the floor when she heard the sound of Ron's Jeep. He was coming to take her to the family, she thought. She walked out to meet him, her legs rubbery, the sunshine strangely cold on her scalp. Ron leapt out of the car and rushed at her.

"It's your fault!" he yelled, pointing at her, his hands shaking. "You told him to take that job. He would be alive if it wasn't for you!"

Alice heard his words like she was underwater and couldn't speak. Buddy had been as excited as a little boy about the job with the big truck. The decision had been all his.

Ron grabbed her by the shoulders like he wanted to hurt her and said terrible things. Go ahead, she thought, looking up at his contorted face. The worst has already happened. Ron pushed her away and doubled over. Alice reached out to comfort him, and he stumbled to the Jeep and roared off.

Those memories rushed back, and Alice was afraid she would be overwhelmed, but she felt the limits of her sorrow then. She let herself relive the pain of that day, which included Ron. It was another loss both separate and part of losing Buddy. She felt that grief moving around inside her, and she knew her body could contain it. She was okay. It was going to be okay. Her sadness worked itself back down inside her into the safe place it needed to live when she was around people.

Alice sat down on the windbreak and looked over the apiary and her remaining hives. This was her home, her place. A fierceness rose in her then, and she felt the urgency of protecting her honeybees. She pulled out the hive diary and jotted down some notes for the beekeepers meeting.

By the time Alice returned to the barn, Jake had helped Harry clean out all the dead hives. She nodded at the material they had collected and examined the frames.

"Nice work," she said. She snapped the lids closed on the bins.

"I need to bring these to the beekeepers meeting," she said. "Harry, will you grab that one?"

"Sure, Mrs.—er, Alice," he said. "Let me carry that. It's heavy, and you shouldn't—"

Wordlessly, she hefted the bin in her arms and strode to the truck. Harry trailed behind her with the other, and Jake followed, snickering.

Now, in front of the library, Alice was surprised and grateful she could laugh about it. She glanced at Jake and noticed he was scanning the sidewalk nervously. She looked at the placard he had hung on the mirror, thinking it might have cost him something to pull it out. She was grateful he'd agreed to come, this surprising new ally. She jumped out of the truck and grabbed his chair from the back, set it next to the door, and waited while he maneuvered his way carefully down and settled himself in. She followed as Jake wheeled up the ramp in front of her and slapped the mechanical door control.

Bee club members, mostly men, clustered along the hallway in twos and threes. Some of them knew Alice, and smiled and nodded. They looked at Jake with curiosity. She didn't stop to talk to anyone. Many were farmers and orchardists, and some were hobbyists like her. There were a couple of large-scale beekeepers like Chuck Sauer, who was currently president of the bee association and also eternally crabby. He volunteered, not out of altruism but in an effort to keep the "idiot weekend farmers," as he called them, from screwing up his commercial hives by spreading mites.

Alice strode to the front of the room, where Chuck stood holding a clipboard and wearing a scowl.

"Hello, Chuck," she said.

Chuck grunted.

"I have an item for new business," she said.

Chuck peered down at her, stone-faced, and said the agenda had already been printed. She should have emailed him a week ago like the rules said.

"I'm sure the members will want to hear what I have to say. And anyway, those rules about the agenda are yours. They aren't written into our bylaws."

She waved her phone at him and read from the screen. "'Any member can introduce significant new business at the end of the meeting with verbal notification to the president.'"

Chuck's frown deepened, and Alice thought of the wizened faces of the dolls her German grandmother once made using dried apples. He waved a hand.

"Fine, Ms. Holtzman. I'll add it on at the end. Please be ready with your commentary. We don't want to waste people's time," he said, spitting his t's.

"Now if you don't mind, I'd like to get started," he said, striding away.

Alice rolled her eyes at Jake, and the two of them sat near the front. Chuck thumped his fist on the podium to call the meeting to order and worked through the agenda with an almost military precision. Approval of last month's minutes. Discussion of a club motto. Plans for the Fourth of July float. Alice checked her phone and glanced toward the door. She saw Stan Hinatsu slip in the back. He scanned the room and nodded when he saw her.

The meeting dragged on as Chuck exhausted the discussion of the parade float beyond the tolerance of even the most patient. People were getting restless, and a few older members had already left, scraping their chairs back and talking loudly as they went.

Finally, Chuck said, "Okay. That's all for the official agenda. I have had a request to open the floor to new business."

He glared at Alice and stalked off to the side of the room.

Alice stood, took out her notebook, and walked behind the podium. She waved a hand at the room.

"Um, hi, everybody. Most of you know me. I'm Alice Holtzman. I'll make this quick, but I know you are going to want to hear what I have to say."

Her voice quavered, and she glanced down at her notes. Her hands shook, and she balled them into fists.

"I've been a member of the bee club for nine years, and I currently have twenty-four hives in the south valley."

People had begun standing and talking as they moved to leave. Alice raised her voice to be heard.

"Yesterday, following a routine inspection, I found that five of my hives were dead. They were the five oldest of the twenty-four."

Chuck was putting his notes in his bag, rustling his papers loudly.

"The five most robust hives," Alice said. Her voice dropped.

Five hives. What was she saying? She saw Jake glancing around the room. Conversations grew louder. Chuck guffawed at something the guy next to him said. They weren't listening. What did it matter? Five of her hives were dead. *How are your bees, Auntie?* Ronnie had asked. *It's your fault,* Ron said. Bud Ryan was her late husband. She was Alice Island. Then she heard her mother's voice, impatient and snappish in her head.

"Alice Marina Holtzman! Stand up straight and stop mumbling!"

Alice came back to herself. Then it was her own voice she heard.

"Hey! You guys in the back! I have the floor. So either get out or sit down and be quiet!"

The room fell silent. Chuck Sauer sat. Those who had been clustered in the hallway drifted in to stand in the back, their arms crossed.

"Thank you," Alice said. She closed her notebook and came out from behind the podium. Her voice was steady.

"Five of my hives died overnight. Two others are ailing. They were strong, healthy hives. I'm almost positive it was the result of pesticide drift from Doug Ransom's orchard."

Mutters rose, and she put up her hands.

"Now, Doug is a friend of mine. He's been really good about working with me—timing his spraying dates with low wind or east wind, and it has worked out fine. He sprayed on Monday, which was windless, so it should have been okay. Only this year, Doug used a new product on his trees. It was a SupraGro sample given to him as a free demo."

The room was utterly silent now. Other orchardists shifted in their chairs, looking at each other.

"I'm sure Doug doesn't know this, but SupraGro's pesticides have been linked to large-scale hive devastation in Nebraska, North Dakota, and Northern California, as well as far-reaching destruction of water-sheds and riparian systems. I'm having my dead hives tested at the extension service for residue, and I'm certain we will find SupraGro neonicotinoids in there."

"Chin up, dearie," Al's voice said. *"They're listening."*

Alice pulled her shoulders back and lifted her gaze.

"In the meantime, I propose that the Hood River County Bee-keeping Association request a temporary ban on the use of SupraGro in the Hood River Valley until we determine if it is harmful to local bee populations. Can I get a second?"

A hand shot up at the side of the room.

"I second!" a man called. "Mr. President, can we get a vote, please?"

Everyone started talking at once. Chuck stood and tried to call the room to order, but voices continued to rise.

"Be quiet!" he yelled, and banged on the table with his clipboard. The room settled to a murmur.

"Now," Chuck growled through his mustache, glaring at Alice, "since we've had a motion and a second, we are obligated by our by-laws to have a discussion. I know that some of you want to get home. Anyone who leaves now is free to do so, but remember you will forfeit your right to vote on the issue. If you need to go, go now," he said.

Nobody left. Chairs creaked. Chuck sighed, sat down, and waved a hand.

"The issue is officially open for discussion," he said. "One at a time, please. And state your name."

Many people rose to speak. The room was full of old men, and old men have strong opinions. Some of them were worried that the county would impose regulations on them if they rocked the boat. Some of them had received free samples from SupraGro. Of course, they didn't want to hurt their bees, but they made a living from the orchards. SupraGro was cheaper, and the science said it was more effective than the pesticides they'd been using. How could they say no to that? Others said they had read that the idea of pesticides hurting bees was a hoax. Some said they should only ban the use on large orchards, not small operations. After the bee club members had spoken, Stan stood.

"My name is Stan Hinatsu. I'm the executive director of the Hood River Watershed Alliance—"

"No nonmembers are allowed to participate in official debate," Chuck interrupted with a snarl.

Alice stood and waved her phone. "Nonmembers are allowed if they are called as experts by another member. I asked Stan to come," she said. "The bylaws say—"

"Fine!" Chuck hissed. "Proceed."

"Thank you," Stan said.

". . . Uppity hippy," someone in the back mumbled, and Stan pretended not to hear.

"Name and affiliation, please," Chuck said with a sigh.

"My name is Stan Hinatsu. I'm the executive director of the Hood River Watershed Alliance. During the past week I've been conferring with other watershed groups and agriculture associations around the West, and I can tell you, unequivocally, that SupraGro is responsible for devastating the bee populations across the western United States."

He told them about the science behind it, how the extra strength of the SupraGro pesticide was nothing more than a double dose of neonicotinoids.

"I won't even get into the rest of it. What it does to the watershed and to the salmon," Stan said.

". . . Going to want to take out the dams next," someone grumbled.

Stan waited till it was quiet again.

"Look, I understand that many of you have orchards or your neighbors do. The orchard economy is the lifeblood of this community. This is not an anti-farming issue."

He paused.

"The most recent data to come out of the University of California shows that in the communities where hives failed, the following spring showed a forty-five percent drop in fruit production due to the absence of local pollinators. In addition, research showed an acceleration in diseased fruit trees and outright tree loss. This is not some left-wing conspiracy. This is information from scientists at the U.S. Department of Agriculture. Here's all the information we have to date."

Stan passed photocopies around the room. Voices rose as the members talked among themselves. Stan fielded questions about data and research sources. Most questions were respectful, but one man, sneering, asked if the watershed group saw itself as impartial.

"Absolutely not," Stan answered. "We are one hundred percent on the side of the wildlife and plant life of the valley and uninterested in supporting big businesses like SupraGro. Thank you for asking."

The man huffed and sat down. Someone asked Chuck how binding their request could be for the county.

"Legally not binding at all," Chuck said slowly, and tugged on his mustache. "But in the past, they have offered a two-week period as a courtesy for topics we'd like to research. I imagine we could ask for that while the extension service looks into this."

Chuck sounded decidedly less grouchy now. He had been a research biologist at Oregon State University before he retired, Alice recalled.

"I don't know about the rest of you, but I've heard enough," Chuck said. "The science behind this and Ms. Holtzman's hives seem enough reason to take this issue to the county. I motion that we put it to a vote."

"I second!" someone yelled.

"All in favor?"

About two-thirds of the hands went up.

"Against?"

Less than one-third rose this time, and some people kept their hands in their laps.

"Motion passed," Chuck said. He turned to the club secretary, Matt Garcia, and asked him to draft a statement for city council.

"Meeting adjourned!" Chuck hollered, and rose to his feet, gathering his things. He nodded at Alice as he left.

"Thank you, Ms. Holtzman," he said.

Alice exhaled. It was a start.

Jake grinned at her. "Nice work, Alice. For an old lady, I mean."

She laughed and stood when she saw Stan approaching.

"Thank you so much for coming, Stan. That was, well, just what we needed."

"Happy to be here, Alice," he said. He sat down next to Jake, and Alice realized what a simple courtesy that was.

"I don't think we've met. I'm Stan," he said, grasping Jake's hand.

"I'm Jake," he said, and smiled. "Alice's apprentice."

Alice laughed and shoved her hands into her back pockets. "I think it's the other way around. Stan, you would not believe what this kid can do."

Someone tapped her on the shoulder, and she turned to see the line of beekeepers waiting to say hello, shake her hand, and thank her. Looking at that queue of friendly faces, well, it felt like some sort of homecoming.

Stan offered to take the hive waste to the extension service for testing.

"I have to meet with Michaels tomorrow anyway," he said.

So they transferred the bins into his car. He waved as he drove away.

As Alice drove through town on the way home, Jake riffled through the tape collection. He popped in a cassette and Tom Petty's voice streamed out into the spring evening: "Time to move on. Time to get goin'. What lies ahead, I have no way of knowin'."

Jake rolled down the window and surfed his hand on the evening breeze.

"Who was that great big guy you were talking to at the door?" he asked.

"Tiny Castañares," Alice said. "An old friend of my dad's. And mine," she added.

Jake looked out the window at their little town flashing past.

"You've got nice friends, Alice."

She nodded, and her heart swelled. She did have nice friends, and remembering that made her see she was coming back to her life. She felt that container inside her. She felt her grief, and around the edges of that grief she felt the rest of her life and everything in it growing like a fine wax comb to buffer her sorrow. She drove south toward the mountain as the sun set over the river and the wind died off. The bees went into their hives, and the people of the valley slept.

19

INTO THE HIVE

Place yourself before a hive, and see the indefatigable energy of these industrious veterans, toiling along with their heavy burdens, side by side with their more youthful compeers . . . Let the cheerful hum of their busy old age inspire you with better resolutions, and teach you how much nobler it is to die with harness on, in the active discharge of the duties of life.

—L. L. LANGSTROTH

Jake jolted awake to the sound of someone yelling. He looked at the ceiling, unsure of where he was and feeling a tightness in his throat. In the dream, he'd been skating along the waterfront with Cheney running alongside him. The dog had cantered into the road and been hit by a car. Relief flooded him then. He was at Alice's, and Cheney was alive. Cheney was right there, stuffing his big wet nose into Jake's hand.

The dream had felt so real, the sensation of speed and movement as he flowed along on his board. He could almost feel the warm spring air on his bare arms and the swing of his hips as he shifted his weight to carve a line. He'd felt so free. As the dream receded, he remembered things were different now. He didn't longboard anymore. He used a wheelchair. His eyes settled on the chair next to his bed, waiting for him like his forever escort. This was who he was now. Instead of a boy with limitless possibility, he was a person with very specific limitations.

But this morning, perhaps for the first time, he understood distinctly that an entirely new world had opened itself to him. In the weeks since he'd landed at Alice's, his sense of who he was and how he operated in the world had shifted, imperceptibly at first but undeniably now. Yes, there were things he couldn't do anymore and he would never walk again. But he had something precious he had never even imagined before—this life with honeybees. He lived with hundreds of thousands of bees. He was learning to be a beekeeper, and he was good at it, better than average. Most amazing of all, he could do something most beekeepers could not. For some reason he had been gifted with the ability to distinguish the bell-like tone of the lovely queen bees, the uber mothers. It rushed into him, the color and texture of his new life. He stretched his arms over his head and smiled.

Cheney thumped his front paws on the bed and pushed himself up in a slow-motion stretch. Then he cocked his ears and wiggled his rump as he eyed the mattress next to the boy.

Jake sat up, grabbed his big ears, and laughed. "Don't push your luck, dude."

Jake shoved the big dog off the bed, transferred into his chair, and rolled into the bathroom. He used a new single-use catheter to empty his bladder, flushed, and washed his hands and his face. The dream still hung over him—the joy of movement and the devastation of losing Cheney again. He shook it off. It was just a dream.

Jake looked at himself in the mirror. He had showered the night before, and his hair hung loose over his shoulders. The blue-black color was fading, and he could see his natural brown bleeding through. It reminded him of those first days in the hospital, when the nurse had tried to cut his hair and he threw a fit. He was all doped up, but conscious enough to fight for it, and his mom backed him up.

The nurse sighed and narrowed her eyes. "Really, Mrs. Stevenson. It's going to be hard enough to manage his care. It's just easier this way."

His mother had insisted, politely but firmly, Jake recalled, and pulled it back in a ponytail. It was a matted and tangled mess. When he was finally able to sit up, it took hours to comb out, and he wouldn't let his mother or the nurses help. He yanked a comb through the snarls an inch at a time. It was weeks before he'd been able to dye it again and months before he could style it upright into that sixteen-and-a-half-inch record-breaking mast.

Now he grabbed the new bottle of Midnight Blue #47. He glanced at the clock and turned on the faucet. He had time to let the dye set before breakfast. He held one hand under the stream of water, waiting for it to warm, and read the ingredients, which he had never noticed before: ammonia, lead acetate, bismuth citrate, intermediate p-phenylenediamine. Jake opened the bottle and sniffed, and the bitter tang of ammonia hit the back of his throat. He'd always loved the smell, which was part of the ritual of his hairstyle. But now it made him think of the days they sprayed out in the orchard, that metallic taste of chemicals in the air.

In his studying, Jake had learned all kinds of things about bees. He'd come across many interesting and archaic traditions in his reading—like if you got married, you had to introduce the bride to the hives. And if a beekeeper died, his friends had to tell the bees. One thing that really struck him was this idea of tending to the bees "absent of vice." He read that they didn't like the smell of onions or garlic. Beekeepers were urged not be "rude or drunken." He'd jotted down, "Tend the hives with cleanliness and sobriety." He noticed that Alice always washed her hands before putting on her gloves and veil, and he suspected she brushed her teeth too.

She wouldn't give him a straight answer when he asked. *"Everyone has their own rituals, kid. You'll have yours."*

He looked at the ingredients on the back of the bottle again. Whatever intermediate p-phenylenediamine was, it probably wasn't free of vice. Jake screwed the cap back on the bottle and dropped it in the trash.

Just like that, he was done with his hair, his record-breaking mohawk, his freak flag, his brand. Jacob Stevenson, who'd had the tallest
mohawk in the history of Hood River Valley High School, had moved
on. At the very least it seemed silly to invest hours fixing his hair now
that he had so many other things to do. He looked at his reflection and
reached for his scissors.

An hour later, Harry banged into the house for breakfast to find
Jake flipping pancakes and smiling under his shiny, egg-bald pate.

"Wow! Whoa! Did you— How did you— Why did you . . . I mean,
no, it looks fine . . ."

Jake grinned and ran his hand over his skull. "I know. Now I look
like a cancer patient. But it was time. Want to feel it?"

Harry passed his palm over Jake's skull, shivered, and dropped
his hand.

"Badass, man," he said.

They sat down to breakfast, and Cheney bumped around under
the table like a small horse until Jake let him out the slider door.

"Go on, Cheney! Squirrel!"

The big dog took off in the wide galloping arc that was his morning ritual. When Jake returned to the table, Harry was wolfing down
his breakfast like he was afraid someone would take his plate.

"Slow down, man! There's plenty more," he said, laughing, and
Harry reddened.

Harry had really grown on him. Though he was six years younger,
Jake felt almost protective of the guy. That day right after Harry got
hired, when they were cleaning out the hives for Alice, he felt his envy
leave him. Harry just couldn't say anything right to Alice. He had asked
that stupid question about her son and then went silent as Alice left
the barn. A dead bee fell and grazed the back of his hand. He yelped
and dropped the frame with a clatter.

Jake chuckled. "Dude. You need to chill out," he said, holding his
hands out, palms down. "Seriously."

Harry swore under his breath and picked up the frame. He scraped the bees into the plastic bin as Alice had asked. Some of them missed and fell onto the floor. Harry scooped them up with gloved hands, grimacing.

Jake nudged the bin closer to the workbench.

"How old are you, Harry?" he asked.

"Twenty-four," Harry muttered.

"Well, Alice is forty-four, so technically she's old enough to be your mom. But not that guy's mom," he said, gesturing to the photo of Bud and Alice.

"I see that now," Harry said with a sigh, scraping the frame.

Jake leaned back in his chair and watched Harry work. He was an awkward guy. But he had brought Cheney back, hadn't he? Jake looked at the dog, sprawled out and snoring in the shop doorway, and his heart flipped over. Jake decided he was going to help him.

"Hand me those frames. I'll brush the bees, and you can do the wax," Jake said.

While they worked, Jake told Harry what he knew about Alice, her job, and her family. Jake told him how she wanted to grow the apiary. Harry listened, alert but not speaking. His eyes widened as Jake described how they had met, truck nearly colliding with chair. Jake glossed over her fight with Ed Stevenson, saying only that Alice had offered to let him come stay at the farm for a little while. He didn't know how long.

"She's cool, Harry. She'll give you a chance if you work hard. Just stop saying stupid shit and try to relax, okay?"

Harry nodded. The two worked side by side through the first brood box. Harry retrieved the second one from the doorway, where Alice had parked them on the cart.

"That your longboard on the porch?" Harry asked.

Jake looked surprised. He hadn't pegged Harry for a skater. He nodded. "Haven't ridden it much lately."

Harry paused, as if trying to decide if that was a joke. Then he said, "I rode a pintail cruiser in high school."

"Serious?"

"Yeah. Old-school, I know. Did you see *Lords of Dogtown?*"

"Hells yeah!" Jake said, and quoted the line from the famous pool skating scene. "'I can't feel my feet! But then again, I can never feel my feet.'"

They both laughed, but then Harry looked at Jake's chair and stopped laughing.

Harry pried another frame out of the box and brushed the bee bodies, less gingerly now, into the waiting bin.

"I was at the waterfront the other day, and I saw this dude long-boarding around the parking lot with a kite. Like a kiteboarding kite, you know. But a really small one? He was hauling ass!" Harry said.

Jake couldn't remember the last time he'd been to the waterfront and adjacent skate park, his old haunting grounds. He missed the water and the sky, the sight of Cheney galloping along the sandbar, chasing seagulls and biting the waves.

"This guy I met said he would teach me how to kite for free," Harry said. "He said he'd lend me gear and everything." His voice rose with enthusiasm and then trailed off. "I don't know, though."

"Can I come?" Jake asked.

"What?"

"To the kite beach. Can I come with you? And, dude, if someone offers you free kite lessons, you'd be stupid to say no. Just saying."

"Yeah, sure. You can come with me. He said come down any day. He's always there."

Jake smiled to himself—the river, the wind, the sandbar. How long had it been?

The two worked together in a companionable silence until Jake left with Alice for the beekeeping meeting.

After that, their household had fallen into a routine of sorts as the days passed. It was uneasy at first. Harry was so awkward, nervous that he was going to say the wrong thing to Alice. He lingered out in the shop unless invited inside. His worry was palpable and made her cranky. One night, Alice came out to call them in for dinner, and Harry dropped the broom with a clatter. She stood in the doorway, surveying the room, which Harry had reorganized neatly. He began apologizing for moving things around, and Alice sighed and crossed her arms.

"Harry, we obviously need some ground rules here."

She laid it out plainly for him. The shop was his domain, and he could rearrange it however he saw fit, and it looked nice and tidy, by the way. He was welcome in the house when he wasn't working. She'd like him to take over table setting and dishes. He could use the computer. He could use the washer and dryer. But he had to stop apologizing every time he opened his mouth. If he didn't stop doing that, she was going to have to ask him to leave. Jake knew this last part was a joke, but Harry didn't.

"Okay, Mrs.—I mean, Alice. I'm sorry— I didn't—" he stammered, and clapped a hand over his mouth.

Alice's laugh rang in the rafters. "Don't worry, Harry. I'll give you that one for free. Now come in for dinner."

Now at the breakfast table with Harry, Jake pulled out the hive diary and told him about how the newest hives were developing. Harry had spent several days just catching up on maintenance around the farm for Alice. Now she wanted him to build brood boxes with top entrances for half of the newest hives so she could track their progress and compare them to the other hives with traditional bottom entrances.

Harry nodded. "I'm building the first ones today," he said. "For Hives Thirteen through Eighteen."

Out in the barn, Harry flipped on the shop lights. Jake rolled up to the workbench and pulled down one of the empty brood boxes onto his lap and flipped it over.

"So how are you going to do the top entrances, exactly?"

Harry explained how he would construct the new brood boxes like the old ones, only the entrance would be at the top. He pointed to Alice's sketch of what she wanted.

"I need to cut top entrances on the new boxes and then router out the ledges for the frames to hang on."

"They're called rabbets," Jake said, showing off. "The ledges."

"Oh. Rabbets. Okay, then I guess Alice is going to move the frames into the new boxes and use the same covers and everything?"

"You don't sound so sure, man," Jake said.

Harry's brow furrowed. "I think that's what she said?"

"I'm kidding, Stokes! Yeah, we're going to transfer the frames. Then we'll turn the old boxes into upper brood boxes. So you'll have to block the old entrances and add the rabbets to those?"

"Yeah, I'll need to make sure the frames hang right in those to . . . ," Harry said.

He put down the brood box on the workbench and stared at it. Then he went outside to look at the hives, then came back and looked at the brood box, mumbling to himself.

Jake watched him.

"Hand me that cover, would you, Jake?"

He passed the cover to Harry, who continued to murmur to himself. He flipped the box over and put the top on, then poked a finger underneath the ridge to measure the space left there. He grabbed a tape measure from the bench and tucked it into the gap.

"What's bee space again? Half an inch?"

Jake shook his head. "Three-eighths."

Harry straightened and grinned. He pointed at the brood box. "One down and five to go," he said, grinning.

Jake looked at him, puzzled. Harry showed him the tape measure.

"There's enough room for the entrance under the telescoping cover. And the rabbets are built into these boxes already. They're reversible. All we have to do is flip them upside down, and voilà, the bottom entrance is the top!"

Jake looked at the box, and his understanding dawned. "That's another one for Stokes! Working smarter, not harder!"

He high-fived Harry and rolled back, looking at the brood box.

"We'll still need to transfer the frames," Jake said, his enthusiasm rising. "If we put the frames from Hive Thirteen in this one, then we can flip that brood box and transfer the frames from Hive Fourteen and so on. Super easy," he said.

These young hives, still only one brood box tall, remained accessible to him. He could do this on his own. He knew he could.

"I think I could change them all out this morning," he said, talking more to himself than to Harry. "I just need to put this one like this, and the other one like—"

He took an empty frame and moved it through the air, trying to sketch the workflow of the transfer from the side of his chair. But it wouldn't work. He couldn't lean over two hives placed side by side on his right. And he didn't have the muscle strength to work one on his left side. Jake felt the bitter edges of his physical limitations then.

He let out a short, unhappy laugh. "Well, fuck. I can't do that."

"Do what?"

"Reach over two box lengths. Or over my lap. It's too far and—"

He tried to laugh it off and turned the frame over and over in his hands. But this was it, he knew. He had reached the end of his time with the hives. These new ones would get their second brood boxes by next week, and they would be too tall for him to work. He couldn't do this last goddamn thing. Disappointment rose in his throat and choked him.

"There's bee space, and then there's Jake space. It's fine. I just—Fuck!"

He threw the frame, which bounced off the shop floor and landed near the snoring dog. Cheney jumped up and slunk out of the barn with a hurt look.

Harry was watching him, perplexed.

Just like my dad, Jake thought. I'm such an asshole. He pushed his chair after the dog, but Cheney had trotted out of sight. He sighed and spun his chair to face Harry.

"Sorry, man. It's just . . . frustrating. I thought I could, but we'll have to wait for Alice. Still, she'll be really psyched that you figured out how to reverse them. Nice job, Harry."

Harry was staring at a spot just over Jake's shoulder and mumbling to himself. He stretched his arms out on either side of him.

"—To be able to slide under it. That's fourteen times two, which is only twenty-eight. Not so bad," he muttered.

"Hold your hands out," he commanded.

Jake complied, and Harry stretched the measuring tape between them and then measured the width of the brood box.

"—Times two. Yeah, that'll work," he said to himself. He straightened up and smiled at Jake. "You just need a workbench, man."

He measured the height of Jake's chair from the armrests and Jake's natural reach, and in half an hour, Harry had manufactured a portable table that could hold two brood boxes, side by side, over Jake's lap. Jake rolled his chair under the table and laughed.

"You're a fucking genius, Stokes!"

The older boy flushed with pleasure. "It's no big deal. Just some wood and nails."

"Dude, you're talking to someone who flunked shop class."

Now Harry laughed, incredulous. "Seriously? How does anyone flunk *shop*?"

Jake leaned his bald head back, looked up at the ceiling, and counted on his fingers. "Let's see: Don't show up. Show up super baked. Show up late and fail to complete the assignment. Oh, and superglue a girl's books to the desk."

That last one had been Noah's idea, but Jake was the one who did it. It had somehow seemed hilarious that day. He laughed, but Harry wasn't smiling.

"Wow. That's weird, man. I just . . . that doesn't seem like something you would do," Harry said.

Jake cocked his head. "Which part?"

"Well, any of it," Harry said. "I mean, you're so solid with everything around here."

Jake realized it was true. He wouldn't fuck around like that at Alice's. Not with the bees or anything at the farm.

"That was before," he said quietly.

Harry nodded and eyed the chair. "But you graduated, right?"

Jake barked a laugh. "Well, I have a diploma! They can't take it back."

He shook his head and looked at the brood boxes, then out at the apiary. This was his new life, he reminded himself. He was assistant to the beekeeper. He knew what to do.

"Listen, Harry. I think I can do this pretty quickly. But I'm going to need some help."

Jake told him to go wash his hands and face, brush his teeth, and change into a clean shirt.

"Just trust me," he said.

When Harry reappeared, Jake pointed to the full bee suit, and Harry donned it without protest.

"Tuck your pants into your boots. Here." Jake handed him a pair of gloves. Harry pulled them on with shaking hands.

"Sit down, man."

Harry sat, breathing sharp, shallow breaths.

"Breathe, Harry."

The older boy inhaled a quivering breath and let it out in a puff.

"Listen. If you are calm, they will be calm. If you freak out and slap at them like you did before, they will release a stress hormone and come after you. And you cannot drop the brood box or put it down fast, okay?"

Harry blinked and nodded.

"Good. I'm going to tell you what to do at each step. You just have to listen to me. Pretend you are in slo-mo. Like you are underwater, like Tai Chi. No joke. Can you do that?"

"Yeah. I can do that."

Jake made him take ten slow breaths, and then he zipped the screened hood over Harry's head.

Cheney lay panting in the sunny grass and watched the two young men enter the apiary—one dressed like an astronaut and the other in an orange T-shirt and jeans, his bald head shining in the sun. Jake guided Harry through prying the first brood box from its stand using the hive tool. Then Harry slowly lifted the box up onto the makeshift workstation over Jake's lap next to the empty brood box. Harry hurried to a safer distance and unzipped his hood. Jake sat with his eyes closed, breathing slowly and thinking through the steps he would take. When he opened his eyes, he saw Harry watching him. He loosened the top of the hive and gently lifted if off. Two or three bees buzzed out and hovered near Jake's face, then around his shirt. One landed on his newly bald head, and he smiled.

"Hello, ladies," he murmured. "The movers are here. Everything is going to be just fine."

One by one, he loosened and transferred the frames into the flipped brood box with the entrance now at the top, and then he re-placed the lid. He waved at Harry.

"Okay, Stokes. This one is done. Take 'er back!"

Watching Jake's quiet engagement with the bees seemed to have emboldened him, and Harry was calmer then. The six brood boxes were transferred in an hour. They could see that the foraging bees were finding their way through the top entrances into the new hives. Jake slapped his palms together.

"Shit, we're done for the day," he said.

He glanced up at the big pines on the edge of the meadow, which were tossing their shaggy branches in the westerly wind.

"Wind's up! I say we hit the kite beach!"

20

Bee Dance

Bees when on the wing intercommunicate with such surprising rapidity, that telegraphic signals are scarcely more instantaneous.

—L. L. LANGSTROTH

Each member of a honeybee colony is united by a common bond—the pheromone of their mother and queen, a scent that spreads through the hive as a mark of belonging. That lemony pheromone is a constant reassurance to each of the fifty thousand murmuring bees that she is home. Humans have no such obvious interconnections, at least outside of their families. And Jake, of course, did not feel a sense of belonging even within his family home. Instead, home was something he yearned to escape, along with the entire town of Hood River.

During his first weeks in the hospital, he'd drawn the map of Hood River over and over again in his mind. The Heights neighborhood where the locals lived and shopped. Downtown's three square blocks of boutiques, bars, and restaurants, where tourists strolled along, coffees in hand, blocking traffic as they meandered through the crosswalks. The waterfront where locals and visitors converged. This last was Jake's playground—the skate park next to the kite beach and the giant sandbar that spilled out into the Columbia. There he had run with Cheney and felt the lick of wind on his bare skin for what seemed like countless hours. Within those borders he had found some good and some bad, but he had expected to escape it all, if not for Seattle, then at least for Portland. But lying there in his hospital room, his hometown loomed on the horizon as a permanent holding tank. The day his mom brought him home from rehab, the streets were sloppy with slush and a gray ceiling of sky pressed down on the gorge. He felt a cold weight settle in his stomach when they turned in the driveway.

As the months wore on, so did the crushing sense of claustrophobia. He would hear his parents and their neighbors leave for work in the morning and then listen to truck traffic barreling down Tucker Road all day. The same neighbors and his parents returned at the same time each evening. Even when he had been at the rehab center in Portland, he was sure that life ticked along unchanged in this small town. In his mind's eye, buses came and went to May Street Elementary. In summer, the Elks Club banner flew over Jackson Park announcing Summer Family Daze. The pool rang with children's voices and youth soccer games took over the playing fields on weekends. There was a pancake breakfast at the fire station, a line of classic cars in the Fourth of July parade, and the annual Wild Weiner Days and Dachshund Dash. Nothing ever changed around here.

But now, driving through town with Harry, something had shifted. Jake had a strange sense that he had been elsewhere for a long time. He gazed out at the familiar backdrop and felt the glimmer of its beauty.

Harry drove Alice's old pickup, which was smaller and lower to the ground than her new truck. He had rigged a strap around the steering wheel to give Jake better leverage for maneuvering in and out. There was plenty of room in the bed for the chair and Cheney, who jumped in and braced himself against the back window, smiling into the wind as they drove out of the valley and into town.

Jake lay his arm along the open window and leaned his head back. As the truck dropped down into town, the view opened and Jake felt his heart crack wide open. He could see the broad expanse of the Columbia River with whitecaps whipped up by the wind, sunshine on the basalt cliffs to the north, and cotton candy clouds climbing into thunderheads to the west. He closed his eyes, breathing in the yeasty smell of pFriem Family Brewers mixed with the aroma of roasting beans from Dog River Coffee. The wind gusted mightily and buffeted the little truck.

At the waterfront, Jake waited for Harry to grab his chair as he took in the scene in front of him. In the skate park, a kid dropped into the half-pipe and landed on the other side with a clatter. The long green swath of lawn was peopled with wet-suited figures pumping up kites. Out on the sandbar, the wide green river lapped at the sandy shore. Jake had practically lived down here during high school. He and Noah usually hit the skate park right after school and then just chilled on the grass until the sunset. In the summer the light over the ridge-line lingered until almost 10:00 p.m. He had logged hundreds of hours here. For a moment, he felt a deep pang of grief for that past life. But then Harry appeared with his chair, and he put the feeling away.

Cheney strained at his leash as they moved toward the grass, and Jake found himself grateful for the ADA accessible path, which he had never noticed in the old days because he hadn't had to. As he pushed his way along, he could feel people looking at him and the chair. If they met his eyes, they looked away like they were embarrassed. It felt like everyone was staring. Jake felt suddenly naked. Maybe this was too much exposure—going to the waterfront for the first time since his accident.

But then he looked at Harry, who was scanning the crowd of kite-boarders, and noticed how pale he was. He hadn't said much on the ride down either. Jake could see beads of sweat standing out on Harry's forehead, and it occurred to him that it was he who suggested they look for Harry's kiteboarding buddy, not Harry himself.

"You know, Yogi might not even be here. So, we can head back, you know, like, whenever," Harry said.

His voice squeaked with anxiety, and Jake felt his own worry diminish with a rush of empathy. Poor Stokes, he thought. He tipped back and balanced on his back wheels, smiling at Harry.

"It's cool," he said. "Let's just hang for a bit."

They moved through the kiters, and Jake unleashed Cheney, who raced toward the sandbar. Jake watched the big dog belly-flop into the channel and then look back for his boy. His throat tightened as the dog sprinted back, sprayed him with river water and kisses, and ran out and away again. He tore along the water's edge, barking and snapping at seagulls. Jake's sadness lightened a bit at his dog's joy. He closed his eyes and smelled the river, felt the warm wind on his bare skin.

"Shit!" Harry whispered.

His eyes were locked on a big dude striding up the grass in a dripping wetsuit, his long hair slicked back. The guy grinned hugely and punched Harry in the shoulder.

"My man! The conditions are perfect, dude. Gonna be epic!"

He looked down at Jake, and the wattage of his smile increased even further.

"Howzit going, brother?" He held out a meaty fist. "I'm Yogi."

Jake bumped the guy's fist. "Jake."

"Good to meet you, brother. Harry is gonna love this shit, aren't you, Harry?"

Jake recognized the quiet terror in his new friend's eyes, but Yogi did not seem to notice.

The big man clapped his hands together. "It's gonna be sick out there! Okay, here's what we're doing today. Equipment intro and kite basics. C'mon. I've got it all set up."

Yogi strode away from the sidewalk toward a cluster of adolescent boys and one girl slouching around a pile of gear on the grass, skinny arms crossed over their chests against the chill of the wind. Jake followed Harry after confirming the ground was navigable. The children stared wordlessly at Jake's chair and his bald head. Then they looked at Yogi.

"Okay! Listen up, kidlets! Rule number one: This is *not* a kite lesson. I am *not* an instructor. I'm simply standing around talking about kiteboarding and you happened to be nearby. Any of you tell your parents I gave you a lesson, I'll kick your little butts. Consider this a public service announcement, all right? All right, Tommy?"

He turned to the closest boy, a pale redhead who looked like he weighed less than Cheney.

"Uh. Yeah. Right, Yogi. It's not a kite lesson," he said in a soft soprano.

"Great. Okay. Rule number two: Know your equipment."

The children leaned in as Yogi showed them the gear: wetsuit, helmet, impact vest, harness, bar, lines, board, and the banana-shaped kite. He talked about how the equipment worked together, showed them the safety releases, and explained the need to take care of your gear. That meant stowing it properly when you weren't using it and not leaving it out in the sun. He unrolled the kite, which was Pepto Bismol pink, and the kids took turns at the pump, their skinny arms going up and down, until all the struts were inflated. Yogi flipped it over so it was facing into the wind and weighed it down with the board to keep it in place.

"Nice job!" he said, slapping his palms together. "Good. Okay. Rule number three: Don't be a douche nozzle on the beach!"

He talked about the wind window, the power of the kite, safe launching and landing, and beach etiquette. He explained where to stand when you were out among the kites on the sandbar and how to be aware of people around you. He told them how important it was to look out for other kiters for safety. The kids hung on to every word.

"What's rule number three?"

"Don't be a douche nozzle on the beach!"

"Right on!"

The girl raised her hand.

"Autumn?"

"What happens if the kite crashes in the water?"

"You gotta relaunch the dang thing," Yogi said. "There's no one right way. Depends on the wind and the water current. One thing is sure, though. Your attitude is everything. If you want that baby to fly, you gotta believe you can make it happen. Make sense?"

The kids nodded, and Yogi grinned.

"Great! Now, you pip-squeaks are too skinny to try this out yet. But Harry Stokes here is going for it!"

He grabbed Harry by the shoulders and shook him. Jake saw Harry's face turn gray.

"We're going to practice launching and landing out on the sandbar. You can come watch, but again, what's rule number one? This isn't a—"

"Kite lesson!" the kids shouted.

"Tommy, you take the kite. Autumn, you grab the bar and lines. The rest of you, follow and get that kite rigged. Harry, get your gear on," he said.

The little crowd took off running, and Yogi picked up the kiteboard and followed them. Harry struggled into the wetsuit, which was far too big for him, being Yogi-size. It sagged in the crotch and bagged around his neck. He pulled on his helmet, his face beaded with sweat, and handed the truck keys to Jake, mumbling, "I don't think . . . Should be back pretty . . . If I . . ."

"Hey, Harry," Jake said. "Breathe, man."

Harry met Jake's eyes, swallowed, and nodded.

From the water's edge, Yogi yelled, "Get yer stoke on, Stokes!" and laughed at his own joke.

Jake watched his friend walk toward the sandbar, his shoulders slumped and his eyes trained on his feet, looking like he was headed to jail. Jake could hear Yogi's encouraging voice over the sound of the wind. He had enthusiasm enough for the two of them, Jake thought. They crossed the channel to the sandbar, and then Jake couldn't hear Yogi anymore.

The spring sunshine warmed his head and shoulders as he looked out at the river. The park was not as crowded as it would be in the summer. About two dozen kites dotted the sandbar awaiting launch, and a handful of windsurfing sails flashed out in the white caps. A barge chugged into mid-channel and blasted a warning as kiteboarders and windsurfers sailed out of its path.

Jake felt an unexpected ease settle over him. No one was staring at him, not really. Sure, people noticed the chair, but so what? That was fine. He closed his eyes and felt the sun heating up his T-shirt. He heard a familiar hum and looked down at the lawn in front of him. A honeybee landed on a cluster of dandelions and crawled through the great puffs of pollen, joined soon by others. One landed on Jake's chest and crawled around, perhaps mistaking his orange T-shirt for a giant blossom, and then returned to the dandelions.

"Hello, there, ladies," Jake murmured.

He scanned the sandbar and saw Cheney charge up to Harry and Yogi and put his paws on Harry's chest. Then the big dog put his nose to the ground and made his way back across the channel and up the grass. He threw himself at Jake's feet, panting and smiling.

Jake stroked his broad head. "Good boy, Cheney."

The big dog dropped his chin onto his paws and fell asleep.

Jake heard the clatter of a skateboard and a prepubescent boy doing a Tarzan call. But it didn't make him feel sad. He felt almost carefree, sitting in a favorite old spot with Cheney. Sunshine, wind, honeybees, and a snoring dog. He tried to put his finger on how he was feeling and was surprised to name the word. He felt happy. Yes, he just felt content to be sitting there in the sun by the river with his dog on a windy weekday. It was just fine.

He watched the bees work the dandelions, and his mind returned to what he had been reading that morning about the bee waggle—that strange series of spins and booty shaking that the forager bees performed to demonstrate the location and quality of a good nectar cache. The better the source, the more enthusiastic the dance. The others would replicate it until they had learned it by heart—how far away, at what angle to the sun, which direction, and how robust. That was all pretty amazing.

The bee waggle had made him think of "Wiggle Waggle," the piece that his jazz sextet had performed at state his junior year. He and Noah were the brass, which played the opening riffs and short punctuations. They were flawless that day—tight and punchy—and they took first place. More than the award, he remembered the way it all felt—the valves under his fingers, the pressure of the mouthpiece against his lips, the regulation of aperture. The other day he had taken his trumpet out of the case and held it in his hands. He raised it to his mouth, but was overwhelmed and couldn't play, so he had put it away again. He felt a deep longing for it now. Maybe he would pull it out when he got back to Alice's and mess around a little. Perhaps he could just run his scales. He wondered what the bees would think if he played "Wiggle Waggle" for them.

Jake took a swig from his water bottle and scanned the sandbar. He could see Harry and the kids gathered around the big pink kite at the north end of the large sweep of sand. He heard a girl laugh, and he glanced back at a group of teenagers standing behind him. He recognized some of them from school. They were all girls and just one guy. One of the girls was Megan Shine's little sister. What was her name? Michelle? She was blond and had the same cheerleader body as her sister. The boy had a Husky on a leash. Michelle leaned over to pet the dog, which was staring in Jake's direction. Cheney bolted upright, growling, and ran straight for it.

"Oh, shit!" Jake muttered. He released the brake on his chair and followed.

"Cheney!" he yelled. "Come, buddy!"

The two dogs stood nose to nose, doing a stiff-legged dance with their tails held high. Cheney offered a deep play bow and then tore off toward the water. The Husky yanked her leash out of the boy's hand and bounded after Cheney. The boy ran after her, calling, "Yuki, come! Yuki! Bad dog!"

Jake sighed and watched them go. He draped Cheney's leash around his shoulders.

"They'll be back," he said to no one in particular.

He could feel the girls staring at him from behind their sunglasses, and he told himself it didn't matter.

"Landon is hilarious," Michelle said, giggling. "I mean, Yuki runs away every five minutes."

Jake moved back toward his spot on the grass.

"Hey! Um, did you go to HRV?" a voice said. A girl with short black hair detached herself from the group. She took a step toward Jake and pushed her sunglasses up on top of her head. She wore a black T-shirt, cutoff jean shorts, and red Chuck Taylors. Her skin was pale, and under her dark hair was a pair of intense green eyes.

"Yeah. Class of 2013," Jake said.

The girl stepped closer and shoved her hands in her back pockets. She slouched and crossed one ankle over the other. She did not look like a cheerleader. Not one bit, and Jake couldn't take his eyes off her—her lanky Bugs Bunny arms and legs, her messy hair, and those green eyes.

"I think I sat in front of you in band?" she said. "I was in the clarinet section. I remember you and your friend, the big one with the curly hair?"

"Katz. Noah Katz," Jake said. "Yeah, Schaffer's class."

"You guys were trouble, huh? I was there that day you poured milk into Matt Swenson's tuba," she said.

Jake's smile disappeared. That had seemed funny at the time. He looked away. "Yeah, well. We were being idiots. Stupid shit."

Her cheeks flushed red. "Sorry! I didn't mean to—"

"Don't worry about it," Jake said, smiling. "I'm the idiot. Not you."

She smiled back at him, her cheeks still red, and her green eyes seemed to darken. He had a faint memory of her from band class. She'd been a freshman. Clarinet. Yes, definitely. Her hair had been longer then.

A brown blur flashed between them, and Cheney shook from head to tail, flinging sand as he wriggled from his big ears down to his rump. The girl squealed.

"Beast!" Jake yelled, throwing his hands up. "Sorry."

The girl laughed and wiped her face with her arm. "It's okay. I was sandy already. He's sweet. What's his name?"

She knelt next to the big dog, who rolled over and offered her his sandy belly.

"Cheney. He's a lover, not a fighter," Jake said.

The boy called Landon stalked back up the lawn with the Husky straining against her leash. Cheney jumped up, whining, and Jake grabbed him by the collar.

"Dude! You know there's a leash law down here, right?" the boy said, glaring at Jake.

"Jesus, Landon," one of the girls muttered.

"Cheney, sit," Jake said, and Cheney sat. He nodded at the Husky. "Pretty dog," he offered. "Looks like they want to be buddies."

"This is a pedigree Alaskan Husky," the boy spat. "She's going to breed champion sled dogs. Not get knocked up by a fucking beach mutt."

"Hey, dude," Jake said, and held his hands up. "Why don't you take it down a notch?"

There was a loud hissing noise as someone deflated a kite. Yuki jumped at the sound and took off toward the water, trailing her leash. The girls laughed as Landon pursued his dog. Jake let go of Cheney's collar and let his dog join the chase.

"Whoops," he said, and the green-eyed girl laughed.

"Hey, Amri!" one of the girls called. "We're going. You want a ride or not?"

"Yeah! Wait for me!" she said.

She turned back to Jake. "Well. Um. Nice to see you again. It's Jake, right?"

He nodded. "Good memory," he said. "Amri?"

"Short for Amrita." She rolled her eyes and pushed a hand through her short hair. "My mom and dad are old hippies."

Jake leaned back in his chair and smiled at her. "I think it's a nice name."

Her cheeks flushed again.

"Amri! Let's go!" her friend called.

"Well. See you around," she said.

"See you around," Jake said.

She ran to catch up with her friends, waved at him over her shoulder, and then she was gone. Jake turned back to the water. He saw the bees in the dandelions. He saw Cheney sprinting back up the lawn. He saw Yogi's pink kite high in the air over the water. He thought of Amri's green eyes, which grew dark when she smiled.

21

REQUEENING

If they cannot find [the queen], they return desolate
home, and by their sorrowful tones reveal their deep
sense of so deplorable a calamity. Their note at such
times, more especially when they first realize their loss,
is of a peculiarly mournful character; it sounds somewhat like a succession of wailings on the minor key.

—L. L. LANGSTROTH

Alice stared at Nancy like she was speaking a foreign language. Behind her purple-framed glasses, her friend's large brown eyes blinked
under blue eye shadow and thick mascara. Had Nancy been wearing the same makeup since high school? Alice wondered.

She'd only been half listening to Nancy chattering away across the
table from her in the conference room as they stuffed envelopes
for the county-wide noxious-weed mailing.

"Really putting our education to use here," Alice had joked, irked
that this job had fallen on her.

The intern was working on some problem with the servers, and
Debi Jeffreys, the office manager, claimed she didn't have room on her
small desk for the mailing job. Last year she filed a workers' comp
claim because she said the filing cabinets were not ergonomically correct and caused her neck pain. Since then the unspoken rule was
whatever Debi wanted, Debi got.

Rich Carlson, who was in charge of all annual grant money from the state, said the mailing had to be posted by midnight to qualify for funding. Alice was not surprised that Rich would micro-manage the mailing without actually helping out, and annoyed that he had waited until the last minute.

"Teamwork! That's what holds this place together," Rich had said, dropping a large box on the table with a thunk.

Alice glowered at his back. The memory of their conversation about her retirement plan was still fresh in her mind.

"Well, I guess old Rich isn't on the team," she said, smirking at Nancy and reaching for a stack of fliers.

"Well, Alice, I'm sure Mr. Carlson has important things going on today."

Alice snorted, but Nancy didn't crack a smile.

"Right!" Alice said. "I'm sure he's in his office right now making a color-coded spreadsheet of his spreadsheets."

Their running joke was how Rich filled up his time without really doing anything. He buzzed around the office, checking up on everyone else but serving no clear function. Everyone knew he collected a level-one salary with a 5 percent annual raise and a yearly bonus built in. Alice hadn't had a raise in four years.

"Sorry, Alice," Bill had said at her annual review in March, wagging his big head and frowning. "The recession, you know. Our budget is frozen. I'd do it if I could. You are invaluable to us."

". . . You don't know what pressures the managers might be under, Alice," Nancy was saying. "They do a lot of work we don't see— important work."

Alice stared. Was she serious?

"Hey, Nance. Hello? That you in there?" Alice knocked on the table. "Invasion of the body snatchers?"

Nancy set her mouth in a prim line and shoved a flier in an envelope, moistened it with a sponge, and smoothed it shut. "I just think you should show a little respect," she said flatly.

Alice sat back in her chair and gave a short laugh. "Well, aren't you a little suck-up?" she said.

Rich banged through the door with another box.

"Thank you, ladies!" he sang out. "Oh, and take a break at ten thirty. We'll need the room for the meeting."

"What meeting?" Alice asked.

"Quarterly all-staff. Don't you read your email, Alice?" he scolded in a teacher voice, wagging a finger at her.

He beamed at Nancy. "I'm sure Nancy read about the meeting."

Alice watched her friend's face twist into a girlish smile as Rich left the room.

"Wow. You are a first-class ass-kisser, Nance."

Nancy flushed. "You think you know everything," she hissed. She jerked herself up out of her chair and left.

Alice leaned back and stared at a brown stain on the ceiling. It was the shape of Florida and had been there the day she interviewed for this job almost twenty years ago. She had been so excited to get hired then. But now she just felt tired. She picked up another flier, this time reading it as she folded it.

"Hood River County Annual Noxious-Weed Program!" it declared, and laid out the dangers of the weed problem: choking wetlands, strangling native plants, harming wildlife. A cartoon of a desperate-looking quail had been drawn by a summer intern about six years ago. They used the same copy every year.

At the bottom of the page, Alice saw a new line: "SupraGro is a proud sponsor of the Hood River County Noxious-Weed Program." Her breath caught. She took a photo of it and texted it to Stan.

"Read the bottom," she wrote.

The extension service's tests on Alice's dead hives had shown a clear saturation of chemicals that matched SupraGro. But the noxious-weed program raised the stakes considerably. This went beyond spraying the orchards, which was bad enough. It was a county-wide project that covered hundreds of square miles and would start at the beginning of summer. It meant that SupraGro's pesticides would be sprayed on every road, park, school, empty lot, and culvert in the entire county. It might kill the noxious weeds, but it would also poison the wild clover, dandelions, asters, and sunflowers. The runoff would then drain from the ditches into the creeks and the rivers until it had contaminated the entire watershed of the Columbia River Gorge.

People began to trickle into the room for the meeting.

Alice's phone buzzed. Stan had texted back: "Lynchpin! Filing joint lawsuit with PDX Riverkeeper. Keep you posted. Thanks!"

That was something. The tightness in her chest eased, and she felt a sliver of hope open up.

Bill lumbered into the room, hitching up his slacks and tugging on his polo shirt before lowering himself into a chair. Nancy slipped in and sat near the front. Bill cleared his throat.

"Thanks, everyone, for making room in your schedules today. This won't take long. Just one or two pieces of business for the quarter."

He put on his reading glasses.

"The first is just a reminder that the new employee wellness plan goes into effect as of June first, so expect to see that in your email soon. It doesn't cost you anything extra, but it includes add-ons like smoking cessation, nutrition counseling, and cardiac health tips."

Bill rattled off a customer service email address and phone number in case anyone had questions about the wellness program. Then he pushed the paper away and leaned back. His chair squeaked, and he chuckled as he peered out from under his thick eyebrows.

"This second announcement won't surprise many of you," he said. "As you know, I've been with the county for almost thirty-five years now. I've watched it grow, and I've taken a great amount of pride in leading my team in shaping Hood River's future. We've grown from a little orchard town nobody heard of to a destination for international tourism and tech business! I'm proud of that. I'm proud of you people."

He gestured out at the room with his plump hands and then curled them into fists on the tabletop. There was scattered applause.

"Thank you," he said. "But it really was all your hard work. I just steered the ship." He paused. "However, all good things must end."

Alice's heart raced. Was this it? She couldn't believe it was finally happening. Why hadn't he given her any warning? Had she missed an email?

"The wife has been after me to retire, and the time has come. I'll be officially leaving the county at the end of this month, at the end of our fiscal year."

Alice sat up straight, and now everyone was clapping.

"Thank you! Thanks, everyone," Bill said. "Really. You are too kind. Now, any transition takes some time. And I want you to know that I'll be leaving you in good hands."

He glanced toward Alice and then away.

Her face flushed. Her breathing accelerated. It had been a long time coming, that was certain. She'd had years to think about how she would manage the department once she was in charge. For now, she would just keep it simple. Be gracious and say thank you.

". . . Leadership in place that is going to carry you into the years ahead and keep Hood River County pointed in the right direction," Bill was saying.

Debi Jeffreys nudged her, and others began to murmur.

"I'll be working hard to help prepare her to step in. But I know she'll have no trouble filling my shoes. It is with great pleasure that I introduce your new interim director—Nancy Gates!"

Bill banged his big hands together and beamed at Nancy. There was a pause, and then other people joined in, looking at Alice and then at Nancy. Nancy giggled and gave a little wave. Alice struggled to catch her breath. Her ears rang.

"Unbelievable," Debi muttered. "Alice, I'm so sorry."

Bill was wrapping things up.

". . . Want you to know I will be here to answer any questions during this month of transition. My door is always open!"

He pushed himself away from the table and stood. There was more clapping. Alice saw Nancy, in her mind's eye, coming out of Bill's office. She also saw what she had refused to acknowledge: Bill's hand on Nancy's ass. The day of the SupraGro meeting when the two of them had disappeared hadn't been the first time Alice had been unable to find both of them.

Alice waited for everyone to leave. Jim Murphy shrugged and shook his head at her as he passed. Others looked at her like they wanted to say something but didn't. When the room was empty, she rose and went back to her desk. Nancy was sitting with her shoulders back and her eyes on her monitor.

"Mr. Carlson would like to see you in his office, Alice," she said, not looking up.

Alice ignored her and knocked on Bill's door.

"Mr. Chenowith went to early lunch," Nancy said, her mouth in a prim line. "You can leave a message with me if you want."

Alice faced her, and Nancy's bravado melted under her gaze. What was most surprising was not Nancy's betrayal, Alice realized, but her own failure to see it coming. Nancy had copied off her Spanish tests in high school. She had let Alice shoulder the workload as Bill did less and less. She came in late, left early, and spent hours circulating the office with a cup of coffee, her tinkling laugh in all corners, gathering gossip. She had something on everyone. Nancy had collected dirt like treasure and tucked it away for later. Alice shook her head, all the pieces falling into place.

"You're a perfect fit, Nance," she said.

Nancy's face quivered, and she gave a weak smile. "Thanks, Alice. I mean, I'm sure you're disappointed—"

"No, you're perfect. You're a suck-up and a do-nothing," she said.

She grabbed her bag and headed for the front door. As she passed the reception desk, Debi gave her a warning look and said, "Carlson's looking for you."

Alice kept walking toward the exit. Like hell she was going to talk to Rich Carlson right then.

As if summoned, he leaned out of his office and smiled at her, his yellow tooth poking out from under his thin upper lip.

"Just the person I was looking for! Please come in."

Alice sighed, walked into his office, and shuddered as he closed the door behind her.

"Sit! Please!" he said.

He tugged at his suit jacket and pulled his chair forward, leaning his elbows on the desk.

"Now, Alice. I'm sure you were somewhat surprised by Bill's announcement today. Perhaps a little disappointed, hmmm?" He made a frowny face, like Alice was a kid who'd just dropped her ice cream.

"Well, no sense in dwelling on it. Your turn will come when the time is right. Bill made his choice, and I'm sure Nancy will do an excellent job, especially with you on board to support her like you've supported Bill so well."

Alice said nothing. She just watched Rich as if from far away.

Rich flipped open a file folder on his desk. "Now, it's no secret that Bill talked about your own candidacy at one time."

Alice was silent.

"And we do appreciate your work. So we'd like to give you a promotion! I've got a new contract here that will go into effect at the start of next month. You will be the planning department senior staff manager, and that gives you a fifteen percent raise! Nothing to sneeze at, is it?"

He pushed the paper across the desk at her, but Alice didn't look at it.

"Senior staff manager?" she said. "Who would I be managing? Who's replacing Nancy?"

Rich grimaced in an attempt to smile. He rubbed his skinny hands together. The sound of his dry skin made Alice flinch.

"Well, we won't be filling the position right away. As part of the reorganization, that gives us the extra money for your raise."

"I see. So you want me to do my job and Nancy's job for fifteen percent more? Is that right?"

Rich looked annoyed and sat back. "That's sort of a glass-half-empty way of looking at it, Alice. Think about the leadership opportunity you're gaining here."

Alice laughed. "What, to lead myself? I'm already doing that, Richard."

Rich didn't like being laughed at. He also didn't like being called Richard, and Alice knew it. He once told her that only his mother called him Richard. He leaned forward again and trained his beady eyes on hers.

"Look, Alice. Quite frankly, you haven't exactly been a team player lately," he said.

He flipped open another file and fanned its contents across the desk. Alice saw the newspaper article and the photo with Stan. She saw emails from Nancy. A cursory glance showed she'd been documenting Alice's remarks and jokes about their director and the other administration members.

Rich sat back in his chair, smiling smugly and tenting his fingers.

"I'm sure you can see how it looks from our point of view," he murmured. "It's really in your best interest to play nice, Alice. You're going to have to work with Nancy, like it or not, and Bill too."

"What do you mean?" she asked. "Bill is retiring."

Rich shook his head, pressing his lips together. "Bill is retiring from the *county*," he said. "He'll be working with us as an outside consultant. For SupraGro."

Alice looked at Rich's receding hairline and the naked edges of his scalp. Bits of dandruff dusted the dark polyester of his shoulders. She looked past him and out the window toward the water. She recalled that day in fourth grade, when she'd said she wanted to be a farmer and the class had laughed. Miss Tooksbury had gotten married and moved to Portland when Alice was in the sixth grade. She'd like to tell her teacher that it wasn't true—you couldn't be whatever you wanted. Life was a whole lot more complicated than that. But she also knew now, with just as much certainty, that you couldn't be whatever other people wanted you to be either.

She pushed the contract back at Rich.

"No thanks," she said, and stood, slinging her bag over her shoulder.

He looked annoyed. "Come on, Alice. This is a great offer. We both know you aren't going to get more than this."

"No, I won't," Alice said. "You're right."

"Well, shall we get this over with, then?" He held out a pen.

"Yes, let's," she said. "I quit."

For once Rich Carlson was speechless. Alice left his door open and walked out of the Hood River County building into the May sunshine.

Alice Holtzman had never quit anything in her life. She was reliable, steady, and loyal. Capable Alice. But now she was walking out, just like that. She felt a stab of joy as she headed down Oak Street. She passed the John Deere shop where she had first met Buddy. She passed the bank, where her father had taken her to open a checking account when she got her first job. There was the library and across the street, Waucoma Bookstore. Hood River had been her home for forty-four years. She owed something to this place.

She must have looked so expectant when she walked into the Watershed Alliance offices that the receptionist assumed she was there for the meeting and ushered her into the conference room.

Stan was standing in front of a whiteboard, gesturing with a dry-erase marker.

". . . File a motion to cease and desist later this afternoon," he was saying to a group of about ten people. He stopped when he saw Alice, and smiled.

"Excuse me for a moment," he said to the group, and crossed the room to her.

"Hi!" His smile dimmed when he reached her, and his brow furrowed. "Everything okay?"

"Yeah, I just wanted to come by and see if there was anything I could do to help."

Stan's face relaxed. "That last bit was really key. We've got Portland Riverkeeper here, the organic growers association, and the outdoor school people."

He turned to the group. "Everyone, this is Alice Holtzman, from the county planning department. I think most of you know her?" Stan said.

Alice nodded at the men and women clustered around the table.

"I don't want to interrupt," she said. "But let me know if there is anything else I can do," she said to Stan. She moved toward the door.

"Actually, we were just looking at a map of the valley," Stan said. "You know most of the orchardists, don't you?"

She nodded and moved toward the map.

"We're trying to figure out where they'll start spraying. We know the county puts them on a schedule, and that it is wind-dependent. Do you have any idea how they decide?" Stan said.

Alice nodded. The permits came through her department, she said.

"Smaller outfits will do their own spraying and can start anytime after April fifteenth," she said, thinking of Doug Ransom. "But the larger orchardists have to file a permit with the county and note their preferred day. We make a schedule dependent on the wind forecast."

People nodded, murmuring.

"Who do they usually start with?" Stan asked.

"It changes from year to year," Alice said, and unslung her bag from her shoulder.

"Why don't we look it up?" she said, pulling her laptop from her bag.

She logged into the system and clicked through to the spray schedule. There it was, neatly color-coded and organized by acreage. Because it was one of Nancy's few tasks, it gave Alice extra pleasure to capture the file and email it to herself, cc'ing Stan.

"It's all there," she said, logging out of the system. "Dates, times, and addresses."

Stan pulled it up on his computer, and those sitting closest to him leaned in.

"They're starting two weeks from tomorrow," he said. "With Randy Osaka's orchard in Odell. That's one of the biggest."

He looked up, triumphant. "We can be ready by then, can't we?"

The group nodded, murmuring in agreement.

"Let's get organized," he said. "Starting with the master task list—legal, community outreach, and media."

Alice rose and tugged her computer bag over her shoulder. "I'll let you get to it," she said, and moved to leave.

"Back to work?" Stan asked, walking her to the door.

"No. Actually, I just quit!" she said with a laugh.

"Wow! Sounds like there's a story there?" Stan said, cocking his head. "You happy about it?"

"Never been happier," Alice said.

"Well, don't rush off, then. We can use your help."

She was glad to stay. She cataloged a list of the orchardists she knew, ranked in order of those who might be receptive to the group's message. Their goal was to force the county to abandon the SupraGro contract and revert to one of many less toxic herbicides approved by the local coalition, which was made up of the Hood River Watershed Alliance, Portland Riverkeeper, the outdoor school, the organic growers' group, and a long list of residents, including doctors and nurses from around the valley. Alice told them about the beekeeping group's petition. She figured she could talk them into joining the fight.

Stan asked her if she'd be willing to approach some of the orchardists. Alice agreed, noticing that at least three of them were also beekeepers and had been at the meeting when she spoke. She was sure they would listen. Others would be tougher, but she would start tomorrow, dropping in on them and talking to them face-to-face. She knew that when needed, she would call upon the memory of her generous father, whom everyone had loved.

She looked at Stan and these other people who were working together to protect this lovely place they all called home. She thought of her little house in the dell, where Jake and Harry would be waiting for her. They were her—what were they? "Employees" wasn't the right word. Jake had called himself her apprentice. Friends, she settled on. They were her friends. Her funny, bumbling, and inspiring young friends. Alice Island, it appeared, could have regular visitors when the drawbridge was down. She thought of them as she drove south toward the mountain, toward the dell, toward the bees, and toward home.

· 22 ·

Swarm Warning

From these considerations, it is evident that swarming, so far from being the forced or unnatural event which some imagine, is one, which could not possibly be dispensed with, in a state of nature.

—L. L. LANGSTROTH

Harry Stokes was a man transformed. At the dinner table Alice observed that his customary reticence and stammering had disappeared as he evangelized about his newfound religion of kiteboarding. Usually the first to finish his food—bent over his plate and shoveling with an eye out for seconds—he now let his dinner grow cold as he sketched the physics of kiteboarding on a napkin. He explained the wind window, the layout of the kite, the power of the lines, and the movement of the board across the water. To Harry, it was nothing short of magical, she could see.

Alice watched him, amused, this usually bumbling young man who'd found confidence in such an unlikely place. Jake smiled at him and shook his head. Harry was as surprised as they were. He relayed how his hands had been shaking as he walked away from Jake and out onto the sandbar behind Yogi.

"I thought I was going to hurl, dude!"

Jake laughed and banged his fist on the table. Alice frowned, and Harry ducked his head.

"Sorry, Alice! But man, I didn't want to embarrass myself in front of all those kids. Yogi said he can have me staying upwind and tacking in two more sessions," he told them, beaming. "He said I'm a fast learner."

Alice, who had watched the kiteboarding craze unfold in recent years, said, "Well, I think you're all nuts. Don't you get all tangled up out there? It looks like chaos."

Harry grinned. "Yeah, it is sort of chaotic. But you just have to hold your line. And people are cool about making room for newbies. It's a generous crowd."

Alice noted that she had never heard so many words come tumbling out of Harry's mouth at once.

"Don't let me dampen your enthusiasm, Harry. I just don't want to call your mom when you break a leg," she teased.

Harry's smile dimmed.

"Hey! I was just kidding. I'm not the fun police."

Harry shrugged. "No. It's just that I haven't called her in a while. I missed her birthday last week. I feel bad, but I haven't bought a phone yet, and there aren't any pay phones in the valley."

Alice sighed with exasperation and scraped her chair back from the table. She reached across the kitchen counter and plunked the cordless phone down in front of him.

"Call your mother, Mr. Stokes. Any time. Consider it an employee benefit. That thing works out in the barn too."

She stood with her plate and silverware and glanced down at Jake. "You might want to call your mother too, Jake."

She set her dishes in the sink. "Thanks for dinner, guys. I've got some work to do, so you boys will have to excuse me."

In her bedroom, Alice took off her shoes and lay on the bed. The tension of the day had settled into her shoulders, and her head pounded.

She hadn't said anything to Jake or Harry about quitting her job. It hadn't been the right time, with Harry over the moon about kiteboarding and both of them so excited about the hives—especially Jake, who had completed the transfer almost on his own. She could see how much it meant to him. And Harry was proud of how he'd figured out how to reverse the brood boxes.

They had grown on her, those two. But the hive expansion, the plan for planting an orchard—that all seemed impossible right now. First she had to find a new job, which, in a town this size, would be no easy feat. She didn't regret walking out of Rich Carlson's office. Not one bit. But the county job had been a bridge to her dreams. Now that she'd burned it, she needed to build something new. She wouldn't be able to afford to keep Harry on, which was a shame. Maybe she could let Jake stay for a while.

Alice sat up, opened her laptop, and tried to log into the county system. Her access was denied, and she smiled grimly. Rich must have finally called tech support. At least she'd had time to get in and download the spraying schedule for Stan's group.

She looked at the list of farms she'd pledged to visit and divided them up by address over the next fourteen days. They had two weeks from tomorrow before the spraying began. That was a lot of ground to cover. But she was ready for it. Boy was she ever. Her face burned when she thought about Bill, about Nancy, about Rich.

She scrolled through the other cache of information, which had come to her in such a surprising turn after the meeting at the watershed offices.

Stan had walked her outside. They stood on the sidewalk in the spring sunshine. Stan clasped his hands behind his back and smiled down at her. Alice noticed again that he had nice eyes.

"We really appreciate your help, Alice. We have a really strong case. That county info was a huge help. Huge! The noxious-weed program on top of the orchardists network is a double whammy. Parks, schools, public roadways. Every parent in this town is going to listen now. I don't know how to thank you."

Alice shifted her computer bag higher on her shoulder. "Buy me a beer at pFriem when this is over, how about?" she said.

"You're on," he said, smiling.

Walking away, she was happy, she realized, happier than she'd been in months. Quitting her job made her feel free, reckless, and excited. She'd screwed up her pension and references by walking out. So what? She would worry about that later. She'd always been so careful, the reliable one, such a worker bee. Where had that gotten her? For once, she was going to enjoy the moment.

Alice walked toward the county parking lot, hoping she wouldn't run into any of her coworkers. It was just before 2 p.m. and the lot was still full. She walked swiftly to her blue pickup, opened the door, and threw her bag across the seat.

As she moved to climb in, she felt a hand tap her elbow. The blood rushed into her ears, and she wheeled around to face Rich Carlson and whatever venom he was going to throw at her this time. But it wasn't Rich. It was the intern, the young carrot-haired student from OSU. He jumped back from Alice with his hands up.

"Oh! I'm s-sorry, Ms. Holtzman! I didn't mean to startle you," he stammered, and reddened.

"Jesus, Casey!" she said, putting her hands on her knees and lowering her head, breathing deeply. "You gave me a heart attack."

"Sorry! I'm sorry! I just—well, I've been waiting for you. I know you quit today. Everyone was talking about it. Everyone heard. We're all on your side. I mean, they gave Nancy your job and everything—"

Alice raised her head and looked at him, stone-faced, and he reddened again.

"I know it's none of my business. It's just— I— You were always so nice to me—"

Alice waved a hand. "No, it's fine. It's just been a rough day. Now, what can I do for you? Do you need me to sign your paperwork or something? Nancy can do that now since she is interim director. You won't have any trouble finding old Nance, I'm sure."

Casey cringed. "No, I don't need anything. I just— I wanted to warn you."

Alice frowned at him. "Warn me? What do you mean?"

Casey took a deep breath and spoke in a rush. "I overheard Mr. Carlson talking about you in the server room." He looked at the pavement. "I wasn't trying to eavesdrop or anything. I was in the back working on the servers, and he came in and didn't see me. By the time I heard what he was saying, I figured it was better to just stay quiet until he was gone."

Her stomach somersaulted. She blinked and saw Rich making a frowny face at her across his desk.

"Tell me," she said.

"He said you were a—" The young man reddened. "He was telling someone that it was personal, you quitting, that they really needed to stick it to you. He said he knew just what would get to you. It didn't make any sense to me, but I figured it would make sense to you. It was about Evangelina Ryan."

When Casey said Evangelina's name, Alice went cold, like someone had poured ice water over her. Evangelina. She stood very still as Casey told her the rest of what he had heard despicable Rich say about Bud's sweet sister-in-law, Evangelina.

"Thank you, Casey. I really appreciate the information. I'm not going to explain it to you. I think it's better that you don't know the details."

He nodded.

"There's one more thing," he said, and held up a small black object in his freckled fingers. It was a jump drive.

"These are all the documents outlining the county's agreement with SupraGro. They had me transfer everything from Mr. Chenowith's computer to Nancy's today, and, well, I made a copy. I saw your picture in the paper with the watershed people, and I thought, I don't know, maybe someone should look at this."

Alice chuckled. "Well! Hood River's Edward Snowden!"

Then, her face somber, she said, "Thank you, Casey. If anyone finds out I have it, I'll say I took it myself. I owe you one, kid."

Casey nodded and disappeared into the building.

"Never a dull moment at the Hood River County Planning Department," Alice muttered as she climbed into her truck.

Now, sitting in her room, she scanned the master file and noted what documents might be useful to Stan's group. Certainly, the details of the SupraGro contract and the authors of their so-called scientific study. They must have paid a pretty penny for the skewed data collected there. Then there were the details of Bill's retirement package, seven figures, and his annual consulting fee, which was more than Alice had made in the last five years put together. Jesus. She thought of Bill's eternal nag about the tight budget. She shut the laptop. She would begin talking to the orchardists tomorrow, starting with her neighbor Doug Ransom. Good old Doug. He would listen.

But first, this thing with Evangelina.

She wished she could have this conversation with Bud's parents, instead of with Ron. It would be so much easier, despite the fact that Alice had not contacted them in over a year. But no, it was Ron she needed to talk to about the danger to his wife.

She remembered Evangelina the day of Bud's funeral. The Ryans were Catholic, so Buddy's service was at Sacred Heart. Alice sat with Bud's parents in the front. Evangelina, Ron, and their kids sat in the pew behind. At the cemetery, Evangelina moved close and put her arm around Alice's waist. It was such a small gesture, but Alice felt immensely comforted as she leaned into her friend's arm. At the rowdy, crowded Ryan family events, it was always Evangelina who drew her in. They enjoyed each other's company, although there were significant gaps between Evangelina's English and Alice's high school Spanish. But in that moment, when there was no language for such loss, Evangelina must have understood better than anyone else how Alice felt losing her life partner too soon. She might have asked herself the same torturing questions Alice did: What was the last thing I said to him? Did I kiss him goodbye before he left for that last trip? Did I tell him I loved him? Was it enough?

And yet Alice felt her own grief eclipsed by the sorrow of Bud's elderly parents. Parents shouldn't have to bury their children. Somehow Alice felt she didn't have a right to show her sadness in the face of their loss. At the house after the service, she hugged them and didn't know what to say. She thought of her own parents' funerals and how she'd had Bud at her side. It was too much to think about. She excused herself to grab a sweater out of her truck, fully intending to go back in the house. Standing in the driveway, she watched extended family and old friends gather around the Ryan family, and it felt like a circle that had closed to her. Before she knew it, she was behind the wheel and was halfway home.

The family called, but Alice didn't answer the phone. They sent young Ronnie down, and he banged on the door for a long time before giving up. They kept calling for weeks. She knew she should call back. Even with the ghosts of her parents shaming her, she couldn't manage it. She was physically unable to get in the truck and drive to her in-laws' house. When the numbness she'd felt wore off, it was replaced by a pain she hadn't thought possible.

She took a month off from work. When she went back, work was the only vestige of her old life. She stopped going to bee club meetings. She let her sailing club membership lapse. She didn't return phone calls. She turned inward. That was when she started going to the grocery store after 9:00 p.m.—when she didn't think she'd run into anyone she knew. It was a lonely crowd she joined there. She began recognizing their faces. Most of them were men, in line with beer and cigarettes or baskets full of frozen dinners. Once she saw Evangelina there with her daughter, the two of them poring over the cold medicines. She turned around at the sight of them and hid in the meat department until she thought they were gone. Coward, she thought now.

She wished she could just talk to Evangelina, but she needed to make sure she communicated this information as clearly as possible. It had to be Ron. She grabbed her phone and texted him.

"Meet me at Twin Peaks tomorrow," she wrote. "You say when. Important. About Evangelina."

She hoped he would think twice before deleting her message. She fell asleep despite the pounding in her head.

The next day she sat with Doug Ransom and mused that her dad would have been the same age now, if he were still alive. Doug was an old gentleman, cut from the same cloth as Al. The two men had been friends long before Alice bought her house next to Doug's orchard. All this made Doug an easy person to start with in recruiting orchardists to boycott SupraGro.

Doug insisted on making tea for Alice. His wife, Marilyn, had been dead for five years, Alice realized as she stood in the kitchen looking at the wallpaper—pigs in cowboy hats with piglets toddling along behind them. She remembered the first time Doug and Marilyn had had her and Bud over all those years ago. Time passed in a blink. She looked at the photographs on the refrigerator while Doug puttered around, gathering cups and spoons. Three kids, several grandkids. Doug smiled when he saw her looking.

"Don't see them as much as I would like. You know," he said, shaking his white head and smiling. "Busy."

They sat on the porch and looked over Doug's apple and pear trees. Alice had watched them blossom each spring with a kind of collaborative joy. She knew her girls were over there pollinating.

Doug waved a hand at her. "You don't have to try to talk me into anything, Alice. I know the bees are helping me. My yield has been better in the years since you and Bud put the bees in," he said. "He was a good man, that Bud Ryan. I sure miss him."

Alice nodded and smiled. She felt moved, but not like she was going to fall to pieces. Buddy had liked Doug too. The two of them had shared a love of decrepit farming equipment. Vintage, Buddy liked to say. Salvage, Alice had responded.

Doug gestured at the petition Alice had brought with her. "I'll sign that. Whatever you want. I'm damn sorry I used the stuff in the first place. I should have done my own research first. I've been in this business long enough to know better."

He passed a hand over his wrinkled face. "Truth is, I'm about done here, Alice. The kids don't want the orchard. They all went west. Tech jobs in Portland and Seattle. They want me to move out there, sell the place."

He raised his wooly eyebrows. "Me in the city. Can you imagine?"

They both laughed. Doug often drove his ATV to the grocery store, backing up traffic as he poked along in the shoulder of the road.

When Alice left, she walked back to her place through Doug's trees. It made her sad to think of Doug selling his orchard. He was one of the old guard, one of the last small orchardists of her dad's generation. She stood between two rows of pear trees and gazed at the blossoms exploding in white clouds on either side of her. She heard the hum above her, a roof of sound, and looked up to see hundreds of honeybees at work.

She wondered if Doug would harvest that fall or if he would have sold his place by then. Properties sold fast in the county. A place like this would be snapped up, and not by a farmer. It was the perfect setting for the kind of country living development that had ruined her parents' place. She tried to imagine what the land around her would look like cleared of trees and crowded with identical boxlike vacation homes. Doug's orchard was bigger, too—at least eighty acres. She sighed. Townhomes for tourists, the little country road clogged with cars, the quiet broken by loud music from drunken bachelorette parties. She couldn't do anything about that, but she could finish this fight.

Her hand closed around the list in her pocket, drawn out in Doug's elegant spidery script. It was a tally of allies—their phone numbers and addresses too, all of which Doug had known by heart. He had handed it to her after he walked her to the end of the driveway. She stuck out her hand for him to shake, but he leaned down and kissed her on the cheek, then tapped her shoulder with his thin hand.

"You go get 'em, Alice Holtzman. You make your parents proud."

23

GUARDING

The defence of the colony against enemies, the construction of the cells, and storing of them with honey and beebread, the rearing of the young and, in short, the whole work of the hive, the laying of eggs excepted, is carried on by the industrious little workers.

—L. L. LANGSTROTH

Harry understood that the physics of kiteboarding had to do with Newton's laws of motion. The combination of lift and drag kept the kite in the air, and the tension between the kite and a person's body weight was a carefully calibrated feat of aerodynamics. It was a tenuous relationship, never a sure thing. Even so, it gave Harry a newfound sense of possibility to have personally felt the embodiment of those principles.

He sat with Jake at the picnic table under the big cottonwood, which snowed fluff down on their heads. A scree of clouds smeared the pale blue sky and the morning wind had picked up, tossing the branches of Doug Ransom's orchard. Harry sketched the mechanics of the leading edge lines and their role in the process of relaunching the kite. Jake was cleaning the disassembled pieces of his trumpet as he listened, and nodded at the diagram Harry drew in his notebook.

"Pretty rad, man," Jake said. "Are you heading down there later today?"

Harry's heart leapt at the idea, and he started to check the wind forecast again, but then Alice walked across the yard to sit with them, and what she had to say brought everything crashing down.

Harry could tell that her resignation was not "two-weeks' notice and thanks for the memories." This was "fuck you, I'm outta here." And although she didn't say so, he figured her quitting was related to this other thing—this protest against the county and the big ag company.

"You two shouldn't get involved in this," she said, turning her coffee cup around in her hands. "Your folks would probably want you to steer clear."

She brought the cup to her mouth and spilled coffee down the front of her overalls. She brushed it off with her hand, and Jake handed her a tea towel. Harry liked Alice, this slightly grumpy bee lady who was almost as old as his mom and unlike any woman he had known—teachers, aunts, and various neighbors. She wasn't a coddler or a disciplinarian or phony-friendly. Even his own mother had a way of overpoliteness with people that Harry noticed. Alice was different. Alice was just, well, Alice.

"My mom does have an opinion about you," Jake was saying.

Alice raised an eyebrow. "Oh?" she said.

"She wanted me to tell you she is praying for you at church. Not just on Sundays. Every day. Her whole prayer group too."

Alice chuckled, saying she was unaccustomed to being remembered in prayers and to please say thank you for her. Her face grew serious again.

"Look, I've lived here my whole life, and I know this town. Things could get ugly. You really should distance yourself from this, from me."

It dawned on Harry that she was concerned about them, about *him*. Other than his parents, Harry couldn't recall the last time someone had worried about his well-being. Alice told Jake he could stay with her for now, but she didn't know what the future held.

She smiled at Harry, and her eyes looked sad. "I can pay you through the month, Harry, but then— Well, I'm not sure what I'm going to do for work myself. I'll give you a great reference, kid."

Harry felt those familiar twins—worry and self-doubt—settle back onto his shoulders then.

"I hate to let you go, Harry. You can stay here as long as you need to while you're looking," Alice said.

Harry wanted to say he would work for room and board. But he needed the money. He still owed his mom for his legal fees. He groaned inside thinking of his mom. He had to call her. But not until he had Uncle H's ashes.

Alice braced her hands on her knees. "I'm going to start visiting farmers today about the watershed petition. Why don't you two work on the next phase of our hive project here? Jake, check on Eight and Nine to see how close they are to swarming. Harry, I'll need hive stands for all the new hives you put together. Same height as the rest of them, okay?"

Alice stood and zipped her windbreaker. "I'll check in later."

They watched her walk away past the apiary and into Doug Ransom's orchard.

Harry could feel Jake's eyes on him. The boy popped a wheelie in his chair and spun in a circle, whistling.

"Holy shit! Wish I'd been there to watch Alice blow the doors off the planning department," Jake said. "Boom! That just happened!"

Harry mustered a smile.

Jake punched him lightly in the shoulder. "C'mon, man. Don't worry about it. You'll find something. There's loads of jobs you can do around here."

Harry shrugged, feeling defeated, and watched Jake slide the pieces of his trumpet together. He held the instrument against his mouth and pursed his lips.

"As for me, I'm going to start a marching band, work all the weddings and quinceañeras around here. Going to put Hood River on the map, yo!"

He put the trumpet to his mouth again, played a couple of lines of "La Cucaracha," and grinned at Harry. "Too creepy?"

Harry could see his friend was trying to cheer him up. It dawned on him that this uncertain future was even worse for Jake, who faced the same problems but with fewer options. Harry could drive. Harry could use his legs. He could get another job doing manual labor pretty easily. He felt like a jackass for sulking when Jake had obstacles he didn't.

"I don't know, man. With that head, you already look like a creeper," Harry said.

"Oh, snap!" Jake laughed. "Just for that, I'll make you second breakfast before we get to work."

Up in the house, Jake rolled into the kitchen and began pulling food out of the refrigerator, singing to himself.

"La cucaracha, la cucaracha. Ya no puede caminar."

Harry grabbed the phone book. He glanced at Jake, started to explain, and then didn't. He called the morgue.

"Hello. Um, my name is Harry Stokes. Yeah. I, um, need to come pick up my uncle. Harold Goodwin. Yes, that's right. His remains?"

Jake jerked his head up from the cutting board where he was grating cheese.

"Right. ID and five hundred dollars. Great. Okay. Thanks."

He hung up and put his hands over his face.

"Dude?" Jake said.

"It's kind of a long story," Harry said.

He started at the beginning, well, almost the beginning, and told Jake about Seattle, the trailer, his uncle's frailty, and the hospital. He didn't say anything about jail.

"Man, when you said your uncle had died, you made it sound like it was a while ago. Does Alice know?"

"Hell no!" Harry said. "I mean, what was I supposed to say? 'Thanks for the job! Can I borrow the truck to go pick up my dead uncle?' I thought I'd have a chance to slip by there on an errand, but it's all the way over in Bingen. I just kept putting it off . . ."

"Wait," Jake said. "When did he die?"

Harry looked up at the ceiling.

"April twenty-ninth? I think."

"The day of your interview?"

Harry sighed and nodded.

"Jesus, Harry! Why didn't you say something?"

Harry shoved his hands into his hair and shrugged. "You don't talk about yourself much either, man," he mumbled.

Jake scoffed. "There's not much to tell, Harry. I mean, you know my story. I was a loser in high school, and I fucked up my legs at a stupid party."

Harry looked at him and didn't say anything. Jake held his gaze.

"I don't blame anyone else. It was just a stupid accident, but I'm the one who was screwing around on the roof. I'm responsible, man."

Jake stared out across the yard, his lips pressed into a thin line. He shook his head and looked back at Harry.

"Look, Harry. I know it sounds fucked up, but I feel like I got another chance here. I mean, look, walking would be way easier than using this chair, right? But the weird thing is, there's a lot about my life that I like way better than before."

He paused. "I like myself better," he said. "I like other people more."

Harry nodded.

Jake ran his hands across the stubble on his head and looked out the window. Harry followed his eyes to the apiary, the air full of golden bullets.

"It's like the bees saved me or something. I mean, so much of my life is still a fucking mess, but when I'm out in the apiary . . . Man, I just feel like I belong there, like I am part of it."

Harry heard the younger boy say this without embarrassment. He was impressed and not a little jealous.

Jake met his eyes. "I want to stay here if I can. I'm going to help Alice. Whatever that means."

Jake's courage was contagious. What did he have to lose, anyway?

"Me too," Harry said.

They were in this together. The thought fired him up, and then his enthusiasm dipped a notch. First things first.

"I'm going to the morgue before Alice gets back. Want to come?"

"Hells yeah! Road trip to the morgue!"

After breakfast they took the little pickup and let Cheney ride in the cab, his big body flopped across Jake's lap with his nose smearing the window. The little engine puttered up the long driveway, through the orchards, and into town.

As they headed toward the bridge, Harry peered out the window at the sandbar.

"Kites up! I see two, three, maybe four. Oh, man! It wasn't supposed to blow today. I told Yogi I would be there tomorrow."

Jake laughed. "You're obsessed, dude."

Harry grinned and banged on the steering wheel with his palm. He felt like the new Harry again. "There's nothing like it, man! I mean, I was a shit-show, flailing around in the water. But when I got up and rode? It was like the sickest longboard ride, but a hundred times better. So smooth. And watching those guys get big air? I can't wait."

Traffic slowed to a crawl behind a logging truck, and Harry gawked out at the river below, scanning the water for the big pink kite. The car behind him honked, and he jumped.

The morgue was located in a decrepit building in Bingen, a small town across the bridge from Hood River. One building housed every major civic office—mayor, police, taxes, health department, and the morgue—and was situated right next to the railroad tracks. Harry parked the truck as a train thundered by. Under the noise, Jake gestured that he would wait outside.

The dim hallway was lit by a dirty yellow light and smelled like wet matches. Harry peered at the directory and saw that the morgue was in the basement. He stepped into the narrow elevator, which jumped when the doors closed and creaked downward. Harry said a small prayer that he wouldn't get trapped. After several long seconds, the elevator paused, bounced, and groaned open.

Harry saw a woman of indeterminate age sitting behind a low counter. The overhead light gave her skin a greenish cast. Her frizzy hair was the color of tuna fish salad. Her broad shoulders filled out a gray medical scrub top.

She glared at a computer screen and banged on a keyboard with her index fingers and didn't look up as Harry approached. He waited, and the seconds stretched out as she continued to type. Harry leaned forward and cleared his throat.

"Excuse me, I—"

Without looking at him, the woman held up one finger and kept typing.

Harry glanced around, looking for something to read, and found nothing. He shifted from foot to foot and listened to the clack of the keys and the hum of the lights. After a long minute, the woman let out a great sigh, pushed her wheeled chair back from the keyboard, and folded her pale arms over her chest. She narrowed her eyes at Harry. "Yes?"

"I— Um. I'm here to pick up my uncle. I mean his re-remains," he stammered. "The name is Goodwin. Harold Goodwin?"

The woman exhaled through her nose, then looked back to the screen. Without a word, she rolled back to the desk and banged away at the keyboard.

Harry waited.

"ID," she said tersely.

He jumped. "What?"

"Iden-ti-fi-cation," she said, drawing the word out like she was speaking to a child. "Do you have your iden-ti-fi-cation?"

Harry struggled to pull out his wallet and dropped it on the floor. He fumbled for his driver's license. She glanced down at it and pushed it back at him.

"Nope," she said.

"Sorry?" Harry said. "It's a New York license, but it's current. See. The expiration date is right here."

The woman shook her head. "You are not authorized to pick up Mr. Goodwin's remains."

"But, I called and they said I just needed ID and five hundred dollars?"

"Yes, and 'they' was me, but you are not authorized to pick up Mr. Goodwin's remains."

"Well—I mean. Who authorizes that?"

"Mr. Goodwin does," she said, barely moving her lips.

"But—he's dead," Harry sputtered.

"Yes. I know. This is the morgue," the woman said. "I'm very sorry that we can't help you."

She didn't sound sorry at all.

"Why?"

"We can only release remains to authorized persons."

She said "persons" like it had a "z" on the end.

"Who is authorized, then? Can you tell me that?"

The woman exhaled through her nose and glanced at the screen. "Lydia Romano."

Harry brightened. "Oh, good! That's my mom. But she lives in Florida. You can call her. Or I can call her."

He cursed himself for not having a phone but knew he could borrow Jake's.

"I'll just grab my phone," he said.

The woman wagged her head from side to side. "Authorized. Persons. Only."

Harry felt his courage wilt. He just wanted to take care of this one simple thing for his mom. It was always like this when he hit a dead end. He couldn't move ahead in the way he had planned, and that was that. His shoulders slumped, and he started to turn away. But then he thought of what Yogi had said to Autumn about relaunching the kite. Attitude is everything, he'd said. You gotta believe you can make it happen.

Harry turned back toward the clerk and smiled tentatively. "Ma'am," he said, "I'm sorry to inconvenience you."

He explained he'd been living with Mr. Goodwin, who was his great-uncle. He was picking up the ashes for his mother because she was in Florida. Maybe he could call Dr. Chimosky at Skyline and ask him to confirm all this for her. Would that work? Or was there a form he could email to his mom to have her release the ashes to Harry?

There must be some process, he thought. He just needed to be patient and follow through.

As he spoke, the woman's face softened. "Chimosky was his doc, huh? Yeah, I think that could work."

Harry produced the number he'd been carrying around in his wallet. She picked up the phone, peered at the paper, and punched the number.

"Thanks," she said, sounding almost friendly.

A few minutes later, she was handing him a small plastic container. Harry signed the release she gave him and thanked her. She smiled, and Harry realized whatever made her so grouchy had nothing to do with him.

"I'm sorry for your loss," she said. "And for your family."

He nodded and thanked her again. He left feeling tremendously pleased with himself. He had honored his uncle. He would call his mother. Harry Stokes was a man who could solve his own problems. He walked out into the May sunshine and back to the truck, where his new friend Jake waited for him. Whatever was coming next, Harry was ready.

24

Hive Splitting

The plan of multiplying colonies by dividing a full hive into two parts, and adding an empty half to each, will be found to require a degree of skill and knowledge, far in advance of what can be expected of ordinary bee-keepers.

—L. L. LANGSTROTH

The Schmidt sting pain index was first published in the 1980s by the entomologist Justin Schmidt in an attempt to catalog and compare the pain inflicted by various stinging insects. The Western honeybee rated level 2 out of a possible 4 and with a typical duration of ten minutes. Alice could not have said for certain where the honeybee sting landed on the scale (somewhere between the tropical fire ant and the red paper wasp), but she did know that the usually gentle *Apis mellifera* only stung as a last resort because it was a fatal act. Once a honeybee inserted her tiny barbed lancet under the skin of an offending creature, she was unable to withdraw it without tearing her body apart in the process. As she released the apitoxin venom through the stinger, she simultaneously emitted a pheromone to raise the alarm among her sisters. More bees would join the fight and bombard the enemy with increasing fury as their own suicidal stings ratcheted up the message that the colony was under attack.

Later, Alice would recall that she smelled the classic banana fragrance of the pheromone that acted as a call to arms. But Jake told her that the thing he noticed was the sound. He heard the contented murmur of the colony shoot up into a pitch of defense. And a moment later, he felt the first of those level 2 stings.

Alice could tell he didn't take it personally. She had run to the farthest edge of the apiary as the bees descended in an angry cloud. She watched Jake slowly turn his chair around and move calmly out of the apiary. By the time he reached the house, he was enveloped in a swirl of buzzing bodies but never once swatted at them. He just took it. She'd never seen anything like it.

Sitting at the kitchen table, Alice dug gingerly at the soft skin under his eye with a tweezer. The area had swelled up considerably while she'd been busy pulling stingers out of his scalp. She swore under her breath as she grasped the tiny barb and finally eased it out. "I think that's the last one."

She handed him an ice pack and sat back to look at him. "Dammit, Jake. I'm so sorry. That was a stupid mistake."

Jake prodded the puffy area under his eye with his index finger. "No, it's all good, Alice. At least now I know I'm not allergic."

She glanced at her watch. "We're not out of the woods yet. I pulled at least twenty stingers out of you. You just sit tight and let me know if you're feeling dizzy or having trouble breathing. You took that Benadryl, right?"

He nodded.

She had wanted to use the EpiPen, but he insisted the ice pack and Benadryl were enough.

They had managed to split two hives before things fell apart. As they started the third, Jake sat, bareheaded and unveiled as usual, waiting for Alice to hand him a full frame. It was swollen with capped brood and loaded with bees. Alice extended it to him, lost her grip, and dropped it next to the wheelchair. It hit the ground, and the bees exploded upward.

Looking at the kid's swollen face, she felt a wave of anger at herself. She felt terrible for hurting the bees and for getting Jake stung. She knew better than to work the hives when she was distracted. She'd been thinking about what Fred Paris said. Arrogant, pink-faced Fred. What had she expected? Even her father hadn't had anything nice to say about Fred Paris, and Al Holtzman had liked almost everyone.

Earlier that day, after her talk with Doug Ransom, Alice had visited Victor Bello and Dennis Yasui, both of whom were on Doug's list of allies. They listened to what she had to say about the lawsuit, asked some good questions, and signed the petition. She felt a rising sense of hope. Maybe it wouldn't be impossible to rally the south valley orchardists to this cause, she thought. Alice hadn't planned to stop at Paris's place. He wasn't on Doug's list, but his mailbox was right down the road from Victor's. She hesitated and then swung in the gate.

She parked behind Fred's white Ford and walked to the back door. She could hear *The Dr. Laura Show* blaring out of the kitchen radio. Fred's wife, Ellen, appeared, looking none too friendly, and pointed Alice toward the barn before letting the screen door bang shut. Fred came out of the barn wiping his hands on a rag.

"Well, Alice Holtzman! Looky here. Haven't seen you in ages."

Fred was about ten years older than Alice, and though he had grown up in the valley like she had, for some reason he affected a Southern accent. Fred always took great care in his appearance. His Wranglers were ironed with a crease, and his boots shone. He wore his ginger hair in a short buzz and favored ornate belt buckles. "The Bantam," her mother had called him. "He's a horse's ass," Al had said, but her father had also reminded her that she didn't have to like everyone, just get along. Fred was a third-generation orchardist. He'd grown up farming with his grandparents. Surely, he'd at least listen.

Alice mustered a smile. "It sure has, Fred. I don't think I've seen you since Dad's funeral."

He nodded and polished the toe of one shiny boot on the back of his jeans and folded the rag into a neat square. "Good man, your father. Don't make 'em like that anymore."

"Thanks, Fred."

"Broke the mold."

Though her father hadn't liked Fred, Fred had liked Al. There were loads of men like that, Alice noted, at the reception following the funeral. Half the county had shown up for Al at the Elks Club, it seemed. People circulated the room, taking her hand and offering their condolences. Some, like Fred, teared up as they told stories about Al. It was a testament to her father's diplomacy, she supposed. She thought of that then as she decided what to say to Fred about SupraGro, hoping his respect for her father might ease the way.

She pulled her clipboard out from under her arm. "Look, Fred, you know my folks sold their place before they died, so I don't have the orchard anymore."

He nodded, folded the rag again, and tossed it on the hood of his truck.

"Still, I care deeply about the industry and keeping these trees healthy."

She hated the way she sounded. Stilted, like she was reading an ad.

"Sure, Alice. I know you do," he said, cracking his knuckles.

Encouraged, she went on.

"It might sound sort of strange, but I've gotten into honeybee keeping in the past few years."

"Is that right?" Fred said, raising his eyebrows.

Alice gave a self-conscious laugh. "It's pretty fascinating, actually. But what's really interesting are the connections between local honeybee populations and the health of the orchards. The USDA did a study on this that showed that orchards near healthy honeybee populations had a twenty-five percent increase in fruit production."

"You don't say."

She nodded. "Yes, those numbers were from 2012. I have a copy of the study here if you want to take a look at it."

She struggled with the clipboard and pulled the flier loose. She held it out, and Fred glanced at it but didn't take it.

"That's mighty interesting," he drawled. "Funny, I was just reading a different study that said orchards increased their yield by fifty per-cent using commercial support. As a matter of fact, this study showed that over time, the yield can increase as much as sixty percent. That's a lot of apples, Alice."

His smile became a sneer. She gripped the clipboard.

"Fred, the researchers who did that study were paid by SupraGro. That's not exactly what you'd call objective science, is it?"

Fred pulled a toothpick out of his shirt pocket and picked his teeth. "Objective? I don't know, Alice. I s'pose it depends on who you ask. Your tree-hugger friends at Watershed aren't exactly known for their objectivity now, are they? Libel and defamation is what I heard."

She shook her head. "What are you talking about?"

"You ask your ol' friend Stan. That lawsuit against the dams last year made a lot of nice folks mad. You people," he scoffed. "'Oh, the environment! The climate is changing!'"

His voice rose to a falsetto, and he waved his hands in the air.

"Just love drama, don't you? I'm stickin' with my friends on this. Chenowith asked me to be a local point person for the spring spray. I said yes, out of courtesy, of course. Friends stick together."

He reached into his back pocket and pulled out a catalog, which she recognized from the CP meeting. He tossed it onto Alice's clip-board. "Have a look at that and let me know if you have any questions, Alice."

He walked away, leaving her standing in the dusty driveway.

Her hands were shaking, and her face blazed. What would her

father have said? For starters, Fred would never have spoken to her dad like that, or any other man, she thought. She dropped the Supra-Gro catalog on the driveway and left. She drove south toward Dan McCurdy's farm, the next on Doug's list, but pulled over and cut the engine and tried to slow her breathing. How could she even reason with someone like Fred Paris? The good old boys' network would trust Bill Chenowith and believe the so-called science of the pesticide company. People thought Stan was a crazy hippy, even though he had a master's in environmental science and a law degree. This town was so small-minded sometimes.

No one was home at McCurdy's. Discouraged, she headed back to the farm. Jake sat at the picnic table, peering at his laptop, and waved as she drove up.

"Hey, kid," she said, and sat down with a thump. "Where's Thing 2?"

Jake pointed to the barn. "He's talking to his mom."

"Ah, good boy."

Jake looked closely at her. "How did it go? With Mr. Ransom, I mean."

Alice let out an exasperated sigh. "Fine! Things went fine with Doug. It's these other idiots I have to convince!"

She banged the map of the valley down on the table.

"People here think global warming is a hoax made up by Portland yuppies who want to turn the interstate into a giant bike lane and dismantle capitalism in favor of socialist communes and replant all the wheat farms with marijuana."

Jake's eyes widened.

"Don't look at me like that. I'm not the crazy one!"

But she did feel crazy, or at least a little unhinged. Quitting her job had made her feel she'd been living wrong. Her life had been compressed during these last years. It wasn't just about Bud either, balling up behind her grief. It was sitting in endless meetings and not speaking up about bad policy. Doing Bill's job for him because it was easier than speaking up. Not telling her father how much she wanted the orchard. Alice had spent years trying not to upset other people. The elation of walking out of Rich Carlson's office had been replaced by an urgency. She had to make up for lost time.

"You also need to calm down, dear," she heard her mother say in her head.

She shook herself.

"Sorry. Bad morning," she said. "How about we tackle those splits on the other side of the yard?"

Jake nodded and smiled, always eager to work. Things had gone fine until she dropped the frame and got him stung all over.

Now Alice looked at his shaved head, lumpy from reactions to the stings, and his swollen face. She laughed.

"Jesus, kid. Look at you! The neighbors are going to call social services!"

He laughed, rubbed both hands over his scalp, and gingerly touched his puffy cheek.

"This is the only one that really itches," he said. "The other ones— I don't know—it feels kind of good."

"All right, now. Don't turn all New Agey on me and become one of those sting healers."

He held up his hand. "Scout's honor, Alice," he said. "Let's go finish up."

When he convinced her he really was fine, they worked through the rest of the afternoon. Jake insisted on returning to the apiary without a hat or veil as usual. Harry came out of the barn and observed from afar before heading off to Ace Hardware. Alice and Jake moved six splits into new hives Harry had built. They matched Alice's old Langstroth hives in style but had been made with great care, every corner a dovetail joint and sanded smooth.

"Harry's a real problem solver, isn't he? Your workbench is pretty slick too."

Jake ran a hand over the platform. "He says he's going to make me a better one," he said. "It's still a little awkward, but I can transfer frames and check them for brood and all. I still need someone else to pull the brood boxes down for me, but it's better than nothing."

She heard a pitch of frustration in his voice, which was unusual. He'd been quieter today, even before the stinging episode, she noticed. She imagined he was still thinking about her news from the morning and the tenuousness of his own future.

"You've got real talent, Jake. You should be proud of your work," she said.

He shrugged.

"Hey, I'm serious! All that business with the sound of the queen. And you are the only beekeeper I know who has worked bareheaded from day one."

Jake glanced at the apiary but didn't meet her eye.

She gestured around them. "Look at what we did today. Six new hives. I couldn't have done that alone. You've been a huge help."

Jake shook his head and looked away. "A monkey could do it," he said.

Alice snorted. "A monkey, huh? Look, kid—I know you might think I'm always showering people with compliments, but I don't offer refuge to rebellious teenagers every day. If you weren't pulling your weight, you'd have been gone in a minute. I might seem like some kind of Mother Teresa, but—"

Jake threw back his head and laughed. "Mother Teresa! That's totally your new Twitter handle, Alice. MomT!"

She laughed too, and her breath caught. She turned back to her tools, her vision blurring. She didn't want Jake to leave. She had grown to care for this funny boy and the other one too—nervous Harry. Alice

Holtzman didn't like very many people. But she realized now that she loved them—these two slightly lost boys who had come to feel like stray nephews.

She could see Jake pretend not to notice her emotion. He opened the smoker and looked at the bottom.

"I know you don't know what will happen with work and all. But thanks for letting me stay for now. I want to help with the lawsuit. I'm committed, Alice," he said, looking up at her.

She met his eyes and nodded. "Thanks, Jake."

She glanced at her watch. It was nearly five. Ron had answered her text, at least. "Twin Peaks, 5:30 p.m.," he'd written, and nothing else. Her stomach flip-flopped. But she thought of Evangelina, which strengthened her resolve. Ron was not her enemy, she told herself, though she might be his.

"I've got an appointment in town," she told Jake.

"Another orchardist?"

She shook her head. "No—just some personal stuff. I'll see you in an hour or two."

At Twin Peaks, Alice found a table in the shade and sat with an iced tea. The 1950s-era drive-in sat across the road from the county airport. A handful of small planes were tethered to the ground like a flock of restrained birds. One had its motor idling. The hatch was open, and the pilot stood on the wing. Alice remembered a summer evening years ago when Buddy's friend Vince flew them into Portland for dinner. Buddy was going with or without her, he said. When she balked, he asked what she was afraid of.

"Um, crashing? Dying? What do you think, you big oaf?"

He laughed and reminded her that statistically speaking, she was more likely to die in an automobile accident than a plane crash. So she went. She remembered how beautiful that evening flight was. It was cloudy when they took off, the west wind clobbering the small plane as it strained upward. Once in the air, they flew smoothly. Alice looked out over the clouds to see the old volcanoes poking up above the white sea. They were lined up in the pink alpenglow—Mount Hood and Mount Jefferson to the south and Mount Adams, Mount Saint Helens, and Mount Rainier to the north. She sat in the back seat of the small plane and looked at her husband's profile. When Vince let him take the controls, Alice felt her worry leave her. She looked down at the river of clouds that snaked above the gorge in a mirror image of the river. She would follow Bud Ryan anywhere.

A car door slammed, and she saw Ron walking toward her in his sheriff's uniform. She stood as he approached. He wasn't smiling, but he wasn't frowning either. She didn't know what to do. Shake hands? Ron seemed as uncomfortable as she felt as they faced each other.

"Hi, Alice," he said.

"Hello, Ron. Thanks for meeting me," she said.

There was an awkward pause. She gestured at his uniform.

"You on duty?"

He shook his head. "Just off. Didn't have time to go home and change."

She nodded and looked at him more closely. Did he look nervous?

"I'll just go grab a—" He pointed a thumb over his shoulder. "You want anything?"

She shook her head. Ron walked to the soda machine and returned with a Coke. He sat down across from her, rolling the sweating can between his hands.

"Long time," he said.

She nodded.

"Yes, it has been," she said. More than a year, she thought, though they both knew that.

She looked into his face, so familiar to her. Ron was six years older than Alice, so he would be fifty that year. His blond hair was grayer now. The crow's-feet had deepened around his eyes. But otherwise he was the same old Ron. There was a time when she had felt a brotherly love from this man. It didn't matter if Ron still hated her and blamed her for Bud's death. She just needed to deliver this message and they could go back to the silence of the past year. But for some reason she kept talking about other things.

"I saw Ronnie," she said. "I heard he joined the department."

"Yeah. Last fall," Ron said, and gave a short laugh, rubbing the back of his neck with one hand. "You know Ronnie. He's still getting his feet under him."

Alice nodded. "He'll be fine," she said. "He's a good boy."

Ron looked away toward the airport and then back to Alice.

"He told me you have a couple of kids working for you," Ron said.

He raised his eyebrows, being diplomatic. Surely Ronnie had told him about Harry's junky trailer up in BZ Corner and Jake's wheelchair and kooky hair.

"They're pretty handy," she said.

Ron nodded. "It's good you have some help around the place."

His voice was stilted.

"You know you can always call us," he said. He looked at her and glanced toward the airport again. "Me and my boys, I mean."

Alice didn't know what to say to that.

Ron cleared his throat and looked down at the table. The silence stretched interminably as Alice waited for Ron to speak. When he finally met her gaze, his face was tight with grief.

"Look, Alice. I said some terrible things to you after—" He stopped and took a breath. "After Bud died. Probably unforgivable things. I was— It just hurt so much to lose him."

Ron stared down at his clenched hands, and she could see the tears gathering in his eyes. His words came out in a rush.

"I think about him every day, and I think about those things I said to you. I've wanted to call you to tell you how sorry I am. I didn't think you would ever speak to me again. I just— I'm so sorry. I should never—"

His voice broke.

Alice saw again how she had failed to appreciate Buddy's family's grief. Locked away in her own pain, she had not considered theirs. They had each other, after all, she'd thought, thinking that somehow made it easier for them. How could she have been so selfish? She reached out and touched his sleeve.

"There's nothing to forgive, Ron. Water under the bridge. Buddy would want us to be friends."

The big man looked up, nodding. He wiped his eyes. "He would, Alice. You're right."

He tried to laugh. "You can't blame me! You know the Ryan family motto: 'Shoot first and ask questions later.'"

Alice smiled.

"Not Buddy, though," Ron said. "He took after Grammy June. Always happy, that guy."

Alice nodded. She felt emotion rise in her. Her heart beat hard in her chest, and she let herself think of his face. Bud's great teasing grin. Her eyes grew wet, but it was okay. She could hold her love and her grief in the same moment.

Ron watched her, crossing and uncrossing his arms as she composed herself.

"Your mom always said the Ryan mean streak skipped your generation," she said, wiping her eyes.

Ron laughed, but then his face grew serious. "So, what's this thing about Evie?"

Alice took a deep breath and told him, as concisely as she could, about the SupraGro contract with the county, Bill's retirement, how Rich Carlson had threatened her, and how she'd quit.

Ron's face grew stormy. "Those two," he spat. "No checks and balances in this town. Always double-dipping."

Alice nodded.

"And Evie? What about Evie?"

Alice chose her words carefully.

"Someone passed this along to me. I didn't hear it myself," Alice said.

She told him how a person had overheard Rich saying that some of Evangelina's employees at the taqueria didn't have their work permits. He said they could shut her down for that and press charges for unpaid payroll taxes.

Alice knew that Evangelina had worked for years to make the restaurant successful. It was popular with Mexican and white families alike—a rare common space for the two communities in Hood River. It wasn't just Evangelina this attack would hurt either, Alice knew. Her longtime employees counted on sending money to their families back home in Mexico.

Ron swore and rubbed his hand over his face.

"Rich said he was going to leave a message on the ICE tip line—as a way to get back at me through you guys, of course. I thought about calling Evie myself, but my Spanish is terrible, and I wanted to make sure she understood. I'm really sorry, Ron," Alice said.

Ron sighed. "It's not your fault, Alice. Rich Carlson is such a little weasel. And you should know none of that is true. Evie runs a tight ship, especially these days. She's practically running a free legal aid firm, helping people renew their work permits and apply for permanent residency and citizenship. You're not the first person to tell me this, by the way. Carlson. The little shit. No surprise he is helping spread that around. Thanks for letting me know."

Alice felt her shoulders relax. So many people thought immigration was a black-and-white issue—legal or illegal. It was so much more complicated than that. Here in the valley they all lived with the gray. More than 25 percent of the year-round residents of the county were Mexican-American. Many orchard workers were Mexicans who worked seasonally in Oregon and went home in the winter. Status was a tricky question. Her father had taught her that it simply wasn't any-one's business.

"These blowhards want to deport every last person who doesn't have a green card," Al would fume. "These families have been here for generations. They pay taxes. They have the right to be here, and we should make it easier for them to stay."

Ron shifted on the bench. His face broke into a smile.

"So, you told old Rich Carlson to take a long walk off a short pier. Good for you, Alice," he said. "What are you going to do now?"

She said she didn't know. She said first she had to see this thing through with the Watershed Alliance lawsuit and the plan to protest the spray Friday after next. She unfolded the map and showed Ron the orchards on the route. She told him about Doug Ransom's list and pulled it out of her pocket, smoothing it with her hand. Seeing Doug's graceful handwriting made her think of her father again, and she felt a surge of optimism.

Ron held out his hand. "Let me see that list," he said. "I want to help."

· 25 ·

ROBBING

Bees are so prone to rob each other, that, unless great
precautions are used, the Apiarian will often lose some
of his most promising stocks.

—L. L. LANGSTROTH

The day of the protest dawned cold, as if spring were unwilling to let
go of the valley even as the blossoming orchards and farms leaned
toward summer. The wind, which had blown all night, had dimin-
ished to a fluting breeze that found its way into all corners of Alice's
farm. The hives were quiet as the bees waited for the sun's warming
to call them forth.

Alice sat on the edge of the bed and surveyed the photographs on
her dresser—pictures of her parents, her nephews, and Buddy. The
most recent photo of Buddy had been taken just a week or so before
he died. He was standing next to the cab of the big long-haul truck
he'd been leasing for months, grinning like a teenager.

"I feel like such a *man* behind the wheel of this thing," he told
Alice that day, laughing.

He stood with his hands on his hips and stuck his chest out. "Go
ahead. Ask to see my *man* card."

"You are an overgrown boy, Bud Ryan," she said. "You watch yourself, or you're going to have every man-child in this valley down here wanting to drive your new toy."

Bud had taken her for a ride through town before he left for his first job, which took him to Salt Lake City and back as a contract hauler for Home Depot. Alice had to admit that the view from the high seat was fine, and she knew Bud, who loved to drive, would have a good time on the open road. When he returned from that first trip, his contagious enthusiasm made her promise to go with him on his next trip down to the Southwest. She'd take a vacation for once, she said. But she hadn't gotten around to it. She was busy; he kept driving. And then Bud took that final trip to Las Vegas, and that had been that.

Alice still couldn't remember the last thing he had said to her or she to him. Surely it was something routine, some kind word. They never fought. She didn't remember kissing him goodbye, though she must have, or what he'd been wearing. During the first weeks after his death, the compulsion to remember such details kept her awake. She wandered her house at all hours trying to remember. But now she understood that none of that mattered. Bud was gone, and nothing would change that, nor the fact that they had loved each other.

Alice ran a brush through her hair. Bud would approve of what she was doing. The thought braced her. The events of the past two weeks were a blur—meetings with Stan and his partners, visits to orchardists around the valley, and texts back and forth with Ron, who, true to his word, had pitched in and called on some of the valley farmers in person. Alice had recruited Chuck Sauer and the bee group to the effort too. Jake's young friend Celia had connected them with the Mexican-American Workers Union. The Riverkeeper people were bringing college students out from Portland. Alice tightened her belt. She felt as if she were marching into battle.

With Cheney riding in the truck bed, Alice drove the boys to the county fairgrounds out near the high school, where the march would begin. About a hundred people stood in groups, chatting as they waited for things to start. Harry retrieved Jake's chair, and Alice told them she would go check them all in at the white tent standing in the middle of the hubub.

As she walked through the crowd, Alice thought the atmosphere felt almost festive—more like a parade than an environmental protest. She waved at some of the guys from the bee club and saw sweet Doug Ransom with his oldest daughter, Victoria.

"Nice work, my dear," he said, beaming.

Alice saw the young women from Riverkeeper, the fish and wildlife folks, and a guy from state parks. As she listed the names of her group for the young woman running check-in, she was surprised to see Casey, the red-haired intern, sitting behind her. He peered into a laptop while simultaneously typing furiously into his phone. He waved sheepishly when he saw Alice.

"Joining the resistance, kid?"

He stood and crossed his arms, hunching forward. "Well, my internship ends next week, so I thought, Why not? I'm doing social media for Stan. I'll be live-tweeting the whole event."

Alice nodded. "I have no idea what that means, but thanks for helping out."

Casey ducked his head and went back to his screens.

Alice found Stan just outside the tent, frowning over a piece of paper. His face brightened when he saw her.

"Alice! Great day for a mutiny, eh?"

Stan asked her to lead the orchardists and the beekeepers during the march and pointed her toward a table where the Portland students had made signs representing the various groups. Alice found Dennis Yasui, Vic Bello, and a handful of other orchardists, along with members of the bee group. She called them together and handed around signs that proclaimed, "Marching for the Bees!" and "Two-thirds of

America's Crops Pollinated by Honeybees!" and "No Farms = No Food!" Soon, Stan hopped up on a chair in front of the tent, waved a hand, and whistled. The voices died down.

"Thank you, everyone! Thanks so much for coming out today to support the Hood River Watershed Alliance, PDX Riverkeeper, and the Clean Air Alliance. We are also joined by representatives of the Confederated Tribes of Warm Springs, the Mexican-American Workers Union, La Clínica del Cariño, and the Hood River County Beekeeping Association. And we want to thank the college students from PSU for coming out to help too. I know you're taking time out from work and school to be here, and I appreciate it. Give yourselves a hand for standing up for the environment!"

The crowd clapped and whooped. Alice looked around at the smiling faces and felt the energy surging through them all. She felt like a part of something good.

Stan outlined the march course. The group would walk down Fir Mountain Road until they reached Randy Osaka's driveway. They would not trespass, but they would block the road so that the spray truck could not get by. Stan reminded everyone that this was a peaceful protest and that no name-calling or violence would be tolerated. He said they could be arrested for blocking the county road. If anyone was having second thoughts about participating, he said, no one would judge them for bowing out. He looked at Alice. She knew this was true. Ron had talked to the orchardists as a private citizen, but he made it clear he couldn't help her beyond that. She stood up straighter. She was sure of this thing. It made more sense than anything had all year.

"All right, then. Let's get going!" Stan yelled.

He jumped off the chair and led the group out of the parking lot. Someone yelled, "Yee-haw!" in the back, and people cheered. Alice heard the beating of a drum. She saw Harry and Jake moving in from the back with Noah. She waited for them to catch up. Cheney, at the end of his leash, reared up and kissed her. People clapped along to the drum, and someone started singing "Give Peace a Chance." Others joined in. The PSU students walked by swinging Hula-Hoops and waving rainbow flags.

The chill left the air as the May sunshine beamed down on them. They passed the high school, where kids stood in the parking lot waiting for the first bell. Several of them loped toward the lineup and joined in. Alice saw a lone figure—a lanky body and a shock of short hair—push off on a skateboard and coast down the hill. She stopped just short of Jake and hopped off. The kid was wearing his heart on his face.

"Hi, Amri," he said.

"I thought it might be you," she said.

"What gave me away?" he asked.

She smiled at him. "The dog, of course."

"I guess you got my text."

"Yes, I did," she said.

"Hey, Alice, this is Amri," Jake said. "Alice is our den mother."

Alice snorted and nodded at the girl. She felt a surge of protectiveness for the boy. Don't break his heart, she thought.

"Nice to meet you, Amri," she said.

The march streamed down the hill and past the golf course. The Mexican-American Workers Union folks had started chanting "*Sí se puede*," and the rest of the group took it up. Passing cars and trucks tooted and waved as the group wound down the county road. Alice saw a Honda pull over, and Pete Malone climbed out. He joined the stream of people, walking backward and snapping photos. A shadow fell across Alice's face, and she looked up to see a large, long-haired man in board shorts and a hoody slapping palms with Harry and then Jake.

"Hombres! It's a revolution!"

This must be Yogi, the kite instructor who wasn't a kite instructor, she thought. His big face split with a grin. He did not try to high-five

Alice, but instead shook her hand politely and then fell into step with Harry.

We look like the Bremen Town Musicians, Alice thought.

As they neared Osaka's farm, the group slowed and bunched together. Stan stood off to one side, directing people to sit. Alice saw Jake pushing toward the front of the group. Cheney whined and strained against the leash. Jake looked over his shoulder.

"I want to be in front," he said. "Hang on to Cheney for me, okay?"

He passed the leash to Harry and maneuvered the chair so he was front and center. Alice followed, and so did Harry, dragged along by Cheney, as well as Amri and Yogi the gentle giant. Alice saw Pete Malone snap a photo of them and she thought the five of them looked like the ringleaders of the ragtag band of protesters—beekeepers, orchardists, environmental conservationists, farm workers, and students. They held brightly colored signs that read "Hell no, SupraGro!" and "Protect Our Watershed." Someone waved a clutch of helium balloons. The drums beat, and people sang "America the Beautiful." Alice laughed as she looked around. It was like a party. That was probably not how it looked to the driver who crested the hill in a bright orange truck and lumbered toward the turnoff to Osaka's orchard, where he was scheduled to begin spraying at 9:00 a.m.

Over the singing, Alice heard the truck's jake-brake chugging as the driver slowed. She saw a look of alarm cross his face as he scanned the scene. He threw the truck into idle, stared down at the crowd, and pulled out his phone. A cheer went up, and Stan yelled at everyone to stay seated.

In the confusion that followed, Alice thought fuzzily that the driver had called Fred Paris. That couldn't have been true. He had probably called his company to find out what he should do since he couldn't drive his truck through a crowd of peaceful protestors, some of whom were minors.

Alice heard an engine approaching from behind. She turned and saw a line of trucks coming from the other direction. They drove onto the shoulder of the county road and around the protesters, kicking up dust, and parked between the spray truck and people sitting in the road. Doors slammed as men jumped out and stood in a line across the road. Alice saw Fred Paris climb out of his white Ford and stand with his hands on his hips. He glared at the crowd and then stalked over to the truck, motioning the driver down out of the cab.

Oregon had an open-carry law, and Alice saw more than one holstered gun. Several of the men had baseball bats. Some people who were sitting began to stand, and others pulled them back down. Their voices rose in confusion. Stan hadn't said what to do in this sort of situation, probably because he hadn't expected a mob of vigilantes. More trucks appeared and drove around the crowd, which sat in the middle of Fir Mountain Road, gamely trying to keep the sit-in going. Alice sat up taller and squared her shoulders. She could hear Stan's voice admonishing everyone to remain calm, but she couldn't see him. Someone started singing "Give Peace a Chance" again but trailed off when nobody joined in.

Fred stalked away from the truck driver and back to the line of men.

"Get the hell out of the road!" Fred yelled. "You're obstructing private property!"

He signaled the line of men forward. They waded into the sitting crowd and began shoving and kicking everyone around them.

Alice heard someone yell that this was a peaceful protest. She saw Yogi jump up and lunge toward the interlopers. Someone shoved Harry, and Cheney reared up, barking. She watched Yogi reach down from his great height and sock Fred Paris in the face. Then she lost track of everyone. People were pushing and shoving to get out of the way. But more of Fred's guys were coming in from the back. Time seemed to slow down. She fought to stand up, and someone elbowed her in the eye. She heard sirens, saw flashing lights, and then someone kicked her in the jaw as she struggled to keep her feet. She fell in the crush of bodies, grappling against them, trying to catch her breath. In the scrum, she looked out and saw Amri, the young woman with the green eyes and dark hair, swing her skateboard and bring it down on the shoulders of a man twice her size, and Alice laughed crazily.

Jake was lying on his side and halfway out of his chair. He tried to pull his head up. He'd lost sight of Amri. Where was Cheney? A large pair of hands reached down, pulled him into his chair, and righted it. Yogi, his long hair stringy with sweat, a bloody gash on his eyebrow, grinned at him.

"Dude! You gotta get outta here. These idiots are—"

A fist caught him in the mouth. Yogi's head bounced, and he growled with joy and clobbered a shorter man. He grabbed Jake's chair and moved him out of the fray.

"I'll come back and get you!" he yelled before jumping back into the fight.

Jake looked for Noah, for Alice, for anyone. He couldn't see them anywhere. People were punching and shoving and yelling. He didn't recognize anyone he knew.

A hand came down on his shoulder, and he looked up to see a middle-aged man in a sheriff's uniform scowling down at him.

"Put this guy in the second van!" the sheriff barked before moving on.

Ronnie appeared at the side of his chair, looking embarrassed.

"Sorry, man! I have to. He's my boss. And my dad," he said, and pushed Jake in his chair out of the crowd.

Right before the sheriff arrived, Harry realized the nasty men were succeeding in clearing a path to Randy Osaka's driveway. The unfairness of it burned in his gut. The crowd hadn't been prepared for a fight, but they were about to lose one. He saw Jake just outside the chaos. He saw Yogi swinging his big arms around with glee. He couldn't see Alice or the dog. Cheney had yanked loose in the scuffle. Sirens blared, and then the sheriff was yelling over the crowd through a megaphone. Harry turned away and looked at the big orange truck, which sat idling in the road.

In the months after his arrest in New York, nobody ever asked Harry why he had agreed to help his friends with the failed heist— why, specifically, he had decided to climb behind the wheel of the truck full of electronics that his friends had decided to steal. His mother had asked him, "What were you thinking?" But that wasn't the same thing as asking him what his motivation was.

Though he'd never been asked, Harry knew exactly why he had done it. That day at the bar with Marty and Sam, he'd actually started to walk away. He drained his PBR and set the empty can on the counter. Then Marty turned to him and said, "It's not like you have a better idea, do you, Stokes? You haven't had an original thought in your entire life. So don't pretend you're better than the rest of us."

Harry didn't say anything, but he was thinking that Marty was right. He was nothing special. What kind of life was he going to have with his associate's degree and living out in the burbs with his parents? The economy was in the toilet, and there was nothing about Harry that would set him apart from the thousands of other unemployed guys his age. So why not do it?

It was a decision, he understood, after thinking about it all those months in jail, made out of self-loathing. It was careless and hurtful, to his parents certainly, but also to himself. You couldn't just stop trying. You had to believe in something. And if you didn't like yourself, how could you expect anyone else to?

Now Harry looked back at the chaos on Fir Mountain Road. He knew Jake would understand if he could explain it to him. Alice would get it too. Maybe he would be able to tell them sometime. In the meantime, he knew what needed to happen next, and this time his motivation was clear as day. It was love.

The truck driver, standing with his back to the road and shouting into his cell phone, didn't notice Harry swing himself up into the cab. He didn't hear Harry throw the truck into gear. By the time the driver turned around, Harry had gained speed and was heading back up the long hill into town.

Harry knew this act was a violation of his parole. He understood he would likely end up back in jail, this time for a minimum of two years. Alice and Jake would find out that he was both a liar and a felon. He would break his mother's heart all over again. But he did it anyway. Harry, who was uncertain about most things in life, who questioned every decision he made and thought of himself as a grade-A dumbass, knew unequivocally that this was the right thing to do just then. Even if it only delayed spraying by a day or two, it would make a statement. Alice and Jake would understand that he had done this thing for them, for the bees, because he could.

And when he crossed the Hood River Bridge and paid the toll, the attendant didn't even glance up from her screen as Harold Courtland Stokes III crossed the river and headed up into the great dark woods of the Gifford Pinchot National Forest in a stolen semitruck full of pesticides.

Far up Highway 141, Harry pulled the big truck into the clearing where his uncle's trailer once sat. He cut the rumbling engine and rolled down the window. He felt the breeze blow across his face, and his body relaxed. The sweet little hollow was now devoid of trash and broken glass. Gone were the tattered "No Trespassing" signs and bits of pink insulation. No sound of loose siding banging around in the wind. He heard the rush of the whitewater highway running behind the clearing. He heard the keen of an osprey fishing over the river eddy. He leaned his head against the door and looked up at the tall dark trees. He thought of the secret lives of creatures this forest held within its heart. He thought how nice it would be to get down from the truck and disappear into those woods forever.

How much time passed? He couldn't say. It felt like a lifetime and it felt like minutes before Harry heard the sound of an approaching vehicle. He looked in the mirror and saw what he'd been waiting for—the sheriff's Jeep with its flashing blue-and-red lights. He sighed and climbed down out of the truck. His heart felt heavy. His heart felt light. He walked toward his future with his hands held up in surrender.

The Hood River County Courthouse was a large, imposing building with neoclassical columns, an ornate façade, and a large mural depicting the harrowing journey of the Oregon Trail—white settlers battling prairie fires, flooded rivers, and snowy mountain passes to reach the verdant, supposedly empty farmlands of Oregon. When first painted in the 1950s, the mural had depicted settlers fighting hostile Native Americans. It had been edited in the 1980s to show members of the Wasco and Wishram tribes welcoming their new white neighbors. That wasn't the whole truth either, but it leaned in the right direction. Local tribes had been curious and helpful when the first whites came. In return they had been misunderstood, abused, and eventually robbed of their lands.

The courthouse builders had clearly anticipated a wilder West and had constructed ample jail space in the courthouse basement. The only other time it had been as full was a day in 1942 when the county had jailed local Japanese-American residents before sending them on trains to internment camps around the country. That chapter of local history was not presented in the mural either.

Jake waited in the courthouse basement with the other men from the incident on Fir Mountain Road. He didn't know any of them, but it was easy to tell who was who. The guys who had started the fight sat together glowering at the rest of them. Jake sat as far away as he could with the PSU students and a guy named Casey who said he had worked with Alice. Casey sat on his hands, as if trying to keep his khakis from getting dirty.

"College boy," one of the older men sneered. His squat nose sat crooked in his face, and his collar was torn.

Casey paled but then turned back to Jake, his face brightening.

"I was live-tweeting the protest," he said, his voice low. "And it was totally blowing up Twitter! We got retweeted by a reporter with the Associated Press out of Los Angeles and Reuters in New York."

Casey said his video of the attack on the protesters had been shared by people all over the country before deputies had confiscated his phone and laptop.

Jake craned his neck around the room. He hadn't seen Noah, Harry, or Yogi since Ronnie had handed him off to another deputy. The guy didn't fingerprint Jake or take his picture. He just asked Jake to sign a piece of paper confirming that he had been processed through the county jail for disturbing the peace.

Jake had refused, his anger bordering on rage. The deputy had hauled him out of his chair and belted him into the front seat of the van, repeating the process in reverse at the jail. Then they bumped him roughly up the stairs into the building. The whole thing felt like an assault.

"I'm not signing that. I shouldn't be in here at all. And you banged the shit out of my chair. Plus, your guys left my dog out there."

"Suit yourself," the deputy said, and pushed him down the hall into the cell. Jake yelled that he'd sue for ADA discrimination, but the guy just walked away.

Jake felt sick thinking of Cheney. He didn't have a tag on his collar. Maybe Harry, wherever he was, still had him. He couldn't bear losing Cheney again. He thought of Amri too, who had been in that clusterfuck because he'd invited her. Was she okay?

The guy who'd sneered at Casey was glaring at him now. He looked Jake up and down and smiled meanly. "Freak," he spat.

Jake felt a wildness surge through him. He'd forgotten all about his chair. He'd forgotten to worry that people might be staring. How must he look to this guy: shaved head, Doc Martens, anarchy shirt, and wheelchair. There had been a time he might have cared what a guy like this thought of him. It seemed so preposterous now. He 100 percent did not give a fuck. Yeah, this is me, he thought. He felt his voice in his throat, and it climbed to a shout. He threw his head back and laughed with an unhinged kind of joy. The guy shrank back. He left Jake and Casey alone after that.

Alice demanded to use the phone.

"I want to call my lawyer," she told the sheriff's secretary. Denise had herded all the ladies into the courthouse staff room. There were only about twenty of them, and she said it seemed impolite to put them in the basement cells with all the men. Alice knew Denise from 4-H years ago. They hadn't exactly been friends, but they'd been friendly enough.

"Come on, Neesie. You can't just keep us in here all day."

Denise shook her head. "Sorry, Alice. You'll just have to wait for Ron. I don't know what they are going to do with you all."

Alice sat back down with a woman from Riverkeeper named Kate and put an ice pack on her jaw. The college students were all sitting cross-legged on the floor talking about their weekend plans and seemed no more worried than if they were waiting for the bus. She guessed they had more practice at this sort of thing.

So much for a peaceful protest. She thought of the big orange truck and its driver. She glanced at the clock on the wall. It was past noon. The truck would have finished Osaka's orchard by now and probably the next two down the road. Her heart sank. She thought of the guys from the beekeeping association who had showed up for her. And sweet Doug Ransom with his daughter. The Mexican-American Workers Union too—people who picked fruit in the orchards and bore the brunt of injury from the chemicals used. It was like none of them mattered, she thought. Money wins again.

She thought about her remaining hives. The large-scale use of SupraGro would inevitably poison whatever her foragers brought home. She could try feeding them, though she didn't think the surplus sugar water would discourage their collecting instinct. Perhaps some might survive the summer regardless. Like her dreams, the bees now faced extinction. She would guard what she had left. It was all she could do.

Jake didn't ask any questions when the deputy called his name and led him out of the basement.

The door swung shut behind him, and Jake looked for Alice but didn't see her. The only other person in the lobby was a man Jake had never seen before. He stood and walked toward Jake. He was a trim man with a kind face, shoulder-length hair, and a white shirt and blue tie. He extended his hand.

"Hi, Jake. I'm Ken Christensen," he said. "I'm Amri's dad."

They shook hands.

"It's nice to meet you, circumstances notwithstanding," Ken said. He held out a manila envelope.

"Here's your phone and wallet," he said. "They gave them to me at the front."

"Thanks," Jake said. "Is Amri in there?"

Ken shook his head, and Jake breathed with relief.

Ken sat down on a bench and pulled out a yellow legal pad. "Did she tell you I was a lawyer?"

Jake shook his head. "She said you were an old hippy," he said without thinking.

Ken laughed, and Jake saw that he had the same dark green eyes as his daughter.

"I'll have to give her hell for that," he said, smiling. "Anyway, Amri called to say her friend had been arrested and might need representation. The intake clerk said you and everyone else were charged with disturbing the peace. Want to tell me what happened?"

Jake explained about the Watershed Alliance, the sit-in, and the attack from the gang of men.

Ken's face grew somber. He jotted notes down as Jake talked.

"Sounds to me like there's potential for assault and battery charges," he said.

"Alice is the one you really need to talk to," Jake said. "She probably got arrested too. Otherwise she would have bailed me out by now. Alice Holtzman. I live with her."

"I'll be right back," Ken said.

He went back inside and returned a few minutes later with Alice, who looked pleased.

"Young Amri has rescued us, then? I guess I must have made a great impression on your new friend."

Jake felt his face turn red and didn't speak.

Outside the courthouse, they found Amri sitting on a bench under a cherry tree exploding with pink blossoms. She held Cheney's leash loosely, and the big dog was leaning his full weight into her knees like he had known her forever. Amri smiled when she saw Jake, and he felt the world crack wide open.

"Hi there," she said, standing.

"Hey," Jake said.

Cheney yawned, wiggled his rump, and shoved his head in Jake's lap like he'd just seen him five minutes ago.

"Thanks for taking care of him. And for calling your dad," he said.

"Well, Cheney kind of found me in the ruckus," she said, scratching his ears. "Anyway, that's what friends are for."

Her green eyes shone, and Jake's heart felt too big for his body.

Amri sat next to him in the back seat of her dad's Subaru while Ken talked to Alice about the protest as they drove back to the fairgrounds. Jake was intensely aware of the proximity of his arm to Amri's arm on the seat. He felt the magnetic force of her nearness like the electric charge that pulled pollen to a honeybee. When the car hit a bump and his arm brushed hers, he felt a jolt run through his body.

By the time Ken dropped them off at Alice's pickup, the story was all over the news. Peaceful protesters had been attacked by a vigilante mob in the Hood River South Valley during a sit-in to protest pesticide use on local orchards. By nightfall, thanks to Casey's live-tweeting, the story had gone viral. Within two days, Stan Hinatsu had fielded calls from reporters in Seattle, Los Angeles, New York, London, Paris, and Berlin. The Hood River story emboldened other small towns around the country to speak out, and within a week, SupraGro was under fierce attack.

At a gathering the following week at the watershed offices, Jake sat next to Alice and listened to Stan recount how SupraGro, not admitting any formal connection to Fred Paris and his goons, had agreed to pay restitution to the people injured in the attack on Fir Mountain Road. The company also said it was reassessing its contract with Hood River County.

"It looks like we have made them hit the pause button. You all did this together, folks! You should be damn proud of yourselves," Stan said.

Stan shouldered his way through the celebrating throng to Alice and Jake. He smiled at Alice.

"So. How about that beer at pFriem?"

And Alice said yes.

Jake watched them, but he was miles away. He was thinking about how he had pulled himself into the truck while Alice exchanged contact information with Ken. As Ken drove away, Amri rolled down her window, leaned out, and waved at him. Jake waved back, and as the car disappeared over the rise in the road, he felt like his heart had gone with it, leaving his body empty, like a fickle swarm abandoning the hive.

BEE DAY

Although when bees commence their work in the Spring,
they usually give reliable evidence either that all is well,
or that ruin lurks within, if their first flight is not noticed, it is sometimes difficult, in the common hives, to
get at the truth.

—L. L. LANGSTROTH

Jacob Stevenson had the highest exam score in the history of the Oregon State University Master Beekeeper Apprentice Program—125
percent, counting an extra-credit question about queen rearing. Even
before it made the program newsletter in April, he was pretty sure
about it. Over the fall and winter, he'd done much of the course work
online and attended local bee group meetings toward his certification.
The day of the test, his mom drove him into the OSU campus in
Portland. It was a Saturday in mid-March. The weather was wild—a
spring chinook blowing rainbows and spattering showers down the
gorge. He watched a squall bluster over the river, and his stomach did
somersaults. However, as soon as he started the exam, he felt very
calm. He knew this stuff inside and out because it mattered to him.
So, although he was pleased to earn a more than perfect score, he was
not terribly surprised.

Of course, the test only accounted for half of the Master Beekeeper certification program. The second half involved forty hours of

community service. For this Jake had partnered with a science teacher at May Street Elementary, agreeing to help the third- and fourth-grade classes develop their own hives. Since January, Jake had been teaching them about the life cycle of the honeybee. Using photographs and drawings, he'd explained about the worker bees, the drones, and the queen. He told the kids how bees turned nectar into honey and about the various threats to a healthy hive—varroa mites, wax moths, starvation, and, most important, human-made pesticides.

As another part of community service, Jake had helped connect local beekeepers with graduate students who were studying the impact of commercial pesticides on honeybees. After the dustup with SupraGro, OSU's extension office hosted a group of graduate students on a tour of the valley. Four students had proposed a study to look at the relationship between local orchard production and honeybee populations. Understanding the symbiotic value of the two ecosystems was a silver lining, Jake supposed.

On this April day, he sat outside May Street Elementary in the butterfly garden where he and the teacher had decided to establish the hives. The garden was part of the new science building, which was state-of-the-art in terms of accessibility inside and on the grounds. Noah had dropped him off and helped him unload the nucs. Jake wanted to drive himself, but his adaptive conversion Subaru, paid for with a sweet grant from the Mobility Resource, wouldn't be ready for another week. He couldn't wait to be behind the wheel of his own car.

His mentor, Chris, had let him practice in his car, a tricked-out Honda Pilot, after Jake had passed his driver's test. Jake had driven them both to Portland for a meeting with his support group. When he pulled onto the highway and accelerated up to speed, he felt a rush of adrenaline and screamed at the top of his lungs.

Chris laughed and punched him in the shoulder. "Don't wreck my ride, little man!" he said.

He knew he was early, but he was happy to sit in the sunshine and wait for the kids from Ms. Unalitin's class. He put a hand on both of the wooden nuc boxes he'd brought and felt the quiet vibration of the bees within. Each nuc contained five frames of drawn comb, honeybees, healthy brood, and a big fat queen. They were already a happy family unit, so transferring the frames would be a quiet affair. Jake could show the kids the capped brood, the uncapped larvae, and the eggs on the frames before he transferred them into the newly painted hives. If they had enough time, Jake would have them look for the queen. Most of the kids would be too nervous to handle the frames, but if any wanted to give it a try, he would show them how to work slowly and carefully, just like Alice had taught him last year.

And just as he'd taught Amri. More cautious than he, she wore a full bee suit the first three or four times and just sat and watched him work. Remembering Harry's introduction to the bees, Jake didn't pressure her. She asked him questions while he examined the frames and documented the development of each new hive. She hadn't fallen in love with them immediately like Jake had, which was like her. Amri felt things deeply, but it took her a while to show her feelings.

In that way she was different from her parents. Like Ken, his wife, Olivia, was a social justice lawyer, but she had been a yoga teacher when she was pregnant with Amrita, whose name meant "nectar" in Sanskrit. The younger children had more earthly names—River, Sage, and Tierra—but Amri's parents were still big on communication and sharing their feelings. The first time they invited Jake over, Olivia had called ahead to tell him the house had a ramp and would be navigable in his chair. Even though Amri had already told him, he thought it was really nice of her. As they sat around the table, they took turns saying what they were grateful for before they ate. Amri rolled her eyes. The younger kids had an easier time with it. Ice cream, tricycles, and unicorn underwear topped the list for Tierra, who had recently been potty-trained and was in love with her little-girl undies. For Jake, whose family had stopped eating dinner together when he was twelve and who didn't have siblings, it was cool. He said he was grateful for honeybees, good friends, and his dog, not necessarily in that order. Still, he understood that Amri seemed reserved on the outside while she felt things intensely. And once he got that about her, he could easily read her affection for him. She loved him, he knew. The thought still made him dizzy.

Last night at the farm she said she wanted to ditch class and come with him that morning, but Jake wouldn't let her.

"Don't be a fool! Stay in school!" he said in his best imitation of Mr. T. "You can come help me after."

She shrugged and leaned down to kiss him before climbing into her car.

"See you, handsome," she said, her green eyes bright under her dark hair.

There goes my girlfriend, he thought. It had been almost a year, but the words still made his heart pound. They weren't rushing anything, but he could tell Dr. Gunheim at his next checkup that everything seemed to be working.

After Amri left, Jake rolled out to the yard to watch the sunset. He pulled out his trumpet. The weight of the polished brass felt familiar and comforting in his hands. He ran through his scales for a while, which always aroused the suspicion of Red Head Ned. The little bantam stalked toward Jake and then patrolled the line between the boy and the chicken coop for a few minutes, as if to remind him who was boss. Jake finished his scales and played "Up Jumped Spring," a piece he'd worked on over the winter. It felt like an appropriate song for the season and for the bees. The phrasing mirrored the quick, graceful motion of the bees and their contented, busy flight patterns up and over the field. Could the queen bees hear it? he wondered. He hoped so. Maybe they would understand what it was—a love song, an offering, a hymn of gratitude for his new life and the unexpected joys it brought forth.

Now Jake looked at the two hives the third- and fourth-grade classes had built to house these two nucs. The third-grade hive was a traditional Langstroth like the ones he first saw at Alice's. The fourth-grade hive was essentially a Langstroth hive laid out horizontally. It had the same number of frames, same inner cover and telescoping top. It was just long instead of tall. Some people might call it a leaf hive. This one was a Stokes hive, he would tell the kids, with a wry grin. Jake was now tending three of them himself, and they were thriving alongside the traditional Langstroth hives, just like Harry had predicted.

Harry said the idea for the horizontal hive came to him after his first kite lesson with Yogi—an invention born of looking at the physics of a problem from various angles. If it were completely horizontal, Jake could add brood frames and supers to the ends. The bees would just build out instead of up.

"They nested for thousands of years in logs and random holes before we made hives, so why not?" he'd said when Jake looked skeptical.

It was an unexpected gift. Harry had given him the hive the morning of the march last May. The day Fred Paris's goons had attacked them. What a fiasco. Stokes. Goofy bastard. Jake missed him.

Jake shivered in the April chill and shifted his chair so the sun fell on his face. He put a hand on one nuc box and then the other. He closed his eyes and listened. There it was—that clear, ringing G-sharp.

The bell rang. The door banged open, and the air erupted with the bright voices of twenty-two third graders, filing out of the building behind their teacher. They waved, smiled, and yelled Jake's name.

On his first day in their class in January, when he rolled into their room, they stared at his shiny bald head and the chair. Ms. Unalitin introduced him and told the kids he was going to tell them all about honeybees. One little girl put her head down and started to cry quietly. The teacher looked embarrassed.

"Now, Ruby," she said. "Remember what we talked about?"

But Jake waved a hand.

"It's okay, Ms. U. Can I call you Ms. U? Most kids haven't seen a wheelchair as fly as mine. They aren't sure what to think."

He turned back to the class.

"Okay, how many of you can ride a bike?"

Several of the kids tentatively raised their hands.

He cocked his head. "Really? Only the six of you? Nobody else in here can ride a bike?"

More hands went up.

"That's more like it," he said. "And how many of you bikers can pop a wheelie?"

Hands shot up again, and kids leaned forward on their desks.

"Awesome!" said Jake. "And how many of you wheelie-poppers can do a manual?"

The kids lowered their hands and looked uncertain.

"A manual," Jake said, "is a wheelie plus a 360."

"Oh!" a plump boy yelled, kneeling on his chair and waving his hand. "My big brother can do that! He goes up and then around!"

The boy leapt out of his chair and whirled himself in a circle. The other kids laughed.

"Sit down, Joshua!" Ms. Unalitin called, but she was smiling.

The kids looked back at Jake.

"Well," he said, "my chair can do even better than that. Watch this."

He popped a wheelie, did a 360 in one direction then back the other direction.

"That's a 720, kiddos! Wheelie with a double manual. Check me out!"

They clapped and cheered and yelled, "Do it again! Again!"

Now they streamed toward him, their small faces so familiar to him. Ruby, the one who had cried, sidled up close and leaned on the arm of his chair. Her breath smelled like graham crackers. The children encircled him and unzipped their jackets in the warming air.

"Hey, chitlins!"

"Hi, Jake!" they yelled.

"It's great to see you today. It's a really special day. Anybody remember why?"

Little hands shot up, and Jake pointed at Barbara, a gap-toothed beauty with long black braids who was a cousin of Celia's. She grew shy when he called on her.

"It's Bee Day," she whispered. *"Día de las abejas."*

"That's right!" Jake crowed. "It's Bee Day at May Street! I've got a queen for you to meet and her hardworking daughters and a few lazy drones. Let's get started."

Alice Holtzman had been in a good mood all morning even before she confirmed that her favorite blue dress fit again. She pulled it over her head and smoothed the fabric down around her hips. She tied the belt at the waist and looked at herself in the mirror, pulled her shoulders back, and pushed her hair behind her ears. It was a nice dress and an old standby for special occasions. When was the last time she wore it? One of the Ryan family birthdays? She loved this slate blue, which flattered her pale skin. But she took it off, deciding it was far too fancy. Slacks and a nice shirt would have to do for her visit to the Hood River County Courthouse today.

Alice hadn't expected the lawsuit that had blown up at the Hood River County Planning Department. Increased scrutiny following the SupraGro conflict revealed major problems within the county budget, and it came to light that Bill Chenowith had embezzled more than a million dollars. Today Judge Weisfield would read out the formal sentencing, which had already been reported in the paper. Bill would be spending the next twenty to forty years in the Oregon State Penitentiary.

Debi Jeffreys had been the one who noticed. Debi the disgruntled office manager. Debi meticulously combed through the county financials and put it together that Bill had been skimming for years. Debi hadn't had a raise in a while either, and she had three little kids to support.

It's always the quiet ones you need to watch, Alice thought to herself.

She put on a pair of shoes—navy with a low heel. They felt tight, so she changed her socks.

She thought of Bill and scoffed. The revelation cleared up a lot of questions, like why the budget was always so tight and how Bill paid for his nice boat that was moored at the Hood River Marina. Nancy was immediately demoted to her old position, and the county was still looking for Bill's replacement. Rich Carlson had emailed her to ask if she would consider applying for Bill's job. When Bill's crimes emerged, he'd had a change of heart, he wrote. He hadn't appreciated what a fine job she'd been doing. He sincerely hoped she would consider coming back, and either way, her pension plan would pay out as planned starting next year. Alice had deleted the email without replying.

Now she walked outside and onto the porch. Automatically, she looked toward the barn, expecting to see Harry. She felt a small jolt whenever she did so and saw the bunkroom door closed firmly like a sleeping eye. She missed that bumbling boy.

She glanced at her watch and saw she had some time before she had to be at the courthouse. She walked down the steps and headed toward where the bee yard used to be—that fenced perimeter that had grown from those first few hives to fifty last year, when Jake had come to stay. She smiled. Last year had been quite a time. She stood at the edge of the fence and looked at the broad expanse where the hives once sat. Now, instead of the painted white boxes set high on their stands, the yard was full of flowers—early bloomers like heather, fox-glove, and heliotrope—that stood out in splashes of pink, lavender, and blue. The air was full of the scent of it, a heavy bouquet of bee-friendly plants. She closed her eyes, breathing it in. Summer would bring salvia, hyssop, lavender, Russian sage, and sunflowers. The flower garden had been Jake's idea. He thought it would be another great tool for teaching the May Street kids.

The air around her was alive with the zinging golden bodies of the honeybees coming across the field to light upon the flowers. By late summer of last year, Alice had understood that one hundred hives was not an impossible goal, despite the losses early in the spring. But she didn't have room for that many in the old bee yard, so she moved them to the Ransom orchard, where there was more space. All hives but one had survived the winter. Now she had the space and the resources to grow as big as she wanted to. With good luck and splits she could have as many as one hundred and fifty hives by July.

Alice gazed out toward the orchard. The trees held tight blossoms that would soon surrender to the warming spring days and explode in a white blanket that would toss around like froth in the west wind. Then those bees would be especially busy. And Alice would too, as she was now doubly blessed in honey and fruit.

Alice had bought the old orchard from Doug at the end of last summer. He suggested it one August day when he and Alice sat drinking tea on his porch. They were talking about the county board of commissioners meeting where Stan had presented a proposal for banning some pesticides in the orchards and limiting others. It wasn't a complete reversal, but it was a start.

"Old habits die hard," she mused.

Doug nodded. "But people can change, Alice. These fellas are good old boys, but they love their trees. Give it time. Now what about you? What's next?"

Alice told Doug she didn't know. She was looking at jobs in Portland, which would all involve a commute, but she hadn't found anything. That was when he made his proposal about the orchard.

"You know my kids don't want the orchard, Alice. And I don't want to move to Seattle. Me in the city? Impossible."

Doug insisted on holding the note so she wouldn't have to take out a loan. Alice tried to refuse this generous offer, but her heart wouldn't let her. Of course she wanted the orchard. It was what she'd always wanted since she had been that fourth-grade girl in Miss Tooksbury's class. Yes, she said, absolutely. Doug would stay in the house as long as he wanted to, as long as he could and rent-free. As part of the deal Alice promised his children she would check on him every day and help him with shopping and errands. And spending time with Doug, well, that was no hardship. He made her miss her folks less.

Alice Holtzman was now an orchardist and a beekeeper. She would have her first crop of pears and apples that fall along with another enormous harvest of honey. It all felt so right, like things had just fallen into place. That was what she'd told Dr. Zimmerman at her final session, when they both agreed that Alice seemed to be healing and moving on.

"*Steering your own ship again,*" she heard her mother's voice say.

"*Tough as a two-dollar steak. That's my girl,*" her father said.

Alice heard a loud yawp and saw the brown body of Cheney streaking across the field from Doug's house. Cheney and Doug were great pals now. The big dog wolfed down the breakfast Jake poured into his bowl and then ambled over to Doug's for whatever tidbit Doug saved for him.

Alice let Cheney into the house. "You behave, big boy. Stay off the bed."

He banged his tail on the floor and trotted down the hall to Jake's room.

Jake was an equal partner in the beekeeping business, which had officially outgrown hobby status last summer when they harvested four hundred gallons of honey at the end of the season. It had taken them the better part of a week, with help from Amri, Noah, and Celia, to harvest and bottle the crop. The shop had been converted into an assembly line where they took turns using the heat knife to cut the creamy wax cappings off the honey frames. They worked together loading the dripping frames into the extractor, monitoring the flow, and straining the thick golden syrup that poured forth. It was sticky, wonderful work. Celia had strained the wax cappings and made candles out of them. The honey sold for $20 a quart at the Hood River County Fair in the fall. After that, they had recruited Jake's mother to set up their books, and Queen of G Honey had taken off. Ron and the nephews helped move the hives to the orchard, and they also built the network of ramps that Jake had designed to run throughout the apiary.

Jake had more initiative than most at his age. He was certainly doing better financially than she had at nineteen, she thought wryly. Thanks to Amri's lawyer dad, the kid had a trust that protected his stake in the honey business and his disability benefits. And lucky thing too. He had plans for queen rearing and cross breeding for mite-resistant bees that would keep Queen of G growing in new directions she couldn't even have imagined. She laughed and shook her head. His enthusiasm never failed to surprise her.

Alice climbed into her pickup and headed up the long driveway into town. She passed the high school and the gas station. She slowed down by the taqueria and made a mental note to call Evangelina and ask what she could bring to her youngest daughter's quinceañera next weekend. The Monday after the extravagant party for the girl was Bud's birthday. It eased her heart knowing she would spend the day before with his parents, Ron and Evie, little Ronnie, and the other nieces and nephews. Her family. Jake and Amri were coming too, and she thought she might invite Stan.

Stan, as she had suspected, was a man worth getting to know. After that first beer at pFriem last summer, they went hiking up on Mount Hood.

"Hiking! A healthy sheen on your brow!" She could almost hear her mother laughing.

Holtzmans had always confined exercise to hard work, but Alice had taken to hiking. Over the summer Stan showed her his favorite trails along creeks and waterfalls up on the mountain. She and Stan were—what would her old-fashioned father have said? Keeping company. Nothing serious.

Alice passed Little Bit Grocery and Ranch Supply, which she no longer haunted on off-hours. Now when she went she looked forward to seeing the people she knew—old friends and new ones. She pulled her seat belt off her neck and loosened the button on her pants, which just felt better. She stuck her elbow out the window and drove through her little town to the courthouse to see a bit of local justice meted out.

Harry waited in line for the shower, holding his clean clothes under one arm and his toiletry bag under the other. He'd learned the hard way that anything left lying around would be filched by one of the other guys.

He leaned against the sink and glanced at himself in the mirror. They'd let him keep the handlebar mustache, for which he was grateful. It took so long to grow in. It would have been a damn shame to have to shave it off for some vague regulation about facial hair.

He looked stronger too. He was proud of that. He lifted weights and ran three times a week these days and felt fitter than he ever had. The work they had him doing was so physical it paid to be as fit as possible so he didn't get injured.

The water in one of the stalls shut off, and Harry heard loud whistling and a deep baritone singing "Shake Your Moneymaker." The curtain swished open, and Yogi stepped out in fresh board shorts and a T-shirt. He saw Harry, dropped his dirty clothes, and launched into an air-guitar solo, whipping his long, wet hair around, finishing with a jump kick.

Harry slow-clapped as Yogi made the faint sound of screaming fans through cupped hands.

"Thank you, South Padre!" he yell-whispered.

Harry laughed.

"You stoked for today, Stokes?" Yogi asked. "We're in charge of that pack of rug rats from L.A. again."

Harry groaned and slouched into the shower. "You have to take those horrible twins, Yogi. They don't listen."

"That's cuz their brains are in their balls right now. They're fifteen. What do you expect? You can handle 'em, Stokes. Know why? Cuz yer always stoked!"

He hollered this last part as he left the bathroom.

Yogi had gotten Harry a job for the season with South Padre Kiteboarding Adventures. The Texas season ran from October to May, which were the dark and rainy months up north. Yogi had worked for SPKA for years. After he'd watched Harry excel over the summer, he offered to talk to his boss. Harry jumped at the chance. He'd had to miss the fall harvest, but Alice said she expected him back at the end of spring.

"All hands on deck this summer, Harry," she said.

He was elated that he still had a place there. He hadn't been sure she would keep him on after he told her about the TV heist and his jail time. He remembered how he stood in the kitchen and recounted the whole stupid story the day he stole the SupraGro truck. He let it out in a rush, staring at Alice's feet. She'd taken off her work boots, and Harry could see she had a hole in one sock.

Alice put her hands on her knees and exhaled when he finished. She looked mad. Harry braced himself.

"Those little shits!" she exclaimed. "Let you take all the blame. Sounds like they both need an ass-kicking."

Harry stared, and Alice shrugged.

"Look, I didn't ask you if you had a record. And you didn't tell me. You gave me references, and I didn't call them. So." She stood. "Who wants more pie?"

She went into the kitchen.

Harry looked at Jake, who stifled a laugh.

It felt good to come clean, although he hadn't really needed to tell her. He thought everything would come out when he was arrested for stealing the truck.

Up at Uncle H's old place, he climbed down out of the cab to face the flashing blue-and-red lights of the sheriff department's Jeep. He didn't regret what he had done, not a bit, even as he faced arrest. He wanted to help, even if his action only delayed the spraying by a day or two. It was something.

The door of the Jeep opened, and out popped Ronnie. He slammed the door and strode toward Harry.

"Dude! What the hell are you doing?!" Ronnie said, his face shiny with sweat. "I've had the lights on since the bridge."

"Oh, I'm sorry, man. I—I didn't notice. I would have pulled over—"

"I can't figure out how to turn the damn siren on!" Ronnie said, miserable. "I think there's a short or something. Fuck me."

Harry opened the Jeep door and located the fuse box. He found the tripped fuse and flipped it. He punched the siren button and let it scream a round or two.

"Jesus! Thank you, dude," Ronnie said.

Harry knew Ronnie would have to take him in. He told him about his previous record and what county Ronnie should call to get the details.

Ronnie leaned against the door of the Jeep, took off his hat, and ran a hand through his short dark hair. That wouldn't work, he said.

For one thing, he didn't want his Auntie Alice mad at him again, and arresting her handyman would really piss her off. Plus, Harry hadn't told anyone about Ronnie misfiring his gun. That could have cost him his job. This siren thing was minor, but the other guys would have teased him about it for weeks.

"I have an idea," Ronnie said.

He picked up the CB and radioed in to dispatch that he had removed the SupraGro truck from the protest on Fir Mountain Road to deescalate the conflict. He couldn't find the driver, so in the confusion he asked a civilian to do it for him. It was an issue of safety, he said. Harry climbed behind the wheel of the big truck again and followed Ronnie back down into town, where Ronnie had the truck impounded at the sheriff's department. And for the second time, Harry was delivered to Alice's doorstep courtesy of the Hood River County Sheriff's Department.

After that, Harry wanted everything out in the open, no matter the consequences. He wanted to be held accountable for his decisions. He understood the power of taking responsibility for his actions. He could make things happen, he realized now. Like his own kiting and the leaf hive he had designed for Jake. And Jake's kiting.

That was, hands down, the greatest accomplishment of Harry's young life. After watching an old-school dude at the beach who was kiting circles around everyone seated in what he called an "air chair," Harry resolved to get Jake out on the water. The boy had plenty of upper-body strength. He just needed an alternative to the board. So Harry tailor-made him an air chair and rigged the harness so they could ride tandem as he taught Jake to fly the kite.

That first day on the water, Harry had a flash of self-doubt as he struggled to position Jake and hook up the harness as the waves broke at his back and the wind whistled through his helmet. But then he looked at his friend's face, wild with anticipation, and confidence enveloped him like a giant hand from above. Yogi launched the kite, and the two young men flew across the river, spraying a rooster tail in their wake. Jake hollered and whooped over the sound of the wind, rushing into an unexpected, incredible new happiness. It was a gift Harry had never expected to receive—being responsible for someone else's joy.

Now Harry showered and changed into board shorts and a rash guard. He walked back to the dorm and dropped off his toiletry bag and hung up his wet towel. He stood in the rollup doorway and looked out at the flat expanse of blue water that stretched into the Gulf of Mexico.

He would wade all day in the warm, waist-deep water, patiently coaching the spoiled twins from L.A., who were there for spring break, about safe landing and launching practices. He would teach them to respect the power of the wind and tell them about beach etiquette, which they were too self-centered to understand. Next month he would pack his bags and board a plane back to Oregon. He would return to the little farm at the bottom of the road where his friends waited, where the bees flew, where the wind sang him to sleep, and all of it called him home.

ACKNOWLEDGMENTS

Writing is a solitary endeavor, but publication is not. I'm grateful for the support and hard work of the many people who helped get this book out into the world.

Molly Friedrich and Heather Carr, thank you for seeing the potential in this story and insisting on the ruthless first edit that made it so much better. You've been with me every step of the way, and I'd be lost without you. Thank you, Hannah Brattesani and Lucy Carson, for all the behind-the-scenes work. Laurie Frankel, your willingness to help a fellow writer made all the difference, and I'm deeply grateful. Lindsey Rose, thank you for seeing promise in the manuscript. Your smart questions and deft editing greatly improved the story. From the beginning I trusted that you would be the best guide for this book. Maya Ziv, thank you for your guidance, support, and diligence. I'm so happy you were there to carry me through. To Emily Canders, Katie Taylor, and everyone on the Dutton publicity and marketing teams, much gratitude for your enthusiasm and hard work on behalf of this book. Vi-An Nguyen, thank you for a beautiful cover.

Several people offered their insights to help me draw Jake's character as faithfully as I could. Many thanks to you all: Mathew Lucero, Lindsey Freysinger, Jessica Russo, Nate Ullrich, and Tina Catania.

I'm indebted to the Oregon State University Extension Service's Master Beekeeper Apprentice Program for teaching me so much about honeybees. Special thanks to my mentor, Zip Krummel.

Acknowledgments

Matthew Lore, I'm so grateful for your support, encouragement, and friendship. Cory Jubitz, thank you for being a great sounding board. Nancy Foley, you are such a generous first reader and the "writers' group" I've always wanted.

Many thanks and much appreciation go to my family and friends who cheered me along the way.

And to Brendan Ramey, bottomless love and deepest thanks. You are my home.

ABOUT THE AUTHOR

EILEEN GARVIN is a beekeeper and writer living in Hood River, Oregon. Her memoir, *How to Be a Sister*, was published in 2010. *The Music of Bees* is her debut novel.